Seeking the Dawn

Book One of The Tethered Thrones

Elisabeth Valienne

Contents

Trigger Warnings

Seeking the Dawn is intended for audiences ages 16 and up. It contains the following potential triggers throughout the text:

- Alcohol (Mentioned)
- Child Death (brief mention)
- Emotional Abuse (moderate)
- Misogyny (mild, none of the MCs)
- Homophobia (brief mention)
- Violence
- Torture (happened off page, but we see the results)
- PTSD
- Sexual Assault (off page flashback)
- Profanity

Please mind your own triggers, and take care of yourselves

To anyone who's ever been rejected or hurt by their family of origin.

Forge your found family together with blood, sweat, and tears; they are no less your family for it.

Prologue - Oksana

It was cold in her cell.

Oksana's limbs trembled as she curled up, making herself as small as she could, avoiding the iron bars that trapped her in the tiny stone closet. Even the smell of them was abhorrent, but the few times she'd brushed the bars as she was dragged out of the cell had shown her exactly how pure the iron was. Fae injuries rarely scarred unless the use of iron was involved, and she would bear the marks of those iron bars on her body for the rest of her life—however long that would be.

Both courts forbade the use of iron even for torture, but she knew that wouldn't stop... Him. *The creature responsible for the aches and pains that even her advanced regeneration couldn't heal in these conditions. The one who'd put her in this goddess-forsaken cell after she woke up for the first time in that warm cave suffused with magic.*

Oksana's whole life since had been nothing but the sharp burn of pain and the hazy chill of the damp cell. She'd never truly seen the sun. Mother D'Vita had ensured that she knew about the sun, its warmth and light, but the secondhand knowledge was nothing compared to seeing it herself. Sometimes, when things were at their worst, she did her best to imagine the sun. Imagine what its rays would feel like on her skin, imagine what it would be like to be truly warm.

But she knew that if he had his way, she'd never leave the bounds of the cell without pledging herself to him— body and soul. A corruption of the lifebond that is intended for her. Corrupt enough that the force of it could destroy their world, be the final piece that truly broke the balance of their world and ended it. Some days, that knowledge was all that kept Oksana saying no, all that kept her from using that one short syllable to stop the endless pain that came day in and day out.

Mother D'Vita had whispered to her of her lifemate, of the male who would come and help her return the world to balance. Almost as if she was shoring Oksana up against the pain of what He was doing to her. Reminding her that there was more out there, more to the world than this iron box and the room of horrors. More to the world that could all be lost if she didn't stay strong.

Some days, she wanted to hate Mother D'Vita for encouraging her to keep fighting.

If He had His way, Oksana would end up just like her sisters, dead before their time. And she was the last.

She could sense that Mother D'Vita was badly hurt by what was happening here. That Mother D'Vita was drained by the pain of losing all of Oksana's sisters over the millennia. The dregs of Mother D'Vita's strength were within her, the little scraps of her spirit whispering in her mind.

If the One Who Was Coming didn't find her in time, the darkness of her cell would soon swallow the entire world...

Part 1

1

Lina

"It's time to wake up."

The curtains around Adelina's bed opened, the sudden change in light jerking her awake. A few hard blinks later, and the sunspots disappeared from her vision to reveal the soft green fabric of the canopy on her bed.

"Adelina," her maidservant, Sofria, called her name to grab Adelina's attention. The demi-fae stifled a sigh, she'd told Sofria that she preferred to be called Lina, but the maidservant was determined to ignore her request.

"Your breakfast is on the desk," Sofria announced, tucking a whisp of hair behind one of her pointed ears. Lina climbed out of bed but stumbled on her way to her desk when she remembered what today was.

Tonight, she would complete her Coming of Age ritual. Her stomach flipped. No one would tell her anything about the ritual, but she gathered it was unique to every fae. The lack of any clear idea of what to expect made it all worse. Lina twisted her fingers together as she approached the desk.

The tray on her desk was much like any other morning: a cup of —thankfully—steaming tea, a bowl of cold, congealed porridge, and a bruised apple. At least it was edible... mostly. Some of the meals she'd been served in the past included raw meat, uncooked oats, and other unfortunate dishes that left her curled up in the bathing room for hours at a time afterward. □

Beyond her meals, Lina seemed to have constant bad luck. Dropped tea trays, cold fireplaces in the winter, small thorns in her favorite shoes, journals and other personal writings disappearing...

There was never any actual *proof* of malice, but the sneers from the servants weren't subtle either. After five years, she'd learned to live with it.

As she began to eat what she could, she wondered at her grandfather's naivety. When she told him the servants disliked her all those years ago, he assured her that they'd "warm up to her soon enough" and that they simply weren't used to having a demi-fae around.

When her grandfather was home, it was easier. The 'pranks' were less obvious, and she got warm food more frequently. But between his job as the Prince of the Southern Highlands and his declining health, he had more important things to see to.

"Hurry up." Sofria's voice cut through her thoughts. "Was breakfast not to your liking?" The hope in Sofria's voice only barely stung this morning.

"It was fine. I'm just not particularly hungry today," Lina assured the crestfallen female, as she did each morning.

"Hm." Sofria pursed her lips but moved on. "Your clothes are on the bed."

"Thank you," Lina replied softly. Sofria took the tray and left.

Lina inspected the clothing, baffled by the differences in how clothing worked in the land of the fae compared to London. The soft, long-sleeved shirt laced at the neck, and the pants were some sort of strong fabric—perhaps leather? And again, tied closed. Tall socks and sturdy boots finished the outfit. Thankfully, the clothes were easy to put on, as Sofria wasn't gentle when she was forced to help Lina dress.

Once her hair was braided back, Lina gazed at herself in the mirror. The braid made the green streaks in her hair more obvious; it was nice that she didn't have to hide them. Here, for fae, the green was normal. Generally, the fae had a wider range of hair colors than humans. In her time here, she'd seen not just green like her own, but other colors, including purple, blue, and even a fiery orange. Though there were also plenty of shades like blonde, brown, or black, Lina wasn't going to be ostracized for the rest of her hair either.

Even with no clue what awaited her during the Coming of Age ritual itself, she knew what would happen after. Her training and education would intensify. Grandfather had spoken to the Council only a few days prior. They'd given their approval, and now he would prepare her for the role of his Prince-in-Waiting, his heir.

Her exhausting physical training would be traded for self-defense, and her general education would concentrate on governance and leadership. And, of course, she'd be training magic she'd unlock after the ritual... Hopefully, anyway.

Lina was more nervous about the magic than the rest. Most of the fae seemed to use their magics regularly. Sofria would levitate heavy burdens to ease her job, and Uncle Donal often created faelights in bright yellow that danced around her on bad days. She'd seen the gardeners coaxing growth out of dying plants on her walks as well, and once, she was sure one of the cooks had toasted bread with her fingertip.

On the other hand, Lina had never used magic in her life. The closest she'd ever been to using magic before her time in the world of the fae was the faded tarot cards her mum found in a charity shop. Even now, nothing. Was the human half of her bloodline too dominant?

The magic was so beautiful, but when it went wrong? It *really* went wrong.

Grandfather had tried to water a plant with a bit of rain a few years ago, and he'd been bedbound for the rest of the day.

Uncle Donal had chewed him out for an hour for that one.

As recently as a few months ago, one of the servants overreached their powers. Supposedly, they were trying to scour the ash from the fireplaces and tried to do all of them at once to finish faster. Instead of going home to see their sweetheart for the weekend, the servant had spent a week in the infirmary.

Squaring her shoulders, she went downstairs to her grandfather's office. The room was very much like her grandfather: warm, comforting, but a bit stuffy. Bookshelves lined the wall to her left, and a deep fireplace sat off to the right. Two elegant armchairs stood in front of the empty hearth. Directly in front of her was her grandfather's desk, with the man—no, the *male* himself. Even after all this time, she sometimes forgot that the fae used "male " and "female" instead of "man" and "woman."

"Good morning, Adelina." Grandfather smiled, bright blue eyes crinkling at the corners. "Are you ready for your ritual?"

"I..." Lina hesitated. "I think so?" She braided her fingers together.

"Be decisive," Grandfather reminded her. "You *are* ready. By believing it, you become so."

"Yes, Grandfather," Lina replied obediently. "I'm ready."

Even parroting the words didn't help. She wasn't so sure she believed in the same "fake it till you make it" mentality that her grandfather did, but it was kind of him to encourage her. She could tell he was exhausted; the dark circles under his eyes were hard to hide. As was the slight slump in his shoulders.

"Yes." He smiled indulgently. "You are. And you'll prove it tonight."

Lina knew her smile didn't quite reach her eyes, but her grandfather seemed satisfied.

"You have a few hours until you have to leave," he told her. "Do you know how to read a map?"

"Mostly," Lina admitted, truthfully not sure of anything right now.

"Then let's begin with that, and we'll ensure that you don't have anything to worry about tonight."

Grandfather continued with the last-minute lessons until after lunch, when her Uncle Donal wandered up from the portal room.

"There's my niece!" Uncle Donal boomed. "All grown up and ready for her Coming of Age!"

Uncle Donal was, without a doubt, the oldest-looking fae she'd seen in her time here. His tan skin was almost weathered, thin lines creasing the outer corners of his gray eyes, his forehead, and the space around his mouth. Grandfather had told her in confidence that he was over ten thousand years old and was the oldest fae on this continent.

She supposed that was why he was the Prince of Aledale City, a position that came with the title of Seneschal of the Seelie Court, stewarding a throne that had been empty for six thousand years.

"Hello, Uncle." Lina smiled slightly, doing her best to cover the nerves.

"Don't fret." Uncle Donal reached over and patted her head. "You'll be fine."

"I'm here too, you know," Grandfather joked, arms crossed.

"Ah, I've got hours to catch up with you, Cor." Uncle grinned. "We can chat after Lina leaves."

And the nerves were back.

After that, Lina's focus went in and out as her grandfather and uncle talked, her anxiety finally getting the best of her. As the sun began to set, her grandfather met her gaze and nodded.

"It's time," he said.

2

Lina

It was eerie leaving Royal Vale behind on foot, rather than on horseback or via portal.

It had been two hours or so since Lina had left and slipped through the city, a deep hood hiding her features. By the time she actually left the city, the sun hung low in the sky. There were quite a few trees on either side of the small road that led from this direction, so the path darkened quickly.

Soft forest echoes were the only sound she could hear other than her own footsteps on the dirt road. Lina was pretty sure there were croaking frogs somewhere, and birds called softly in the distance. Trees lined the path, dripping in moss, but little undergrowth impeded her view of the sides of the low hills.

As she had a more and more difficult time seeing, a troubling thought occurred to her.

"Oh, no," she whispered into the darkness. "I can't make light."

Most fae could summon simple faelights even before their Coming of Age. And even if not, the fae saw significantly better in the dark than she did.

Grandfather and Uncle Donal had probably forgotten that her eyesight was worse than theirs. Understandable, but it meant that currently she was alone in the dark with now mostly useless memories of a map and no light source.

Lina bit her lip and hoped desperately that the path actually ended at the grove where it was supposed to end. And that she wouldn't *lose* the path. With the lack of undergrowth, it would be incredibly easy to veer off the path completely. She could feel her heart beating faster, breathing becoming uneven.

She had *nothing* in this forest. She went into the woods "as intended," which meant with nothing but the clothes on her back. And her clothes were of the simplest make.

It could be worse, she reminded herself. *A few generations ago, they did this naked.*

A soft crunch behind her had her spinning around, but her weak, human eyes saw nothing. Unintentionally, Lina whimpered. The noise was small but seemed to echo in the emptiness and sudden silence of the wood.

Her grandfather's words echoed in her mind suddenly.

As long as the woods aren't silent, you're safe. If everything goes quiet, that's when you should start looking around for bigger things than you.

All I can do is move forward, Lina thought to herself, turning back around and straining her eyes for the edges of the path. When she was fairly sure she had it, she began to walk again. Her palms were damp where she held the edges of her sleeves in a tight grip.

Another tiny noise escaped her when more crunching sounds came from behind, but she was careful to keep moving forward and not turn around.

Keep going.

Breathing came from behind her. Even her dull human senses could tell when she was being hunted.

Keep going.

Lina strained her eyes to see something, *anything* that she could use to defend herself on the path. A rock, a stick... There had to be *something* in this bloody forest.

There! A reasonably sized stick. Lina dashed over to pick it up, but before she reached it, an invisible rock tripped her up. She landed heavily on her hands and knees, which managed to save her as something *leapt* through the spot where she was standing.

With a gasp, she crawled over on her bruised knees and scraped palms to grab the stick before the creature could reach her. It irritated the scrapes on her palms, but Lina struggled to her feet, holding the stick in the closest thing to a defensive stance she could. The creature's eyes glowed in the dim light of the crescent moon that was *finally* starting to peek above the treetops. A soft growl emanated from its throat.

"What do you want?" Lina's voice sounded weaker than she wanted it to, but she did her best to look threatening, showing her teeth in an attempt to intimidate.

The creature growled again, taking a deliberate step forward. Despite the realization that her whole body was shaking, Lina stood still. It took another step. And another.

Whatever it was seemed to be examining her. It tilted its head sideways, then dipped its chin to her.

Lina almost dropped the stick in her surprise. Had the creature... bowed?

It met her gaze again, then moved until it was behind her, ignoring her flinch when it pressed a... soft? Head against her back and pushed her forward.

"You're... helping me now?" Lina asked. The creature pushed her again. "I'm going to take that as a yes." She shrugged, moving forward. The creature moved to walk beside her, giving Lina ample opportunity to try to figure out *what* exactly was helping her. The color wasn't any indication: it looked silvery in the sparse moonlight. The outline suggested some kind of normal forest animal, and its liquid grace suggested cat.

It couldn't be a mngwa; those *hated* the fae. Perhaps... Was this a fae-lion? But her tutors had said that they were vicious...

Maybe they were wrong about the fae-lion, like they were about Unseelie and mixed-blood fae. Lina put the issue out of her mind for now; she could figure it out when she returned home.

She and the fae-lion walked for a while before the path stopped at the edge of a well-lit clearing. Her eyes said it was a normal forest clearing, moonlight trickling through tree branches and moss to create an oddly perfect circle in the middle. But something else, something *older* within her, said it was so much more. Said that the perfect circle in the center of the clearing was exactly where she was supposed to be.

"Thank you," she murmured to the fae-lion. "I think I'm supposed to go on alone now."

Lina had no idea where that came from, but she trusted her intuition. For all her body was mostly human, she was still part fae. The fae-lion made a soft noise that sounded to her like agreement, and took a step back as she took one forward. Then another. And another.

Before she knew what she was doing, she was in the exact center of the circle, letting the moonlight fall over her.

"What is it you seek, half-human?"

Lina didn't know how she knew the voice was female, any more than she knew how she understood it. The voice was split, layered, with the lower registers louder than the higher ones. The layers spoke at different speeds, creating an almost painful dissonance. It was a fight not to wince or cover her ears.

"Who... who are you?" Lina asked, hesitantly.

"I am the goddess D'Vita. I am the source of magic itself," the voice said to Lina. *"I say again, what is it that you seek?"*

"I wish to come into my power and my heritage." Lina's voice sounded more sure than she actually was. Especially after coming face-to-face with a goddess. "I'm here for my Coming of Age."

"If you do this, you will not be able to return to your home," the goddess warned.

"This is where my family is," Lina told her. It was true. After losing her mother, she had no more urge to return to the world she was born in.

"If I do this, if I awaken your power and gift you your truename, what will I get in return?"

Lina blinked. Grandfather and Uncle Donal hadn't said anything about anything like this when they told her about the Coming of Age! They should have *warned* her that she'd have to trade! She'd have brought... something?

"Half humans and changelings require more power to change. Full fae are made of magic, so they power their own change. I must draw from myself to change you," D'Vita told her, as if in answer. *"I have little to spare right now."*

Lina swallowed. If the goddess was the source of magic, she should have more power than this! Changing Lina shouldn't be hard for her, even though the task required more power than a full fae!

"The balance has changed." D'Vita was definitely reading her thoughts. *"My darkness, like the darkness of the world, is strengthening. The light fades."*

"But why?" Lina asked, aghast.

"The King they call Lifebringer is unleashing death upon all. He seeks out my daughters and destroys them. Even now, the Queen of Light suffers under his hand."

"Wait, there's a Queen?" Lina asked. "A new one?"

Uncle Donal was one of the only fae left who had met the former Queen. He'd told her a few stories, but the Seelie fae just didn't talk about their lack of a Queen. It was a wound that had never truly healed.

"There must be balance," D'Vita said again. *"Without balance, the order is destroyed."*

That... made a surprising amount of sense. Grandfather had told Lina just recently that if a member of the Council died without naming a successor, the magic—apparently D'Vita—would choose one. Why wouldn't it—she—do that for the Queen? Was it normal for it to take so long?

"This is not the first new Queen," D'Vita told her. *"But she will be the last. My power wanes; the darkness surges. Balance must be restored."*

"What do you need from me?" Lina asked.

"Find the Queen. Bring her home. She must take her throne."

Lina bit her lip. Even without her own Coming of Age ritual at risk, she would want to help the goddess. But she didn't know enough. She'd been in the fae world for less than a decade; even children—faelings—knew more than she did.

"You needn't take this on alone, faeling. Ask for help, but be careful who you trust."

Relief filled her. She didn't have to tackle it alone.

"Then I accept the offer." Lina bowed her head. "I will do my utmost to find the Queen in exchange for my birthright."

"So mote it be."

Before Lina could thank the goddess, her whole body erupted in pain from the inside out. It felt like every part of her was on fire. There was nothing but the burning and darkness. Lina wanted to scream, but she couldn't speak, couldn't even move.

Centuries later, Lina wouldn't be able to tell you how long she was drowning in pain. She came out of it just barely long enough to realize that she'd collapsed in the dirt before the burning resurfaced.

As it began to slowly abate, the voice echoed in her mind once more.

"Your final gift is your truename, which you will be unable to speak aloud or tell another being for a full turning of the seasons."

Lina couldn't respond; she could only listen and hope that this gift hurt less than the last.

"You are Orla. The Golden Prince. Arise, Orla, and take your place amongst your people."

Even after the voice and presence of D'Vita left her, Lina stayed on the ground for a few moments longer. Her bones still ached with the phantom remnants of the burning, and she needed to gather her scrambled wits.

It was that befuddlement that caused her to take a good ten minutes to realize that the clearing was now crystal clear. It wasn't bright or brightly-colored, but every detail was silver-cast and clear within her range of vision.

"Whoa," Lina murmured, sitting up slowly. When she looked down at herself, she felt as though she'd been *stretched*. The legs of her pants came up higher, leaving a thick strip of her skin visible between the top edge of the boots and the hem of the pants. Her shirt was in a similar state, the ends of the sleeves coming halfway down her forearms. She definitely wasn't as tall as full fae like her grandfather or even Sofria, but she was longer than she had been.

Her shirt hung wrong on her torso as well. Upon further inspection, she realized her hips and chest were a bit narrower, and she just felt... stronger.

Lina stretched, attempting to get used to the unusual length of her limbs and body before trying to stand.

As she did so, the creature from before, which was *definitely* a fae-lion, female from the lack of a mane, reappeared. She chuffed a bit, rubbing her face on Lina's shoulder.

"Hello," Lina murmured to her. "I'm glad you recognize me. I don't know if I would right now."

The fae-lion made another small noise, then poked Lina with her nose, as if attempting to stand her up.

"Alright, I'll get up," she promised the fae-lion, following through.

Despite her balance being off, Lina managed to stand easily, likely due to the grace she'd acquired during her transition. She hummed, stretching her whole body again before turning back in the direction she'd come. Faint traces of an oddly familiar smell assaulted her nose. Upon sniffing her clothes, she realized it was herself. There was a hint of rot to her scent that seemed to have vanished; was that her humanity? If so, that was a bit eerie.

Deciding not to dwell upon it, Lina decided to instead take advantage of being able to follow her own scent back home. The fae-lion stayed close by as Lina took a few wobbly steps, not expecting the smoothness with which she was able to move.

"This is so cool," she murmured to herself. "So, so cool."

Her strides were obviously longer, but the additional strength made her faster as well. She was back on the path in a much shorter time than she had expected. The fae-lion stayed with her, chuffing a bit every once in a while.

"What do you think?" Lina asked the fae-lion. "An improvement?"

She gave Lina a frankly impressive side-eye, making her chuckle.

"That's fair." She nodded seriously, as though the lion had responded. "It wouldn't have been hard."

The fae-lion sneezed.

Lina giggled.

"Are you going to stay with me when I go back into the city?" Lina was actually legitimately curious about the answer to this particular question. The fae-lion sneezed and shook her head. Lina supposed that meant 'no.' "Well, I'll miss you," Lina admitted. "Even though you *did* attack me at first."

The fae-lion stared at her, clearly incredulous. An uncomfortable thought dawned on her.

"You didn't attack me," she stated. "Oh God. I have no idea what you scared away, but *thank you*."

Now the fae-lion managed to look pleased with herself. Lina

didn't blame her, frankly. She had no idea what was in these woods, but it likely wasn't good for a lonely human with no means of defense or the ability to even *see*.

It was a surprisingly short walk back to Tricities, which Lina attributed to a combination of her new strength, her longer legs, and the company she was currently keeping.

Unfortunately, it wasn't to be for much longer. The fae-lion snuffled against her hand, then stopped. Lina turned around and smiled sadly at her.

"Time for you to go?"

She just bowed her head. Lina's chest tightened slightly.

"I'll miss you," Lina said in a choked voice. The fae-lion leaned forward and rubbed her face against Lina's forehead before bounding off into the forest and disappearing from sight almost instantly.

Lina had to stay where she was for a few moments to collect herself, not wanting to go back to the city in tears. The fae preyed upon weakness.

After a few moments, Lina managed to stuff her emotions in a neat little box to deal with later, leaving her to focus on her homecoming. Idly, she wondered what sort of magic she would have. Would it be like her father and grandfather's? Or would her humanity affect the heredity?

How would she even *know?*

She couldn't even feel the power right now. If it wasn't for the new, fae-like body, she'd wonder if she had even gotten anything. Maybe her power wasn't very vast. Many fae had minimal power.

But what did that mean for her status as a royal? As the Prince-in-Waiting? You had to be royal to be part of the Council. If she wasn't royal, then... What *was* she? What would she be? Would her grandfather finally get tired of her? Even her mum had eventually faded away and left, long before Lina's father had destroyed her.

For all she'd made mistakes with the Unseelie fae, she wasn't stupid. Lina saw the looks the other fae gave her when she ventured into the market quarter. She hadn't missed the expressions on the faces of other royals when she was around. And even if she'd missed those, she *definitely* wouldn't have missed the rotting tomato that was thrown at her the only time she went to the market quarter alone.

There were *reasons* Grandfather didn't let her go to the markets in Aledale City when they visited. There were *reasons* she had contact with so few fae, and why she'd never truly *met* another around her own age. She was half-human. A *mongrel.* Her father was completely disgraced, the bastard. His punishment made him incapable of repeating the decisions that had led to her conception and that of her older siblings, who were—as the fae said it—now returned to the earth and the Magic. Lina still just called it dead.

If her magic wasn't to the level of a royal, she was completely screwed. Completely.

Lina bit her lip as she snuck back into the city as the sun rose. How long had she even been gone? The streets were mostly empty, and Lina did her best to avoid anyone she *did* see. Tradition dictated that the people who saw her off to the grove were the first to see her upon her return.

To her surprise, her grandfather and uncle were camped out by the back gate she'd exited from. Her grandfather was sleeping, judging by the snores coming from a nearby tent, but Uncle Donal was awake and poking at a banked fire, a dissatisfied frown on his face.

"Uncle?" Lina said quietly.

Even with how quiet she was, her uncle jumped a bit.

"Lina?" Uncle Donal squinted at her, then brightened. "Welcome back, youngling!" He reached behind himself and smacked the tent. "Cor! Wake up, sluggard! Your granddaughter is back!"

"Huh?" Grandfather looked half asleep as he stuck his head out. He blinked a few times, then his gaze locked on her. "Lina! You're back!"

"Hi, Grandfather." Lina smiled shyly, all too aware of how her clothes were too short, her pants were a bit ripped, and there was probably all sorts of grass and other nasty bits in her hair.

Her grandfather gave her a rather wan version of the indulgent smile she was so used to.

"Welcome back, youngling," Grandfather said. "I'm proud of you, even if you did scare me to death."

"Scare you?" Lina asked, confused.

"You were gone for about a week," Uncle Donal told her bluntly.

Lina gasped.

"I was gone that long?"

"It never feels that way, does it?" Grandfather asked knowingly. Lina just shook her head. She was incredibly overwhelmed and wanted to have a good cry.

"Come on," Uncle Donal said to her. "Let's get you inside. You need a hot bath, a warm meal, and a nap. Your formal celebration is going to be tonight, though it won't be a large gathering."

"Okay," Lina murmured. "That sounds good."

It *was* good. The meal gave her enough energy to finish her bath, and the bath warmed her from a cold she hadn't realized she was feeling. She fell asleep as soon as her head hit the pillow.

3

Sasha

Sasha *really* didn't want to be here.

He was sure the demi-fae was nice enough, but her grandfather, Prince Cormac, had always seemed a bit... obnoxious. The fake happy expression the male always kept up unsettled Sasha, especially after finding out the older male was *losing his magic*. How do you get out of bed and be joyful with that going on? It just felt like a lie.

But Dad wanted to help train the demi-fae after hearing about Prince Cormac's illness, so here they were. Socializing.

When they arrived at Prince Cormac's lavish manor house and found it pretty much empty despite a potential Prince-in-Waiting's Coming of Age, Sasha understood Dad's insistence. They were the *only* attendees.

Sasha stifled a sigh as he followed behind his parents. Da and Dad had their fingers intertwined, Iron making a snuffling noise on his dad's other side. Sasha was happy to follow them; he wanted a chance to gauge things for himself. Especially if this faeling was going to be spending a great deal of time with his family in the coming weeks and months.

He took in the surroundings carefully, the intricate artwork and stuffy-looking decor annoying him a bit. It all felt exactly like he would have expected of the Prince of the Southern Highlands, uppity male that he was. A fairly snotty butler escorted them to a room that was a bit less stuffy this was a private family event, then. Very private.

Da greeted Prince Cormac cheerfully, announcing their family with no fanfare and allowing Sasha the chance to dip his head respectfully before continuing his examination of the room. Dad, who noticed what Sasha was doing, artfully engaged Prince Donal in conversation as a form of distraction.

The paintings in this room were more relaxing, soft river and lake scenes in midsummer. The furniture was all clearly well-made but just as clearly well-loved. Chairs dotted the room, most clustered near a couple of small tables and around the large fireplace. An open set of double doors led to a comfortable-looking dining room set for six.

They really *were* the faeling's only guests.

Against his will, Sasha felt bad for the female. From what he could remember, she'd been here around five years, and they were the only ones other than her family attending her celebration. Even he had a few acquaintances and friends from both Skovfore and Aledale City. And it was odd that Prince Cormac hadn't invited the rest of the Seelie nobles, or at least the Southern Highlands nobles.

Before he could think more deeply into the question, the guest of honor arrived. Adelina looked... incredibly different. In his memory, she was small and curvy, practically a human. While she definitely didn't look full fae, her fae heritage was incredibly obvious now. Her ears were pointed, though less obviously than his own. The very subtle streaks of green in her hair were darker, the same leafy green color as her eyes. Her whole body was longer and slimmer; someone had clearly dressed her in a way that wouldn't require an entirely new wardrobe in a day but didn't look obviously too small either.

She also looked exhausted, despite the smile that was clearly pasted on.

When the female saw the three of them, she looked over at Prince Cormac and Prince Donal in obvious confusion.

"Cor." Prince Donal glared at his friend. "Did you forget something?"

To Sasha's amusement, Prince Cormac looked sheepish.

"Sorry, Lina," Prince Cormac said to his granddaughter. He placed his hand on the middle of her back. "Delwyn," Prince Cormac said, nodding to Da, "offered to train you, along with Aleksandr." Prince Cormac nodded to Sasha now. Even after all these years, it was strange hearing his full first name. Most of the people he spent time with used the diminutive, Sasha.

"He did?" Adelina turned to Da with surprise. "You did?"

"Given my... condition," Prince Cormac said with a wince, "and my vast difference in fighting style, I agreed. While I could easily hire tutors, the *incident* with Lady Mara left me a bit leery."

Sasha was incredibly curious about said incident, especially since Adelina first went pale, then flushed and looked at her feet.

"Your grandfather agreed it would be a good idea," Da said cheerfully. Adelina blinked, clearly thrown off after having only met him in the Council room. Da was always on his best behavior when he was working, so seeing his normal, happy-go-lucky personality rather than the focused, detail-oriented male she'd met before was probably a shock.

"Thank you for coming," Adelina said to them in a low, clear voice. "And for being willing to train me," she added with a short bow.

"Oh it's no trouble." Da grinned. "We wanted to introduce ourselves in a more relaxed environment before we start training you." Da turned and extracted Dad from his conversation by the simple expedient of grabbing his arm and tugging. "This is my lifemate and partner, Mikhail Mngwalord," Da introduced. "And our son, Aleksandr Mindwalker."

"It's lovely to meet you all properly." Adelina smiled slightly.

Her gaze suddenly caught on Iron, and her eyes widened in a combination of awe and... something else. Longing? "Who's this lovely fellow?"

Iron, knowing he was being spoken about, sat proudly, flicking his tail.

"This is Iron," Dad replied. "My familiar."

"Is he... is he a mngwa?" she asked. It wasn't an unfair question. Most mngwa *hated* the fae.

"Well, that would explain Misha's surname," Da teased, triggering a blush. Sasha noticed the slight confusion in her gaze. It didn't sound like anyone had told her about Unseelie names and diminutives. *He* knew that Misha was his dad's nickname, but it would be a stretch for a Seelie or Seelie-raised fae to know any better.

"I'm sorry; that was terribly rude," the female murmured, looking down at the toes of her boots.

"No apologies necessary," Dad assured her, glaring almost playfully at Da. "This idiot uses all of his brains when he's doing Prince business and then spends the rest of the time making us wonder how in the world he manages."

Adelina covered her mouth, but a *real* smile peeked around the sides of it and crinkled her eyes. She turned to Sasha as if to escape.

"H-hello," she said. "It's nice to meet you."

"It's good to meet you, too," Sasha said, surprised to find that he meant it. "Properly, at least, now. You never see someone's true self in the Council Room."

"Truer words were never spoken," Prince Donal grumped. "Can't get anything useful done in there. It all gets done before and after." Adelina smiled at the older male.

"So you've said, Uncle Donal." She rolled her eyes good-naturedly. "Every time you go."

Uncle? That explained his presence. Sasha didn't realize that the Prince of Aledale City and the current Prince of the Southern Highlands were so close, but it made sense. Prince Cormac had been

Prince Donal's Prince-in-Waiting at one point or another, so of course they were close. Particularly given what had happened with Prince Cormac's family.

With that, their group migrated into the dining room where Prince Cormac's snobby butler gestured for an assortment of brownies to place serving dishes on the table. He served them all himself, but Sasha noticed how Adelina shrank away from the male slightly. And considering that the only other person he seemed to look down his nose at was Sasha, suspicion about the male's prejudices grew.

In an attempt to distract the younger female, Sasha decided to make conversation from where she was seated across from him.

"How are you feeling after the ritual?" he asked.

She thought a moment before answering, seeming to want to answer truly rather than give a surface-level answer like most would have.

"Exhausted," she said finally. "And a bit... off."

"Off?" Sasha was curious; his own Coming of Age had been mostly ceremonial.

"My reflection is incredibly unfamiliar right now," Adelina murmured. "And my body feels weird. I went through a lot of changes in a very short time, apparently."

"That makes sense," Sasha admitted. "Most full fae don't change too much during their Coming of Age. It's usually fairly mild until someone discovers their magical specialization."

"Discovers?" Adelina perked up.

"Yeah." Sasha shrugged. "We can all do the basics before our ritual, but at some point after, we figure out what our specialization is." Sasha paused, brow furrowed. "Did you not know that?"

Adelina huffed, clearly frustrated.

"I lived in the human world until I was thirteen," she admitted. "And then I came here and have been here ever since. I haven't had the *time* to learn as much as I'd like."

"How old are you?" Sasha inquired.

"Nineteen," Adelina told him. Sasha's eyes widened slightly.

"Damn," he said. "I'm eighty-seven. I did my Coming of Age at sixty. I guess humans really do age differently. I'd read about it, but it's different seeing it."

"I looked a bit younger than most people my age did," Adelina mused.

"That makes sense," Sasha told her. "Most fae your age are still children. Faelings."

"By human standards, I was an adult." Adelina shook her head. "The problem isn't even the age; it's that by the time you did this ritual, you'd had decades to get used to your magic and learn things. *Live.* For full humans, a lifetime is around eighty or ninety years."

"I can't imagine that's an easy shift in thinking," Sasha mused.

"It comes with its challenges." Adelina shrugged.

"I hope we're able to help ease the transition for you when you train with us," Sasha said, more earnestly than he expected.

"I hope so, too." Adelina's shoulders slumped slightly. "I look forward to understanding things better."

"Good luck." Sasha shook his head. "I still get fairly confused sometimes, and I've been here for my whole life."

Adelina snorted, then covered her mouth and nose.

"Lovely," she sighed, taking a bite of her food.

"We'll get there," Sasha encouraged.

"We never know everything about the world," Da said, cutting in. "Did you know everything there was to know about your human world before you left?"

"No," Adelina admitted. "Not even close. Even the elderly didn't know anywhere close to everything."

"Exactly." Da pointed a fork at her. "You will always have questions. They're a part of life."

"Thank you." Adelina smiled slightly, looking a bit more relieved now.

"That's what I'm here for," Da replied breezily, turning back to his food and his conversation with the older fae.

"He does that," Sasha told the female, correctly interpreting the bemused expression on her face.

"I definitely appreciate it," she admitted. She was quiet for a moment, then spoke again. "I hope this isn't a terribly inappropriate question to ask. If it is, please tell me, and I'll leave it be. But when did you find out about your magic?"

Sasha tilted his head sideways.

"I don't mind answering, but for future reference, most fae either bring up their magic themselves, or it is asked about in reference to magical assistance. Most commonly in battles or war," he informed her. Sasha held back a wince at the sight of her countenance falling a bit. "My magic is in mind control. It's not uncommon for Unseelie fae to lean toward mind magics."

Adelina nodded, seeming to be listening intently, for all there was definitely a hint of pink on her face.

"Is that one of the primary differences between Seelie and Unseelie?" she asked.

"Yes, actually," Sasha replied. "Type of magic is one of the ways those differences manifest. From what I've learned, the Seelie fae are associated with springtime, summer, and daylight. Unseelie fae are associated with autumn, winter, and nighttime."

"We're often nocturnal too," Dad said dryly.

"Wait, that's... that's it? Difference-wise?" Adelina blinked, staring. Some of her practiced politeness fell in the face of her confusion.

"Well, there's the fact that the Unseelies have a high King and the Seelie fae always had a Queen and the Council," Da added.

"What the heck," Adelina whispered before speaking louder. "That's what people get upset about?"

"They get upset because of the whole 'the Unseelie King assassinated the Seelie Queen' thing too." Donal shrugged. "But the people forget that King Lifebringer mistreats his own people, too."

"Exactly." Dad nodded. "Most Unseelie fae don't like him. Well, most of the Unseelie royals do, but they're thriving under his rule."

Adelina looked, frankly, baffled.

"This is still completely ridiculous," she said.

"Agreed," Dad said. "People turned *very* quickly to hatred only a couple of generations ago."

"Fae and humans aren't all that different then, I guess," Adelina muttered. "Not that most fae would be happy to hear that."

Sasha caught the sight of the flash of distaste on the butler's face as she spoke.

"People rarely want to believe things that conflict with their worldview," Da told her with a frown.

"Fae or human," Adelina added. "That particular issue is riddled throughout their history."

"Ours as well," Da replied. "You seem quick to catch on to things."

"She's very bright." Cormac smiled at her. "It was one of many reasons why I knew she'd make a great successor for me."

Adelina was very flushed, seemingly unused to so much praise, as she played with the food on her plate. Sasha, following an impulse he didn't entirely understand, met her gaze and made a silly face at her. She didn't respond overtly, but he did get a hint of a smile.

As he turned back to his meal, he caught Da smirking at him. Sasha shot the other male a glare, then focused back in on the rest of the conversation.

Once they finished eating, they made their way back into the sitting room.

"How did you plan to move forward with Adelina's training?" Donal asked Da directly as they walked.

"That's up to her and Cormac," Da replied honestly. "The easiest way would be for Misha and me to foster her for a time so she doesn't have to do daily portal travel. But if she would rather stay here, where she's familiar with the environment, that's entirely understandable. My family and I would happily support that."

"Where would you be starting?" Donal prodded further.

"Twofold," Del admitted. "We'd be focusing on defensive fighting and figuring out her magic at the same time. For her, those are going to be *vital*."

"Good call," Donal approved. The male looked over to where Sasha and Adelina were sitting quietly. Usually, Sasha would have made conversation, but the little female looked exhausted, so he was just keeping her company.

"Lina," Donal called. The female startled, but looked up.

"Yes, Uncle Donal?"

"Are you comfortable staying with the Northern Forest fae while you're learning?"

"That's fine." Adelina nodded.

"You're welcome to travel back here via portal whenever you'd like," Da added.

"Thank you," she told him.

"It's no problem." Da waved her off. "Your comfort matters. Give yourself the rest of the week to recover, and we'll work on getting you moved into the house after."

Once everything was arranged, the party slowly dissolved. Sasha and his family were quiet on the walk back to the Southern Highlands portal room, everyone lost in their own thoughts. After they were through the ornate portal and back in the safety of their own home, Sasha spoke.

"Dad," Sasha said, grabbing the male's attention.

"Hmm?"

"I'm glad we're going to help her," Sasha admitted. "She seems really lonely."

"I agree, kiddo." Dad wrapped an arm around him and squeezed. "Adelina needs more people in her corner."

"Yeah." Sasha frowned, worrying a bit about the little female and how she flinched away from the servants. Dad slumped down on the couch, curled in Da's arms.

"Get some rest, Sasha-sweet," Da said with a little smile, perching his chin on Dad's hair. "We'll start preparing for Adelina tomorrow."

4

Lina

Lina was rather grateful for the reprieve she'd been granted by Prince Delwyn and Consort Mikhail in regards to her training. Not only had she not realized *exactly* how hard her Coming of Age ritual had been on her body, but she really needed to get started figuring out her mission from D'Vita.

She found it odd that she'd not heard of D'Vita before, so that was her first step. And anything else she found out about the Seelie Queen would likely be helpful as well.

Two days after her Coming of Age, she felt much more well-rested, so she decided that now was a great time to find her grandfather's library. It would have been nice if she could have gotten into Uncle Donal's—or rather, the Seelie Queen's— but she didn't like asking. It was much easier when she could do things herself.

It was probably better to start with a smaller library anyway. The one in the Seelie Queen's palace was reportedly absolutely massive. Where would she even start?

Her grandfather's library was nice enough, a moderately sized room with wooden furniture and light, warm fabrics. There was, thankfully, a card catalog against the wall, which was alphabetized. Unfortunately, her initial search for "D'Vita" led her nowhere.

"Goddess" was also nonexistent. When she found "magic" in the catalog, she realized that many of the titles were going to be pretty useless.

She was definitely going to need some paper and a pen.

Walking a bit deeper into the library, Lina noted that there were a couple of little desk nooks along the back wall. When she inspected them, she found that they were loaded with supplies like glass pens, ink, the charcoal sticks used here in place of pencils, paper, and even more.

Extracting a little stack of paper, a pen, and a bottle of ink, Lina returned to the card catalog to write down titles that weren't immediate rejections. Unfortunately, that left her a *lot* of titles to write down. That took a good hour or so on its own, and then she went looking for the books. After grabbing the first one and flipping through it, Lina realized that she was *also* going to have to figure out if the books with promising titles actually were promising.

Lina emerged from the library a few hours later with nothing but a bunch of crossed-off titles and towering frustration.

"This is ridiculous," she muttered, throwing some scrap paper into her fireplace rather aggressively. With a sigh, she pulled on the rope that would summon Sofria.

"Yes?" The maidservant looked a bit annoyed.

"Can you have a pot of tea sent up here?" Lina asked. Not something she often did, but an indulgence Lina decided on to alleviate her frustrations. Sofria immediately sighed and disappeared. Lina fidgeted and bit her lip as she waited. A few minutes later, a brownie showed up with a tea tray.

"Thank you," she said to the little creature, who simply bowed to her and went back to its duties. Thankfully, something coming directly from a brownie was going to be fresh and delicious—they didn't care about heritage—just that people felt cared for in their homes.

Lina tucked her feet underneath herself as she settled into her couch with a cup of fresh tea, taking small sips as she thought. There had to be a different way of figuring this out.

It seemed fair to assume that most of the fae didn't know about D'Vita. Even Uncle Donal had never mentioned the goddess, and he was the oldest fae she'd heard of on this continent. So obviously, the name being mentioned wasn't normal during a Coming of Age ritual.

While most of the fae she'd overheard treated magic as something sentient, they *didn't* treat it like it was tied to their religion or belief system. As far as she knew, the fae didn't *have* religions the way humans did. They were mostly just very naturalistic and all that.

So, assuming this was once something everyone knew, *when* did the knowledge disappear?

And why did D'Vita's name sound so familiar?

The second question was the one Lina most wanted the answer to, but unfortunately, it was the one she was least likely to actually *get* an answer for. She mentally placed it on a back burner to simmer while she addressed the main question of when the knowledge disappeared.

While there was a good chance the knowledge just wasn't available anymore, it was worth redirecting her search out of the magic section of the library and into the history section. The magic section was focused on specific techniques and powers, which was not what she was looking for right now.

Something D'Vita said stuck with her: *without balance, the order is destroyed.* What was out of balance? She supposed it could be the balance of power. Something about the balance created by an Unseelie King and a Seelie Queen. But the Seelie fae had their Council; what did the Unseelie King have? Did that affect the balance?

Lina had so many questions, and her lack of answers was getting incredibly frustrating. Idly, she wondered if Aleksandr would have any of the answers to these questions or if he was someone that she could trust enough with what she heard during her Coming of Age. D'Vita had told her to be careful who she told, and the male seemed okay so far. Perhaps she'd get a better idea over the time she was going to be spending in the Northern Forests.

Once Lina was revitalized with tea and snacks, she returned to the library. This time, she began digging in the card catalog for history books. There were, again, many, but there was enough information on the cards that she was able to remove some of them very quickly. It only took another hour before she had a short list of about a dozen books and their locations. Within less than thirty minutes, she had narrowed the twelve down to about five books that had promise.

"Thank goodness," she muttered, placing the stack on the slightly dusty desk she'd gotten paper from that morning. The first book, *A History of the Affairs of the Seelie Fae,* smelled of old parchment and a touch of mildew. Lina hummed, flipping through the beginning introduction. Her nose wrinkled in annoyance; deciphering this was going to be annoying. It was written in a variant of the language old enough that she doubted even her uncle would understand it easily.

From magick and earthe we are made, and to magick and earthe we will go.

That sounded a bit like something that would go on a tombstone, in Lina's opinion. But it was the very first thing written in the introduction, so it had to mean *something.*

I, Galdar Storypen, am writing this tombe to preserve our years past. Our people are dying of a mysterious ailment that none have found the cure for. We aren't able to pass along our fair historie to the future generations. Even the Queene's line is beginning to forget our fair lineage.

Our very being is made of magick. Unlike the magicless humans that spill into our lands like the pestilence they likely brought with them, our smallest parts have been knit together with the magic and the earthe.

The humans say they were created by a single creator. A distant god for their people, who created their entire world out of nothing. But how? They have no magic to their bodies. Unlike us, the faerie, whose Goddess formed us from the vast oceans of power available on our fair land.

It is because of us. Our people. We found the magickless apes and gifted them with knowledge that could move them forward. It broke us that they had no magick. We wished to share it with them, so we began to help them grow.

And then they betrayed us. They took the iron we taught them to make, and they twisted it. Ever since they brought their blasted pestilence with them into our lands in an effort to escape it, the iron has betrayed us. Perhaps we were not to play god with these little mortals; perhaps our Goddess has punished us for seeking to rise to her level.

However it is to be explained, we attempted to do good and were given nothing but sackcloth and ashes in response. It resists the very touch of our magick, and seems to be no longer one with the earthe. The iron burns us all, all but those who have been born of a mixture of us and those cursed creatures.

Lina stared. The humans had visited this place before? When? Apparently, they'd brought a sickness with them, one that even the fae weren't immune to. It seemed like something had happened during the sickness that made the fae unable to touch iron.

It was even weirder to consider that the fae gave humans the ability to smelt iron in the first place. This explained why the fae hated humans and part-humans so much.

Flipping to the front of the book, Lina was relieved to find the book dated. Unfortunately, it was dated over twenty thousand years ago. Below that, Lina found a note stating that it had been copied from a much older manuscript. It made sense that it was old, but Lina was fairly certain that human history didn't have information that far back. So, it was likely that time ran a bit differently there than it did here.

Lina tucked that information away on the off chance that it was useful later and kept reading through Galdar Storypen's words. As she worked her way through the beginning of the volume, she read about the goddess she'd met, whose name by this point had been forgotten. She also read about the goddess's secret island and how fae and humans both had sought it out.

By the time the sun had set and the candles had burned low, she had finished the book. Flecks of ink scattered like freckles across her hands, and a stack of paper full of notes and questions cluttered the desk.

She wasn't sure why, but Lina suspected that leaving this out would end in disaster. She tucked the papers in among the pages of the book and the book itself in a particularly dusty nook in the desk. The other books went on a dark, low shelf by the desk.

Before she could get too preoccupied with her thoughts, Lina's stomach growled. When it did, she realized that she hadn't actually eaten since breakfast, aside from her little tea tray earlier in the afternoon.

Detouring from her route to her suite, Lina headed down towards the bottom floors of the manor, where the kitchens were located. One of the cook's assistants usually stayed awake late to be available for anything the family might need. The trek was much easier with her fae eyes; she usually managed to see obstacles before tripping over them now.

Finally, she arrived in the warm kitchens, the only light being the low fire in one of the smaller hearths. A single kitchen servant was working on what looked to be preparatory chores for the next morning. He looked sharply at Lina, gaze only barely softening once he recognized her.

"What do you need?"

"I'm afraid I missed dinner," Lina apologized. "I lost track of time. Is there anything I could have before I head to bed?"

"I'll see if there's anything left," the servant said with a sigh. He left his work and went to check for something to eat.

As she waited, Lina edged closer to the warm hearth. The evenings were cold, and the kitchens had to be particularly well-ventilated to prevent the workers from sweltering. Unfortunately, that usually meant that it was cold on evenings like this one. The room was a bit frightening in the dark; it was a large, low-ceilinged room dotted with hearths and ovens large enough to feed hundreds of people at once. Down the center of the room went a large, wooden countertop for preparation. Utensils, pots, and pans hung from hooks attached to the ceiling, and others were stored on shelves beneath the counter. From what she'd seen on other visits, the food and drinks were stored in massive closets that were buried in the ground to keep everything from spoiling. The whole room currently smelled of warm bread and traces of some kind of meat and vegetables.

Before Lina could figure out what else she was smelling, the servant reappeared with a bundle of food wrapped in a cloth.

"That's all that's left for today." He dismissed her, turning back to his prepwork.

Lina dipped her chin.

"Thank you," she told him, leaving as quietly as she could to avoid disturbing him. Lina unwrapped the food and found a thick sandwich made of brown peasant bread spread with soft cheese and some sliced meat between the pieces of toast. The servant had also added some slightly bruised fruits that Lina couldn't remember the name of.

She chowed down on the food as she walked back to her suite, getting more and more exhausted as she filled her stomach. By the time she got back, all she had energy for was to clean the fruit juice off her fingers and face, change into the nightgown that Sofria had left her, and curl up in a warm ball in the middle of her oversized bed.

The next morning, Lina's plans to continue her research were interrupted by Sofria waking her up early.

"Wake up," the female commanded. "His Highness would like to see you at breakfast."

Her grandfather wanted her to join him for breakfast? That was rare. He usually used breakfast for his important meetings related to the business of running the realm. She wasn't his Prince-in-Waiting yet, so why was she being summoned?

Lina slipped out of bed quickly, rubbing her eyes and yawning.

"And I'll thank you to *not* leave your clothes on the floor at night," Sofria added with a sniff.

"Sorry." Lina hung her head slightly, feeling like a chastised child. "I was exhausted last night and wasn't thinking."

"Think next time," Sofria advised. "Your clothes are ready."

With that, the female swept away, leaving Lina blinking herself awake in the middle of her bedroom. Slowly, Lina made her way to where her clothes were, barely noting that they were built more for comfort than for style. Once she took a quick moment to tidy her hair, Lina quickly made her way to her grandfather's formal dining room.

To her surprise, the first thing Grandfather did when he saw her was hug her tightly.

"I'm so glad you're alright," he murmured. Lina just blinked at him in confusion. Reading her expression, Grandfather frowned slightly. "I don't know where you were tucked away yesterday," he told her. "But I'm incredibly grateful for it. Yesterday, a pair of..." Grandfather made a face. "I hesitate to call them true assassins; they were barely better than ruffians. They broke into the manor and cau-sed havoc looking for you."

"They were *looking* for me?" Lina whispered, horrified. Her time in the library had literally saved her life yesterday.

"They were." Grandfather nodded solemnly. "One of them got into your room, and the other came in through a side door that was left unlocked. We're unsure if it was left that way on purpose or not."

Lina, for all that she was trying to keep her cool, started to shake. As tired as she was, she hadn't noticed anything amiss in the suite when she got in there. If they hadn't dealt with the assassin, she could have been killed on her way to bed.

Grandfather cupped her face in a hand. "It'll be alright, Lina, dear. We'll find them," he swore. Lina blinked back tears. Her grandfather wasn't particularly demonstrative, and sometimes she felt a bit distant from him. Moments like today, though, reminded her that for all he wasn't very good at *showing* it, he did care about her.

"In the meantime," a familiar voice said from behind Grandfather, "you'll be coming to stay with us a bit early to ensure your safety."

She peeked around her grandfather to see Prince Delwyn, his green eyes hard. Lina shrank into herself a bit.

"I'm sorry to be a bother," she murmured, looking down.

"A—Oh no, you're not a bother at all." Delwyn's voice softened significantly, enough that Lina felt brave enough to look up and read that he didn't look as angry anymore. "Sorry, my family has dealt with any number of assassins who attempted to hurt my son. I take a dim view of political assassination, frankly."

"We're going to leave most of your things here so that we can keep up the illusion that you're still living here," Grandfather told her, grabbing her attention again. "But if you have any small things you'd like to take, go get them now. Here's a backpack; bring only enough to fit in this."

Lina nodded, knowing that most of the space would be taken up by those five books and her notes from the day before.

"Go ahead, child," Grandfather told her, a tired smile on his face, before he dismissed her. "We'll be here when you return."

5

Mikhail

Mikhail wanted to throttle the assholes who had tried to kill the little faeling. When his partner had received the panicked message from Cormac about the incident, Mikhail had to resist the urge to follow Del through the portal to check on the child for himself.

In lieu of being able to do so, Mikhail found Leander and made him aware of the new circumstances. The two males found a suitable room for the female in the family wing of the house, giving her a room with a view of the vast, dark forests and low hills. Leander had been sent to find appropriate clothing for her, and Mikhail made himself a menace to Cook. The faeling would need some food when she got here as well, and Mikhail wanted to ensure it was, at the very least, moderately comforting.

"Shoo," Cook told him finally, a frown on the brownie's face. "Take your mother henning elsewhere. You've ensured that the faeling will have a good breakfast, so now go do something else."

"I don't *mother hen*," Mikhail hissed, sounding very much like his familiar.

"You do," Cook told him, unimpressed with the male's theatrics. "And it's unnecessary. Go. Shoo," they repeated.

Mikhail glared at the brownie, though without heat. In response, they simply handed him a mug of relo brew and a delicious-smelling something wrapped in cloth. Taking it for the dismissal it was, Mikhail made himself scarce, finding Iron and curling up with the mngwa in a dissatisfied manner.

"I don't mother hen," he informed the mngwa.

Iron looked distinctly unimpressed.

"I *don't*," Mikhail insisted.

"Talking to the mngwa who isn't going to answer you again?" Mikhail would swear for the rest of time that he did *not* jump at the unexpected sound of his son's voice, thank you very much.

"I don't know what you're talking about," Mikhail sniffed. He had his dignity to think about.

What little was left.

"Yes, you do." Sasha's eyes sparkled with mirth as he dropped down onto the couch across from where Mikhail was curled on the floor with the mngwa. "But we'll come back to that, because it's completely too damn early for you to be awake. Where's Da? What's happening?"

Sometimes, Mikhail forgot that strong emotions, particularly if all the members in a group *shared* said emotion, got through to his son. He made a face.

"He got a message from Cormac this morning," Mikhail told Sasha, who immediately looked a bit alarmed. "There was an assassination attempt on Adelina."

"Is she okay?" Sasha asked immediately, looking significantly more awake.

"She's fine," Mikhail soothed the younger male (and reminded himself). "Apparently, she wasn't where they expected her to be. The assassins couldn't find her before they were caught."

"Who sent them?" Sasha's mirth was long gone, anger hiding behind his usual deadpan expression.

"They killed themselves before they told," Mikhail growled.

"Fucking cowards," Sasha muttered. Mikhail nodded in agreement.

"So Del is actually going down there to get her," he continued. "They're moving her up here sooner, and leaving most of her belongings to point the assassins down there rather than here."

"That makes sense," Sasha admitted. "And explains why you look like you got exiled from the kitchens. You were worrying Cook again, weren't you?"

"I don't do that," Mikhail muttered.

"Whatever's in that cloth would say otherwise." Sasha nodded to the almost-forgotten food. Mikhail unwrapped it to reveal steaming cheese biscuits. Sasha leaned over and snatched one before Mikhail could protect them.

"Go get your own," Mikhail muttered, hunching over the remaining biscuits.

"You've definitely been mother henning again." Sasha smirked. Mikhail glared.

"I don't mother hen," he insisted.

"So you've said," Sasha mused. "Would now be a good time to ask where Leander is?"

Mikhail glared again.

"Well?"

Mikhail sighed.

"He's getting clothes for the faeling," he admitted. "She can't bring much of anything with her."

"Mother hen." Sasha pointed at Mikhail, then took a bite of his biscuit. "Holy. You'd better eat those before I steal them."

"You better not," Mikhail growled, nibbling on the end of one and almost melting. "These are *mine*. Go get your own."

"Wouldn't want to steal Adelina's," Sasha said cheerfully. "She's been through enough. But I can steal yours easily."

"That's what you think." Mikhail hunched over his biscuits. He was so focused on protecting the cheesy deliciousness that he didn't realize Sasha's *true* goal.

The relo bark brew.

Sasha stole the mug of relo brew and took a few steps away before giving Mikhail a shit-eating grin.

"Give it back," Mikhail warned.

"Give me another biscuit then," Sasha teased. "It's a good trade."

"There's no need to trade if you *give me my relo*," Mikhail growled, gaze locked on the mug.

"You were the one who said I couldn't steal your biscuits," Sasha pointed out. "You have no one to blame but yourself."

"That logic doesn't add up," Mikhail pointed out despite himself.

"Is that so?" Sasha leaned against the wall, a few drops of the delicious beverage coming too close to the lip of the mug for Mikhail's comfort. "Explain."

"It doesn't count if I give you one or *trade* one to you," Mikhail said. "You have to steal it properly."

"A con is proper thievery." Sasha smirked. "And that's exactly what's happened here. You've been had, Dad."

"Give. Me. The. Mug."

"Come get it," Sasha challenged.

Before the whole thing devolved into blows, Del appeared at the doorway with the little faeling in tow.

"What's going on in here?"

Mikhail glared at Sasha and the mug in his traitorous hands.

"Anyone?" Del prodded, hands on his hips.

"He took one of my biscuits," Mikhail felt compelled to explain, a hint of disappointment in his partner's gaze making him crack faster than his son. "And then stole my relo!"

Del's brow rose as he turned to Sasha.

"He said I couldn't steal the biscuits." Sasha shrugged. "It was a challenge. Now he's saying that a con isn't proper theft."

Del sighed exaggeratedly.

"Did you already steal a biscuit?" he asked his son.

"Perhaps," Sasha replied cagily.

"Then you've had yours," Del told the younger male. "Give Misha his relo brew back, and go get some of the biscuits from the kitchens. You and I both know they'll give you whatever you ask for."

"Mean," Sasha replied with a grin before walking back over and handing Mikhail the mug. "Saved by the bell."

Mikhail didn't even bother to remind the younger fae who was boss. He *trained* Sasha. When his precious relo wasn't in the equation, it was a very obvious win. And when it was? Oh, then neither Sasha nor Mikhail could say whether or not Del's house would survive the carnage.

"Hey, Adelina," Sasha said to the anxious faeling. "Glad to have you, for all I hate that you have to deal with that bullshit. Assassins are the worst."

That comment actually got Mikhail's son a hint of a smile.

"I can't believe I didn't even know they were in the house," Adelina admitted. "I was very focused yesterday."

"I imagine you were, if you missed assassins," Mikhail said dryly. The faeling flushed, looking down at the toes of her shoes.

"Relax." Del bumped up against Adelina's shoulder. "You're safe here. None of us will hurt you."

"Del's right," Mikhail pointed out. "You're safe here." He gave the faeling a tiny smile. "Have a seat. I'll check on breakfast."

Adelina perched awkwardly on the edge of a chair as Mikhail left, thankfully finding Leander close by so he didn't have to go down and get scolded by Cook again.

"Is breakfast going to be ready soon?" Mikhail asked. "Adelina just got here."

Leander nodded sympathetically.

"I'll go check on it, but I suspect it will be," he informed Mikhail. "I'll be back soon."

When Mikhail came back into the room, he stopped short. Del was *also* staring in complete bafflement. Iron was curled up, wrapped around Adelina's feet, and purring loudly enough to vibrate the entire chair.

"What the *hell,* you oversized housecat?" Mikhail finally said, causing Adelina to flinch.

"I'm sorry!" she burst out, freezing when Mikhail put his hand up.

"No, no, nothing to be sorry for," he corrected. "If anything, *I'm* the one who should be apologizing for that idiotic ball of fur there. People think mngwa are scary, but they're truly just oversized housecats. With all the brains of one." Mikhail gave Iron the side-eye before continuing. "The reason they're so frightening to most is that they tend to be born from housecats who are tortured or mistreated by their owners—human or fae. Obviously, they have a strong, negative reaction to the ones who harmed them."

"Then... why does he like people?"

"Ah! A question!" Del teased, the only sign of his concern was a tightness around his eyes. "I was wondering when we'd get one."

"Shut." Mikhail pointed at the other male. He turned back to Adelina. "He was my pet when I was a faeling." He flushed slightly. "That's why he's called Iron. I named him when I was all of... twelve? I was still barely better than a baby at the time. I wanted to name him after something scary."

Adelina covered her mouth with her hand, but Mikhail could still see the smile in her eyes. Mikhail began to make his way over to the couch Del was on, sitting next to the other male.

"He became a mngwa while he was protecting me from the assassins that killed my birth parents." A tiny, sharp, familiar pain sparked through his chest at the thought. He barely remembered his parents, but what he remembered was good. He still missed them some days. Adelina's gaze sparked in understanding as Del sent love and sympathy over their bond, but she said nothing, just leaning down to scratch his ears.

"I'm still surprised Iron likes you so much," Del cut in, allowing for a graceful subject change. "It took him a century to warm up to me. Less for Sasha, but still."

Adelina looked between the two of them, Mikhail getting the distinct feeling of being measured, before she looked back down at Iron.

"Cats have always rather liked me," she said quietly, leaving Mikhail feeling somehow cheated.

Before the conversation could continue, breakfast arrived. Leander appeared with a tray covered in warm, comfortable dishes. Mikhail mentally thanked Cook; they knew exactly what was needed without anyone having to tell them.

"Thank you." The faeling dipped her chin to Leander. Mikhail narrowed his eyes in thought. She was even more deferential to servants than she was to him and Del. Not that either of them cared; he was more concerned about *why* she was so deferential toward them. It was odd behavior, and not something common to the Southern Highlands.

Mikhail kept his eye on the little female as he poured himself another cup of the bitter relo brew. She seemed to particularly enjoy the potato cakes, though even he wasn't entirely sure. For his part, Mikhail enjoyed a few more of those cheese biscuits and let Del bully him into eating some fruit with only a few pointed looks. Overall, Adelina spoke very little as she ate, just watching their antics with something that Mikhail might have called longing.

"Adelina," Mikhail spoke quietly to get the faeling's attention, but she still flinched at the attention before she met his gaze.

"Yes?"

"Do you need anything else?" The faeling had only eaten a single plate of food, and Mikhail had noticed that longing expression being pointed towards the food as well as them.

"I..." She flushed slightly. "I'm sorry; it's been a long time since I've had a meal served like this. Either I eat alone in my room, or I eat a more formal meal with Grandfather." Adelina's shoulders drooped slightly.

"If there's food left, eat," Mikhail said firmly, ignoring how much he wanted to address the fact that she mostly took meals alone. "I don't care how much you eat unless you're stuffing yourself right before training. And that's just because it'll make you sick."

Adelina smiled hesitantly.

"Thank you," she murmured, then reached slowly for the potato cakes again. To his joy, she ate another plate and a half before she sat back in her chair with a drowsy expression. Sasha met his gaze and mouthed "mother hen" at him, Mikhail resisting the urge to hiss.

"Would you like to rest this morning?" Del asked the faeling. "You had quite the scare when you first woke today."

"Yes, please," Adelina said, gratitude written openly in the lines of her face.

After Adelina and Del disappeared, Mikhail glanced over at Sasha. For once, his son's emotions were playing fairly clearly across his expression.

"She's so lonely," Sasha murmured. "Even with the fucking *fortress* she's constructed around herself, I could feel that."

"I kinda figured," Mikhail sighed. "I don't have to tell you to be gentle with her."

"What do you take me for?" Sasha's brow rose, and he crossed his arms across his chest.

"Sorry." Mikhail ran his fingers through his hair. "I'm just... worried."

"We can tell." Del's gentle teasing alerted the other two to his presence, and delicate fingers detangling Mikhail's hair helped release the tension in his shoulders.

"I've got a good feeling," Sasha said, an impish grin on his face. "Don't worry, Dad."

"As if that would stop him," Del chuckled. Mikhail just sighed a very put-upon sigh and relaxed into Del's calming hands; the other two could banter just as well while he napped.

He wanted to be at his best.

6

Lina

For the first time in several hours, Lina felt a bit more like herself again. Breakfast was more delicious—and *warmer*—than anything she'd eaten in years. The relaxation brought on by a stomach full of hot food sent her straight to sleep after Prince Delwyn brought her to a comfortable room with an even more comfortable couch.

The room was thankfully empty of anyone that she could see when she woke up, the sun high in the sky and shining in through the windows. A tiny bit of movement grabbed her attention and told her that she hadn't been completely correct in her initial assessment of being alone. Her gaze locked on a tiny brown kitten stretching in a patch of sunlight on the floor.

"Oh." She made a tiny, pleased noise. The kitten just looked at her, eyes narrow in the judgmental expression so common in cats. "Here, kitty," she cooed at the little creature, rubbing her fingertips together at what she judged to be its nose level when it stood.

It looked at her for a bit longer, letting her prove that she wasn't going to move yet, and then stood and meandered over to her. It sniffed the tips of her fingers before blessing her with a head butt. Obediently, Lina petted the kitten, rubbing her finger in the space between its ears. It responded with an uneven purr, sounding a lot like the beater of a car that her mother had driven when she was a little girl.

"That's Cheese Biscuit," a voice startled her before she could decide if she wanted to try to pick up the cat. "We call her Bissy. She's a menace, but she's so cute she can get away with anything, unfortunately. We're all weak to her charms."

Lina looked up to see Aleksandr leaning against the doorframe. The male was, unsurprisingly, relaxed, as he was at home. Lina hadn't realized how long the male's hair was the first times she'd seen him, or how it seemed to be more of a violet-tinted black than a full black.

"How is she with being held?" Lina asked, looking wistfully at the kitten.

"Depends on her mood." Aleksandr shrugged. "Give it a shot. Worst case, she scratches a little. It'll heal up in less than an hour."

Lina nodded, trying not to startle at the reminder of her now-accelerated healing. She leaned over and picked up the kitten, cuddling it against her chest. The cat took matters into her own hands, clawing her way up Lina's shirt painfully, then draping herself happily in the spot where Lina's neck and shoulder met.

"Well, that answers that question." Aleksandr smirked. "She likes you. All the cats do, from what I've seen. They're good judges of character, though, so I'm not surprised."

With that surprising and vaguely confusing note, Aleksander stood up straight, coming closer to her and dropping into a nearby chair.

"How are you feeling?" he added.

Lina paused to take stock.

"More settled," she decided. "I think I was in shock this morning."

"Understandably so," Aleksander sighed. "The first time is always the worst. I don't know how you missed it, frankly. Where even were you?"

Lina hesitated for a half second, her gut telling her to share with the other male for some reason. At least a little something. He didn't have to know all of it to be potentially helpful.

"I was in the library, trying to find some information that I suspect is buried in fae history somewhere," she told him finally. Aleksandr's brow rose.

"I'm not the best scholar of history, but I might be able to help," he invited.

Lina bit her lip, brow furrowing in consideration. Did she want to offer him more? Sofria had been kind at first, too, before her true feelings shone through. So had Aisling, all those years ago.

She decided to just ask a question that she was *fairly* sure wouldn't come back to bite her in the ass.

"Does the name D'Vita ring a bell to you?" she asked.

Aleksandr narrowed his eyes in thought.

"It sounds familiar," he said finally. "But I'm unsure of why."

"I thought the same thing," Lina admitted. "I *know* it's familiar. I just don't know why."

"Do you have anything else that could jog either of our memories?" Aleksandr asked.

"Not yet," Lina mused. "But I brought the books I was using with me, so I'm probably going to research in my free time."

"Let me know if you need a hand," Aleksandr told her.

"I will, thanks." Lina smiled slightly, internally deciding to drop it. "I appreciate it."

"It's no problem." Aleksandr waved a hand. "But research makes sense as a reason to somehow miss an entire assassination attempt. My first one was out in the marketplace; someone tried to stab me in the back with a knife. I only escaped unscathed because of my specialization."

"Your specialization?" Lina asked.

"The magic I'm most comfortable with. In this case, mind reading." Aleksandr looked down at his feet. "I can't do it without trying, but I do get a sort of aura off of people. I usually try to block most of it out, but really strong feelings come through anyway.”

“That makes sense,” Lina replied thoughtfully. “I bet that’s saved your life a few times.”

Along with making him hated and ostracized, most likely.

“It has.” Aleksandr relaxed slightly into his chair. She looked down at her hands which she was unconsciously wringing together, as she realized that he had been waiting for her to be frightened.

“I’m sorry you have to deal with that,” Lina told the male. She didn’t tell him how brave she thought he was for being forthright with her, but her respect for him increased all the same.

“And I’m sorry you do too,” Aleksandr came back with a smile hovering at the corners of his mouth.

Both of them were quiet before Aleksandr spoke again.

“I thought you’d be a bit more snobby,” the male admitted.

“Why?” Lina blinked in surprise. Her? Snobby? She was just... Lina.

“Your grandfather is...” Aleksandr paused to think. “Stiff. He’s a good male, don’t get me wrong. He’s a very good male. But he doesn’t seem to like Dad much, and he has always seemed very straight-laced.”

Lina reached up and gently rubbed the sleeping kitten between its ears with a finger, thinking about how to explain her grandfather.

“Grandfather was very different when I first met him,” she said finally. “He was a lot more like the person you’re mentioning. Straight-laced. Traditional. When I first met him, he wouldn’t have believed anything I told him if I didn’t have a birthmark like his and my father’s. I don’t think he *wanted* to believe after I told him. But the proof is hard to deny.”

Lina didn’t tell him how desperate she’d been for a father, how much she’d wanted to believe that if she could just *meet* him, her father would love her. She didn’t tell him how her father had instead brutalized her mother after he was sentenced and exiled, either. Or how he'd threatened her and turned the household against her even more than they already had been from her being half-human. Or how cruel Grandfather had been before he believed her.

Aleksandr didn't need that kind of ammunition against her. No one did.

"I think he just felt guilty initially," Lina said. "He and my grandmothers blame themselves for who my father became. What he did. But over time, some of that softened. For him, at least."

"A reality check for him," Aleksandr summed up, brows furrowed.

"Precisely." Lina shrugged, then refocused on petting the sleeping cat.

Things went quiet, Lina casting around for something to say so she didn't have to wallow in her own thoughts. Finally, she asked a question of her own.

"Are you Prince Delwyn and Prince Consort Alexei's biological child?" she queried. It wouldn't be the oddest thing she'd ever heard since moving here, frankly. Magic was weird.

Aleksandr *stared*.

Before the male could answer, both of his parents walked in, chatting together. Prince Delwyn froze when he saw the expression on Aleksandr's face.

"Sasha?" he asked.

"She... I..." Aleksandr's voice was a bit strangled.

"What happened here?" Prince Consort Mikhail's voice was a bit more demanding. Aleksandr made another noise, this one like a dying animal. Lina blinked, but obliged the older male since Aleksandr seemed unable to.

"I asked Aleksandr if he was your biological child," she repeated plainly. Maybe Aleksandr hadn't heard her correctly?

"You *what*?" Prince Delwyn practically shrieked before exploding into breathless laughter. Prince Consort Mikhail looked... done. Lina didn't really know what was so funny, but the males all seemed confused by her question. The world was weird; magic was weirder. Who's to say it was impossible?

"What the fuck," the male whispered.

"Is... that not something magic can do, then?" Lina asked, nerves making her stomach flip. This conversation had just gone into awkward "questions you don't ask" territory, and she was regretting even asking. Why did Grandfather choose her anyway? Literally anyone else would have been able to carry on a normal conversation with the other fae.

Aleksandr buried his head in his hands, and Prince Consort Mikhail looked a bit like he was praying.

"No, kid," Prince Consort Mikhail said finally, amid his partner's snorting laughter. "No, it's not. There are... limits. Physically."

"Got it," Lina cut in before the male could say anything else. She'd gotten this talk from her grandfather about three years ago; she did *not* need it again from a veritable stranger.

"Thank the Magic," the Prince Consort muttered. He turned to his partner. "Are you quite finished with your carrying on?"

"No," Prince Delwyn giggled, wiping tears of laughter off his face. "No, that's the best thing I've heard in decades."

Lina flushed.

"Sorry," she muttered, fingers twisting around each other.

"No, no, no." Prince Delwyn shook his head. "Please don't apologize. That was the funniest shit I've heard in a while."

"Idiot," Prince Consort Mikhail muttered. "We actually came to see if you were awake and if you were hungry."

"Um..." Lina evaluated. "A bit, yes. Mostly, I'm thirsty."

"Noted." The male nodded. "Well, there's lunch in the dining room, so we should head there if you're hungry. These two will catch up."

With that, Prince Consort spun on his heel and left the room, Lina deciding immediately to follow, cat in tow.

7

Mikhail

Mikhail kept an eye on the faeling during lunch, ignoring the occasional chortling his partner let out. And on Sasha, who still looked like he had been hit in the head with a stick. Privately, he thought the whole thing a bit funny himself, but the faeling looked so anxious at their reactions that he stifled it. He'd laugh about it later, privately with Del.

To be fair to Adelina, she had no context for what magic could and couldn't do. None. Which was why they needed to get going with her education as soon as possible. Tomorrow, if she was up for it.

He also really wanted to figure out why she seemed nervous whenever Leander showed up. She was almost painfully polite to the servant, even more so than to them. It almost seemed like she was afraid, but that would be silly.

Wouldn't it?

There was one thing for sure: Adelina would fit in with them well once she relaxed a bit. Mikhail was fairly certain that she'd forgotten about Bissy curled up on her shoulder, which was easily one of the most adorable things he'd seen in a while. He couldn't deny being a touch envious; Iron got very jealous and upset when Mikhail spent too much time with other cats. That usually ended in destruction. The last time Iron had gotten jealous, they'd needed a new bed. The mngwa had ripped up the bedding with his teeth, then used the posts to sharpen his claws.

Mikhail had to rethink his decision that she'd forgotten the kitten when he saw the little female look around nervously, then grabbed a tiny piece of chicken with no sauce off her plate and held it up to the tiny, brown kitten's mouth. Bissy snatched it and—based on Adelina's delighted expression—started to purr. The next two bites of chicken vanished behind tiny white teeth just as quickly, but when the dessert course came out, Mikhail regrettably had to stop things.

"Cats can only have milk from other cats," Alexei said quietly to the female sitting across from him, holding a finger saturated with milk carefully on its way to the kitten's mouth. The faeling flinched, the drop of milk falling into her lap.

"Sorry," she murmured, eyes downcast.

"Don't be." Mikhail shook his head. Adelina still looked upset. "Hey," Mikhail said in a soft voice, causing her to look up in surprise. "Don't sweat it. A drop wouldn't have hurt him alone, but it's better you know so you don't give him a bowl of it later or something. But even if you did, the worst that would have happened is that the little beggar would have gotten a stomachache. No harm done."

The female graced him with a tiny, relieved smile.

"Thank you," she whispered, rubbing the kitten's head with a gentle finger. "I don't want to hurt him. I don't know much about cats."

"Never had one for a pet?" Mikhail asked. He was curious after the way Iron responded to her.

"I used to feed strays sometimes when I was little, but our landlord didn't want animals on his property." Adelina looked a little sad at that.

"Well, I'm glad you like them," he told her. "We have tons of the little creatures wandering around."

As he'd hoped, her smile grew.

"If you find one that's not been claimed," he said, lowering his voice, "and you can convince Cormac, you might can take it home with you."

Alexei felt very satisfied by the sparkle in the faeling's eyes when she met his gaze.

"Thank you," she murmured. "I'll keep an eye out." Then her countenance fell again. "I don't think the servants would be very pleased if I brought a cat back, though," she muttered, something Mikhail probably wasn't supposed to hear. He responded anyway, given how alarming the statement was.

"You're the heir," Mikhail pointed out. "Helping you and your family is their job. That's what they get paid for."

"They have plenty to do with helping Grandfather and keeping the manor," Adelina sighed. "My personal handmaiden is nice enough, but she's very busy and I wouldn't want to bother her. I make a lot of work for her on my own; adding a cat would just be cruel."

Made a lot of work for her? If the handmaiden had more jobs than working directly for Adelina, it was because the servant *wanted* them. And was likely avoiding her duty to her mistress. Mikhail wasn't sure if the servant was lazy or malicious, but there was definitely something. He was leaning toward malicious, given how she seemed to feel around servants in general. And from what he knew of the human world, she probably had never had any kind of house servants or workers. It was incredibly rare there.

"You're allowed to ask for another servant, you know," Mikhail said gently. "I may be wrong, but I'm thinking that you didn't have servants growing up. It's more than acceptable, especially if you don't get along with someone who's supposed to work for you specifically."

"But they're all so busy..." Adelina trailed off, looking a bit distressed. Mikhail heard, rather than saw, Sasha and Del's conversation trail off, both of them focusing on the faeling. Mikhail pretended that they weren't paying attention, doing his best to keep Adelina's focus on him rather than the other two. A gut feeling told him that bringing more people into this would make the faeling feel frightened and cornered, and he *really* didn't want that.

"You should have someone assigned to you and your needs who is willing to actually meet them," Mikhail told her bluntly. "That is literally their job. Them doing their job should not be an inconvenience. I don't know you well yet, but I'd eat my boots if you actually inconvenienced a servant, especially with what I've heard servants consider to be 'normal' actions from royals."

"But I accidentally left my clothes on the floor a couple of times," Adelina whispered. "And got cosmetics on the couch when I faceplanted on it or napped on it. And I ask for food and drinks outside of normal meal hours."

Mikhail's brow went up.

"You never had servants before coming to our world, did you?" It was more of a statement than a question, confirmed by the faeling's shaking head. "That sounds right," Mikhail sighed, making a face. He was so tired of prejudice. And that was all this was: fae who were so convinced that she didn't deserve personhood that they acted like it was an inconvenience when she actually got it. "So, all the things you're referring to are normal requests and normal things to have happen. Your servants are convincing you that you're making their lives difficult in order to avoid you or something of the like. Most servants would be desperate to work with someone as low-maintenance as you are."

"...Oh." A flash of depthless sadness crossed the faeling's face before a neutral expression settled. "I... I wondered. Sofria has been snappier since my Coming of Age."

Mikhail's heart twisted in his chest. The faeling was practically a baby, and he *hated* seeing how she'd been mistreated. It bothered him as much as the way Sasha's village treated *him.*

"Kiddo." Mikhail hesitated. "A couple of questions."

Adelina met his gaze with no hesitation now, he noticed absently, ignoring the warm fuzzies this gave him.

"Does Cormac know about this?"

"Sort of?" Lina shrugged. "I told him that they didn't like me. He said that they would get used to having me in the house."

"Did you tell him what they do?" Mikhail pressed.

"...No," she admitted. "There's no *proof* that it's them, and they've been there longer than my mother was alive. Why would he believe me over them?"

Mikhail felt his heart break slightly.

"Kid..." Mikhail sighed. "Your grandfather and I have had our differences over the years. But he's a good male. And it's obvious how much he cares about you. I've only known you for a few days, but even I know you're not one to tell tales."

"You... You think so?"

"I do." Mikhail nodded. "If you don't feel comfortable telling him, I'd be happy to."

"I'll think about it," she whispered.

"That's all I ask on that." Mikhail dipped his chin at her. "Second question, would you be willing to chat with Leander if someone were there with you? I trust him to give you a *realistic* idea of what is considered a true inconvenience and what the actual job of a body servant is. He technically runs the house here, but he started as Del's manservant."

Adelina looked deep in thought for a few moments, fiddling with her fork.

"I think I can do that," she murmured.

"Thank you, kiddo." Mikhail nodded. "And just so you're aware, even if you have a specific place where you usually put your clothes, it's *normal* for you to sometimes leave them on the floor.

Everyone does that. And accidentally getting cosmetics on fabric because you forgot you were wearing them is also a common issue.

"Finally, you should *always* ask for food or drink if you're hungry or thirsty. I don't care if it's just after sunrise, if we just ate a meal, or if the sun has been down for so long that you think it might be closer to breakfast than dinner. We want to take care of you, and this is part of that."

The faeling's eyes widened, and he thought he saw tears gathering in her eyes, but she clearly swallowed them down. For all that Mikhail wasn't a fan of tears, he wished she would let them go. It seemed like she probably needed a good cry.

"Thank you, Your Highness," the girl managed.

Mikhail's eyes widened.

"Please, no titles," he begged. "I ran *away* from titles. I'll use it if I have to, but just call me Mikhail. And this idiot," Mikhail said and tilted his head in the direction of his partner, who was practically smothering him in loving pride through their bond, "will want to be called at *least* Delwyn if you're not comfortable calling him Del."

"Okay." Adelina gave him a tiny smile, which he felt was a win. Especially with how little she wanted to share.

8

Lina

After not sleeping well the night before, Lina was absolutely not ready to start whatever "training" Mikhail had in mind for her. All she could hear were the kids who chose her last in gym as a child and laughed when she tripped over her feet. She wasn't graceful, she wasn't elegant, and she wasn't very strong. Likely, this was going to go *very* poorly, and Mikhail was going to give up on her in disgust.

After a few minutes of quiet, she decided to get up and face the music. The faster this started, the faster it could end. Before she could get very far, there was a knock at the door.

"Yes?" Lina called out.

"Dad says it's time to get up," Aleksandr called back. "Wear something comfortable that you can move in."

"Thanks," Lina replied, feeling a little queasy.

"Breakfast in ten?" the male asked.

"I'll be there," Lina promised. She began to dig around in the dresser across the room (her room? that they'd prepared for her?) until she found leggings and a comfortable shirt. After lacing up her boots, she crept through the mostly-quiet house until she came across a puddle of light and noise in the dining room.

"Good morning!" Del called cheerfully from where he was having a cup of tea. Aleksandr was also having tea, but he was a bit more subdued. Mikhail looked like he was still asleep with his head in his crossed arms.

"Good morning," Lina said to Del politely.

"Have a seat." He gestured to the well-laden table. "Have some food. You'll need your strength today."

Lina hesitantly found her seat and pulled a plate of warm bread closer. It proved to be those same cheesy scones from the day before. One or two of those, some sausage, a few pieces of fruit, and a cup of tea was a good place to start.

"Make sure you get a second plate," Aleksandr advised. "You'll need the energy once Dad starts working with us."

"You're training too?" Lina asked to distract herself as she took his advice and added a bit more to her plate.

"I'm probably going to be doing different exercises than you," Aleksandr admitted. "But I'll be around."

A servant appeared suddenly and placed two rough-hewn mugs of something dark in front of Mikhail. Once the earthy scent of the drink hit the male's nostrils, he tilted his chin up and opened his eyes. Privately, Lina thought he looked like a cat stalking a mouse with his yellow eyes locked on the mugs. Suddenly, he *moved.* He grabbed a mug and, without even stopping to blow on it, chugged the liquid inside. Lina felt her eyes widen. She had *so* many questions, but decided it was prudent to keep her mouth closed.

"Oh, good morning, Adelina," Mikhail said, starting to fill his own plate. Lina froze.

"Um... good morning," she managed after she swallowed her bite of fruit.

"Don't worry," Aleksandr murmured to her. "He does this. It's a bit eerie, even after having seen him do it for half a century or more."

The thought crossed Lina's mind that there was going to come a day when she was that blasé about decades and centuries. That existential worry quickly faded back into the depths of her mind; she was more concerned about what the hell the earthy liquid was.

The whole thing was definitely terrifying, more so because it seemed to have summoned Mikhail's normalcy from... some layer of hell, most likely.

Mikhail slowly met her gaze, and she quickly turned back to her breakfast.

"You didn't warn her that mornings aren't my strong suit," he rumbled to Aleksandr and Delwyn.

"I forgot," Aleksandr admitted.

"I thought it was hilarious," Delwyn added cheerfully.

Lina was starting to realize that Delwyn was a bit of a chaos entity. She was reminded of one of the Norse gods she'd learned about in middle school, Loki.

"Ass," Mikhail muttered, glaring at Delwyn, who grinned.

"Dad isn't a morning person," Aleksandr told Lina. "Likely due to being full Unseelie fae."

"Unseelie fae are nocturnal, usually," Mikhail said. "There's a reason we created relo brew."

"What's relo brew?" Lina asked curiously.

"It's something that Unseelie fae brew out of a tree bark that wakes you up. Not unlike how tea does, but... more." Mikhail took a sip out of his mug, apparently the relo brew.

"It's one of the nastiest things I've ever tasted." Delwyn made a face. "I don't know how you drink it."

"It's not terrible once you get used to it," Aleksandr argued. "I prefer tea—"

"Heathen," Mikhail cut in.

"But it's not the worst," Aleksandr finished as if his dad hadn't cut him off.

"Unseelie fae are weird," Delwyn decided with a grin.

"Says the male who welcomed two into his home," Lina pointed out hesitantly.

Aleksandr burst out laughing, to Lina's delight. Even Mikhail grinned briefly.

"I like this one," he decided.

"You wanted to keep her as soon as you realized how much Iron likes her," Delwyn snorted.

Mikhail narrowed his eyes at Delwyn but didn't argue.

Lina looked between them but decided not to say anything. The warmth that statement gave her was something that she only got in tiny doses when her mum wasn't having one of her... episodes. Lina didn't dare name it, but she knew Grandfather didn't really... know how to give it.

"Alright," Mikhail said. "Are you kids done eating?"

"Not a kid," Aleksandr muttered.

"Hush." Delwyn pointed at him.

Mikhail ignored both of them and looked to Lina for her response. She looked down at her mostly empty plate and nodded. If she ate any more, she'd throw up from nerves.

"Let's go." Mikhail stood, Lina following quickly and Aleksandr groaning as he did the same.

"Bye!" Delwyn's cheerful voice sounded like a portent. "Have fun!"

Surprisingly enough, they went into a yard behind the house. The yard butted up against a forest, but there was a decently clear area between the two that Mikhail led them to.

"Sit." He pointed at the ground.

Lina was a bit hesitant but followed easily when she saw Aleksandr settle into the damp grass.

"Go ahead and start, Sasha." Mikhail nodded to the younger male before turning and sitting in front of Lina. "Have you used any magic yet?" he asked her.

Lina looked down at her lap.

"No," she admitted.

"I'd have been surprised if you had," Mikhail told her. "You've been able to access it for all of three days, and you have no framework for it. I just wanted to be sure. Do you know why demi-fae can't access magic before their Coming of Age?"

Lina shook her head, already riveted by the direction the conversation had taken.

"Iron," Mikhail said succinctly. "I don't know how much you know about humans in general, but they have iron in their blood. Because you are a demi-fae with a human mother, your blood was close in iron content to a full human before your Coming of Age."

Lina's mind spun with the implications.

"Wait." She felt her brow furrow. "What happens to fae females who bear half-human children?"

Mikhail sighed, rubbing his face with a hand.

"Most of the time, either the female's body won't be able to carry the child to term, or the iron in the child's blood kills their mother during birthing," he admitted. "It's... always a tragedy."

"That's awful." Lina put her hand to her mouth.

"Most of us believe that the females who manage to survive likely have a touch of human heritage somewhere," Mikhail told her.

"So, iron is a problem for the fae?" Lina verified. "I've heard it a few times, but I don't know *why*."

"Neither do we." Mikhail shrugged. "But what we do know is that iron seems to repel our magic. Full fae of any kind can't touch it without getting burns or rashes. The purity of the iron matters, though; iron mixed into other metals is tolerable, but it will cause a rash. That's why we don't use steel like humans do. From what the research has shown, part of the Coming of Age process for both demi-fae and changelings involves most—if not all—of the iron being burnt out of their blood."

"Does that mean I can't touch iron anymore?" Lina asked.

"Oddly, no," Mikhail answered. "It seems like your body retains its immunity to iron, though it does dampen your magic if it's touching your bare skin. Not completely, but somewhat. Even though you no longer have iron running through your blood, you are capable of wielding it."

"That's handy," Lina decided. Maybe she could have an iron nail or something as a line of defense.

"Indeed," Mikhail told her gravely. "My goal is to get you an iron weapon to have on you as a last resort. Probably a dagger."

"Iron dagger?" she asked. "I was thinking of a nail or something."

"You need to learn to fight," he told her. "Later. But for now, magic."

"I don't know how..." Lina protested, worried.

"Of course you don't," Mikhail replied. "That's why we're here. We're going to help you find the magic inside you."

Lina bit her lip but kept quiet and listened.

"Get comfortable," Mikhail instructed. "Sit easily, and then close your eyes."

Lina did so, feeling a little bit of the stress leave the line of her shoulders.

"Focus on my voice," Mikhail told her. "Breathe on my count."

Slowly, Mikhail led her through breathing exercises, focusing her on her breath as he spoke. She felt surprisingly calm after only a short time.

"Now, I want you to imagine that you are connected to the earth," Mikhail said. "We are of earth and magic, and to earth and magic we will return." The hair on Lina's arms stood up at the use of the phrase from the book she'd been reading the day before. "Inside you, there is a place where you can find stability and peace. That is the earth inside you, providing you shelter from the power of your magic."

Lina turned inward, seeking out this mysterious peace of which Mikhail spoke. A place of stability. Inside herself, she currently felt nothing but a whirlwind of fear and anxiety, nothing stable or safe.

"Many fae find this stability in similar places." Mikhail's voice was a surprisingly comforting sound in the maelstrom of her emotions. "Some find it in their feet, some in their minds, and some in their hearts. Of course, there are those who find their stable places elsewhere, but if you're struggling, I'd look there first."

Mikhail went quiet, letting Lina seek out that stable place. She tried her feet first, but there wasn't any stability there. Her mind was next; there was a bit of stability, but not as much as she hoped for. Before committing, Lina tried her heart. Turning inward, she somehow managed to find a tiny island of calm in her inner landscape.

With a gasp of surprise, she lost the relaxed, meditative state she was in. Her eyes opened, finding Mikhail in the same relaxed position he'd been in previously.

"I found it!" she cried, excited. Mikhail nodded proudly.

"Good, well done," he told her. "Now, when you go back and find it, steady yourself on it and then take a thread of power and lock yourself to that grounding."

Lina closed her eyes again, turning inward and finding that core sense of self. She "stood" on it carefully, then grabbed a thin tendril from the maelstrom and fed it through herself and into the stable place. She managed to nod slowly, indicating that she felt like she'd done it.

"How it feels to use your power is unique to every fae." Mikhail spoke again, in that same soothing tone. "Some feel as if it's similar to their affinity. Some feel it as raw power. Some feel it as something else entirely. The core of it is that to get the best results, you and your power must work *together*. You can attempt to force the power, but you will burn incredible amounts of energy trying to do so. Your power is part of you; it can guide you to where you're trying to go.

"Now, what I want you to do, is I want you to make a faelight," Mikhail finished. "I don't care about size, shape, or anything else. Control comes later, after you can access the power."

Lina "looked" around that emotional landscape, standing on that small circle of stability amongst a whirlwind of power. She focused intently on the idea of a light, of her memories of the faelights she'd seen over the past few years.

After a bit of looking, she found one that glowed ever so slightly brighter than the others. Lina held her hand out, beckoning the strand to herself gently. When it touched her hand, power surged through her body. She gasped with the rush of it, letting herself get used to the sensation before she cupped her hands together instinctively. A light grew in her cupped palms, tinted green and barely bright enough to see.

"Adelina." Mikhail's voice almost startled her out of her contemplation of the light. "Open your eyes."

Obediently, Lina's eyes fluttered open. She found her hands to be in the same cupped palms position, and to her joy and shock, a small, green ball of light hovered above her cupped hands. She felt a smile creeping up over her face as she *finally* started thinking that maybe—just maybe—she was going to do okay. That things were going to work out.

"Now let the magic go," Mikhail instructed. On an instinct Lina didn't understand, she did just that. She released the magic and allowed it to snap back into the rush of power surrounding where she stood on the central island.

"I did it." Lina beamed. "I really did it!"

"You did." Mikhail nodded proudly. "Well done."

"You did great!" Aleksandr praised, a gentle elbow on her arm reminding her of his presence.

"You're a really good teacher," Lina insisted. She'd never considered herself dumb, but the speed with which she'd caught on to this was beyond anything she'd experienced before.

"I, well..." Mikhail blustered a bit. "These are basics. And you grasped them quickly."

Lina narrowed her eyes at the older male, one of the nicest people she'd met in a long time. She didn't say what she wanted to say, which was that he deserved the compliment because he *was* a good teacher.

Aleksandr snorted a laugh, interrupting her worry about the Unseelie male.

"Never seen that before. Good going," he told her.

"Shut." Mikhail pointed at Aleksandr.

"I'm telling Da," the younger male sang.

"You wouldn't dare." Mikhail's eyes narrowed now.

"Oh I absolutely would," Aleksandr replied.

"He won't protect you, Sasha," Mikhail vowed.

"Oh, I know." Aleksandr smirked. "But it'll be worth it."

Lina, meanwhile, was giggling behind the hands covering her mouth. According to Lady Mara, it wasn't polite to laugh properly in public, but she was having a hard time staying straight-faced with these two. Well, three really—Delwyn was even worse.

"Alright," Mikhail finally said. "Get back to your meditation. I need to keep working with Adelina."

"Fair enough." Aleksandr shrugged and grinned before shutting his eyes and deepening his breathing.

"Alright." Mikhail turned back to Lina. "Do you think you could do that again with less guidance?"

"All I can do is try," Lina replied bravely. With that, she worked her way back down to that safe spot. Knowing where it was made it easier to find, but she was also closer to it anyway. She sought out the power for light quickly, then cupped her hands and opened her eyes.

There, yet again, sat a soft green ball of light.

"Yes," she hissed victoriously.

"Good job," Mikhail praised. "That's what you'll be doing today. Creating that light, and then letting it go completely before doing it again."

"Okay." Lina nodded, determined, and set to it.

9

Mikhail

Mikhail found himself impressed with the faeling as she carefully summoned her magic, created a faelight, and then dismissed it smoothly. She caught on quickly. He'd likely be using the faelight as a means for her to learn control before moving to more complex magics.

He couldn't really get a read on her feelings about learning to fight. Was she hesitant because she was taught not to fight others? Because she was a pacifist? Because she didn't believe in herself? Mikhail could definitely tell she was hesitant, but what he didn't know was *why*.

Something tightened in his chest as he watched the faeling continue to summon faelights with a determined expression. The same thing that had convinced him to take Sasha home with him, rather than finding a new family who would love and care for him. Even though the younger him had doubted his ability to be a parent (though never Del's), he'd done it. He'd known it was the right thing to do just as he'd known that Branwen and... and Faolin's parents would care for him—the Unseelie faeling.

Mikhail didn't know everything about the little female, but he knew enough to sense a kindred spirit in her and enough to recognize that she was kind and genuine. Part of him wished that Cormac

hadn't found her—not because he begrudged her her family, but because he would have loved to have given her theirs.

Of course, there was always the chance that Del was right about
the two younglings being mated, but he wasn't convinced. It didn't
feel... right.

After letting Adelina and Sasha practice for just over an hour, he
decided that it was time to take a break.

"When you release this one," he told the female, "we're taking a
break."

Adelina nodded, focusing carefully on releasing the magic in a
controlled manner, a way that he'd never seen anyone do without
being explicitly told to do.

"You've done well," he told Adelina, who practically *glowed*
with the praise. "I noticed that you were able to find and summon
the faelight much faster by the end; it took less direct energy than
previously. That's a very important step. Eventually, little magics like
this will be second nature and take next to no power.

"Now, I don't mind you practicing these on your own, but *be
careful*," Mikhail warned her. "Magical burnout is a real and terrible
thing that I don't want you to have to deal with any time soon.
Sometimes, overuse of your magic is expected, a bit like when you're
training and you ache the next day. But you shouldn't *constantly* be
overworking your magic. You'll hurt yourself."

"What are the signs of burnout?" Adelina asked, eyes wide and
fingers twisting together.

"Be gentle on yourself," Mikhail said instinctively, giving her
twisting fingers the side eye. All that twisting looked painful and
couldn't be good for her hands. "Grab some grass or something;
you're not going to hurt that." He waited until she'd snagged a few
pieces of grass and began shredding it before continuing.

"Now, as for burnout, the signs aren't all the same for everyone.
The most common ones are, of course, aching and difficulty using
your power. Some describe that difficulty as if you're trying to dig a

hole in wet sand. Or as if you're trying to walk up a muddy hill in the rain. It's technically possible, but it takes more strength, and you slip often. Others describe it as losing their grip on their grounding. If you lose your grip on your grounding, drop your magic *immediately*. Do you understand me?"

"Yes, sir." Adelina nodded frantically. Mikhail relaxed.

"Using your magic without grounding is dangerous for both you and the people around you," he lectured. "Some call it 'wild' magic, but that's a misnomer in my opinion. It's, more accurately, just uncontrolled magic. At that point, the magic is capable of controlling you rather than the other way around. Which can, at best, cause untold destruction of both you and the surrounding areas. Worst-case scenario, people die. Neither of which are acceptable outcomes."

"Okay, yes, sir." Adelina nodded again, a bit less frantically this time.

"Good." He gave both faelings a small smile. "Alright, well, if anything about your magic feels weird or off, *tell* someone. We'll let you know if it's burnout or something else."

"Alright, I will," she confirmed.

"Excellent." Mikhail rolled his shoulders a bit, working some of the stiffness out. "You two will be out here right after breakfast. Sasha will meditate and help us as needed, and you'll work with your power. Once we've done that for a while, I'll send you back inside, where Del will torture you with books until lunch and about an hour after. Then we'll work on combat until dinner. After dinner, your time is yours to do with what you will.

"I ask only that you not leave the property alone for now. We're fairly certain no one knows you're up here, but I'd rather not have you get caught alone by assassins before we can help you keep yourself alive through an assassination attempt."

"Do... do I have to learn to fight?" Adelina asked, then bit her lip. "I shouldn't be questioning your methods. I apologize."

"You are *always* welcome to ask questions," Mikhail told the female. "And you *at least* have to learn to defend yourself."

"It's a lot harder to defend someone who can't defend themselves," Sasha told her sympathetically, quoting Mikhail from so many decades before. "I didn't want to learn to fight either. I thought it would turn me into a bully."

"I... I don't want to hurt people," Adelina murmured, staring at the grass. "It feels... wrong."

"Good," Mikhail told her, surprising her enough that she looked up. "You shouldn't want to hurt people," he clarified. "While the occasional desire for violence in retaliation is a normal response to being hurt, straight-up being ready to beat the shit out of someone just because isn't.

"And by ready," he added, "I mean, 'looking for a fight' ready. Being prepared is not just good; it's vital."

"Dad trained me before the first time someone tried to kill me," Sasha said. "I hated it. I told you about my affinity." Mikhail felt a rush of pride in his son. He rarely discussed his affinity; it usually went poorly. "I feel people when I have to hurt them, no matter how much I shield. After that first time... it was weeks before I could train again."

Mikhail remembered that. Sasha had sequestered himself away for days, barely eating. It took them ages to pry out of him that *he felt his assassin die.*

"I thought I was..." Sasha shook his head. "I don't even know. A lot of those days are a blur. But then Da said something to me. I'm going to say it to you. Is a cornered wolf evil?"

"...No." Adelina tilted her head.

"If someone attacks an animal they cornered and it fights back and kills them, is the animal wrong? Should they kill the animal?"

"Of course not!" Adelina shot back, almost glaring at Sasha.

"Then why would you be wrong for ensuring your claws are sharp in case *you* are cornered?" Sasha asked.

Adelina blinked.

"I never thought about it like that," she murmured.

"I hadn't either," Sasha admitted easily.

"Sasha's right," Mikhail told her. "Being able to defend yourself and your people is the goal. Not for you to start fights or kill indiscriminately."

"Alright," Adelina acquiesced.

"Now, inside with you both." Mikhail shooed both faelings inside, taking a moment to watch them talk to each other as they walked back into the manor. Something was growing there, with the faelings. Mikhail was surprised at how much he wanted the little female to trust them. Sasha must have felt similarly, given that he confided what he did about his first kill.

With another long-suffering sigh, Mikhail got up from the cool, damp ground. Iron would likely be lounging around somewhere, and if the faelings were with Del, it was the perfect time for a quick nap.

10

Sasha

Sasha privately was willing to admit that after this morning, he was worried about Adelina and how she'd handle the physical training with Dad. She seemed... apprehensive about fighting. At best. Even knowing intellectually that she needed to learn didn't change the thought processes she was accustomed to.

The kicker was, she *had* to learn. Dad was right; even though she'd probably have guards or other fighters around for most of her life, she'd be both forfeiting her right to any independence *and* making it more than slightly difficult for anyone to protect her in the future.

Still, he hated how nervous she was. Considering how hard she'd clearly been working to hide basically all of her feelings, the fact that he noticed her nervousness said a lot. Adelina picked at her food at lunch and seemed really distracted during the shorter second lesson with Da afterwards.

Having been briefed by Dad, Da was gentle with her today. Sasha knew that if the attention issues continued, Da would address it, but for now, he decided to wait and see if the issues resolved themselves with familiarity. They all suspected that Adelina would feel better once she got used to the schedule.

"You're going to do fine," Sasha murmured to her as they walked up the stairs to the flat rooftop space that they used for training when they couldn't get to the larger training gym they had access to in their central Skovfore home. Well, house; that place never felt like a home to any of them.

"I can't do this," Adelina whispered.

"You couldn't make a faelight this morning," Sasha pointed out. "You just had to learn. That's all that's going to happen today. Putting a weapon in your hand doesn't change who you are. And you're not going to have a weapon in your hand today, anyway. Dad is probably just going to evaluate you."

"You think so?" Adelina asked, fingers twisting. Remembering what Dad had done that morning, Sasha tapped on her fingers until she stopped twisting them.

"You'll hurt yourself," he told the female. "And I know so."

"Hopefully." Adelina moved to twisting the edge of her shirt between her fingers, which was a significant improvement.

"Afternoon," Dad greeted them with a nod.

"Hey." Sasha grinned at his dad, trying not to bounce on his toes in excitement. The look in his dad's eyes promised a spar, and Sasha had *almost* won their last one.

"Good afternoon," Adelina said quietly.

"You won't be fighting today," Dad told her. Sasha saw and felt her relief through his ever-present shields. She probably didn't realize how much he could sense; he tried not to make a big deal over what he noticed from others. "I need to evaluate where you are physically and see about building up a good foundation for you. But before that, I'd like for you to back up to the edge of the balcony. Sasha and I will be giving you a demonstration of a spar, or practice fight."

Sasha grinned, fairly certain it was a bit feral but not minding much.

"We use semi-blunted weapons," Sasha told her. "Obviously, we heal fast enough that a few little cuts and bruises are nothing to worry about, but we don't want anything that's going to cause the loss of limbs or anything." He paused. "Da would murder us both."

"You've got that right," Dad muttered under the sound of Adelina's soft chuckles.

Both of them made their way to the storage box on the far end, grabbing their favorite practice weapons and readying themselves. Sasha felt something in him relax as he began strapping on his assorted daggers. One on each thigh, throwing knife sheaths on his wrists, smaller daggers on his ankles, and a longer dagger sheathed at his waist that he readied.

Dad, on the other hand, was apparently going all out today. His sword on his hip, his rope dart coiled in his left hand, and if he had that, he definitely had his machete sheathed around the back of his sword belt. He smirked at Sasha as he unsheathed his sword.

"You ready, Sasha?"

"Let's go." Sasha narrowed his eyes at his dad, grinning broadly and unsheathing his largest dagger.

The world narrowed down to himself, his weapons, and his dad in front of him. The male stood deceptively still, sword tip low to the ground. Sasha could see the tips of his dad's pointed ears twitching slightly at every noise since the male's hair was tied back away from his face for once. Sasha stayed just as still as his dad, knowing that the first movement he made would get countered with that thrice-damned rope dart and he'd get taken out immediately.

"You going to attack, or are we going to stand here all afternoon?" his dad asked, deceptively mild-toned.

"Oh, I don't know," Sasha replied, forcing himself to sound bored. "I thought it would be a nice day for sitting in the sun."

His dad smirked slightly.

"Come on, son, show me what you've got!"

With those words, Sasha finally understood the point—today wasn't just a show for Adelina. Sasha was being evaluated, too.

He burst into motion with the framework of a plan, faking toward a direction and leaping out of reach of the ankle-cracking weight on the end of the rope his dad held. The attempt was successful until he tried to get a scratch on his father, whose sword blocked the dagger with the clang of metal on metal.

Spinning away using his own momentum to get out of reach, Sasha crouched under another swing of the rope weight and then *leapt* to get a bit of height on his dad, coming down on him with a grin. His dad jumped back, letting Sasha land with a roll that he used to trip his dad.

Unfortunately, it backfired, and he got tangled in the other male's ankles, but not before he managed to pickpocket his dad's machete. He now had two knives in hand, not to mention the ones sheathed all over his body. Sasha disengaged from his dad, skidding backwards to get some space and a quick breath before that magic-forsaken rope showed back up, trying to tangle his daggers together.

Regrettably, this lost him the machete, but Sasha kept moving and didn't stop to grab his pilfered weapon. He had plenty. After all the moving around, his dad was, unfortunately for the male, in a spot where Sasha could actually *use* his throwing knives without hurting him.

With a flick of his wrist, a delicate throwing knife spun out of his fingers and pinned his dad to the door of the storage closet by his shirt. Another followed shortly after, with Sasha quickly running behind the second dart and going in with a gentle jab to the side, leaving a thin cut that Sasha could barely see, but a cut nonetheless.

"First blood." His dad nodded proudly, lowering his weapons. "Well done, Sasha; that was well fought. You've learned a lot since the last time."

"Thanks." Sasha was panting slightly, but grinned as he yanked the throwing knives out of the wall and freed his dad, who frowned at the cuts in his shirt.

"I should have worn a different shirt," he muttered.

"Da can fix it," Sasha pointed out.

"Yes, but he'll fuss." Dad made a face. "He always gets upset when one of us gets hurt, even if it's an easy fix that won't be problematic long- or short-term. Silly male."

Sasha just snickered, then turned to Adelina, who was watching both of them with wide eyes.

"Thoughts?" Sasha asked.

"I've never seen anything quite like that before in my life," the female responded, eyes wide. "It was incredible!"

"You'll eventually be learning a hybrid of these two techniques," Dad explained to her. "I'd like you to at least have a passing knowledge of a sword, throwing knives are vital for someone who has assassins after them, and I think an iron dagger would be a good backup weapon for you."

"Okay." Adelina nodded.

"I can't actually *make* the weapon for you," his dad admitted. "But I think there's someone in the Eastern Mountains who would take on the challenge. Eventually, I'd like for you to learn how to make them yourself, even if smithing isn't one of your magics. It will always be hard for you to find iron-based weapons here."

"Smithing?" the female asked.

"Many of the fae have a particular ability to smith weapons with magic in them," his dad explained.

"Dad's a smith, technically," Sasha cut in proudly. "He learned with Liam."

"The Prince of the Eastern Mountains?" Adelina asked, eyes wide.

"That's the one," Sasha replied.

"Sasha, there are plenty of smiths," his dad protested.

"Not many Unseelie ones," Sasha pointed out. Dad sighed.

"I suppose not, since the King killed most of them or pressed them into service somewhere in the mountains," his dad muttered. Sasha winced.

"Fair," he admitted, shoulders drooping.

His dad shook his head, then ruffled Sasha's hair, to his embarrassment.

"Cool off," he instructed, before turning to Adelina. "Your turn, kiddo."

11

Lina

Lina was happy to admit that she was both intimidated and oddly excited about the idea of learning how to do what the other two were doing. It had looked like a dance of some kind, the two of them ducking and weaving to a melody she couldn't hear yet.

Aleksandr was stretching on the other side of the mostly bare rooftop balcony, having removed the numerous daggers he'd put on before the fight—spar?—he'd had with Mikhail. She bounced on her toes slightly as Alexei came over to where she'd been waiting.

"You look more ready," he noticed.

"It looked... really elegant," she admitted. "Like a dance."

"Good." Mikhail looked pleased with her comment. "It *is* a bit like a dance, yes. There's a rhythm and pattern to battle that you'll eventually need to learn. But the fact that you saw it in my spar with Sasha bodes well for your success."

"Thank you." Lina felt her face flush.

"In the meantime," Mikhail said, "I'd like to evaluate your physical abilities."

What followed was the sort of gauntlet of physical tests like she hadn't experienced since she'd left the human world. It honestly reminded her a bit of the tests they'd run twice a year in the physical education classes. Mikhail had her do push-ups, sit-ups, and squats until she couldn't anymore. She picked up heavy items and put them back down, and she had to stand in increasingly intricate poses to evaluate her flexibility and strength further. Lina even had to walk on a narrow board to test her balance.

Finally, she got a break. Aleksandr handed her a flask of water, which she drank deeply from after she got to sit for a moment.

"You're doing well," Mikhail said. Something about the way he said it made her a bit nervous. "Only one more test left," he assured her before turning to Aleksandr. "Sasha, suit back up. We're doing the distance run."

"Got it, Dad!" The younger male nodded, heading back over to the storage box close to the shed built against one of the edges of the balcony. Once Aleksandr had his daggers back on, he met them close to the stairway.

"There's a path through the woods we're going to take," Mikhail informed them. "We're all three going in order to protect you, Adelina."

"I'm sorry," she muttered. "I'm going to slow you down."

"Better that than you getting hurt," Mikhail said seriously.

Lina just ducked her head shyly and followed the two males through the house and into the backyard.

"Sasha, you know where we're going, right?" Mikhail asked. The younger male nodded. "Excellent. You're leading. Adelina, you're after him, and I'm going to be behind you. Sasha, be careful that you don't leave her behind."

"Got it, Dad." The male looked serious. "Ready?" he asked her. Lina gave him a flat look.

"Absolutely not," she sighed. "But let's get this over with."

"That's the spirit!" Sasha grinned, then turned and started jogging down a track in the woods.

For all Lina felt like she was going to die of air loss, she was really enjoying finally seeing the beauty of the Northern Forests. In this part of the region, there was a gorgeous combination of evergreens and deciduous trees. The latter were just barely starting to change colors; the only non-green visible was in the early-changing bright yellows. Warm afternoon sunshine filtered through the leaves onto the forest floor, which was dotted with plants, rocks, and occasional clusters of undergrowth. Even with the three fae moving through the forest, Lina could hear distant bird calls and rustling in the bits of undergrowth. The whole thing smelled fresh and green, relaxing Lina more than she'd expected.

A small smile crept over her face as she enjoyed the meditative aspect of running in the beautiful forest behind the house. Maybe one of the others would walk with her out here sometimes? It was really beautiful, and she wanted to explore it further.

Unfortunately, the beauty of the forest couldn't sustain her forever. Lina felt her chest tightening as she pushed herself, and her limbs shook. She made a halfhearted waving motion at Mikhail as she slowed to a stop, panting.

"Breathe, kid." Mikhail put a hand on her back. "That's it; relax a little." His voice rose. "Sasha, we're done."

Aleksandr spun, jogging back with a worried expression.

"She okay?"

Lina nodded silently, attempting to get her breath back.

"You sure?" Aleksandr prodded.

"...Yeh," Lina managed, breathing finally starting to even out.

"That's better," Mikhail sighed, sounding relieved to hear her speak. "Let's head back."

Aleksandr led their line in the opposite direction at a moderate walk, allowing them all to cool off as they walked.

"Sorry about that," Mikhail said from behind her. "I didn't explain myself well. I wanted to see your best, not for you to completely wreck yourself, kid. Don't get me wrong, you work hard, but you shouldn't destroy yourself for a basic assessment."

"But... that *was* my best..." Lina protested quietly, in deference to the scratchiness in her throat.

"There's a point where pushing beyond your limits like that will just hurt you," Mikhail explained. "Your best doesn't mean pushing beyond your limits; it means finding out what those limits are. I should have realized you were struggling much sooner than I did, sorry."

"No, no," Lina protested. "You don't need to apologize. I was distracted. It's beautiful here." And she didn't want to look weak in front of the other two capable fae. She was behind, behind by *years*. Decades, even. Aleksandr alone was older than many humans reached, and she had the gut feeling that Mikhail and Delwyn would had generations of humans pass.

"We'll take it easy tomorrow," Mikhail promised. Lina felt a frustrated ache in her chest.

"I can do it," she insisted.

"You don't need to get injured." Mikhail stood firm.

"But I..."

"Just take the break," Aleksandr recommended. "Dad is more stubborn than you are, I promise."

Lina's shoulders drooped. She wanted so badly to be successful, to be *good enough*. She had failed so many; she couldn't fail this family, who were going out of their way to help her.

"Okay," she murmured, no longer focused on the scenery, but instead on the swirling inner frustration at her own shortcomings.

The rest of the walk back was quiet, with Lina stewing in her own mind while the two males guarded her until they hit the yard behind the house.

"Go bathe, Sasha," Mikhail instructed. "Adelina, stay back with me for a moment."

Aleksandr turned just long enough to meet her gaze and give her an encouraging smile. Lina let the edge of her mouth quirk up a bit, but couldn't force anything further.

"We're going to stretch a bit," Mikhail rumbled. "Just to do what we can to prevent soreness."

Lina nodded silently, following along as Mikhail led her in a series of simple poses that stretched the muscles in her legs and core. The tension that had been winding in them, unnoticed, relaxed significantly as she moved.

"Wanna tell me what you're thinking?" Mikhail prodded, leaving the floor open.

Lina was quiet, considering the pros and cons before answering.

"I'm sorry for overdoing it," she said to the older male.

"Easily forgiven," Mikhail replied. "Just don't make a habit of it. Your body may be more durable and able to heal faster, but it's not invulnerable. And you *can* permanently injure yourself doing basic exercises."

"Sorry," Lina said again, even more quietly.

"Relax, don't worry about it," Mikhail told her. "We just want you to be safe. That's why I push anyone I train. I want them to be safe. And besides, pushing is one thing; breaking is another. I don't make a habit of breaking my students on purpose. As a matter of fact, I do everything in my power to *avoid* doing so."

Lina nodded again.

"Sometimes, this place doesn't seem too dissimilar to the home I grew up in," she said, barely aware of what she was saying. "But sometimes, it's so completely different that I don't know what's up and what's down. Even after six years here, I still feel... lost."

"You haven't had much of a chance to assimilate, what with people trying to other you all the time," Mikhail pointed out.

"True," she admitted.

"It'll get easier," he promised. "You'll figure out where you fit here."

"Hopefully," Lina mumbled.

"You will," Mikhail replied. "You absolutely will. Now, go bathe. A nice hot bath, and take your time. Then, go to bed early. I'll have dinner sent to your rooms."

"Thank you," Lina said gratefully, smiling tiredly before heading off to the space that was already, even after only a day or two, starting to feel more like *hers* than any part of the Southern Highlands ever had.

12

Lina

With a schedule, Lina found that the days went by quickly. Often, she was moving from the moment she woke up to the moment she fell asleep that night. Even on the rest days that her foster guardians insisted on, Lina found herself being snuck back to the Southern Highlands for a visit with her grandfather and sometimes Uncle Donal.

Most days didn't stick out, but a few moments were cemented in her memories. The morning after she'd hurt herself that first day, a gorgeous little pendant with a leather thong had been sitting next to her plate.

It was a coin-sized pendant. The whole thing was golden wire, expertly wrapped and arranged to look like tree limbs, and the leaves were made of chips of pink, orange, and red sunstone.

She sensed... something, from the delicate piece. Something of safety and care. After she asked, Aleksandr told her it was from Mikhail and that she should wear it if she wanted to. After that, she only took it off to bathe.

Another moment that stuck out was the first time she'd gotten a punch in on Mikhail. It had been an accident, but he'd still gone out of his way to tell her he was proud. She'd been warm the entire rest of the day.

Meeting Prince Clio a few weeks into her training was another type of eye-opening. The female was brash, unapologetic, and fun—despite beating the shit out of them in training. It was a relief to properly meet her after being smothered by the expectations of females like Lady Mara.

Her magic training was being split between Mikhail and Delwyn, who were both very talented mages. Both Delwyn and Mikhail were constantly saying how well she was doing in her magic training.

Lina wasn't sure she'd ever been complimented this much in her life. Mum was so focused on *hiding,* on moving at least once a year, that praising Lina's accomplishments was clearly not even on her mind. Never allowed to play at other children's houses, never allowed to eat food her mum hadn't prepared herself, never living anywhere long enough to put down roots... While Lina now knew that there was *some* credibility to the hyper-paranoia her mum had exhibited, it had robbed her of a childhood.

Lady Mara, on the other hand, had always been tough on her, never bothering to give her a kind word. None of it was like the kind of legitimate praise she'd been getting from Delwyn, Mikhail, and Aleksandr. It was addictive, truly.

She'd been settling into her new routine for close to a month before she realized that she hadn't touched her research on D'Vita since the day she'd arrived. Her blood chilled; what if the goddess took her immortality away if she wasn't able to do what she wanted? Lina didn't want to risk that happening, so she decided to work on her research in the evenings after dinner.

That night, Lina dug out another book from her grandfather's library, this one titled *Legendary Epics.* She wasn't particularly a fan of epic poetry, but given that it had been in the history section, Lina assumed that the poetry was more of a semi-dramatized retelling of certain pieces of the Fae's history.

The first poem was titled *"From Whence We Came."* Lina grinned in triumph; this was the creation of the fae!

In aeons past, the goddess found
herself inside the magick.
Oceans wide and deep
of power personified.

Her hands, she cupped
and opened wide.
The magick spilled out
b'twixt her fingers
the warmth of earth upon new-formed ground

Her fingers dragged through the dirt,
green things sprouting in their wake.
A shake of hair
became the rain. And filled the oceans deep

Puddles of power, she coaxed and shaped
to become the creatures great
and small
In waters and above, in forests dark and mountains high
The world was filled with fauna.

She walked among them to and fro
Their company, she craved.
But for all the familiar spirits there
her shadows they became—
She wanted ones to share the power with
who'd call her by her name.

In cupped palms, she held a bit

of the earth she'd made so dear
And blew the magic soft upon it
To shape it oh so fair.

Two pairs she made, to help her
to rule the land with her
each sang with different magics
the duties in care were split.

The first, she made upon the day
with earth and leaves and buds
Spring flowers and summer breezes
spawned in their souls

The second pair was for the night
Of cold and snow and stars.
Their strength was in their clever minds
and in reading others' hearts.

Lina stopped there for a moment, writing furiously on the sheets of paper she'd removed from her bag along with the book. At this point, her notes and questions were books in themselves, it felt like. She sighed. It seemed like everything she learned gave her more questions, and trying to figure out what actually mattered was horrifically time-consuming because there was just *so much* that she didn't know.

She wondered if it was time to try to bring Aleksandr into this. He'd been kind to her, *truly* kind. And she felt as though she was finally starting to relax in his presence. And that he could, perhaps, be something of a friend. A proper friend, not in the way Sofria was her friend. Her gut said she could trust him, and the goddess *had* said she didn't have to do it alone.

Aleksandr would be a good one to bring in, in her opinion.

Once she had her notes and books in neat, semi-organized piles on the desk in her suite, Lina sought out Aleksandr. The male wasn't in the living area, nor was he in the yard or on the rooftop training area. She did, however, see Delwyn as she passed by his open office door a few times. After the fourth pass, the male called out.

"You okay over there?"

"Hmm?" Lina peered into the room, which was somehow professional, cozy, and a mess at the same time.

"You okay?" Delwyn repeated.

"I'm looking for Aleksandr," she said quietly to the Prince. Delwyn smiled kindly.

"He's probably in his room if you can't find him in the public areas of the house," Delwyn pointed out. "Or in the library; it takes up most of the top floor."

"Okay." Lina smiled softly. "I'll try the library first."

Delwyn just gave her a happy grin before turning back to his paperwork. Lina left him to it, finding the closest staircase and heading all the way up. Well, *almost* all the way. She'd skipped this floor when she had checked the roof and hadn't actually been here yet.

The room was absolutely *gorgeous*. The walls were paneled with a warm wood and dotted with windows. Shelves ran through the center of the room, made of the same wood as the walls and stuffed with books. Desks capped the ends of every other shelf, seeming to hold stationery supplies. Soft chairs and couches dotted the outer edge of the room to create little reading and studying nooks.

In one of those nooks was Aleksandr, thankfully. He was draped over a chair with a book, a tea tray on a little table by his elbow. The male was, adorably enough, *covered* in cats. Bissy snuggled in his hair. A larger gray cat that Lina hadn't met yet made biscuits with the blanket on his lap. A black and white cat that had been introduced as Wheeze snored from where he was curled up on the back of the chair. Another black and white one with different patterning—this one by the amusing name of Hisspot—sprawled on the floor. A tiny all-white kitten they called Fiddle, with eyes the same color as Delwyn's, was tucked into the spot where Aleksandr's shoulder met his neck.

"Aleksandr?" Lina called softly, hoping not to disturb the male or the cats.

Thankfully, Aleksandr was gentle when he looked up, not dislodging any of the felines.

"What's up?" he asked.

"Can... can I talk to you?"

"Sure." The male carefully closed his book after marking his place, gesturing to the seat across from him. Lina took it gratefully, sinking into the soft cushions with a little sigh.

"Remember when I told you a little bit about my research?" she asked him.

"Yeah, the day you first got here." Aleksandr nodded.

"There's... a lot more to it than that," Lina admitted, launching into the tale with no further prompting.

13

Sasha

Sasha hadn't been expecting Adelina to show up when he curled himself into a pile of cats in the library, but she rarely sought him out anyway. He'd have assumed she was afraid of him or something if he hadn't heard her apologize anytime she asked a question—or even spoke—clearly fearing "bothering" them to some degree. It would take time for that to change.

He particularly hadn't been expecting the literal shitshow that she laid at his feet, with trusting eyes that made him want to knock his head against the wall.

"Let me get this straight," Sasha said after she'd finished speaking. "The magic not only spoke to you in the normal fashion, but it also *told you its name* and made a request of you?"

"Her," Adelina corrected. "Her name. But yes."

"No one ever gets requests like that…" Sasha trailed off. "But you said that the goddess—D'Vita, right?" Adelina nodded as he continued. "That she was low on power."

"She said something about the balance being off," the female confirmed. "And that there was a new Seelie Queen? I don't underst-and that part. at all."

"Balance *is* vitally important," Sasha admitted. "It's why the Seelie and Unseelie fae are opposites. To balance each other out.

"I know the Seelie fae had a Queen once," he added. "But it's been around five thousand years since the last one."

"It sounds like there have actually been more," Adelina told him. "From what D'Vita told me. "

"That would make sense," Sasha told her. "When a member of the Council dies without an heir, the magic chooses one for them. Why wouldn't it— *she* do so for the Seelie Queen and Unseelie King?" He was quiet, choosing his words carefully. "I am... unsurprised at the fact that there is something fishy going on with the Unseelie Court. Everything I've heard about the King there is terrifying. If he has been trying to destabilize everything by kidnapping all of the Queens before they could rule, well... it's working."

Adelina nodded.

"I've been reading a bit about history, trying to figure out who D'Vita is and when the knowledge of her as a goddess was lost," she told him. "I found a book that was supposed to be a history of the Seelie fae, and then I was reading another book that's basically epic poems about the origins of the fae."

"That sounds fascinating." Sasha tilted his head sideways. "All of it does. Do you mind if I read them?"

"Not at all." Adelina shook her head. "I have notes and questions that I wrote down, but I feel like there's some cultural context I'm still missing. D'Vita said to be careful who I told, but I... You guys have been teaching me to listen to my intuition, to my magic, and it says I can trust you."

Sasha ignored the flush on his face to the best of his ability.

"Do you want to go get them?" he asked her. "We can take a look at everything tonight, and I'll see what I can come up with."

"Sure!" The female beamed, then disappeared down the stairs to get her things.

Alone again, Sasha let the information he'd been given turn over in his mind. Little of it truly *surprised* him; but some of it was a bit unexpected. The magic being personified didn't entirely surprise him, people had always treated the magic like a sentient entity. D'Vita being both the magic and the source of the magic made perfect sense to him.

Even less surprising was the information about the Unseelie King. There'd been rumors that he had been continuing in his efforts to destabilize the monarchy here in the Seelie Court since he'd destroyed the last Queen, but nothing concrete. Likely because no one—or very few people at least—had made the connection between the magical line of succession and the fact that after five thousand years, they *should* have a new Queen. The Council shouldn't be handling it all. It should truly be the Seelie Queen.

What had thrown him for a loop was the part about iron. Don't get him wrong, he fully believed that the fae as a people were petty enough to blame the humans for the loss of their ability to manipulate and wield iron tools and weapons. What surprised him was that the fae had given humans the iron in the first place. Had that been the first great betrayal? Had the fae been believers in a base goodness before they were "betrayed" by the humans?

It would explain why it sounded like this loss went so far beyond the loss of the ability to use a metal. There was definitely a clear shift in the culture after that, as the fae had to find a metal that wouldn't hurt them. And the humans, whom the fae had apparently once tried to mentor and help grow, became mortal enemies. Partially because of the iron, but primarily because of an assumption of betrayal that Sasha wasn't entirely sure he believed. *Had* the humans purposefully corrupted iron? Or had it just been terrible timing?

His musing was interrupted by one of the brownies dropping in to see if he wanted more tea.

"I'd love some," Sasha assured the little creature. "Can you get Adelina some, too?" he asked. "She just went to her room to fetch something, but she'll be returning soon."

"Of course." The brownie dipped his chin and disappeared.

Before he could get more deeply involved in his thoughts, Adelina returned, carrying a stack of books with bits of paper sticking out.

"Wow." His eyes were wide as he stood, shedding angry cats as he did, to help her carry the books and papers. "Want to move this to a table?"

"Sure," the female agreed. Sasha placed the books on a nearby table and went back for his blanket and the remaining cats. Unfortunately, only Bissy, in his hair, and Fiddle, on his shoulder, hadn't scattered in annoyance.

"Sorry," she added, noticing his peeved expression as he glanced at each betrayed feline.

"Nah, they were leeching my body heat anyway." Sasha waved it off, grabbing his tea tray and placing it on the end of the table. "I have some more tea coming for both of us," he added. "It'll help us think."

"Good idea." Adelina beamed, then handed him the two books she'd already read. "My thought is that perhaps you could first look through my notes and see if you know any of the answers to my questions? Then we could move from there?"

"Makes sense to me." Sasha pulled the books closer, then pulled open one of the thin drawers in the table to find a different color of ink than she'd used, as well as a pen to make his own notes with. Unfortunately, he didn't have as many answers as he wished, and said as much.

"I'm sorry to say that very little of this is common knowledge." Sasha felt his brow furrow as he kept skimming. "I don't know a lot of these answers." He pointed at something she'd written down. "I do know that the date on this document you're referencing isn't exactly accurate—or rather, that it's a copy. Well, knowing the way the historians of the fae are, it's likely *very* accurate. The historians are... careful."

Sasha made a few more notes—additional information and the like. He paused at one of Adelina's notes.

"What's this note here?" he asked, pointing.

"About the plague?" she verified.

"Yes." He nodded.

"I was referring to what the humans call the 'Black Plague,'" Adelina explained. "It's a pretty major part of history. There was a really nasty pandemic that spread throughout the entire known world at the time."

"Not the Iron Plague?" Sasha frowned.

"What's the Iron Plague?" Adelina asked.

"This." He tapped on the passage from Galdar Storypen's work. "The plague where so many of the fae died. I've read about it before—it mentions that it was the humans' fault, but no more details. It looks like a lot of the details were lost outside of volumes like this one."

Adelina blinked, staring.

"They called that the Iron Plague?" she verified.

"Yeah," Sasha answered absently, skimming more of the work. "I never understood why, but now I know."

"Maybe it was the Iron Plague," Adelina replied. "It makes more sense since the timelines don't really line up. Humans don't have history this far back; we've lost a lot of it."

"And how short-lived they are doesn't help." Sasha nodded, understanding. "We lose history too, just not as frequently. Our historians called the last great loss of life the Assassination of Elders. It was carried out a couple thousand years ago by the Unseelie King, and it's why we have so few ancient fae anymore."

"That makes sense." Adelina nodded. "If the fae have lost most of this history, then why is it still called that?"

"Because the fae are traditionalists." Sasha made a face. Adelina nodded.

"Got it. So what do most of the fae do for... belief systems, I guess?"

"What do you mean?" Sasha focused on Adelina's confused expression.

"So, according to this," Adelina said and pointed to Galdar Storypen's work again, "the fae once worshipped D'Vita as their goddess, inseparable from the magic. But the knowledge dwindled until they lost the name of the goddess, and then ultimately, they lost the knowledge of the goddess. What do the fae believe in now?"

"Now's a bad time to ask that, frankly," Sasha replied. "There's been a lot of talk about the magic abandoning us. Basically, we believe in the magic. Many of the fae personified the magic. I thought it was a bit bonkers until you brought up what you'd learned and been told.

"There are cults hiding around in different places, in the depths of the Eastern Mountains, on the coasts of the Northern Forests, and a few dotted in the Unseelie Kingdom —though they hide better. And I *think* I remember hearing that the centaurs worship a goddess as well.

"Otherwise, it's just the magic." Sasha shrugged. "And right now, with the way things are going, many of the Seelie fae think the magic is abandoning them as well."

"Based on what D'Vita told me," Adelina said soberly, "it sounds like she very well could be, though not on purpose as much as from a lack of power."

"Given that she extracted that promise from you," Sasha began, "I would definitely agree. I do think that the loss of the Seelie Queen is alarming, especially with what you were told about the Unseelie King having her. Eventually, we're going to have to go out there and get her. And you're not ready for that yet."

Adelina's eyes narrowed.

"I've improved a lot..."

"You have," Sasha interrupted. "A *hell* of a lot. But from what

I'm told, the Unseelie Court is cutthroat. Dad's parents were exiled to the Wild Hunt because they were *too kind.* Your biological father lives in their capital city *openly.* And he's completely welcome."

Adelina was silent.

"You have grown a lot." Sasha lowered his voice. "You've learned so much, and you can hold your own significantly better. But I need you to wait just a little bit longer. Fuck, *I* don't feel ready yet, and I've been here my whole life. I know we don't have that kind of time, but I also don't think we need to feed you to the Barrow-Wights."

Adelina stayed quiet for a moment, long enough that Sasha began to wonder if he'd irrevocably fucked up. She'd taken months to open up to him, and he may have ruined it all in a moment of overprotectiveness.

"Alright," she finally agreed. The words were followed by Sasha's deep sigh of relief.

A brownie popped in and placed a fresh tea tray on their table before grabbing the old one and disappearing again. Adelina looked over to where the creature had both appeared and disappeared, bemused.

She sighed softly.

"I understand where you're coming from," she added. Adelina stopped, hesitant, but seemed to push through. "I can't deny, though, I'm *terrified* that if I don't do this fast enough, she'll take it all away."

Sasha's chest tightened. He'd seen bare moments of vulnerability from Adelina before, but this... Instinctively, he knew she was trusting him with something huge. Not just the moment itself, but the potential for more moments of vulnerability. The potential for friendship. The potential for her to give in to the heartbreaking *yearning* he felt from her sometimes, when he'd met her gaze and her eyes were at once ancient and ever so young as she watched him with his family.

Adelina looked down at her now cupped hands, summoning a soft green faelight and dismissing it in a breath.

"The magic... It's *beautiful*," she murmured, staring at her now-empty palms. "I don't want to give it up."

"That makes sense." Sasha nodded sympathetically, knowing his own response would matter. He carefully placed Adelina's teacup in front of her before taking his own. "But keep in mind, time passes differently for the fae. We think in decades and centuries. A year is nothing. Five years is nothing. Our people aren't even adults until we're in our fifties."

"That's a good point." A tension that Sasha hadn't noticed lining the female's shoulders relaxed. "Thank you."

"Of course." Sasha sipped his tea, allowing himself to also relax.

"I... have a question," she prodded tentatively.

"Go ahead," Sasha replied.

"What's the Wild Hunt?" Adelina's voice was quiet.

Sasha felt his lip curling.

"They're an *infection*," he spat. "A *blight* upon the magic itself." He calmed down enough to properly explain. "They are a group—almost like a cult. But they answer only to the Unseelie King, and if you join, you forfeit your soul forever. They have a ritual to force people to join, and it's disgusting."

Adelina winced.

"They travel through the shadows," Sasha continued. "And they can even leave the boundaries of our world on the days when the veil is thin. Special holidays and such."

"You know, I don't know much about fae holidays," Adelina changed the subject deftly, face tinted almost green.

"There's not much to them." Sasha shrugged. "They're linked to the seasons, of course; we always celebrate the transitions. The thing is, the Seelie Court and the Unseelie Court celebrate differently. The Seelie Court celebrates the coming of spring as the new year, and then the coming of summer as the triumph of light. Or magic," he added. "And the Unseelie fae celebrate autumn as the new year. They celebrate the coming of winter as the triumph of the darkness and a time of great feasting and all that."

"That makes sense." Adelina nodded. "I'd noticed it being tied to the seasons, but I never noticed much in the way of traditions."

"Oh, there are some." Sasha grinned. "They're just different by place and by family. For example, here, we have a festival every spring where every female gets flowers, and every male gets fruit. If you don't have a partner—or even if you do— your family or friends will give them to you."

"Oh!" Adelina's eyes lit, and Sasha continued, wanting to banish her worries.

"In the summer, there's a huge festival in the capital," Sasha described, "with vendors and musicians and storytellers during the day. In the evenings, there's dancing and bonfires.

"The Unseelie Court has a massive masquerade ball for the winter solstice; it lasts the entirety of the longest night of the year." He smiled wistfully. "Even those who don't go into the city have small masked festivals on the solstice. For the autumn, they have a festival like our summer fest in Aledale City."

"That sounds incredible," Adelina replied wistfully. "I wonder why Grandfather never took me to any of the events."

"Safety," Sasha replied regretfully. "There's always a lot of alcohol, and it's easy for you to get separated from him. I also don't know if he celebrates anymore. I haven't heard about him being at any of the festivals in decades."

"So he may just not be thinking to do so," Adelina finished with a nod. "That wouldn't surprise me at all." She was quiet for a moment, staring into her tea. "I think he was turning into a ghost of himself for a very long time."

"What happened with your grandmother and your father..." Sasha trailed off, looking for words. "From what I'm told, it really changed him. While it seems to be a positive change, that doesn't make it any easier. He's been very sad for a long time, if I had to guess. I do think he cares about you; I just think he's truly forgotten how to live. Especially with his illness."

Adelina's shoulders slumped.

"Yeah," she murmured. "I wish... I wish I could do more for him. But whenever I'm there, I get glared at for breathing. I hate it sometimes. I hate how they treat me, and how much they hate me. I know it's mostly my father's fault, but... they should know better."

"They're adults," Sasha verified. "And can make their own choices. It's not your fault they're the wrong ones."

The two sat in quiet, sipping their tea and alone in their own thoughts for a while before Adelina spoke again.

"Where should we keep the books and notes?"

"I'll hold on to them for now," Sasha decided. "We can swap them back and forth between our rooms."

"Perfect." She nodded. "I think, with that, I'm going to go to bed."

"Goodnight." Sasha gave her a half smile.

"Goodnight, Aleksandr." She half-smiled back before heading back down the stairs, leaving Sasha deep in thought.

14

Lina

In the four months since she'd left the Southern Highlands, Lina had only been back to her grandfather's house twice. She felt guilty, but everyone there *hated* her, and the longer she spent around people who didn't hate her, the more sensitive she was to the hatred that surrounded her there. And the harder it was for her to go back.

But it had been too long, and Lina decided to take a rare free day she'd been given to go visit her grandfather. Once Delwyn had verified that Grandfather didn't have any meetings that day, she made her way into the basement and slipped through the portal and into her grandfather's travel room.

To her relief, Ronin was *not* anywhere nearby. Meaning that she could exit the portal mirror and go find her grandfather without as much fanfare, and with less risk of being sent to her room to "wait for him." Even if she'd verified his presence in advance, the Southern Highlands Fae liked to make her wait to see her grandfather if he didn't have a specific time he was expecting her.

Every time she went back, the entire household reminded her forcefully that they did not want her there. No matter how fae she looked or how much magic she waved in their faces, to them she'd always be human; she'd always be the one who had the "true" heir sent away. She kept trying to tell herself that her father's actions were his own, but that didn't alleviate the coldness she received.

Sometimes, Lina considered not taking the position. The servants didn't want her; who was to say the people did? Part of her really didn't want to spend the rest of her long days working to make life better for the people who hated her and would rather see her dead.

But then, on the other hand, she'd been spending a lot of time with Aleksandr recently and his particular brand of humor. There was something rather ironic about making life better for the very people who hated her so fiercely. It was something that she was fairly sure Aleksandr would appreciate if nothing else.

Either way, she needed to make more time for her grandfather, and today was that day.

Using the skills that Mikhail had been drilling into her, she made her way through the house as silently as possible, avoiding everyone she could to keep on her way unimpeded. On the third floor, she found her grandfather's study door cracked open.

"Grandfather?" Lina called out as she knocked on the door.

"Come in," Grandfather replied.

Lina opened the door to the familiar room; the whole thing was furnished with light woods and deep green fabrics. Her grandfather was behind his massive desk, finishing up some paperwork. He flashed her a soft, indulgent smile as she walked closer, which she returned with a smile of her own before going to browse the bookshelves.

None of the titles looked terribly interesting, though some looked like they could potentially help her with her research. Not enough to ask to borrow them, but enough that she tallied them mentally on the off chance she stalled out.

"Adelina?" Her grandfather's voice broke her train of thought, but she spun, blinking.

"Yes?"

"Find anything you like?" Grandfather smiled again.

"Nothing I'm interested in right now." Lina shrugged, but smiled back. "Thank you though."

"Come, let's chat." Grandfather ushered her over to a couch by the fireplace. She curled into one side of it while he sat on the other. "You seem to be progressing well," he continued. "I've heard nothing but praise from Delwyn."

Lina flushed, her smile growing with the warmth in her chest.

"I enjoy it," she admitted. "I've learned a lot."

"Good!" Grandfather enthused. "I'm glad." He was quiet for a moment before speaking up again. "I know I probably don't say this often enough, but I'm very proud of you."

Lina flushed again.

"Thank you, Grandfather," she murmured, pleased. "I'm happy to *make* you proud."

He smiled, reaching over and patting the top of her head delicately.

"Now, I have a bit of a surprise for you today." Grandfather grinned.

"A surprise?" Lina had to keep herself from bouncing in her seat.

"Someone who was once a friend of your father's." Grandfather's expression saddened. "He was furious after everything came to light. The youngster comes and checks on me when he can."

"A friend of my father's." Lina hid her frustration. She got the feeling that he would like her about as much as the servants did. "How long will he be staying?"

"Oh, a day or two." Grandfather waved off the question. "Thankfully, I'm feeling a bit better than I have in a while, so I'm up to entertaining. I know you only have today, so I thought it might be nice for us all to dine together so he could meet you."

"Of course," Lina replied smoothly, bottling up her frustration at the loss of time with her grandfather. She'd deal with it later. "I'd be happy to meet him."

"Excellent!" Grandfather beamed. "He'll be joining us for

lunch. In the meantime, tell me *everything*," he added. With a smaller smile, Lina spoke, filling up the hours between her arrival and the elegant lunch her grandfather had doubtlessly planned. She relaxed slightly in the time between his announcement and the meal, but not completely.

It turned out her instincts were completely correct. The male waiting in the dining room for them was... slimy. He wasn't hideous, with his blue eyes and soft brown hair; he was actually rather—dare she say—pretty. But there was something incredibly off about him. The male's smile felt more like a baring of teeth at her, something that she had never actually seen the fae do.

"Hello, you must be Adelina *Halfhuman*," the male said to her. "I'm Egan. Egan Ghoulbane." Something about the way he said her surname sat very wrongly with her. Her instincts were *screaming* at her in a way that they never had before. There was something very, *very* wrong with this male.

"Hello." She nodded politely. "Yes, I'm Adelina. It's nice to meet you." For once, she felt no qualms about lying.

"I can definitely see Darek in you, youngling." She wanted to bristle at the nickname; it felt more condescending coming from Egan than from Mikhail or Delwyn.

"I wouldn't know," she demurred, falling back on Lady Mara's training. Even though she'd have rather chosen Mikhail's and put a dagger through the male's throat.

Part of her was aghast at the casual way she considered violence, but her survival instincts, so much stronger than they were before her Coming of Age, were making it hard to hold back.

"Well, I would," he replied. "And I can." Egan turned to Grandfather. "And you're planning to put her on the Council?"

"Of course," Grandfather replied, having them sit down together. Unsurprisingly, Adelina's first plate was stone cold.

"Is she being trained for the position?" He frowned. "I wouldn't want our fair land to go into the hands of an amateur."

"I am," Lina cut in, nibbling on her lunch. She knew she shouldn't have; she should have let Grandfather lead the conversation. This... *creature* was liable to get more out of her than she wanted to release.

"By whom?" Egan raised a perfectly manicured brow.

"I sent her north," Grandfather replied. "She's working with the Prince of the Northern Highlands and his family."

Egan looked infuriated for half a blink, so short a period that Lina wondered if she was seeing things.

"North?" he replied. "What prompted you to send her there?"

"Delwyn offered to help train her," Grandfather told the other.

"You don't think that he's got ulterior motives?" Egan might look worried to most, but Lina could tell it was fake. While she did her best to ensure her face showed none of it, she was inwardly seething. Delwyn, Mikhail, and Aleksandr had been nothing but kind and decent to her the entire time she'd been there. The little pendant she wore under her shirt warmed slightly. She relaxed slightly at the reminder of her... her *family*.

Why did the world-shattering realization of how much she cared for the Northern Forest Fae have to happen *now*, of all times? When she was trying desperately to survive this meal?

"What on earth would those motives *be*?" her grandfather asked. For once, Grandfather's semi-naive perspective would work in her favor.

"Well, he's mated to that Unseelie fae," Egan said. "Who's to say he's not in their pocket? In the Unseelie King's pocket? And they have that *mutt* that they call their son..."

Lina called upon every speck of patience she possessed to keep a civil tongue in her head at hearing the name Egan called Aleksandr.

"I'd prefer if you *didn't* use that sort of language here." Grandfather frowned at Egan. "I made a point to meet with them and ensure they didn't have ulterior motives. Delwyn is a fellow

Council member, and his son is Prince-in-Waiting. Council business is important to all of us, so it only made sense."

"Why not send her to Prince Clio?" Egan asked, sounding worried, even as Lina got the feeling that it too, was fake.

"I've actually been to train with Prince Clio," Lina spoke up again, staying just as polite as she could. "She's an incredibly intellig-ent Council member; I have much to learn from her."

"See?" Grandfather beamed, missing the look of vitriol Egan sent Lina. "She's fine, doing excellently, even."

"Of course, sir." Egan dipped his head deferentially. Lina wonde-red how Grandfather missed the hungry expression in his gaze. "You're the Prince, after all."

"None of that, Egan." Grandfather waved off the clearly false deference. "I appreciate you trying to do your best by us."

"I wouldn't do anything else." Egan put a hand over his heart. "It was awful, what happened with Darek. Under other circumstances, I know he'd want to be here with his family, so I'll do my best in his stead."

Bullshit, that's what he was spewing. Her *father* had murdered children. Faelings. And humans as well, for all that most of the fae wouldn't give a damn. And what he'd done to her mother after his crimes were brought to light? She still had nightmares about what she saw in her house.

Lina wanted to go home so desperately that it was painful. This wasn't home; this place with cold food and colder servants and this male whose cruelty knew no bounds. Home was the little kittens cli-mbing her leggings and Aleksandr's deadpan humor and the soft expression in Mikhail's eyes when he saw Delwyn.

"Thank you, Egan." Grandfather smiled again. "It's good to have my family here, together."

"I'm glad we could come back to an understanding," Egan said. "Family is important, after all." Something about Egan's words and the sideways glance he gave her made her wonder exactly what happened here. But she had no way of asking without drawing more attention to herself. And with this dead-eyed creature here, she had *no* interest in doing that.

Cormac seemed to relax as the lunch went on, but Lina felt herself becoming more and more tense. After the meal and the conversation that followed, her grandfather had to excuse himself.

"I apologize, younglings." He shook his head, slumping into his couch. "I find myself completely exhausted for some reason. I believe I ate something that didn't agree with me. Adelina, dear, you're welcome to stay, of course, but I know you have training again in the morning."

"It's alright, Grandfather," she said softly, smiling at him. "I'll head back and see if I can get ahead on my reading. I hope you feel better."

"Of course, youngling." Grandfather smiled wanly in return, before looking to Egan. "Egan, would you mind walking her to the travel room, please? We had assassins in here after her a few months back, and I wouldn't want anything to happen to her."

"Of course." The male's smile was sleazy, but Lina refused to rise to the bait. Both stood, Lina making sure she was standing close enough to the male for politeness's sake as they walked toward the stairs. Egan didn't speak to her until they reached the staircase.

"You'll be lucky if you live to see the autumn again," he said cheerfully. Lina's blood ran cold, but again, she didn't respond. "And even if you tell Cormac about this, he won't believe you." The male's face darkened. "I don't know what he was thinking, making someone like *you* the heir. *I* should have been the heir." His eyes narrowed, glaring at Lina. "I've been tricked out of a crown once, by your *precious Delwyn*," he spat, "and his little *slut* of a lifemate and their peasant heir. I will *not* be denied again." Egan grinned, the expression causing goosebumps to break out over Lina's skin. She refused to show fear.

"Oh? Nothing to say?" he taunted. "No defense for your *friends*
? Perhaps you're more like your father than I thought."

The words struck her in her soul, but she kept her mouth shut
by the simple expedient of biting the inside of her mouth and fisting
her hands so tightly she could feel the bite of her nails on her palms.
She could *not* show this male weakness. She knew it like she knew
her truename, like she knew how to walk in this body. He was attempting to appeal to her baser instincts, to make her feel like prey rather than the *predator* that D'Vita had made her into. Her necklace
warmed again, reminding her of the people waiting for her. What
this male said *didn't matter.*

Lina reminded herself of that over and over as they walked, as he
continued to spill vitriol at her. As the servants looked down their
noses at her and smiled at him. He'd made himself at home here, in
her home. Her place. This would be *her* manor. She *would* live. He
wasn't a foreseer; he was simply a male who felt wronged. Just another angry royal.

Finally, they arrived in the basement.

"Thank you for walking me down," she said calmly and clearly,
her clenched hands the only sign of her fury. "I wouldn't want to
draw the attention of assassins or other unscrupulous characters."

"You've already been corrupted by *Prince* Delwyn, I see," Egan
drawled. "You seem remarkably resistant to my taunts. Why is that,
do you think?"

"I wouldn't know." Lina shrugged, disguising how *desperately*
she wished for a weapon. This male needed to be put down. He was
a threat.

"Safe travels." He smirked at her, at the fact that she was forced
to turn her back to him to enter the mirror. Lina knew that if her
hands weren't in tight fists, they would be shaking. But she tilted her
chin up and spun around toward the mirror.

"I thank you" was her only reply.

"Do tell the royal *couple* that I said hello," Egan said as she left. "And that I long to finish the discussion we began a few centuries ago."

Lina didn't respond, walking through the mirror and into safety.

15

Sasha

For once, Sasha could feel Adelina coming without mentally looking. She was emanating a fury that he'd never felt before. He half stood, startling his fathers where they were dozing in front of the fireplace.

"What—"

"Adelina," Sasha interrupted, knowing his anxiety was written all over his face, but unable to stop it.

"What's wrong?" Dad asked succinctly.

"I don't..." He trailed off as the little female stalked into the room, the fury he could sense from her written all over her body.

"Does anyone," Adelina ground out, not seeming to realize how much more of her emotions were showing than usual, "have something breakable that they'd not care to have replaced?"

Silently, Da stood, walked over to a dark corner, and grabbed a frankly hideous vase, then handed it to Adelina.

"Thank you," she said with a slight dip to her chin before she spun on her heel and threw the ornament with more force than Sasha had ever seen her exert, even in training. The throw was paired by an ear-splitting shriek of "fucking *BASTARD*" that rang out with the sound of shattered crockery.

A touch of bright, shimmering red grabbed Sasha's attention, and he realized that Adelina had held her hands in fists so tightly that her nails had cut into her palms. The female finally turned, eyes bright with unshed tears.

"What happened?" Dad asked. Sasha could tell the other male was just as thrown off as he was.

"Egan. Fucking. Ghoulbane," she ground out between clenched teeth. Dad's eyes narrowed, and even Da's face darkened uncharacteristically.

"What the *fuck* was that *useless excuse for a male* doing there?" Da hissed.

"Apparently," Adelina spat, "he was my *father*'s best friend. Sounds like birds of a feather and all that. He wanted to visit Grandfather."

"That's not good." Dad crossed his arms, leaning against the wall. Sasha gave his dad the side-eye. There was something off about his calm.

"He waited until Grandfather asked him to walk me to the portal to threaten me," she said. "Said I wouldn't live to see another autumn."

Dad's eyes narrowed further; his jaw was tight.

"That's what *he* thinks," Da spat between clenched teeth.

"He sent me with a message for you. He said…" At this, Adelina hesitated, clearly worried about passing the message on. "He said he 'longs to finish the discussion you began a few centuries ago,'" she said. She couldn't get anything else out, because Da *snarled*.

Sasha could feel his eyes were wide, and he was completely frozen. Da was no longer the male he'd known for all these years; he was a full-blown predator. There was no light in his eyes; they had all the life of a pair of ancient emeralds. Da's face was carved from fury as he whipped out a dagger that Sasha had no clue the male carried and *threw*. The blade whipped through the air and sank hilt-deep into the wood paneling.

And Dad… Dad looked *small*. In a way that Sasha had never

seen before. Dad's shoulders were hunched, and he was curled into himself. He *shook*. The anger from before was completely gone, fading into an ageless fear.

"I will carve the very skin off of his bones," Da growled. "And bathe the wounds in iron dust. He will *suffer* if he is back on this continent."

Sasha's eyes darted over to where Adelina was cowering, neither of them able to move so much as a muscle. She was clearly as terrified as he was, but neither of them matched the mind-melting fear that was emanating off of Dad, and the fury of a mated fae coming off of Da.

Finally, Dad seemed to realize that the two of them were basically frozen in terror.

"Del," Dad whispered. Da spun, eyes raking over him, and tugged Dad close to his chest. "Del, you're frightening the faelings."

Sasha didn't protest being called a faeling as he usually would; anything that would help break Da out of... this.

Da just hissed, pulling him closer.

"Come on, Del." Dad's voice shook, but he kept trying. "Let's leave the faelings alone. You're scaring them."

Da growled, glaring at both of them, then grabbed Dad and held him close before running up the stairs and likely shutting them both into their room from the sound of the harshly closing door.

It took both of them a good few moments of quiet before they could break out of the paralysis the fear had on them. Adelina, who'd clearly had an absolutely atrocious day, burst into tears.

"I'm sorry!" she wailed. "I didn't know what it meant. I shouldn't have said anything."

The sound broke Sasha out of his own paralysis. He went over to the distraught female and pulled her down onto the closest couch. Adelina cried into his shoulder, so distraught herself that she didn't notice that she was actually initiating contact. Or the fact that Sasha was shaking violently. Absently, he rubbed her back as he tried to reconcile what he'd just seen with his happy-go-lucky Da and stern but kind Dad.

Da had always been protective, but he'd *never* seen anything like that. That was the feral rage of a mated fae. *Something* had happened with Dad. Sasha had no clue what it was, but he knew it was bad. Bad enough to reduce his strong, amazing dad into an anxious, shaking mess. Sasha couldn't stop *seeing* his dad... how completely terrified the other male was. He'd never seen his dad as *small* before. He'd always seen the male who saved him as larger than life in a way. But today... Today, his dad had shown something *broken,* and Sasha didn't know what to do about it.

Of course, he knew that someone who was approaching a thousand years of life was bound to have some skeletons in the closet, some pains that had been buried for centuries. But this was something else entirely. This was... Sasha had no words for it.

Leander appeared, clearly having been alerted to the disaster by someone else among the staff.

"What happened here?" he asked.

"Adelina met someone who was friends with her father," Sasha replied, arm tightening around the still sobbing little female. "Someone that apparently Dad and Da have history with."

"Who threw the ornament?" Leander asked.

"Adelina, but Da handed it to her. She asked first."

Leander nodded.

"Who was it?" Leander asked.

"Someone called Egan Ghoulbane," Sasha murmured, afraid to say the name too loudly. Leander's eyes darkened, his hands opening and closing, then he sighed.

"If I may," Leander asked, "I can shed at least *some* light on this mess."

"Please?" Sasha begged. He was confused beyond all belief. Leander nodded, perching on the edge of the seat across from where the two of them were sitting. Adelina had finally begun to calm and had pulled partially away from him. The tip of her nose was still violently red, as were her eyes.

"I'm sorry," she repeated, voice still thick with tears.

"No, child." Leander shook his head. "You had no way of knowing. I wouldn't be surprised if you were set up, honestly."

"Set up?" Sasha replied.

Leander sighed again.

"Egan is... old," Leander said. "His mother was the sister of the former Prince of the Northern Forests. The entire former royal family here was murdered when your fathers were barely older than you are now. Before then, Delwyn, Mikhail, Branwen, and Faolin were just villagers. They weren't royals." Leander's smile was sad. "They were my mother's neighbors."

Sasha blinked, but stayed silent.

"When the former Prince was murdered, the mantle fell to Delwyn, to everyone's surprise," Leander continued. "No one expected it, least of all Egan. He was convinced that since he was related to the former Prince, he would be next. Unfortunately, the rest of the royals agreed, treating him like the Prince, assuming the power would soon appear.

"But then Delwyn showed up, the son of an artisan, with the power of a royal. He informed everyone that he had been told he would be the new Prince, and they could sense the power in him. Most of the royals accepted it as well, as could be expected.

"Egan, however, was infuriated. He felt entitled to the Council seat."

"He said he'd been tricked out of a crown once," Adelina whispered in a shaking voice. "And that he wouldn't be denied."

"That male..." Leander shook his head. "There's something broken in him that he enjoys suffering. He... hurt Mikhail. I won't go into any more detail, as it's not my story to tell, nor my place to tell you the story. But it is something that Delwyn has felt guilty and angry about for centuries." Leander looked at Adelina, worry shining in his brown eyes. "If he's after you, little faeling, be *very* careful."

Adelina nodded, eyes filled with tears once again. Sasha hugged her again, and Leander reached over and patted her hair gently. Leander's eyes saddened as she almost absently flinched away.

"We'll protect you," Sasha promised, almost rashly. "You'll be safe here."

"For now," Leander predicted soberly. Sasha gave the other male a half-hearted glare as Adelina wilted at the words.

"Don't worry, youngling," he added. "As long as you stay in the house, you'll be fine. I suspect you'd even be okay in town, though I'm unsure."

Adelina nodded silently.

"I'll send you two some food up to your rooms," Leander promised. "I think it would be wise to retreat for the evening."

"Do you want to stay with me until you go to bed?" Sasha offered to the female. "So you're not alone?"

Adelina nodded again.

"I'll send both of your meals to Sasha's suite then," Leander replied, standing back up in a fluid motion and dipping his chin to both of them.

"Come on, Lina," Sasha encouraged, the nickname feeling like the right decision when the female relaxed minutely. "Let's go upstairs. I'll loan you a book and put the cats on you." An attempt at a smile danced around the corners of her mouth, and she nodded.

With worry creasing his face, Sasha led her upstairs, wishing desperately that he could check on his parents as he did. But his da's attitude told him everything he needed to know; in this case, it was "stay away."

But he couldn't help but worry, even as he spent a good couple of hours cheering Adelina up enough that he felt like she could manage the rest of the night alone. Even as he nibbled on his dinner and curled up in his big bed with most of the cats in the house.

Even so, he worried.

16

Delwyn

"Oh shit," Del muttered, arms tightening around Misha. His memories of the day before flooded into his awareness. He remembered every bit of what had happened when Adelina had returned from the Southern Highlands. "Oh *shit*." He buried his face in Misha's hair. "Fuck, fuck, *shit*," he added, the words muffled in the other male's hair.

"Shhh, it's okay," Misha murmured, clearly mostly asleep but trying to soothe his partner anyway. Del melted slightly, but not much could cheer him today.

"Misha, I hate to do this to you after yesterday." Del removed his face from Misha's hair and smoothed the silky black locks out of his lifemate's face. "But we need to check on the faelings. I fucked up."

This had the intended effect; Misha's yellow eyes appeared, attempting to read his partner's face and figure out what had gone wrong. His confusion made Del even sadder; the loss of memory meant it had been a bad episode. Misha hadn't had an episode that bad in centuries.

"What do you mean?"

"Yesterday..." Del replied reluctantly. "When I went... a bit feral? I think I terrified the younglings."

"Shit." Misha's pale skin turned even paler, worry dancing across his features. "And they have literally no idea what's going on."

"None," Del confirmed grimly.

"Well, today is going to be... fun," Misha responded in the same tone.

"I can talk to them." Del stroked Misha's hair some more in an attempt to comfort his clearly upset lifemate. "I was the one who went completely feral. I think I even scared Sasha."

"I don't mind being a part of it," Misha replied softly.

"I won't make you relive any of that," Del swore. "You dealt with enough with that flashback." Del frowned. Misha had cried himself to sleep after they were locked in the safety of their rooms. All Del and Iron could do was cuddle up with the stressed-out male and let him get it out. Del had spent half the night singing lullabies in an attempt to help Misha sleep. Fruitlessly.

"It wasn't Adelina's fault," Misha reminded him. "She had no way of knowing, and, frankly, she's in danger from *that male* as well."

Del nodded, frowning again as he remembered how upset she'd been the previous day. He needed to thank her later; that vase was hideous, and he'd been looking for a reason to get rid of it for over a century.

"She is," he admitted. "And he obviously knows she's with us. Probably Cormac's doing, if he trusts that creature."

"He has no reason not to, if the bastard is up to his old tricks again," Misha growled softly.

"You're right, as usual." Del held his lifemate closer and sighed. "Thank you, love."

"No problem," Misha drowsed. "I'm going to sleep some more, I think."

"Good." Del pressed a kiss to Misha's forehead. "I'll go talk to the children and straighten this all out."

"Mmm, okay," Misha murmured, fading back into sleep as Iron curled around his back.

With a sigh, Del left the warm bed, dreading the task ahead. He wouldn't be surprised if there was some lost trust between him and the faelings… but he would do his best. Even if he didn't admit it to anyone else, *he* knew that he dilly-dallied in dressing for the day, but it was time to face the music.

Del slipped out of the room, closing the door softly so as not to wake up Misha. He went directly downstairs to find the common areas of the house empty of all except Leander.

"How is he?" the servant asked, worry flashing in his eyes.

"Sleeping," Del sighed. "And feeling better this morning."

"And how are *you*?"

"…Still angry, but currently more worried about the faelings than angry," Del admitted.

"I hope you don't find it too forward but," Leander hesitated. "I gave them the basics of what happened last night. No specifics about Mikhail, but where his hatred and vendetta began."

"You told them?" Del asked. Leander dropped his gaze.

"Again, I hope you don't find it too forward, but," he repeated. "But Adelina looked terrified, and even Aleksandr looked unnerved. I didn't wish for them to worry needlessly."

"Thank you." Del smiled slightly. Leander relaxed at the words.

"Of course." Leander dipped his chin. "The faelings are in the library if you'd like to speak with them."

"Thank you again," Del told the other male. "I think I'll go down and grab some tea and then go speak with them."

"Tell Cook that you're taking a tea tray for all three of you," Leander advised before heading off to his duties.

Del took Leander's suggestion seriously, passing the information along when he went down to the kitchens. Cook nodded, seeming pleased, and put together a tea tray with little bits of breakfast on it, faster than Del had expected. The male took the heavily-laden tray and went up the stairs, hesitating at the door to the library before opening it and looking around.

The faelings appeared to be in deep discussion, a short stack of books next to each of them, and pieces of paper were scattered across the entire surface of a large table. There were empty teacups near each youngling's dominant hand, and Adelina had a bit of ink splattered across her face.

When she caught sight of him, she froze mid-word, leaving Del's heart in pieces. Sasha turned in his chair when Adelina froze, but didn't speak either.

Mate bond rage was clearly a mixed blessing.

"May I come talk to you two?" Del asked, voice gentle in an effort not to frighten them further. "I brought some more tea."

Sasha looked to Adelina, seeming to gauge her mood. She gave Sasha a tiny nod, hand reaching for... was that the pendant Misha had made her? Del's chest ached at the sight. Part of him was overjoyed at her clearly growing trust in Sasha—and in Misha. But the rest of him wanted to cry at how hesitant she was. Sasha, in return, turned back to him and nodded, gesturing at the table.

In an effort not to break the youngling's trust any further, Del made a point to *not* look at whatever it was that they were studying. He just shifted the tray to the palm of one hand and carefully made space for it with the other. Sasha helped silently.

Del handed each faeling a cup of tea before taking his own, then gestured to the basket as he thought of how he wanted to say his piece.

"I'm sorry, younglings," he said finally, a rasp in his voice. "What happened yesterday was a complete clusterfuck, but it was *neither* of your faults. Yes, that includes you, Adelina," Del added, seeing doubt flit across the faeling's face. "You were passing along a message and had no idea it would happen that way. It *shouldn't* have happened that way. I'm sorry again." Del hung his head.

"What... what happened to Dad?" Sasha asked hesitantly.

"I know Leander told you both a bit," Del said after a moment of thought. "The phrasing caught Misha by surprise and sent him into a flashback. Do either of you know what a flashback is?"

"When you get trapped in a memory," Adelina answered soberly, large green eyes locked on him.

"Yes." Del nodded. "That's what happened to Misha. How much do you two know about mating bonds?"

"Only what you've told me," Sasha admits, Adelina just shaking her head.

"For you, Adelina," Del said and turned toward the little female, "they're bonds created between two fae who have the potential for lifebonding. It's not required, even if you've the potential for it, but there's usually an element of compatibility to it. Usually, you know as soon as you meet someone, unless one or the other of you hasn't gone through your Coming of Age yet. You can't bond until after, because part of the bond includes your truename."

Adelina nodded, seeming to absorb the information.

"Part of this bond is an emotional and mental bond," Del continued. "A bit like what you can do, Sasha." He took a quick sip of his tea. "But stronger and focused on one person. All that to say, Misha's flashback hit me as well, but instead of the emotions *he* associates with the memory, because it happened to him, I instead was tipped into a bond rage," Del sighed. "It's one of the downsides of the mate bonds. If your lifepartner is threatened severely, you can go completely feral. All of your higher reasoning shuts down, and the only thing that matters is protecting your partner."

"So that's what happened yesterday?" Sasha prodded.

"Yes." Del nodded, shoulders drooping.

"What... what did that *creature* do?" Adelina's voice was horrified, for all she spat her title for that bastard Egan. Closer to her, Del could verify that she was, in fact, playing with the little pendant that Misha had made. To his surprise and—frankly, delight— there was a rage buried in her gaze.

"He..." Del took a few deep breaths, making sure to control the tidal wave of rage that surged in his soul, not wanting to wake Misha. "He felt as though, because Misha was Prince Consort rather than the Prince, that he was somehow weaker. He wished to... *take advantage* of that."

Del hoped desperately that he didn't have to go any further; the memories of what was done to his lifemate would haunt him for the rest of his days. The emptiness in Mikhail's eyes and the *fear* he could feel from his partner for years afterward. It was months before Misha would show any affection outside of some private hand-holding. Years before he was willing to go alone anywhere. Almost a decade before his partner felt safe again. Misha hadn't really come back to himself until after that year spent up north at the assassin's camp, where he learned to defend himself and others.

Thankfully, it seemed both of the faelings understood. Sasha looked a bit ill, horror plastered across his son's face. Adelina... Adelina's eyes were bright with fury, her jaw set. Del got the peculiar feeling that if Egan was anywhere in her vicinity any time soon, the male would find himself with a mouthful of his own teeth. Del let it get quiet, gaze dropping into the warm brown tea in his cup.

"Thanks for letting us know, Da," Sasha finally said quietly.

"Of course, youngling." Del gave his son a half smile. "If I'd been in my right mind, you wouldn't have so much as left the room without that information."

"Yes, thank you," Adelina murmured, her gaze absent as though she was deep in thought.

"Copper for your thoughts?" Del asked the faeling. She turned her eyes on him, giving Del the odd notion he was being measured.

"Just... thinking about how different things are here," she finally said with a shrug. Del would bet his whole library there was more to it than that, but he'd forfeited the right to her thoughts with his actions the previous night. "It's super rare for humans to have those kinds of reactions to things." Her brow furrowed. "Except mothers in response to threats to children, now that I think about it."

"The bond between mates is... in some ways comparable to a bond between a mother and child," Del responded after a moment of thought. "Not that bonds between non-blood kin can be any lesser, but..."

"It seems like you lose all sense of reason," Adelina finished with an intuition that surprised him more than it should. "Which isn't very common with even mother-child bonds. Not unless the kid is in life-threatening danger, and even then, most humans don't react quite like that."

"Exactly." Del nodded. "I lost all sense of higher reasoning. All thought. I was nothing but instincts last night."

"That makes sense." Adelina nodded.

Del gave the little female a sad smile. She was being incredibly kind, all things considered, but he could feel the distance that he'd painstakingly closed over the past four months had increased again. Her fingers were worrying at her pendant again, and whether she realized it or not, she was absently tracking all of his movements.

As if he were a threat.

Del buried the heartbreak. Sasha seemed to be handling things a bit better than she was, but the youngling had the benefit of almost a hundred years of knowing him. Adelina didn't—almost all she knew were threats. It had taken them close to a full month to get her to relax at all. Another to get her to laugh properly. Months of seeing her eyes go sad whenever they bantered with Sasha or showed him affection. Months of slowly, carefully making her feel safe.

Destroyed in moments by—as Adelina had so aptly put it the previous day—Egan *Fucking* Ghoulbane.

Resisting the urge to sigh, Del sought a new topic.

"What are you two working on?" he asked.

The two faelings locked eyes, seeming to have an entire conversation with just body language (and not Sasha's powers; Del could usually tell the difference). Sasha nodded, and so did Adelina, then the female turned toward him.

"I'd like to tell you and Mikhail at the same time," she requested softly.

Del's curiosity was even more piqued at that, but he respected her wishes and didn't push further.

"Alright," Del acquiesced. "I can wait. Do you want some food while you work?"

Sasha just gave him a *look,* then reached over and snagged a cheese biscuit off the platter.

"Thank you." The little female gave him a tiny smile before reaching over and grabbing what looked to be a sausage ball.

The three of them devoured the snacks on the tray and realized afterwards that they were all still hungry.

"Shall we go look for something a bit more substantial?" Del offered.

"Yes," Sasha stated, looking longingly at the empty plates.

Del stood, grabbing both empty trays and stacking all of the crockery on them. He held the stack on the palm of one hand and, with the other, pulled out a necklace that was just a little wooden flute. Summoning the magic, he played the tiny little ditty he had titled "Follow Me, Little Soldier," which made the stacked trays float and follow him.

Adelina's eyes were wide; he realized that he hadn't done much specialized magic around her, and she'd never seen what bardic magic looked like.

"My magic is a bit unusual," he told her, continuing to feed power to the spell. It took a bit more than usual since he wasn't continuing to play the song. "It's tied intricately to the music I play and write and how I feel about it. This little song is a bit of a 'follow me' type song."

"Like the Pied Piper," she murmured.

"The who?" Sasha stared. Del grinned with something almost

resembling his usual cheer, taking up the little song again as the three of them trooped down the stairs to the sound of Adelina telling them the human legend of the Pied Piper. Del's bond with Misha warmed as they got closer to the dining room, informing Del that his partner was likely having a meal of his own.

Lo and behold, there was Misha, on what was likely his third or fourth cup of relo, with an empty plate in front of him that Del figured probably had contained some of his favorite foods. The male raised a brow as he saw Del coming in with both dishes and faelings following him like ducklings.

17

Mikhail

Mikhail saw the slight hesitance in Adelina's bearing as she followed Sasha, keeping the younger male between herself and Del, even as she had her gaze trained on the dishes in fascination. His heart broke for his lifepartner.

"Morning, kiddos," Mikhail yawned and stretched. Adelina jumped slightly at the sound of his voice, eyes widening. Mikhail watched her clearly argue with herself for a moment before rushing over to him and surprising him with a fierce hug.

"I'm really sorry," she murmured into his shirt. "I know it was an accident, but that doesn't mean it didn't upset you."

Mikhail absently wrapped his arms around the faeling, feeling a bit like he'd been hit in the head with something. Why... why was the faeling apologizing?

"You don't have anything to apologize for," he reminded the female.

"I can apologize for my actions inadvertently harming you," she replied fiercely before stepping back. "I do hope I didn't overstep," Adelina added softly, flushing.

"No, you're fine, kiddo." He gave her a little smile and ruffled her hair like he always did Sasha's. She smiled more brightly than he'd ever seen, then beelined for Sasha's usual seat next to him, leaving Sasha and Del bemused in her wake.

Did she just... That was Del.

She has a kind heart, was all Mikhail said to his partner as Del and Sasha followed Adelina's example and found their seats. His heart ached at the sadness in Del's gaze as he clocked Adelina's change of seating, but neither of them said anything.

"Leander," Del called quietly. The servant smiled as he saw the group of them gathered around the table.

"Snacks couldn't hold you lot anymore?" Leander asked the other three. They all shook their heads. "I'll get something made up," he promised, grabbing the dishes that Del had abandoned on the edge of the table and left. It only took a moment or two for a brownie to pop in and leave a tray of teacups on the table, a silent command for Mikhail in the fourth teacup.

He sighed, leaving his empty mug and grabbing the tea that was clearly meant for him.

"Cut off?" Del asked, brow up.

"Maybe," Mikhail replied, not meeting the male's eyes.

"You could have slept more, you know," Del told Mikhail softly.

"I didn't want to sleep anymore."

Code for nightmares. Del sighed softly.

I'll sing to you again tonight.

Thank you.

Thankfully, Leander was as good as his word, and food for all of them came fairly quickly. Mikhail suspected that Cook had put together something delicious that they could eat as they felt up to it, but wasn't positive. Perhaps the other three just had lucky timing.

The meal was quiet, everyone lost in their own thoughts as they ate. The quiet persisted as they moved into the living room, curling up on couches and chairs. Eventually, Del spoke up.

"Adelina, did you want to explain what you were talking about in the library?" he asked the female, still treading delicately around her.

Mikhail barely registered it at the realization that there was a *puzzle* here. His foresight was trembling like a leaf in the wind, helping him make connections that he never would have otherwise made.

The female took a deep breath, then met each of their eyes in turn before she began speaking.

"Magic is a goddess, and she told me her name," Adelina said. And she began to weave the tale of what had happened to her during her Coming of Age, everything she'd been researching since, and even the reasoning behind the millennia-old hatred of humans that Mikhail had never quite understood.

"And last night…" Adelina sighed. "She's losing power. She sent me a dream last night. Basically told me that I needed your help. I spoke to Aleksandr a while back, but… things are moving quickly. It was time."

Mikhail had the gut feeling that something more had happened in that dream, but knew not to press.

"Well, I don't know what I was expecting," Del broke the silence that descended after Adelina stopped speaking. "But it wasn't that."

Adelina cracked a tiny smile before turning her eyes—the ones that reminded Mikhail a bit of Del's—on him.

"The Isle of Vita," Mikhail murmured.

"The what?" Adelina said. Sasha spoke at the same time.

"*That's* why D'Vita sounded so familiar!" his son shouted. "I've seen that name on maps before."

"Maps? It's a place?" the female asked.

"The Isle of Vita is a holy place," Del explained. "We're not technically *forbidden* to go there, but it's highly frowned upon."

"Wait, wait, back up." Mikhail held his hands up as something Adelina had said earlier finally penetrated his brain. "You're seeking the Seelie Queen."

"That's what the goddess asked of me," Adelina told him.

"And this is the last chance for the Seelie to have a Queen?"
Mikhail verified. She just nodded.

"Wait, didn't you say something about balance?" Del asked.

"Yeah, D'Vita said her darkness was out of balance," Lina
explained.

"The mural," Del said, brow furrowed. "The mural in the library in the Aledale City palace."

"What about it?" Mikhail asked his partner.

"I think it's D'Vita," Del replied urgently. "I always thought it
looked less shadowy when I was younger, but dismissed it as me just
imagining things. But what if I wasn't wrong? What if I wasn't seeing things? If it's D'Vita, it could reflect her in some capacity."

"That could mean there's more information in the palace
there," Adelina brought things to their logical conclusion.

"Do you think the Queen could still be on the island?" Sasha
asked. Del shook his head.

"I think that it's very likely the Unseelie King knows about the
island. It sounds like he already has the Queen, and he wouldn't
keep her somewhere he couldn't control."

"Where would he have her?" Adelina asked.

"In Stroyne with him." Mikhail didn't really know exactly what
was coming out of his mouth, but he certainly wasn't going to stop.
"Kingsfort is a ruin, Fyedor Peak is too volatile, and he wouldn't be
able to access her if she were left with the Wild Hunt. They answer
to him, but they're just as likely to go rogue. They prefer apologies
over permission."

Del *stared.*

"Was that..." he trailed off.

Mikhail just nodded, a bit terrified of the new evolution of his
power.

"What's going on?" Sasha demanded.

"Please trust me when I tell you that we can't tell you right
now," Del begged his son, who looked... a bit hurt. The expression

was a dagger to Mikhail's heart, especially after what had just happened, but he couldn't. Not yet. Not while that King was still alive. Not while there was a possibility that people could overhear them.

"Please, Sasha." Mikhail's voice was hoarse after his foresight took control. "I promise that I'll tell you when it's safe."

"Safe for *who*?" Sasha crossed his arms.

"Safe for *me.*" Mikhail's shoulders dropped. Sasha's demeanor calmed immediately.

"I'm sorry, Dad, Da." He looked down. "I shouldn't have pushed."

"It's fine." Del waved Sasha's apologies off. "I understand. I would have likely done the same."

"So... are we going to have to go to Stroyne?" Adelina asked in a small voice.

"Eventually," Del admitted. "But not right now. You're not at a point where I'd want to risk you sneaking into a city that's designed to be impenetrable." Adelina winced, but acquiesced, thankfully.

"What we can do," Mikhail added, "is go see this mural that Del is talking about. Anyone up for an adventure today?"

The faelings nodded.

"Weapon up," he instructed. "But make it subtle. We won't be going into the Council chamber, so we don't need to be completely weapon-free, but we don't want to look like we're trying to storm Aledale City either. Sasha, help Adelina."

"Will do," Sasha replied, grabbing the female by the hand and whirling toward the stairs. Mikhail waited until he could no longer hear them before turning a panicked expression on Del.

"What the *fuck*," he said. "What the *fuck*."

"I could tell your voice was off," Del whispered, coming over to Mikhail and grasping his forearms. "I don't know if the younglings could, but..."

"That was awful," Mikhail murmured. "I had no control over

my voice; it was like someone else had decided to speak for me and through me."

Del just pulled Mikhail close, perching his chin on the shorter male's head.

"I hate this for you, Misha," Del murmured. Mikhail just did his best to relax into his partner's arms.

"I wish I could tell Sasha," Mikhail admitted. Del leaned down, pressing his forehead against Alexei's.

"I know," Del breathed. "And we will. As soon as it's safe."

Mikhail closed his eyes and breathed in the calming smell of his partner. Of the woodsmoke smell that lingered in the male's office, of the woodsy undertones that always reminded Mikhail of the tiny village they grew up in. He allowed his shoulders to drop slightly from where they'd found themselves tucked tight to his ears, and he consciously relaxed his jaw.

"At least I can remember what I said," he finally responded. "It's better than those foggy visions that I only remember impressions from."

"True," Del admitted. "And you seem less exhausted."

"I'm a lot less exhausted," Mikhail agreed. Both fell silent for a few moments, bathing in each other's presence.

"Let's get ready to go to Aledale City," Mikhail told Del. His partner stood, gave him a soft smile, and took him by the hand before leading him up to their private weapons stores.

They didn't go *anywhere* unarmed.

18

Lina

Lina caught sight of herself in the mirror and inhaled sharply. While she hadn't been *avoiding* mirrors over the past few months, she hadn't been seeking them out either. Her face was a bit sharper, looking more fae than ever with all of the exercise she'd been getting. The pointed ears visible from where her hair was wound into a messy bun always took her by surprise. As did the now bright green that wound through her hair.

The clothes Alexei and Delwyn had given her were incredibly comfortable: a long, soft tunic in green, brown leather pants that tucked into perfectly fitted boots, and a matching, close-fitting leather vest that—according to Aleksandr—had panels of a fae-created metal called dwilium sewn into the inside to protect her vital organs. Leather greaves around her forearms also had hidden dwilium panels.

Instead of the sword she'd only barely begun to work with, Aleksandr gave her several weapons he called 'beginner-friendly.' A dagger was sheathed at her lower back, its placement making it easier for her to grab than a more traditional hip placement. Well, at least according to Prince Clio, who had also adjusted how Lina wore her sword. Getting it off her back took some practice, but she had to admit it was easier than trying to reach across her body.

Aleksandr had also delicately handed her a few pins that were currently holding back strands of hair and decorating her bun. They were tipped in iron. Another thin dagger was sheathed on her thigh underneath the tunic she wore, and in a pocket was a set of brass knuckles—these were also made of iron and had come wrapped in a thick cloth.

"You ready?" Delwyn peered in her open door, but didn't come any closer. She appreciated the space. D'Vita's words to her in her dream the previous night had echoed the feelings she'd begun to accept during the ill-fated lunch with her grandfather, but... but. Even though she was trying, it was hard to forget the furious, snarling creature that she knew instinctively had been angry at *her*.

She wasn't frightened of him the way she was of Egan, but wary? Definitely wary.

Trust them, dear heart.

D'Vita's words echoed in her mind as she gave Delwyn a little smile.

He didn't look much different, aside from the not-quite-guitar slung over his shoulder. Well, that and the thin band of gold around his forehead that she hadn't seen since the Council meeting where she'd met him.

Lina just nodded, worry making it hard to speak.

"Thank you for the gear," she murmured finally.

"Don't thank me yet." Delwyn smirked. "Thank me one day when it saves your life." The words drew a little grin onto Lina's mouth as well, helping her relax, as the older male doubtlessly intended.

"I'll do that," Lina promised. "What's that?" She pointed toward the instrument, curious enough to ignore the wariness.

"It's a sitar," Delwyn explained. "It's one of my favorite instruments to play. Primarily, I pluck the strings, but I can also tap on the body for a different sound if I need it."

"I've never seen one before," she admitted.

"If you want, I'll teach you to play one day," Delwyn offered.

"One day." Lina tried to smile, leaving her room and walking with Delwyn down to the living area where the other two waited.

While Lina could only see one dagger on Aleksandr's waist, very like hers, she knew from seeing him train that the male had daggers up his sleeves, under his tunic, in his boots, and anywhere one could feasibly (and sometimes unfeasibly) place a dagger. Mikhail was just dressed in his usual dark clothes. He had a sword strapped across his back, but no other visible weapons.

"Everyone armored up?" Mikhail asked, looking both of them over. He walked over to Lina and, at her permissive nod, adjusted her greaves a bit so they sat over her forearms properly. "These are strong," he told her. "If someone comes at you, don't be afraid to block with your forearms. It's a lot easier to fix those than a heart-shot."

Lina nodded, swallowing. The nerves were back.

"Good." Mikhail shot her a small smile and nod before moving to lead the way down to the portal room. When they reached the portal, Mikhail and Delwyn shifted places without a word, the dark-haired male sliding back a step to walk just behind Delwyn's shoulder like a shadow made flesh.

Aleksandr walked next to her and behind the two older fae as they all came through the portal and into the travel room of the palace at Aledale City. A butler and a guard appeared in tandem.

"Prince Delwyn." The butler bowed. "How can I help you today, Your Highness?"

"We wish to visit the Royal Library," Delwyn informed the male.

"Prince Donal will wish to speak with you," the butler informed him, sniffing subtly at the sight of the rest of his party.

"Of course." Delwyn smiled brightly, clearly disarming the stuffy butler who reminded Lina so much of Ronin that they could be brothers. "Allow me to walk these three to the library, and then I'm happy to go see Prince Donal."

The butler frowned, eyes narrowed.

"Can the... *hybrids* and the Unseelie not find their way alone?" he challenged. Lina went cold, then hot with fury. How *dare* he?

"*Prince-in-Waiting* Aleksandr and *Prince-in-Waiting Candidate* Adelina will be doing an assignment for me and have never been to the royal library before. I wish to at least explain their assignment first." Delwyn's voice was icy in a way that Lina hadn't heard before. It was nothing like his usual jovial tone, but nothing like his unhinged feral episode from the night before, either. His defense of her warmed her a bit.

"What's the Unseelie doing here, then?" the guard interrupted. Lina had to resist the urge to throw her (iron) brass knuckles at the male.

"I suspected that Prince Donal would need to speak with me," Delwyn sniffed. "*My Prince Consort* will be staying with the other two as a resource to ask for help as needed."

"Hmph," the guard snorted, but ultimately moved out of the way. The butler glared but did the same.

"Could you bother to tell me where Prince Donal is at this hour?" Delwyn asked, cheerful tone restored.

"In his office," the butler answered shortly.

"Thank you." Delwyn smiled beatifically, then swept from the room with the rest of them in tow.

Delwyn led the way through the halls, chatting happily to a quiet Mikhail, both of them seemingly well practiced in ignoring the looks they received from the palace servants and other lurking royals. Thankfully, the hall they sought was empty of servants.

The library itself was even emptier of people. A single, bored librarian ignored them from where she read at the front desk, somehow completely uninterested in the cavern of knowledge she resided over. The room was at least two stories tall, with stairs and ladders lining the floor-to-ceiling shelves that covered three of the four walls. A balcony ran along the halfway mark of the shelves, under which were more shelves. Along the back, Lina could vaguely see color and an open space.

Delwyn led them through the additional shelves into the open space. Lina caught only the barest glimpse of tables and chairs dotting the space before the back wall caught her attention.

Mural wasn't even the right word; this was a massive stained glass window that took up two stories and the entire back wall. Lina froze when she came upon it, something painfully familiar about the figure. The figure was female, with a lithe, curvy figure covered by a sleek dress. Shadow covered a majority of the body, only a touch of green and gold hinting at the actual color of the dress. The oddest part was that the figure had two faces on one head, almost like Janus from Roman mythology. The larger face was pale, with red eyes and white-blond hair. Near the edge, the second face held something warmer—green eyes, golden yellow hair, and olive-tanned skin.

She held her hands out, one to either side of her. The hand on the side of the red-eyed face reached toward a figure that was clearly a corpse, swirls of darkness taking over a majority of the rest of the stained glass. Hints of color tinted the darkness, but the traces of purple, red, and deep blue were muted. Her other hand healed a barely-visible fae figure. Vivid vines and flowers crawled across the little bit of the glass that wasn't smoked out in blacks and grays.

The four of them stood silently, scanning the mural for a few moments before Aleksandr spoke.

"There," he whispered, pointing to a place where the colors meshed poorly. As they watched, the darkness snuck up the vine, leeching the color out and shrinking the area covered in bright greens.

"It *is* growing," Delwyn murmured in horror. "This *is* D'Vita."

The rest of them were quiet, watching until the creeping of the darkness across the mural finally stopped.

"Stay here," Delwyn ordered quietly. "Research if you'd like; see what you can find in the history section. Misha, you know where it is. I'm going to go make nice with Donal for a while." He looked at Lina. "Would you like to go greet your uncle?"

She just nodded, unable to speak after having someone else finally see what she'd been trying to find proof for all along.

"Take a few moments," he suggested, a hint of sympathy dancing in his gaze but invisible in his expression. "Unless you want to tell him about this, take a moment and gather yourself."

A few deep breaths later, she nodded at the blonde.

"Let's go say hello," she said, carefully pasting on an excited expression as she took a step closer to Delwyn. "I'm sure my uncle is curious about what brought us here; he shouldn't have to wait any longer."

Pride shone in Delwyn's eyes as he shot her a quick smile.

"Then let's go," he replied, turning to lead her out of the library.

19

Sasha

Part of Sasha wanted to be appalled at the way Da was talking to Lina, but he knew that it was a necessary part of their jobs. *All* of their jobs. Da's, Dad's, his, and soon, one day, Lina's. They couldn't show weakness, especially because they were expected to fail. So many of the Seelie fae assumed they'd fail because they weren't full Seelie, or Seelie at all, or even full fae. So they had to be better. They had to show the rest that they weren't weak links.

Sasha looked at his dad, who nodded once at him to have him follow. The two of them wound deep within the stacks until Dad stopped.

"This is the earliest part of the history section." He gestured at where he stood, and then to the far end of the shelf. "Let's start looking."

Starting at the opposite end of the section from Dad, Sasha began skimming titles. Books with no title were pulled out, opened, flipped through, then replaced. Unfortunately, he wasn't finding much useful information. Oddly enough, the Aledale City palace didn't have anywhere near as much information as Sasha had expected it to, at least not on *this* subject.

Had the history been removed? Was it hidden somewhere?

The questions flitted about in his mind, distracting him from his goal as he crept further and further back in time with the books. Notes in the fronts of the books listed them as copies of books whose originals had either been lost to time or weren't available to the public. The authors cited protection of the manuscripts, but... was that even truly the case?

Sasha knew it was theoretically possible for books and other perishable materials to be suspended in time and still usable. It was how many of the small villages in the Northern Forests operated; they cast spells on the trees, or even just parts of the trees, and used them as part of their homes. The trees were still trees, but they were able to be lived in without hurting the flora.

So why didn't they do that for the books?

"Dad," Sasha whispered. The other male looked up sharply, a distracted expression on his face. "Dad, I don't think we're going to find anything here."

"Why not?"

"Look at the notes." Sasha showed his dad the note at the beginning of the book in his hands. "You and I both know they could protect original manuscripts from pretty much anyone. So why remove them?"

Dad's eyes narrowed in thought, staring at the book.

"You're right," he said suddenly. "So where are they keeping the books?"

"I don't know," Sasha admitted.

"Let's sweep the place," Dad decided, placing the book back on the shelf. "You take the left, and I'll take the right. Meet back at the mural. Don't be seen."

Sasha nodded, heading off to his side of the stacks to search with no further fanfare. There wasn't much initially; a lot of dust, a few little insects, and even a large spider crossed his path, but nothing incriminating. He walked up and down the aisles, checking the walls as well when he arrived at one.

He'd almost given up on finding anything interesting on his side when he saw the door.

It was set deep into the wall, hidden in the shadows of the bookshelves around and above it. There were few lights in this corner, as if the faelights in all of the surrounding sconces had chosen to go out at once. Curious, he climbed up on one of the shelves until he could see the sconce, seeing that someone had melted the runes right off.

Continuing to climb carefully, placing his toes on the very edge of the bookshelf, Sasha made his way over to another sconce so he could verify that yes, those were burnt off too. He reached out mentally, seeking his dad's familiar mental presence.

Found something. Back corner.

Once his dad had verified that he'd be there soon, Sasha climbed down from the bookshelves, carefully wiping the shelves so that his boot prints weren't visible. Dad appeared right as Sasha was brushing the dust off of himself, raising a brow at his son's vaguely dusty state.

"Someone melted the runes off the faelight sconces," he told his dad, whose eyes immediately flickered to the sconces, then back down. "And there's a door."

His dad immediately went over to the door, holding his hand just a breath away from actually touching the door. The older male glared at the door and said something under his breath that Sasha suspected was actually a curse.

"It's just locked," Dad muttered, reaching into his pocket and bringing out a thin leather wallet that, when he opened it, turned out to be full of lock picks. Dad swept his hair out of his face and then delicately began to work with the lock. It only took him a moment or two to get the door unlocked with a soft click. Sasha crept over at Dad's soft nod, both of them peering in as they pushed the door very, very carefully.

The room was completely dark. Sasha summoned a tiny violet

faelight and sent it through the door. Dad's faelight was an eye-burning red, and it followed Sasha's into the room. In the dim lights, they both realized it wasn't a room; it was a vault. Books covered the shelves, not a speck of dust anywhere in the room. Dad jerked his head toward the barely opened door, then slipped inside, Sasha following.

Sasha browsed a few of the titles.

These are some of the same books that are out there, he sent to Dad.

Originals?

Sasha pulled one off the shelf and opened it, the message about it being a transcription gone. He met Dad's gaze and nodded. Dad grinned, a bit maniacally, and opened up his belt pouch, stuffing books inside.

How the hell do those fit? Sasha sent to Dad.

I extended the inside of the bag a few years back.

Sasha resisted the urge to chuckle, instead skimming titles as fast as he could in order to find something helpful. His finger snagged on a work titled *The Annals of Seelie Queene Kimia Warmhearted Volume One.* Sasha grabbed the book, as well as the subsequent volumes, and passed them to Dad. Just as the last volume slid into the bag, Dad stood abruptly in response to something Sasha hadn't heard. Suddenly, he grabbed Sasha's wrist and pulled him out of the room before locking the door.

"Hide," Dad hissed, before vanishing.

Sasha, finally hearing what his dad must have already heard, panicked for a split second before he saw the railing of the second-story balcony. After a quick check with his powers for another presence, where he found no one, Sasha scaled the shelves as quickly as he could without making noise. The voices were almost on top of him when he vaulted the railing, crouching behind a pillar and listening as hard as he could.

"That idiot said someone came over here," a masculine voice complained.

"I'm just glad she was wrong," a feminine one retorted. "His Highness needed to make sure that no one had discovered the archives."

"Check the door," the masculine voice said shortly. Sasha's heart was in his throat as one of them checked the door. He heard a rattle. "Magic too," the masculine voice added after the noise.

"Nothing," the female reported. "No magical interference on the door, and it's still locked. His Highness still has the key."

Prince Donal? Prince Donal knew about this? Sasha reached out to Dad, informing him of the most recent development.

A sigh interrupted him.

"Thank magic," the male said. "Ress, you stay around here. I need to figure out where in blazes those damn Unseelies went. Whoever authorized that brat on the Council ought to be put outta their misery."

"It was probably the Northern Forest Prince in cahoots with the Western Lakes Prince and the Eastern Mountains Prince," the female, apparently Ress, snorted. "I've heard rumors that the Unseelie fae 'trains' with Prince Clio."

"Yeah," the male chuckled. "I'm sure they get plenty of training done."

Sasha smothered a rising fury at the turn the conversation took, biting his lip so hard it bled.

"Of course they do," Ress replied in a suspiciously reasonable voice. "Had to train up Prince Clio so she could make sure that Prince Liam did their bidding."

Sasha could feel his body shaking with the fury that was too big for his body. His magic swirled around him; it took every bit of his energy to keep it locked down. The implications in what the two of them said... did his dads know about that? About how these people felt? Why had no one told him?

He knew well that people hated his Unseelie blood. Saw his hair, and worse—his magic—and didn't trust him. But this...? It was worse than he'd ever thought. And the idea that his da would *whore* Dad out like that? No. Just... no. Especially after what he'd heard about Egan's treatment of Dad. Sasha's pulse pounded in his ears, and every ounce of his self-control was currently focused on locking down his magic to keep it from escaping in a vengeance-filled fury.

It had only happened once before, but Sasha had learned things about himself that day that he had buried in a box in the back of his mind.

The hatred confused him, frankly. Or it did on a normal day... Today, it just infuriated him. He focused on his breathing, avoiding listening to them mutter until he heard the male walk off. He ignored the female's chuckling and crept off until he was browsing in the poetry section when he heard someone stomping up the ladder to the balcony.

Sasha correctly assumed it was the male from earlier. The Seelie fae was wearing the traditional green uniform of the Queen's Guard, which enhanced the male's brown hair and eyes, as well as his bronzy-toned skin. Frankly, the male looked pissed.

"What are you doing?" he demanded.

"Looking at the books," Sasha responded mildly, continuing to lock down the fury and feelings to the best of his ability. "I rather like epic poetry."

The male snorted.

"Yeah, sure."

"Is anything wrong?" Sasha asked innocently.

The male narrowed his eyes at Sasha.

"What do *you* think is wrong?" the male demanded. "What makes you think *anything* is wrong?"

"You came up here and wanted to know what I was doing," Sasha pointed out. "Rather urgently, at that. It seems rational to think there was something wrong."

The male crossed his arms.

"You probably read my mind, you fucking leech," he muttered.

Sasha focused again on his breath. This male was testing him. He didn't respond; he knew there was no way to win with this guy.

"I'm sorry, I didn't quite catch that," Sasha replied politely.

"Oh, fuck off," the male snarled. "Just get out of here, you have no right to be in here."

"I thought that the library was open to all five of the Princes?" Sasha queried.

"You're not a Prince, mongrel," the male sniffed.

"I'm a Prince-in-Waiting," Sasha pointed out. "That means I have most of the same access. Unless something changed in the past few days, that means I'm permitted to be here."

Sasha reached out mentally. Thankfully, Da was almost to the library.

Second-story balcony, he sent to Da before refocusing on the current conversation.

"Did you or did you not hear me?" The male adjusted his stance like he expected a fight. "I said, *get out.*"

"On what grounds?" Sasha pushed.

"Because *I said so,*" the male ground out, taking a step closer.

"What's going on here?"

Sasha had never been so happy to hear Da's voice. They may not like or respect him or Dad, but Da, they at least tolerated. Mostly because they assumed he was using them both, but it would serve them well here.

"Prince Delwyn." The male dipped his chin.

"I'm waiting." Da crossed his arms and frowned at the guard.

"This... *person,*" the guard replied, "refuses to obey a direct order from the Queen's Guard.

"What was the order?"

"To leave the library," the male admitted.

"From my memories," Da said as his green eyes flashed, "all royals are allowed access to the library. And when I mentioned that he was in here to *Prince Donal,* he said nothing to me about the rules changing."

The guard glared defiantly at Da but didn't respond.

"Name?" Da demanded.

"Arollyn," he replied. "Captain Arollyn."

"Dismissed, *Captain*," Da jerked his chin toward the door. "And don't think I won't be having a chat with your superior officer about this."

Both Sasha and Da just watched the defeated guard captain nod stiffly, then stalk off. Neither spoke again until Sasha nodded that there was no one within hearing range.

"You okay?" Da murmured to Sasha. Sasha just shook his head mutely. "What happened?"

"They..." Sasha swallowed, biting his lip to help control his emotions. "Da, they said *awful* things about Dad. I was up here and I overheard them. Him being rude to me was annoying but expected, but Dad..." Sasha trailed off. Da's gaze was sympathetic, a hint of the same titanic fury from the other night hiding behind his eyes.

"I know, Sasha," Da said, reaching over and putting a hand on the younger male's shoulder. "I know."

"The things they said..." Sasha whispered, unable to say it at any kind of full volume. "They implied... they implied that Dad was just being *whored out* for political reasons, and I couldn't decide if I wanted to throw up or kill them where they stood."

That titanic fury in his Da's eyes came further to the front for a moment, but the older male took a breath and seemed to *physically* force himself to relax.

"I have spent..." Da trailed off for a moment. "*Centuries* attempting to teach people that there is fundamentally no difference between the Seelie and the Unseelie fae. I had hoped that people would eventually warm to the idea once Misha proved himself not just a friend to the Seelie, but someone who works for our people's good. Some days, I feel like I'm making progress. Others, days like today..." Da shook his head. "Other days, I wish I could leave them all to rot."

Sasha's shoulders drooped.

"They're always going to hate me," the young male whispered.

"I don't know," Da replied starkly. "I hope not, and I hope that time will help. But... I truly don't know. Just as I don't know if they'll warm to Adelina."

"I almost want to warn her away from the job," Sasha murmured.

"I know, Sasha-sweet." Da squeezed his shoulder. "I know. Sometimes, I do too."

"Can we go home?"

"Yeah." Da nodded. "Let's go home."

20

Mikhail

As soon as they were safely ensconced in their own living room, Mikhail stumbled back a step when Sasha threw himself into Mikhail's arms. His son's slight-looking figure was stronger than one might expect thanks to his training, and Mikhail knew he wasn't too far off from some bruising thanks to the force of the hug. But he didn't move, instead wrapping his arms around the faeling and meeting Del's gaze with a question clearly written across his face.

His lifepartner just shook his head and sighed, eyes darting to Sasha and back just quickly enough for Mikhail to infer that he needed to talk to Sasha about what happened instead of hounding Del. Mikhail nodded to show his understanding, and focused back on Sasha as Del guided the other faeling into the kitchens for snacks and tea.

Mikhail settled his chin in Sasha's wild, deep purple hair in a manner reminiscent of what Del always did for him when he was stressed. Soft bits of hair tickled his skin and nose, but Mikhail just wrinkled his nose a bit to relieve the itch without releasing his son. Even Iron sensed Sasha's distress, pushing his cool, damp nose into the back of the younger male's neck. Mikhail glared halfheartedly at the mngwa as Sasha flinched.

"What happened, little storm cloud?" Mikhail was careful to

use a soft, coaxing tone instead of the worried snap that he knew his voice would otherwise have. His baby nickname for Sasha seemed to relax the younger male a bit further. Sasha turned his head enough that he wasn't burying his face in Mikhail's shirt anymore, and he could be heard clearly.

"I..." Sasha's voice cracked, and the faeling sniffed a bit. "When you left. I couldn't go anywhere but *up*."

Mikhail hummed, letting his son know he was listening without interrupting.

"So I climbed up to the balcony to hide. And I *heard* them," Sasha said, something raw and wounded in his voice.

Dread crept up Mikhail's spine as he wondered what the youngling could have heard from the two soldiers.

"I knew..." Sasha paused, then looked up at Mikhail. The older male was shaken to see tears brimming in his usually unflappable son's eyes. "Dad, I've had literal assassins come for me. I've seen the looks. I've been ignored in shops and had penniless orphans look down their nose at me. I've been spit on, and I've had people wash their hands after shaking mine. The people I grew up with tried to literally kill me. *I know hatred.*"

Mikhail *really* didn't like where this was going.

"But what I heard today..." Sasha trailed off. "I don't think I've ever heard anyone be so casual about their hatred. They really do hate us, don't they?" Sasha met his gaze, seeming to almost stare into his soul.

Mikhail's heart broke at the defeated, sad expression on his son's face. He couldn't speak, just nodded, feeling that defeat within himself. Sasha leaned forward, bracing his forehead against Mikhail's chest.

"I shouldn't have agreed to do this," he whispered. "I'm going to fail. I'm going to fail Da, and I'm going to fail the people. How much can I even do when I'm hated so much? The only Prince who will be hated more than me is Lina."

Mikhail held his son closer to his chest.

"It won't be easy, Sasha," Mikhail murmured, trying to speak around the lump in his throat. "It won't. It hasn't been easy for me as a Prince Consort, and as a Prince, you'll likely have it even harder. I don't want to sugar coat it for you." Mikhail smoothed down the back of Sasha's hair as the faeling's tears began to dampen his shirt and a subtle shaking rattled his shoulders. "But remember. I knew what you'd face. I knew. And I still told Del that I believed you'd be successful. And I stand by that statement."

The youngling kept crying, holding Mikhail even tighter.

"You and Adelina both," Mikhail continued. "You'll have each other, and you'll be able to make so many great changes to this world."

"You... you really think that?" Sasha asked, voice shaky.

"I've always thought that," Mikhail answered immediately, no hesitation. "You can check my mind if you're worried."

"No, I don't need to," Sasha croaked out. The words coaxed a smile out of Mikhail, who smoothed Sasha's hair back out of his face again.

"Dad..." Sasha's voice trailed off, sounding worried.

"Yeah?"

"I think... I think Prince Donal knows what's in that room," Sasha told him in a small voice.

"What makes you think so?" Mikhail asked, stifling his rising worry at the words. Unfortunately, Sasha's response didn't help as he reported that the two soldiers had been sent on word of the seemingly distracted librarian, and by Donal himself, nonetheless.

"They just ended it by saying incredibly cruel things," Sasha finished up, guilt suffusing his expression. "I couldn't let them see me and know I was hearing."

The apology in his son's expression told Mikhail that it had been about *both* of them, and Sasha felt terrible for not standing up for him.

"Don't worry, son," Mikhail tilted Sasha's chin up so their eyes met again. "Remember, I'm the one who has always told you to keep your anger to yourself around the Seelie fae. If you want to get revenge, be *smart*. Revenge is best served cold, remember?"

A tiny smile flickered across the youngling's face at the memory.

"I think Da took care of part of it," Sasha admitted. "I think he's having the captain demoted, at least."

"Good." Mikhail knew his smile had more teeth in it than most people cared for, but he wasn't going to hide in front of his family. Especially not when Sasha echoed the expression.

"I'll take care of the female," he promised. Mikhail kissed the faeling's forehead.

"I believe you."

The two of them stayed quiet for a few moments more, both calming down from the stress of the day before doing anything else. The quiet was broken by a gurgling noise coming from the vicinity of Mikhail's stomach. Sasha snickered quietly as he pulled away from Mikhail.

"Snack time?" the youngling asked.

"Yeah," Mikhail admitted, a little bit embarrassed. "Snack time."

Instead of the snack time they had expected when they stumbled upon Del and Adelina in the kitchens, they found a full meal had taken over a small table in a nook off the main kitchen. The two were having an energetic discussion about the research and reading they'd been doing over the past few days. Mikhail smiled fondly; Adelina seemed to be slowly opening back up to Del after the disaster yesterday. His smile faded into embarrassment when his stomach growled again.

At the sound, Del looked up, alarmed, then slid over enough to make space for him.

"Come sit, Misha," Del patted the wooden bench. "Have food."

Mikhail sat, Cook appearing immediately with a mug.

"Thank you," he murmured to them. They nodded briskly,

then frowned at Sasha until he also sat down. Once he had a steaming teacup in front of him, Cook vanished as brownies do.

Before he could do much of anything else, Del took the plate he was sitting in front of and dished out food for Mikhail. A pile of potato cakes, sliced summer sausage, and some steaming green beans appeared in front of him, which he dug into with no hesitation. Sasha had gotten his own and was eating similarly well.

"Cook wouldn't let us leave with just snacks," Del explained with a little smirk.

Mikhail shrugged and went back to his food, keeping an ear out on the conversation now that he was feeling a bit better.

"Why do you call Mikhail by a different name than everyone else?" Lina asked, almost hesitantly, the expression on her face suggesting that this had been something she'd been wondering about for a while.

"His usename, like Sasha's, is Unseelie," Del explained with a grin. "Their names tend to have more unique nicknames. Misha *is* a nickname for Mikhail. But Misha prefers that I'm the only one to use his. And Sasha is a nickname for Aleksandr. It's his call as to whether he's comfortable with you using the nickname. Nicknames like those are called diminutives and are commonly used only by the closest of family, friends, and partners."

"To clarify," Mikhail cut in, "the only people who'd ever used the diminutive for my name before Del were my parents."

"We grew up together," Del added. "And I didn't know the diminutive of his name until after our mating. Notwithstanding the fact that we'd known each other for over a century at that point."

Mikhail fought not to blush. When he and Del had left the sacred site they'd chosen for their mating, the other male had loved having something of Mikhail's to tuck away in his heart, but bemoaned not being able to actually use it to mark how much he loved Mikhail. The silly male. After some thought, Mikhail had hesitantly told him about the diminutive.

Del had *personally* punched the first person who disregarded Mikhail's preferences on the matter, and Mikhail the second. After that, the rest of the world figured it out.

"Oh, okay." The little female looked thoughtful. "Thank you for explaining it to me."

"You can always ask questions," Mikhail promised. "You have a good heart, and we know you well enough now that anything awkward or poorly worded won't offend any of us."

"Thank you." Lina beamed brightly before turning to her dinner and getting back to it.

"Ignorance doesn't fix bigotry." Mikhail shrugged. "Knowledge and truth are the only ways we can hope to fight it."

There was little conversation after that, just the quiet sounds of utensils against plates and cups being picked up and put back down a little emptier than before. Finally, they were left with full stomachs and fresh cups of their warm beverages. Sasha met his gaze, and Mikhail nodded solemnly.

Do you want to tell them, or should I?

The words floated into his mind as if someone had spoken them in his ear, even though no one was close enough. Sasha.

Instead of answering, he took the decision out of the youngling's hands; this was one conversation that needed handling a bit delicately.

"Adelina," Mikhail got the female's attention immediately. Something twisted in his chest; the female had so few that she trusted, and he was about to take one of them away from her. Instead of a verbal answer, she just tilted her head slightly, the way many of the fae did. "Sasha and I found some... interesting and potentially unpleasant things in the library after you and Del left. Do you want to go ahead and hear it, or would you like to wait until tomorrow?"

Lina hummed, clearly thinking based on her furrowed brow. After a moment of quiet, she turned to answer him.

"I'd rather just get it over with," she admitted. "Then I can sleep it off, whatever it is."

Foreboding grew in his chest, causing Del to throw him a worried glance.

"Let's go into the living room," he sighed. "Grab your tea, and we'll go get comfortable."

21

Lina

Lina was afraid.

She didn't pretend to be an expert on understanding her guardians' facial expressions and how they corresponded to feelings, but someone would have to be completely clueless to miss the tension growing between Mikhail and Aleksandr. She was afraid to know what they'd learned.

She settled into the corner of one of the couches, boots leaning against the edge of the cozy furniture and feet tucked underneath herself. The delicate teacup was cradled to her chest to allow the warmth to seep into her skin through her shirt.

Aleksandr was in a nearby chair, sitting a bit rigidly with his own teacup held almost as a shield. Delwyn and Mikhail were on the couch across from her, the two males cuddled into each other. Mikhail never fully lost the furrow in his brow, though, even as they both mostly relaxed otherwise. Then Mikhail sighed.

"There's no easy way to tell you this," he told her. "But it looks like Prince Donal is involved in whatever larger conspiracy is afoot here."

"Uncle Donal?" Lina echoed in horror. "Wait, no. Uncle Donal wants to *help* people!" Her hands were tight around the delicate porcelain of her cup, though she was aware enough not to crush it. Her fae strength was not always a blessing.

"When Sasha and I were in the library, we were looking at some of the history books," Mikhail told her solemnly. The sadness and regret in his tone frightened her; this wasn't the tone of someone telling a bad joke or trying to sow discord in a family. This was the tone of someone who hated what they were saying but wouldn't hide a hard truth. "Sasha and I both wondered why the books in the Seelie Queen's library were transcriptions. With magic, it's incredibly easy to preserve books for future generations. So why would the biggest library in the country have only duplicate copies of books?

"We looked around, and Sasha found a shadowy corner where the runes for the light spell had been melted off the sconces. There was a door hiding there, locked only by a normal lock. When we got in there, we found the originals. Some of which we managed to grab."

"You've got original books?" Delwyn sounded far too excited for the topic at hand, something Mikhail clearly agreed with based on the look he shot his life partner. "Sorry," he added, looking abashed.

"Long story short," Mikhail continued, "two soldiers came to check on the room, and we both hid. Sasha was close enough to overhear them, and the higher-ranked one mentioned 'His Highness' wanting to know if the books were still locked up."

Lina's eyes were burning with tears, both devastated and furious. This... this was a betrayal the likes of which she'd never felt before. The closest she'd ever come was when her mother told her about Darek. At least then, her mum had told her exactly why she'd waited to tell Lina about her heritage. With this, she couldn't *ask* Un—Prince Donal why he'd acted the way he had. She couldn't do anything. She couldn't even warn Grandfather, because between Prince Donal and bloody *Egan,* they likely had been manipulating him in his illness.

Now, with this knowledge, she was second-guessing everything the male had ever done for her family. Everything he'd ever said or done to or with her.

And it *hurt*.

Something inside her was ripped open, it seemed. There was an ache. It wasn't too dissimilar to how she'd felt when she'd found her mother in pieces in their apartment. But worse, because the loss, the grief, was tinged with anger and self-loathing at how she *missed* it.

In a way, that was it: the final loss. She was like one of those balloons that children lost from fairs. Unmoored. By this point, her family was gone. Mum was dead, her father was... frankly, she didn't care where Darek was. Hopefully dead. Uncle was hiding things that were clearly important. Grandfather was not only dying, but being manipulated by Egan, the staff at the manor, and possibly even Uncle.

How deep did this even go?

"We don't know, kiddo." Mikhail's voice cut into her processing. "I'd like to say it's probably something small or not relevant to what we're doing here, but..." Mikhail sighed as her gaze refocused on him. "I don't believe in comforting lies. Not unless someone's on their deathbed. And no one here is."

"Thank you," Lina murmured. That was one thing she had always been frustrated by with her mum. The lies meant to comfort, even when Mum's fear was shredding them to pieces, she still lied about it. A terrible truth was always better than a comforting lie.

"All we can do," Aleksandr said as he met her gaze with sympathy, "is find out how deep it goes. We can't make any decisions until we know. And ultimately, as important as this is, you were given a command from the *goddess* of *magic*. We don't know what kind of sense of time she has or when she'll consider you to have defaulted on her deal." Lina winced. Aleksandr was right. She wanted so desperately to immediately dig into this to find out what her uncle was doing. But she couldn't.

"We can't focus on this," Aleksandr unknowingly echoed her thoughts. "If that mosaic shows the current balance—or lack thereof—we don't have much time to figure this out. Even if the goddess isn't timing you, that *is*."

Lina felt her shoulders droop, though she tried to keep most of the rest of her emotions off of her face and out of her body language.

"We'll keep the whole thing in mind," Delwyn promised. "I, for one, may split my time. As a member of the Council, this is... alarming. The fact that we weren't told bothers me quite a lot."

"Clio," Mikhail murmured.

"Good call." Del nodded. "I'll see if she can come by soon to chat. Once I get through some of this and verify that we're right, that things are being hidden from not just the general populace but the *rest of the Council,* I'll bring Cleo in. And maybe Liam."

Her grandfather's absence in that list was loud, at least to Lina. But he was likely compromised in one way or another. Between his naive trust in Egan and how close he was to Prince Donal... he couldn't be trusted yet. If at all. Her heart broke for the male she knew—the kind, though vaguely naive, grandfather who clearly did his best to love her even when he didn't understand her.

"Okay," Lina managed to get out around the lump in her throat.

"We'll figure it out," Mikhail told her in a soft voice. "It's going to be okay."

Her mouth moved faster than her brain, and for once, she replied with exactly what was on her heart. She was tumbling off a cliff; what had she to lose? What more could these people do to her that her family had not already done? In some ways, it was easier to trust these near strangers. If they broke her, it would only be par for the course.

"What if it's never okay?" The words fell off her tongue; she felt like she wasn't quite in her body. "I... what family I have left is falling apart in my hands."

"It will be okay." Mikhail's tone didn't have a shred of doubt in it; neither did his face. "I know you must feel adrift and scared. Family isn't just blood, Adelina. Don't forget that."

Lina felt her lip tremble as she attempted to stifle the tears. To gather herself back together and present a better front, as Lady Mara said she must.

"We'll be your family," Aleksandr promised. "We may not be able to see you as often later on, but we'll still be your family."

"Yes," Mikhail echoed simply.

"Of course we will," Delwyn added, green gaze fierce as it locked on her.

At those words, a tear or two finally overflowed her eyes. Lina felt the cool path they cut down her face as she looked into each face, finding nothing but honesty and caring. Even Delwyn, who had frightened her so strongly... he'd *apologized.* No one apologized.

Part of her was terrified that they would attempt to use or hurt her the way her blood family had. Her gut said these three had no agenda, that they just truly cared about her. It was... exhilarating. Terrifying, yes, but exhilarating.

"Thank you," she forced out from around the lump still in her throat before she hid her face in her hands to hide the tears. She didn't realize that Aleksandr had sat next to her until she felt an arm wrap around her shoulders and tug her closer. The abrupt memory from the previous day when she'd cried into his shoulder startled her, but not more than his next words did.

"You're like the little sister I never had," he told her. "And no matter what happens with Council business, that's not going to change."

"That room is yours at this point." Delwyn's quiet voice filtered into her awareness. "That's not a guest suite, that's *yours.*"

"Iron likes you," Mikhail said easily. "And he has excellent judgement of character."

At that point, the tears came thick and fast.

She'd given up on any sort of dream of a proper family once she met Grandfather and Darek. Especially after the loss of her mum, there was nothing there for her at this point. Part of her had felt as if she had lost her opportunity for a good, happy family. All she expected now was a dysfunctional mess. But when these three inserted themselves so neatly into her life, they'd changed *everything*.

Part of her wondered if D'Vita had placed her in their lives, knowing that she would need them and need their help.

Whether D'Vita had or hadn't placed them in her life, she had a family who cared for her and would do their best. It was a blessing from the goddess either way.

Family is more than blood. Family is those vitally important people who she knew cared about her. No more, and no less.

Aleksandr was rubbing her shoulder comfortingly with a hand. When she finally felt ready to leave the safety of her palms, he was sitting next to her with a sympathetic expression. His next words echoed the sentiment.

"Losing blood family is hard," he murmured. "My mother died having me, and my father died when I was still a faeling. I think I was your age. The rest of the villagers left me mostly alone while Father was alive, but when he died, it was open season."

"I was fairly nearby, luckily," Mikhail took over. "Took care of things and brought him home. My parents were sacrificed to the Wild Hunt, but before Lifebringer's soldiers got to them, they made me run. I only survived because Iron turned into a mngwa when the soldiers caught up to us."

"He managed to get across the narrow sea up North," Delwyn mused, usually joyful face uncharacteristically serious. "The village I grew up in was close to Queensrest, and that's where the poor kid washed up. My cousin and her half-brother found him and brought him home, just like they had me when my parents died of a pestilence."

"All that to say," Aleksandr brought it back around, "we get it.

Not quite to the same degree." He shrugged slightly. "But we know what it's like to lose blood family in one way or another."

"My cousin is the only blood I have left." Delwyn shrugged. "And she's deep undercover right now. Has been for a long time."

"I haven't actually met her," Aleksandr mused.

"Hopefully you will one day." Delwyn flashed a weak smile.

"Thank you guys," Lina whispered, a few more tears tracing down her cheeks. "I... I don't know what I'd do without you."

"Well, you don't have to find out." Aleksandr squeezed her shoulders in a one-armed hug.

"My cousin would say that we've been missing a female's energy around here." Delwyn winked. Lina sputtered out a damp laugh, her tension around the male starting to fade a bit.

"Well, since you're family," Aleksandr said with a grin, "that means you get to call me Sasha. If I had a blood sister, she'd have grown up calling me Sasha like Dad and Da do."

Lina grinned back before rubbing her eyes on her sleeve.

"You look exhausted, kiddo," Mikhail noted.

"I am," Lina admitted. "It's been a busy couple of days."

"You're not wrong." He made a face. "We all need an early night tonight."

"Absolutely," Delwyn cut in. "All four of us. The past two days have been stressful and hard on everyone. We can take an early night, and then in the morning, start in on the new information we got today."

"Nope, training tomorrow," Mikhail corrected. "*You* can start on this, but the faelings need training. Lina in particular needs to work on her training; eventually, we'll have to send her to Stroyne, and I want her to be as ready as possible."

"You make a fair point," Delwyn admitted, leaning back on the couch with his arm around Mikhail's shoulders. He looked over at them. "You're training in the morning. I'll be reading through the books that were... *borrowed* from the library."

"Without permission," Alek—*Sasha* cut in with a grin.

Mikhail chortled as Delwyn made distressed noises. As Delwyn and Sasha went back and forth, she found a giggle or two bubbling up as well, which earned her warm smiles as the two older fae shooed them off to bed.

22

Lina

Mikhail had told her not to be alarmed when Delwyn hadn't shown up at the breakfast table that morning, and he'd taken both of them to the rooftop to train for a while. Lina had worked hard, sweaty and gross by the time they went in for lunch, but her nerves came back when Delwyn was *still* not at the table.

It was hard not to worry when someone vanished. After leaving her mum safely at home and coming back to find her in *shreds* across their living room, it was hard to ignore the clammy palms and dry mouth. Her toes tapped gently against the floor as she did her best to ignore the fear for someone she cared for more than she'd realized before now.

Even after the Incident two days ago, he was still *Delwyn*. Still the goofy male who walked her and Sasha through scenarios they may face as rulers, who had been angry *for* her after the attempted assassination, who always dropped a kitten on her when he felt she looked sad.

"Da is probably just in the library," Sasha assured her with a gentle bump to her shoulder, correctly interpreting her nervousness.

"He is," Mikhail confirmed. "I think he got up at some awful hour and has been in there ever since."

"Has he eaten?" Lina frowned, remembering how hungry she

was after her own day of research. And how no one had bothered to check in on her or wondered where she was. No one deserved to be ignored like that; she wanted to make sure Delwyn didn't feel abandoned like she did.

"Usually, the staff leave him food and tea," Mikhail soothed. "But after lunch, you can take him a tray if you'd like; he needs a break anyway."

"Okay." Lina relaxed a little bit. She considered for a half second how nice it would have been if the servants at her grandfather's manor had left her food and tea, but then again, if they had, it would have probably all been poisoned.

After lunch, Mikhail led her down to the kitchens, asking for a tray for them to bring to Delwyn. Cook smiled softly at her, then bustled around and put together a tray of food and tea before handing it to her.

"Thank you," she said.

"You're very welcome." Cook gave her a satisfied nod before going back to whatever they were putting together for dinner.

Lina could sense Mikhail behind her, despite his silence, as they walked up the stairs. Sasha had chosen to go read in his room, just telling them to tell Delwyn 'hi' from him.

"Should I knock?" Lina murmured as she approached the closed library door.

"He wouldn't hear you," Mikhail told her, reaching over her shoulder to open the door. "Here, I'll show you where he'll be." Mikhail shifted, walking in front of her and leading her through the stacks efficiently.

When they emerged on the other side of the massive room, Lina almost stopped short. The corner looked like an entire additional library had exploded. A comfortable-looking armchair seemed to have been abandoned, the bag Mikhail and Sasha had filled slouched in the seat. A tray filled with empty and mostly-empty dishes was balanced slightly precariously across the arms as well. A large table had been moved, as well as a single accompanying chair. Behind the chair was a pile of books that all seemed to have been discarded. The table was covered in books and papers as well, most either lying open themselves or being held open by assorted bits of things. Including Delwyn's little panpipes, something decorative that likely had been on a shelf somewhere, a bookend clearly robbed from a nearby shelf, and an empty bowl.

Delwyn himself didn't even seem to know they were there. Bits of black ink spattered across his face like freckles, and he was muttering around a pen between his teeth as he skimmed the book in his hand.

"Del," Mikhail prodded gently.

"Hmm?" the other male hummed absently, seemingly unable to not answer his lifemate.

"Del," Mikhail said again, in the same gentle tone.

"Le'me fin'sh..." Delwyn trailed off, voice muffled around the pen.

Mikhail waited until Delwyn went to swap from his book to notes.

"Delwyn," he said, a little sharper this time.

"Huh?" The pen dropped out of Delwyn's mouth to the floor as his head shot up. He looked between them in confusion.

"You've been in here too long," Mikhail scolded, but even Lina could tell his heart wasn't in it. "What time did you get up?" Delwyn's brow furrowed absently, and he began counting on his fingers. Lina could see the dark circles under his eyes; it must have been early.

"Second hour after midnight?" Delwyn guessed, looking sheepish.

"So you've been in here almost twelve hours." Mikhail crossed his arms. Delwyn winced.

"Sorry." His shoulders drooped, the exhaustion that he'd likely been staving off with work seeming to hit full force. His dark circles and eye bags seemed to have doubled in size and darkness in the course of a few seconds.

"Come here." Mikhail grabbed Delwyn's hand and tugged him over to a table and chairs halfway across the room, out of sight of the mess. Lina followed, placing the tray in front of Delwyn, pushing it toward him. "Lina was worried about you," Mikhail added, crossing his arms and glaring until Delwyn grabbed the tea and took a sip.

Delwyn then looked at Lina and offered a wan smile.

"I'm okay, sweet," Del promised. Lina felt her brow furrow and her heart beat faster, but spoke anyway.

"You don't seem very okay." Lina bit her lip, nervous about talking back but not enough that she'd ignore her worries about Delwyn's health. This was her family; he was one of her people. Even though he'd scared her half to death.

She ignored the part of her that said she wouldn't have done this if Mikhail weren't with her.

"Just got really focused," he told her after wolfing down the sandwich on the tray. "I woke up in the middle of the night, and the lure of the books was too much. After that, I just ended up getting buried in the work and losing track of time. I'll take a nap soon."

"Good." She relaxed a little bit.

"Can you tell me what you're working on?" Mikhail asked. Delwyn froze; his food slid between his fingers and back to the plate as the question brought everything to the forefront.

"Misha." Delwyn shuddered, then looked over at where Mikhail sat next to him. "Misha, I found the Unseelie King's usename. I'm trying to dig up his truename."

Lina had never seen Mikhail speechless like this. She suspected that if he hadn't already been seated, his legs would no longer have supported him. That he would have just collapsed on the spot.

"You..." Mikhail swallowed, staring at Del in bafflement. "You found his *usename?* He destroyed all mention of it... Hell, millennia ago? How in the realms did you find it?"

"Those books," Delwyn told them. "One of the books was a journal from one of the last Queens. During her time, the Council of Princes was... fucking corrupt, honestly. They killed her parents, and then I suspect they killed her, though there isn't any proof that I could find. Openly, too. The monarchy was not doing well during that time period. Once I had some timing, I was able to dig up some royal lines and track them down to the end."

"That's..." Mikhail shook his head. "That's insane."

"I'd tell you, but honestly, I'm not sure he doesn't have a listening spell on it," Delwyn admitted.

"No, no, please be safe," Mikhail agreed. "I don't want to know. I can't believe you *found* it after all this time."

"Me either," Delwyn admitted. "And honestly, I'm probably going to need to take a break soon and just process the mountain of information I've consumed in the past twelve hours."

"That's a good idea," Lina piped up.

"I'll be okay," Delwyn promised with a wan smile. "I've done it before. I just need food and sleep."

"He really will be okay," Mikhail added. "It doesn't become an issue until he's done it three or four days in a row. Which he doesn't do anymore." The last words were more of a warning to Delwyn than a comment to her.

Delwyn shook his head aggressively.

"Nope, once was more than enough," he said, a little too cheerfully.

Lina silently wondered *what* had happened, but decided not to ask. Instead, she just nodded and gave Delwyn a little smile. Which he returned with an utterly blinding grin. Something about the conversation confused her, though.

"Um... why are these names so important?"

"Well," Delwyn began, putting down his food and focusing on her, "the fae tend to have three names. Our usename, which is the name our parents give us, our surname, which often tells you something of note that one of us has done or something about the individual.

"Like mine is 'Sirensong' because I'm a bard," he continued. "And Misha is 'Mngwalord' because he's the only person to have ever bonded with a mngwa. A trait and an action.

"The third name is our truename." Delwyn took a sip of tea, staring into it. "Your truename holds power over you. It's the name given to you at your Coming of Age. In a perfect world, the only one who ever hears your truename is your lifemate during your mating ritual. Otherwise, you have to be incredibly careful who hears it."

"The thing is," Mikhail took over, "the only way a truename cannot be forced from you is if it's yours or your lifemate's. If, for example, you told one of us your truename, it wouldn't be impossible for someone with a power like Sasha's to find it and control you with it. But that same person couldn't rip your truename from your own head."

Lina nodded slowly, remembering the voice of D'Vita in her mind during her Coming of Age.

"And you can't tell anyone your name for a full year," she said.

"Exactly." Delwyn nodded, smiling with pride as he usually did when she answered a question correctly. Lina smiled back, turning the information over in her mind as she sat with the couple.

She and Mikhail stayed with Delwyn as he ate until he conceded defeat on the matter of more research. Once Delwyn had left the library, Lina left the pair. Delwyn was in good hands with his lifemate, and Lina wanted to see if Sasha would spar with her again. She had an idea for a good tactic to take him down.

23

Sasha

Sasha was more surprised than he probably should have been by how quickly Lina had taken to fighting, despite her misgivings. He expected that getting her to fight and practice would take dragging her, and that she'd struggle with the idea of hurting someone. And sometimes, she did. It was obvious that she didn't *want* to hurt people, but she also seemed to have a real talent with the sword. Daggers weren't her best weapon, though they were working on her close combat and improving her aim with throwing knives.

Even when she wasn't a natural, though, Lina fought hard. She had a level of tenacity that sometimes surpassed even Dad. Though smaller than her peers, Lina was sturdier, thanks to her human blood. And that served her better than either of the two males could have anticipated. Blows that would have made one of them stumble, she could just *take* and move forward.

Beyond that, sometimes, she really managed to *get* something, and it impressed Sasha. And Dad, for that matter.

Like today, for instance.

After managing to help Dad pry Da out of the library, she had come to find him to "practice." The look in her eye told him that she had an idea, and Sasha was always up for making sure his little sister could look after herself.

To his pleased surprise, they were on their second sparring round before she summoned a faelight right on top of his nose, the
bright light taking out his vision just long enough for her to duck in
under his guard and hold her sword to his throat.

"Well done!" Sasha grinned at her as he blinked the spots out of
his eyes.

"Thanks." Lina grinned back.

"I've actually used that on someone before," Sasha admitted,
rubbing his eyes with the back of his hand. "About... twenty years or
so ago? They tried to get the drop on me. Not even assassins, just
ordinary cutpurses." He snorted. "Didn't realize I'd known they
were there from the start. I was trying to scare them off instead of
having to kill them, but they were a stubborn bunch."

"Oof." Lina made a sympathetic face.

"Yeah." Sasha rolled his eyes. "I tried, but they didn't want to leave me alone."

"Thankfully," Dad cut in from where he was standing in the
doorway of the rooftop access, "it was obvious what had happened.
And even still, he left most of them alive."

Lina flinched in surprise, but relaxed when she recognized Dad,
even giving him a little grin.

"Well done," he added. "I was going to start working your magics into your fighting now that you're more comfortable with both,
but I'll admit to having been curious about whether you'd do it on
your own."

Lina was flushed a bright red between exertion and discomfort
with compliments; it was only because Sasha could sense her on an
emotional level that he knew that she wasn't embarrassed. The poor
little female always seemed shocked and pleased when she received a
compliment, and then rode the high for hours afterwards.

Sometimes, Sasha wanted to just go beat Cormac over the head
with a frying pan or something similar. His inability to see how Lina
was wilting in his manor made Sasha incredibly frustrated, and the

few stories she *had* told him were enough to infuriate even the most even-tempered.

"Thank you," Lina managed with a proud smile that she couldn't hide.

"Da get to sleep?" Sasha asked with a smirk. Dad rolled his eyes.

"Finally," he said. "The idiot had been up since the second hour after midnight or something."

"Gross." Sasha made a face. "He hasn't gotten focused on anything like that in a while. Everything okay?"

"He..." Dad swallowed. "He says he may have found Lifebringer's usename."

"Um... how will that help?" Lina ventured a quiet question.

"Well, there are quite a few ways." Dad leaned back against the doorframe and crossed his arms. "One way is that we can trace his family. His history. Figure out more aboutwhat makes him a *person* instead of a villain out of myth. It also might help us find the Unseelie King-in-Waiting, figure out if he's someone we can help rescue from Lifebringer, or if he's going to be an additional obstacle." Dad shrugged. "Knowledge is power. Usenames don't have the power that truenames do, but they can lead you to truenames and other information."

"He's erased everything about himself," Sasha jumped in. "And we don't know how much of it is important and how much of it is hiding the things that are."

"That makes sense." Lina's expression was contemplative.

"He doesn't want to lower himself to being one of us," Dad told her. "He wants to put himself above the average fae, even above the royals. My mom and dad were part of a very long list of people who tried to remind people that Lifebringer was one of us. Not some type of god, just one of the fae."

"He's a tyrant," Sasha spat, flipping one of his knives up and catching it with the blade neatly between his finger and thumb. Lina's eyes widened when she saw him do the trick.

"Sounds like it." Lina's response was distracted; her gaze was locked on how he was fiddling with the dagger. Sasha grinned and stopped.

"You're gonna need to get better with daggers before I'll teach you this stuff," he told her. Lina flushed again, embarrassed to be caught out. Sasha sheathed the weapon and showed Lina his hands. Her eyes widened as she mapped the latticework of scars on his fingers and hands from badly caught knives. "This is what learning that cost me, and I had a much better grasp on daggers and knives than you do."

Her shoulders drooped.

"Hey." Sasha put his hand on her shoulder. "You're not bad," he encouraged. "Remember, I'm a little over eighty years old. I've been training since I was..." Sasha trailed off, then looked over at Dad.

"Right around her age now," Dad finished.

"Exactly," Sasha turned back to Lina. "So that's sixty years of experience. I wasn't comfortable enough with daggers to even consider it for almost thirty years. I didn't start trying to learn until another ten years after that."

The worry faded from Lina's gaze, and she relaxed under his palm.

"Will you teach me one day?"

"Sure." Sasha grinned and winked. "When you're ready. Want to practice?"

"Yes." Lina's eyes grew focused, and she sheathed her sword down her spine, where she preferred to keep it when she could. Her dagger sheaths were placed uniquely as well; instead of a hip placement, the daggers were sheathed on her lower back. The handles pointed to either side instead of the front as well.

Her weapon placement in general had completely changed after a meeting with Prince Clio a few weeks ago. The Western Lakes Prince had taken Lina to her manor and evaluated her. According to

Dad, Clio's goal was to ensure that Lina's style took advantage of the differences between males and females.

Sasha grabbed his blades and dropped into a ready position, his bright grin mirrored on his opponent's face. Lina followed his lead.

After Dad counted them in, Sasha stayed mostly on the defense, letting Lina practice her more offensive moves. In general, her style leaned toward the defensive, a reaction to her not wanting to hurt others or fight at all if she could help it. But even if she didn't *prefer* to do either, she needed to know how. The life of a Prince-in-Waiting was more dangerous than most of the fae would want to believe. Especially for fae like Sasha and Lina, who didn't fit into the rest of the Seelie Queendom's mold.

Lina's face darkened as she realized what Sasha was doing.

"Fight me for real!" she yelled. Sasha saw Dad about to intervene, but Sasha shook his head minutely. He kept moving, weaving around Lina's blades. She became more and more reckless, finally *throwing* one of the daggers toward him in an ill-planned move to piss him off. The dagger was easy to dodge, and Sasha used his momentum to grab her wrist and wrap it around her back, dagger uselessly pointed upward along her sheathed sword. To really drive home his point, Sasha opened his mind up to Lina's, stopping every movement before she could even make it.

"*Damn* it!" Lina yelled, and—to both of their surprise—burst into tears. Sasha divested her of the dagger, but before he could do anything else, she collapsed to her knees. Dad practically skidded on the roof trying to get to her. Sasha gave them enough space that he wasn't intruding, but could still hear, and sat down.

Dad tugged her to his shoulder, much like he'd done for Sasha any number of times over the years. Sasha stayed quiet, tracing a finger over the rough stones. Her reaction had surprised him. It wasn't common for him to misjudge someone so thoroughly, especially with the mind link he'd opened up.

His intent was to remind her that he was *training* her. That fighting her with all of his weapons wasn't the point; instead, it was to practice her weak spots and help her get better. Putting her in the dirt over and over wouldn't help anyone. He just wanted to remind her of that.

Sasha pulled his knees up, wrapping his arms around them and dropping his forehead down as something ached in his chest. He stayed there doing his best to breathe until a familiar hand on his head had him freezing. Sasha bit back tears as Dad smoothed his hair.

"Care to come out of there?" Dad rumbled soothingly.

Sasha did *not* care to come out of there, but he knew that while Dad's phrasing was that of a question, it was more of a strong recommendation. And he knew that Dad wouldn't humiliate him in front of Lina.

Which he suddenly realized wasn't a courtesy he'd extended the little female who was practically his sister.

Tentatively, he removed his face from its hiding place against his knees and found both Dad and Lina seated close to him.

"I'm sorry." Sasha looked Lina in her bloodshot eyes and tried to ignore the urge to stare at the stones again. She just tilted her head sideways, brow furrowing.

"Why?" she asked. "I'm the one who lost my temper. I got frustrated because I'm so far behind. Throwing the dagger at you when I'm untrained was dangerous. That whole exchange was dangerous once I lost my temper."

"I shouldn't have let it go on," Sasha admitted. "I should have forfeited or something. Stopped the match. I was trying to remind you that I'm just training you, not fighting for real. Hell, if we were fighting for real, you'd be using your sword. You're far better with it."

"I don't know about that." Lina broke eye contact. "I don't know if I was in any place to accept a forfeit. I... I'm so *frustrated*. I feel like I have to fight for scraps of people's respect. It felt like you were playing with me. Like you didn't respect me as an opponent."

"Lina." Sasha stared at her. "You've grown in leaps and bounds since you started working with us. Your growth is faster than mine ever was. You have natural talent with a sword; you're already better than I am. I was *never* playing with you; I was focusing on defense to let you work on your offensive moves. That's it." Sasha shook his head.

"I have nothing *but* respect for you," he said, more softly this time. "You work your ass off every single day. I'm sorry it seemed like I didn't."

"...Oh." Lina looked and sounded like she'd been poleaxed. "I'm sorry I misunderstood and lost my temper."

"Forgiven." Sasha smiled tentatively, receiving an equally soft smile in return.

"Alright, kiddos." Dad, who Sasha had forgotten was also nearby, placed a palm on each of their heads. "I think it's time to go back inside. A break will do you both some good."

Sasha and Lina's gazes met again, and they nodded, following Dad quietly back into the house to rest.

24

Lina

When she woke up after Mikhail sent her and Sasha back to bed that morning, Lina felt significantly more refreshed. Mikhail's only requirement for the day was that they left the house. Lina wasn't arguing; she was excited to go see Skovfore, as she'd not been in the months she'd been in the Northern Forests.

While Lina knew her training was important, vitally so, but with the restedness came the realization that she'd been overdoing it for at least a month straight.

Well, probably longer. Since she'd found out about Un—*Prince* Donal. Since her life had been so upended that the last trustworthy family member she had was pulled out from under her.

But her new family, these three males, was far superior. Part of her didn't even quite understand *why* she hadn't let herself be cared for by them before. But she was letting them now, and she was starting to relax, to *believe* them.

For a few moments, she just lounged in bed. One of the cats was curled up in the vee of her knees, purring in its sleep. You only have to wake a sleeping Iron to try to get him to move once before you learn how much of a bad idea it is to wake a sleeping cat. Lina just snuggled into the blankets, the warmth of the bed encouraging her to rest a while too.

The next thing she knew, she was waking up again. The extra little nap had been nice, but she was incredibly excited about visiting the center of the city; she'd wanted to see it ever since Sasha had described it to her. Lina hadn't visited a place like that since she had left England. She'd missed the hustle and bustle of the city, even though she knew it would be different.

Lina regrettably slid her knees away from the sleeping cat, carefully getting out of bed without waking them. After a few quick stretches to help warm her body up as she woke up her mind, Lina began looking through her clothes to decide what she wanted to wear to the market. As she browsed, she heard a knock at the door.

"Come in!" she called, turning back to her wardrobe.

"Sleep well?" Mikhail's deep voice surprised her; she'd expected Sasha. Lina turned back to the door, head tilted in confusion, and nodded.

"I needed that more than I thought I did," she admitted.

"That's how it usually goes." Mikhail shrugged a bit. "Glad you're feeling better. I brought you a couple of things."

"Really?" Lina was really curious now. Mikhail nodded. The first thing he handed her was made of the same material as her clothes from their adventure to the palace.

"This is... I don't really know what to call it." He looked almost embarrassed. "I know that female fashion is a bit different, so you can't wear your full leathers all the time without looking like you're afraid, a weakness you can't afford to show as a potential Prince-in-Waiting. But this can go on over or under your clothes, however you prefer, and it'll at least protect you some from any major surprises."

Lina examined the garment. It almost seemed like some sort of corset, albeit one that laced up the sides under her arms. It was made of that same sturdy, flexible material she'd noted on her other clothes, but looked feminine enough that it wouldn't be completely odd to see outside of her clothing if she chose to wear it in that manner. The back was high enough to protect her from a heart shot to the back, though the front would sit low under her breasts. A little smile curved around her mouth as she saw the delicate floral design carved into the leather-like material next to the seams.

"Thank you," she told the male with a grateful smile.

"Of course." Mikhail almost seemed to shrug off her gratitude with this air of "of course." It made her feel warm and cared for in a way she never realized she needed. Mikhail then handed her a delicate bracelet with a single pink stone. "This is a bit like the amulet you have. It's protective. I don't entirely know if it does anything else, but like I've said, this magic thinks for itself sometimes."

Wordlessly, Lina held out her wrist to him in request. Easily, he finagled the delicate clasp and got it around her wrist. Once it was around her wrist and she felt the protective magic that felt so like the male himself fall around her, she shocked herself and Mikhail by giving him a fierce hug.

After a beat of what Lina was fairly sure was surprise, Mikhail returned the hug.

"You're welcome, youngling." His voice was a bit gruffer now, but Lina just squeezed his middle one more time before pulling away. "Now, let me see your necklace and make sure it's powered up."

Lina pulled it out from under her shirt, placing the carved crystal of the pendant on his palm. Mikhail frowned a bit, closing his hand around the stone. Eyes shut, he furrowed his brow in concentration until a flash of light emanated from inside his closed hand.

"There." Mikhail nodded decisively. "Now, whatever you choose to wear, make sure you also have your battle leggings on and never go anywhere unarmed."

"I will, and I won't," Lina promised. She felt incredibly touched—Sasha had told her about his dad's habit of "mother-henning" at odd intervals, but she never thought she'd be enough a part of the family to receive that level of care. Seeing Mikhail fussing over her reminded her strongly of how she'd always wished her mum would act, and she was hard-pressed to keep her emotions at bay.

"I'm going to go check on Sasha," Mikhail said, reaching out and giving her head a little pat before disappearing from the room, shutting the door behind him.

Mindful of his warnings, Lina tugged her leggings on first, then found a pretty, knee-length dress that actually looked okay with the dark brown leggings. It was a gentle pink fabric that was soft and comfortable. The corset immediately went on over it, providing a cinching that made her feel more feminine. In an attempt to balance femininity and practicality, she braided part of her hair from temple to temple. It looked a bit like a headband holding the rest of her hair back.

Then came the weapons. A throwing dagger in the bag she'd carry over her shoulder, two more in sheaths that would be hidden by her boots, a couple of very sharp, pointy pins placed in her hair to look like nothing more than flowers in her braid, and her sword sheathed down her spine.

Lina stood in front of the mirror and gave her reflection a faint smile. She definitely had gotten more used to the angularity of her features and the willowiness of her frame. Even the more pronounced green in her blonde hair no longer bothered her. Fluffing the curls hanging down from the braided crown, it occurred to her that she looked like what her mother would have looked like as a faerie.

She strode out of the room, leaving her thoughts behind her, and excitedly headed for the main area of the house where she knew Sasha would be waiting for her.

As she expected, he was waiting. He was also wearing leathers, but a tunic softened the look and made him look less warlike. Del and Mikhail were nearby. If she didn't know better, she'd say they looked *worried.* But that would be absurd; they were the ones who suggested this particular outing.

"You ready?" Sasha asked with a hint of a grin on his face, the rest of it in his eyes.

"So ready!" Lina beamed, bouncing on her toes.

"Well, let's go!" He gestured to the door. "Bye Dad, Da. We'll be back later."

"Be safe," Del ordered firmly.

"Yes, sir," Lina said, saluting as Sasha dragged her out the door and into the street in front of the house. "I assume there aren't a lot of others who live out here?" Lina asked as they began walking.

"Not really." Sasha shrugged. "Don't get me wrong, we're not far from town. But the distance gives us a chance to have some privacy. We do have a manor in the city itself, but it's publicly known as a property of the Prince, and we rarely stay there. Really, we're only there when we have a guest that needs to be kept out of our private spaces."

Lina read between the lines and was warmed by how easily she'd been accepted into that more private part of their lives. Even before she'd accepted them back.

"That makes sense." She nodded, smiling up at the sun, then at the shady forested area they were traversing. She tilted her head back and closed her eyes, soaking up the sun's warmth like a plant. "It's so beautiful here," Lina murmured.

"Autumn is best," Sasha told her, pointing toward a tree whose leaves looked like they were starting to turn yellow. "And now is one of the best times to go to the market. There's tons of delicious food, lots of goods people have been working on all summer, and the harvest has been good this year."

As Sasha talked, Lina nodded, getting distracted as she saw the city appear on the other side of the hill they'd just reached the top of. She couldn't see much, but she could tell that the buildings tended to be low, spread out much like Tricities. The roads were fairly clear, moving figures visible in the distance, but not so cluttered that you couldn't see the road itself. The forest wrapped around the city like a hug; the sharp contrast of the green and brown made both of them pop. Beyond the forest was a jewel-bright lake fed by a river.

"Pretty, isn't it?" Lina could hear the grin in Sasha's voice.

"Much prettier than London," Lina admitted.

"What was the human realm like?" Sasha asked curiously.

Lina paused, thinking of how to respond as they began to descend the hill and approach the city gates.

"Both very like here and very different," she said finally. "Like here, there were lots of types of places. Cities, towns, little villages, farms, lakes, beaches, stuff like that. There were many different types of people. But humans have a different sort of technology. Iron was a sort of springboard for them; they've created a lot of things that automate life in similar ways to how magic can."

"Really?" Sasha looked intrigued now. Lina nodded.

"It's... It's hard to explain some of it," she admitted. "I don't know a whole lot about the inner workings. But iron smelting led humans to be able to dig into the earth for other minerals and rocks and things that we found could be powered with..." Her voice faded out in thought as she tried to figure out a way to explain electricity. "Energy. It's really all just energy in different forms."

"Magic is energy too," Sasha reminded her.

"Yeah, it's just a different type," Lina countered. "It's harnessed with physical things and different metals."

"Like a focus?"

"What's a focus?" Lina asked, distracted.

"Some fae have insane power levels." Sasha shrugged. "To the point where they really can't use it alone. So they funnel their power through a focus so they can better regulate the power itself."

"Do you know anyone who has one?" she asked.

"I don't know," Sasha admitted. "Most fae don't advertise it. If they can't control their power, they take great pains to make it look like they can."

"The fae are very proud," Lina noted.

"It's true," Sasha allowed.

"It's strange," Lina mused. "Most of the differences between the Seelie and Unseelie fae seem like they're in the way they look. Obviously, the magics are somewhat different, but there are similarities too."

"Like smithing," Sasha said. "Or the non-specialization magics."

"Exactly!" Lina gestured enthusiastically. "Beyond that, it's just that Seelie fae thrive during the day and Unseelie fae thrive at night. No one's ever been mad at a house cat for preferring the night or a dog for preferring the day."

"You make a good point." Sasha shrugged. "People are frustrating when it comes to this stuff."

"Very." Lina pouted, though not for long, as the dirt path changed abruptly into cobblestones.

It wasn't a city the way she'd known them, with tall glass and steel buildings and smoggy skies; this was a city like those that had existed thousands of years previously. There were no cars, and not really any carriages. Instead, it was mostly fae and the occasional horse. A few carts were scattered here and there, universally carrying goods. The streets were surprisingly neat, stones set into place carefully. Many homes had neatly-kept flower beds in front of them, the bright flowers and green leaves setting off the dark wood that made up most of the houses.

"This is beautiful," Lina whispered finally, wide-eyed and smiling so hard her face hurt.

"Just wait until you see the market." Sasha grinned, elbowing her gently. "Watch where you're going."

25

Sasha

Sasha didn't expect his warning to be so timely, but then, he didn't expect for someone to pull a dagger on Lina in the middle of the street either. The assassin thankfully missed the heart shot he was trying for, instead getting the arm that Lina was fast enough to use to block.

He heard her hiss in pain, but couldn't focus too hard on her when he realized that at least half of the people on the street right now were trying to kill them. Two of them began converging on him, blocking Lina from sight.

With a snarl, Sasha flicked throwing knives from his hidden wrist sheaths. One would-be assailant went down with a blade in the throat; the other got caught in the thigh, going down, but not for good. A frustrated growl was all he allowed himself at the mistake before the next attack came.

Sasha sensed this attack more than heard it, dropping down to one knee in a crouch that allowed him to grab another dagger out of his boot. His arm slashed out automatically, drawing blood from his adversary's shins, but not knocking them over.

While the assassin was unbalanced, Sasha leapt up, slashing out again. This time, he caught the other's blade instead of their face. Being on the dagger side of a sword versus dagger fight wasn't how

Sasha would choose to spend his afternoon, but thankfully, Dad had trained him very, very well. The sword wielder didn't manage to injure him with any of the deadly assaults they attempted, but Sasha caught them with a well-timed kick right to the slices across their shins.

As their legs collapsed out from under them, Sasha made a matching slice across their neck. Blood fountained up and half-drowned him as he dropped the dead body. He took a moment to spit the coppery blood out of his mouth and check on Lina.

Thankfully, she was holding her own nearby. A feral snarl followed one assailant's attempts to take her down with a sword, the sound wholly fae and the least human thing Sasha had ever heard from her. She swung with precise sword strikes, doing Dad proud with her focused, intense expression and careful footwork.

Just as he thought that, the other fae got under her guard.

Fear broke her focus as she saw the blade heading for her neck, threatening a harsh decapitation. Before Sasha could so much as shift his weight to move, the blade seemed to skid off to the side of her neck, repelled by an invisible force. Relief hit him like a brick before he refocused on his own battles.

More assailants began to dogpile both of them, forcing Sasha to lose another two daggers to the incoming fae. He was about to slice another throat when his particular assassin screamed in pain, color leeching from their face. When the other collapsed, he saw Lina, a dark scowl on her face, and one of her iron hairpins in her shield hand. Sasha nodded at her before taking the short breather to strip his daggers from the dead.

Sasha didn't see Lina again for an indeterminate amount of time, another group of assassins heading in his direction. He dispatched two with ease, but the third, fourth, and fifth got the drop on him. Absently, he was rather glad that this was what did it. He wasn't sure *Dad* would have been able to get out of something like this, not with the short time he had.

Two of the assassins held his arms, and another stalked toward him with a knife and a grin. Sasha, in an action completely fueled by fear and survival, *reached* with his mind. Nothing. The assassins were all shielded against his specialization so well that there was no way he could get into their minds fast enough. The knife-wielding assassin smirked.

"Can't do much now, can you, little leech?"

Goosebumps crept down his arms and spine at the sight of the blade—and the words—and his struggle renewed. He fought even harder as he both heard and felt Lina realize his dilemma. His heart broke as he heard her *scream*. The sound was one he'd take to his grave, a combination of fear, horror, and fury that reminded him distantly of the scream he'd heard from Da the time Sasha was scratched with that iron nail.

To his surprise—and the surprise of the assassin who was about to slit his throat—Lina's scream was echoed by a roar.

Something golden leapt between him and the assassin, taking his assailant's throat in its jaws and *ripping* in a way that reminded Sasha almost unnervingly of Iron. The golden creature—which, upon further inspection, appeared to be a fae-lion—startled him enough that he forgot about the fae holding his arms for a moment.

He was forcefully reminded by an entirely different ripping as he felt something in his elbow tear in half. As he fell, his other arm still imprisoned in the second fae's grasp, the first kicked out. The resulting *snap* echoed through the street a breath before pain stole Sasha's breath. The second fae left his own mark with a dislocated arm before they ran off.

A low groan was all that he let escape at the pain as his knees hit the stones of the road. Both of his arms were useless, and the slight jarring that falling to his knees gave them almost caused him to lose consciousness.

His pain-fogged vision cleared just slightly as a figure knelt in front of him.

Lina.

Sasha clung to the sight of his friend—his sister. He had to get her home. Had to get them *both* home.

"Okay?" he managed, attempting to focus enough to see if she was injured.

"I'll be fine." She brushed him off. He had no way of knowing if she was hurt either; his gaze wouldn't clear up. "We need to get you home."

Sasha couldn't do more than make a noise now. And a pathetic one, at that. The stabbing-ripping-burning pain was taking over all of his senses. He didn't really know if he could walk right now. And as strong as Lina was, he wasn't sure if she could carry him with the awkwardness of both of his arms completely out of commission.

"I'll be right back," Lina promised, worry pinching her expression as she turned. Sasha made an abortive move to stop her, but instead, blackness crept in around the edge of his vision until he froze again in an effort to prevent further pain. He wished she hadn't gone; he didn't want to be alone.

Before he could work himself up too much, Lina reappeared with a board in her hand. Likely one from the carnage around them. Absently, Sasha wondered where the people were. Where *his* people were. Had they done this? A different ache flashed through his chest, but he couldn't *focus*. Goddess, he just wanted his dads... He wanted it all to stop hurting.

"You're not going to like this," Lina warned. Sasha didn't understand when she tore up the skirt of her dress into strips, nor did he understand when she placed the board against his mangled arm.

Unfortunately, once she started wrapping it with the strips, pressing the breaks flat against the board, he understood.

With a pained scream that he couldn't have stopped no matter how hard he tried, Sasha succumbed to the numbness of the dark with only a flash of green to accompany him.

26

Mikhail

The sound of his name screamed out in the little faeling's voice would echo in his ears for weeks to come.

"MIKHAIL."

Then his partner's.

"DEL."

In the blink of time between Del's movement and his own, fear flowed through his blood, almost freezing him in place. But Mikhail shook it off as his lifemate sprinted toward the sound, taking out a thin flute as they ran. He paused only momentarily, telling Leander to call Maryn. He didn't know what was at the door, but he knew it wasn't going to be good.

The sight at the front door was more terrifying than he expected. Lina had somehow managed to open the door as she leaned on a *giant fae-lioness* that was carrying his son. His son, who was unconscious, with a dislocated arm and another that was bound to a board.

Del skidded to a stop in front of the faelings, evaluating them both. Mikhail stood back a little, letting the male examine both of the faelings with a muttered curse.

"Get Lina," Del barked, before beginning to play a melody that

Mikhail recognized, one to immobilize injured fae. As Del and Sasha made their way to the infirmary, Mikhail scanned Lina.

She was pale, her freckles standing out on her skin. The way she held herself suggested a few broken ribs, and she'd bandaged a cut on her arm as well. He realized that she'd cut bits off of her dress's skirt, which hung in tatters around her leather leggings. There was a scrape on the leathers at her side, though it hadn't gone through, and she had a blooming black eye.

The poor little female looked like she was in shock, one arm over the back of the fae-lioness, clearly her familiar. She was gazing off into the distance, likely looking for Sasha.

"Lina, kiddo." Mikhail used a gentle voice to bring her back to herself. "Let's get you to the infirmary. That's where Sasha will be going with Del."

Slowly, Lina nodded. Mikhail lifted her arm gently and put it over his shoulders, supporting her as they walked through the house. The fae-lioness followed almost silently.

When they arrived in the infirmary, Del had just popped Sasha's arm back into place. Mikhail got Lina settled on the bed next to Sasha just as his son asked about her.

"Lina?"

"Right here," the female said quietly. Mikhail scanned the room for her familiar, finding the feline being groomed by Iron. He ignored the warmth he felt at the sight and refocused on the others.

"I'm going to put you back under," Del said to Sasha. "I need to deal with this arm, and I suspect it's not going to be fun."

Sasha's already light skin paled further before he nodded.

"Cover your ears," Del warned them both. Mikhail stuffed his fingers in his ears, gesturing for Lina to do the same. Neither of them could hear the muffled melody, but Sasha was soon asleep, and Del was examining the younger male's injured arm.

"Did you do this?" he asked Lina.

"Y-yeah." She swallowed. "Is it okay?"

"You may have just saved his arm," Del admitted. "If it had been allowed to set as wrongly as it looks like it was sitting, we would have had to completely rebreak it, and the magic itself only knows what we'd be dealing with then."

"Is he going to be okay?" The little female's voice was fearful.

"Yes." Del nodded. "We have a family physician that I'm going to go send a message to shortly—"

"Already done," Mikhail interrupted. "Leander is sending one of the messengers. Probably already has."

"Thanks." Del nodded to him with a trace of a smile. "But yes, I put him to sleep to help with the pain. There's little else I can really do until the physician arrives now that I got his dislocated arm back in place."

Lina just nodded, tears dripping almost absently down her face.

"Misha," Del said, looking at Mikhail with worried eyes. "Want to grab her a drink? I think she needs one."

"On it." Mikhail nodded. Before he could leave Lina's bedside, she snagged his sleeve. He stopped, looking at the little female quizzically.

"Thank you," she said fervently. He just stared, confused. "Thank you," she repeated. She winced as she reached up with her injured arm and tugged the necklace he'd given her out of her shirt. "You saved my life."

Mikhail blinked.

"I should be dead," she repeated. "He had a clear line to my neck, but you protected me. I should be *dead*."

Mikhail sat down abruptly on the side of the bed, wrapping his arm around Lina. Absently, he saw Del get up, likely to get the alcohol himself.

Mikhail was somewhat glad Lina was shaking, because it masked the fact that he was *also* shaking. He'd never had anything like that happen before. Usually, the little trinkets he made were either sold anonymously to people in the city or given to the people he cared most about.

Now, *he'd* seen them work, but usually, the charms were a lot more subtle than directly stopping a blade. Most of the time, his charms changed the future he saw. The person who got it never knew the difference.

But Lina, too-young Lina, who'd bonded to her fae-lioness finally, saw.

Something most people didn't know about his little trinkets was that they required belief. It was why he was so careful who he gave them to—giving them to someone who didn't believe in them was a waste of magic.

The precious faeling who held their whole world in her hands believed so wholly in his work and in his desire to protect them that his enchanted necklace was able to stop a *blade*. And not an accident, either—an assassination attempt.

Mikhail stroked Lina's back as she soaked his shirt in tears and snot, holding back the burning in his eyes by sheer will. The faeling needed him.

Before Del even appeared, Mikhail felt himself relaxing slightly when the other male reentered the room. He handed Mikhail one of the cups he had floating next to him.

"Sweetheart." The endearment slipped out of Mikhail's mouth before he could stop it. "Can you drink this for me?"

A very large, very green eye appeared from where it had previously been hidden in his shirt; the other was swollen closed and bruised. He coaxed the brandy down her throat, following it with some water, then gently wiped the tears off her face with a cool, wet cloth. Another cool cloth went over her black eye. Soon, Lina slumped back over on Mikhail, drowsing.

When he went to get up, the faeling's fingers twisted in his sleeve.

"Stay?" she asked.

"Sure, kiddo." Mikhail sat back down, settling in this time, and the little faeling tucked herself in next to him.

"'anks, Da," she murmured as she fell asleep.

Mikhail blinked, and then blinked again, feeling his face heating. He didn't look at his lifemate, who was very obviously staring and probably making heart eyes at him or something equally gooey. Instead, Mikhail snagged the pendant that was outside Lina's shirt and charged it up again, topping off the magic that had managed to save her life. Afterwards, he leaned back against the wall, drowsing and trusting Iron and Del to keep them all safe.

It wasn't until Maryn, their family physician, showed up that he found himself awake.

"Thank you for coming so quickly," Del said to the female.

"What happened this time?" Maryn sighed as she began to examine Sasha.

"Another assassination attempt," Del said bitterly. "For both of them."

"Who's this?"

"Adelina," Mikhail answered with a grunt. "She's Prince Cormac's granddaughter."

"Ah, I remember hearing about her now," the female said, tossing a sympathetic look at the faeling. "I'm disappointed but not surprised."

"I was hoping they could at least go to the market without a disaster," Del sighed. "What's the prognosis on Sasha?"

"I don't know who healed his arm, but they saved him a lot of surgery," Maryn said.

"Wait, healed?" Del blinked. "Lina splinted it, but *healed* it?"

"Not fully," Maryn admitted. "But it's further along than it should be. At least on the outside. It's obvious this is the work of someone untrained. But powerful." Both males were baffled by what happened, but they just stayed quiet as the healer did her work. Mikhail couldn't watch the healing process; it made him ill, so he watched Del's face instead—analyzing the other male's microexpressions to ensure that their son would be okay. Relief soon shone on Del's face, echoed on Sasha's sleeping visage.

"Done." Maryn double-checked her work, then stood up and came over to where Lina was starting to stir. The faeling just blinked up at the physician with a vague gaze.

"Hello there, youngling." Maryn smiled softly. "I'm Maryn. I just healed up your friend, and now it's your turn. Can you tell me what hurts?"

"Here." She attempted to point at her torso, but winced at the movement. "Arm." Lina held up the offending limb. "Eye." The faeling was quiet for a moment before speaking again. "Sasha's my brother."

Maryn held her hands over Lina's ribs.

"Good," she told the younger female. "He needs a female to keep him out of trouble. Or save his arm." Maryn winked. "You did an excellent job. Do you happen to have any talent with healing?"

"I... I don't know," Lina admitted, relief blooming on her face. Mikhail absently wondered if she knew she had a death grip on his sleeve still. If she didn't, he certainly wasn't going to be the one to tell her. Suddenly, her eyes widened, and she looked around abruptly. "Where's Fiadh?"

"Who?" Del asked, head tilted sideways like a confused puppy. But Mikhail understood.

"Iron is with her," he assured the youngling. "He's doting on her like she's a kitten. You said her name is Fiadh?"

"Um... I guess so?" Lina bit her lip. "The name just seems right."

"Check with her," Mikhail recommended. "But that's probably her name."

He reined in his slight nausea at the sight of Lina's black eye going through every stage of healing in a few seconds and just sighed in relief when her gaze was clear again.

"They'll need to rest tonight," Maryn instructed. "I'm leaving a pain tonic and a sleep tonic for both of them, though I'm unsure exactly when Alexsandr will wake up. He may sleep through the night and not need it."

"Thank you," Mikhail told her. "Leander will pay you for your time and supplies." She waved him off and headed out of the infirmary. After she was gone, Del came over and pressed his arm against Mikhail's for a moment, then leaned over and kissed Lina's forehead.

"I'm glad you're okay, sweet," he told her with a soft smile.

"Thanks, D—Del," she flushed, looking down at her hands, then her face was tomato red, and she was untangling her fingers from his sleeve.

"If I were bothered," Mikhail said in a dry tone, "I wouldn't have stayed." He also leaned over and kissed the top of her head. "I'm glad your pendant saved you, kiddo. And I don't know about this idiot, but I don't care if you call me Dad. You're just as much my daughter as Sasha is my son."

Lina's face was still flaming, but she gave him a tiny smile and snuggled in closer.

"I don't mind either, sweet," Del added. "I'm with Misha on this one."

"Thank you," Lina whispered, tears beginning to fall. "Dad. Da." The little female was quiet. "I wish I'd found you guys before my blood family." The words sounded choked, like her throat was clogged. Mikhail just wrapped an arm around her.

"We can't change the past, little one," Del murmured. "But we can be with you for the rest of the future."

The two of them sat with Lina, ultimately getting her to eat, then take her pain and sleep tonics. After she fell asleep, Del laid his head on top of Mikhail's.

"What a day," Mikhail choked out.

"It's shit," Del stated, stroking Mikhail's hair. "Do you need me to cancel on Clio? Stay with you and the kids?"

Mikhail shook his head.

"We need to get more people on our team," Mikhail said. "I've got Iron and Fiadh to help care for the kids. Not to mention Leander and Cook."

Mikhail was glad to hear Del laugh as the other male left the room.

27

Sasha

"It's time," Da said soberly when he returned from his meeting with Prince Clio.

"Time?" Sasha asked, having only been awake for long enough to eat and hear where Da had gone. Dad was still sitting between him and a currently sleeping Lina and was paler than Sasha had ever seen him.

"No, Del, they need more training." Dad sounded like he was *begging*. But that would be absurd; he didn't beg for anything. Not as far as Sasha had ever heard.

"They were attacked by assassins practically in our front yard, Misha." Da wasn't smiling, wasn't joking. He was more serious than Sasha had ever seen him, even in the Council room. Sasha reached over absently, grasping onto Dad's sleeve as he listened to the discussion. "This is the best way to protect them."

"By sending them into a damn gorgon's nest?" Dad snapped. "They're not. Ready. Hell, *I* wouldn't be ready."

"That's the problem," Da said gently, kneeling in front of Dad. "You're not ready. They're as ready as they can be. But *you're* not ready for them to go."

"That city is a place of nightmares," Dad whispered, head hanging in defeat. "I can't send them there."

"They'll be okay, Misha," Da whispered, forehead to forehead with Dad now. Sasha looked down at his blanket, letting them whisper now.

Sasha wasn't expecting they'd be sent to the Unseelie territory for months—years, even. But from what Da was saying, it sounded like they'd be sent there soon. That it was time to find the Seelie Queen.

His heart raced at the thought. Dad's reaction scared him. The only other time he'd ever seen Dad even close to this afraid was when Egan was brought up a few weeks back.

And then there was the tiny voice in his mind reminding him that it had been over fifty years since he had been away from his parents longer than a week. Reminding him of the week he spent with Prince Clio all those decades ago, how he cried himself to sleep most nights, and how he'd been homesick the whole time.

The training was supposed to have been for a month, but Prince Clio talked to his dads, and they brought him home after a week.

Sasha tightened his twin grips on his sheet and his dad's sleeve. This grabbed both of his dads' attention.

"Shit," Da swore, regret coloring his features. "Sorry, Sasha-sweet. You shouldn't have had to hear that."

"Oh no." Sasha made his voice deadpan to stop the fear shaking it. "My parents are real people who can love each other and disagree at the same time. How ever will I go on."

Dad chuffed out a laugh, pulling his sleeve out of Sasha's grip and tucking the younger male under his arm.

"Where did you get that attitude?" Da raised a brow, trying to make a scolding sort of face that kept getting ruined by a grin breaking through.

"From you," Sasha said, tilting his head sideways. "Obviously."

This prompted a rather strong snort from Dad.

"I blame you." Da glared at Dad, though the expression had no heat.

"Who's getting blamed?" Lina had woken up, sounding exhausted still. Sasha looked over, and she did look as tired as she sounded. The poor little female hadn't even sat up, instead just having opened her eyes and turned on her side to face them.

Da sighed, clearly realizing he had to tell her now.

"No one," he said softly. "But... I just told Misha and Sasha. I think it's time for you and Sasha to go to Stroyne."

Lina gasped, her already pale face lightening further.

"But... I'm not ready," she whispered.

"You're as ready as you're going to be," Da said grimly. He went over to her and crouched down. A hand went to her shoulder. "You are as prepared as you can be. If you don't go now, it'll be decades. And I don't think you have decades. If you're killed here just trying to live, you'll never fulfill the goddess's mission."

Lina swallowed audibly.

"Now that you're both awake, I'll tell you the plan," Da said before settling in on the floor.

It was going to be a long night.

Over the next several days, the preparation began. Prince Clio's idea of glamouring them to look like half-Seelie and half-Unseelie fae who needed asylum was nothing short of brilliant.

The Unseelie who did their glamours had been incredibly impressive. The male had an eye for detail and had mixed Sasha's and Lina's features rather interestingly. Both of them now had Lina's olive-tinted skin tone and pale blue eyes that were almost gray. Sasha's own purple-black hair looked, frankly, strange on the usually blond-and-green-haired female. And Sasha didn't know what the other male had done exactly, but Lina somehow looked *more* fae. Sharper somehow.

The story they'd come up with was sprinkled liberally with truth from Sasha's own history—though edited. Their mother was an Unseelie assassin who knew a Seelie was her lifemate. They stayed together for less than a century, long enough for them to have two children. Both of them were assassin-trained by their mother, and then she was killed. They couldn't find safety in the Seelie Court and decided to beg for asylum.

Impressively, this explained the Unseelie trinkets they got from Dad, their fighting expertise, and their sibling relationship. And it allowed them both to make the trek to Stroyne. So now that they were newly dubbed Grigory and Raisa, Dad and Da were prepping them for this journey.

"I'm scared," Lina whispered from where the two of them were tucked into the library, reading everything they could get their hands on about the Unseelie Court, Stroyne, and the Seelie Queen.

"Me too," Sasha admitted.

"I don't think I'm ready." Lina looked down at her hands, the fingers looking longer and thinner than they used to.

"I don't think there's a way to be ready for this," Sasha told her reluctantly.

"There's not, I'm afraid." Da appeared. The worry that eclipsed his usually joyful face worried Sasha more than anything else. Da reached out a hand to each of them, smoothing hair back from their faces. Sasha felt some of the tension leave at the soothing movement. "Come down to the living room. We've got a few last-minute things to go over before we smuggle you out tomorrow night."

Sasha and Lina followed Da back downstairs. Dad was sitting on the couch, Iron at his feet, and Fiadh was curled up next to Iron. They'd even glamoured the fae-lion, making her (with permission) look more like a fae-panther. Fae-lions were really only native to the mountains in the Seelie Queendom, whereas fae-panthers were fairly common across both continents.

The worry on Da's face was echoed across Dad's, but only visible if you knew him well. Sasha almost absently reached over and took Lina's hand, squeezing it before they moved to sit on separate chairs. Fiadh's head immediately went into Lina's lap for the little female to stroke. Sasha could tell it was relaxing Lina, too; contact with your familiar was said to be restorative.

"Alright," Dad said, taking a deep breath. "We've got a contact of Branwen's waiting for you outside Stroyne, but please know her usename in the Unseelie Kingdom is Nadya. Someone she trusts there will be taking you in, and they've been briefed on the story you will be telling. They know that it's a tale, but they don't know who you truly are or your real names. Once you cross, don't use any names other than your assumed ones, even in private.

"The King has eyes and ears everywhere," Dad continued. "It's dangerous there. Unfortunately, the circumstances have shown us that it's just as dangerous here. Both of you were lucky to escape that assassination attempt; it was frighteningly well-planned. So you need to get undercover and start searching for the Queen."

"Why..." Lina hesitated, then fell silent.

"Ask, sweet," Da encouraged.

"Why aren't you going?" she managed.

"We can't," Dad replied bluntly. "Del is too visible, and it will be obvious if he isn't around. And one of the downsides of our bond is that we can't be more than a few miles apart for any length of time. The longest we've been apart since we declared was a week. And it was torture by the end."

Lina's shoulders drooped.

"It's a fair question," Dad added. "And we considered trying it anyway, but it's going to take you weeks to get from Queensrest to Stroyne since you're not sailing."

"Will we have any way to contact you?" Sasha found himself asking. He hadn't been away from his parents for more than a week or two at a time since they'd brought him home.

"Not properly," Da admitted, worry rising in his green eyes again.

"I have these," Dad added, holding up an arm. A thick leather bracelet was on his wrist, two rounded crystals caught in the braiding. "It'll let me know if you're hurt. And these." He dropped his hand into his pocket and took out another tangle of leather. Separating it out, he revealed two long leather thongs with a simple crystal pendant on each one. "These are for emergencies only. If you're in serious danger, you can use these to immediately transport to me. Each one can hold exactly one other person."

Sasha and Lina looked at each other with wide eyes. That was a huge, tricky piece of magic. They each grabbed a pendant and pulled it over their heads, tucking the crystals under their shirts.

"Thank you," Lina told him fervently.

"It was nothing." Dad waved her off, but Sasha saw how the male's dark circles had deepened over the past few days. It hadn't been nothing, but having a way out, an emergency portal, would help both of them. "Just be sure you're not magically burned out when you use them," Dad added. "They pull from one or both of the people being moved. Whoever has more available power."

"Got it." Sasha nodded.

"Stay up late tonight," Da told them, uncharacteristically sober. "You need to swap your schedules to the night. I know it's going to be hard on you, Lina, in particular, but after a few days, you'll be feeling better. That's why we're starting now."

She just nodded.

"Tonight, pack," Dad instructed. "Pack lightly. We'll have clothes and basic supplies for you when we get to Queensrest, but pick a couple of personal effects to bring. Remember, you're refugees, essentially."

"And after tonight," Da finished the conversation effortlessly, "you're no longer Aleksandr and Adelina, no longer Sasha and Lina. You're now Grigory and Raisa. Grisha and Raya. Until you come home to us."

Part 2

28

Sasha

It had been almost two weeks since Sasha had seen his parents.

They'd left Lina and him in the ruins of Queensrest, packs heavy with supplies: clothes, food, jewelry that looked aged enough to belong to the parents from their cover story. Even Fiadh had a pack that she'd consented to wear, on the condition that it was glamoured so that only he and Lina could see it.

That bag was where most of their weapons were hidden.

Crossing the water was easier than expected; there were a surprising number of little rowboats hidden in the ruins. Dad and Da helped them get launched, then waved them off. The crossing itself was fairly easy, as everything hadn't iced over yet.

But that first night? That first night was harder than Sasha had ever expected.

They'd been tucked into the ruins of Queensrest's sister-castle, an imposing building called Kingsfort. They'd let the fire go out, and the sun was coming up. Something in Sasha's heart broke as he realized he didn't know when or if he'd ever see his dads again. It would take weeks for them just to get to Stroyne. And then they had to find the Queen. It could be weeks, or it could be months; hell, it could be *years.*

Sasha had curled into his bedroll and cried, trying to stay quiet and not wake Lina.

But the second night found them curled up together with damp eyes and a mothering fae-lion to keep them company through the homesickness.

A couple of weeks later, he happened to look over to where Lina was drooping across the fire from him.

"Raya," he said, noticing her eyes slowly flickering up to his face. "Yeah?"

"You okay?"

"I'm exhausted," she admitted. He frowned.

"I'll make a relo sun brew while we sleep," he said. "I think you need the boost. There's some ground relo bark in my pack."

"Thank you." Lina smiled quietly. "Can you show me how?"

"Sure." He gave her a quick smile, then proceeded to dig the bag out of his pack. "Basically, what you're doing is putting the grounds in a bowl of water and letting them steep in the sun. Much like tea."

"That makes sense," she admitted. He sensed her following him to the back of the cave they were in, where a cool spring had allowed them to refill their water. He scooped up water to fill the pot, then brought it back over to the fire. A couple of scoops of the ground-up bark went into a little cloth pouch, which Sasha tied shut and dropped into the pot.

"Now, I'll just put it outside, in what's going to be a sunny spot in a few hours," he finished his instructions. He stood, slipping outside their cave. The sun was bright enough to make Sasha squint, even just barely beginning to rise. He found a hidden spot in the middle of a nearby clearing for the bowl and set it down. When Sasha stood, gray ash and smoke filled the distant horizon.

Feydor Peak.

The Unseelie heir resided in the massive, lonely volcano. Brainwashed and broken, if the rumors were to be believed.

Lifebringer never let people see the heir, likely to avoid assassinations to destabilize his rule.

Privately, Sasha wondered if the heir even existed at this point. Was there even a King-in-Waiting? Or was it all a ploy by Lifebringer? It seemed odd for someone who was convinced they'd rule forever to permit the existence of a potential threat like an heir.

Sighing, he dropped down next to Lina, where she stared into the fire. They'd have to smother it soon; wouldn't want anyone to see the smoke and know someone was hiding in these mountains.

"What's on your mind, Grisha?" she asked, a slight furrow in her brow as she looked over at him.

"I miss them," he admitted, albeit reluctantly.

"Me too," she replied, shoulders drooping.

"Today's officially the longest I've been away from them," Sasha whispered after another moment of silence. Lina's head dropped down on his shoulder, the warmth of another body welcome against the chill of loneliness and homesickness.

"We'll be okay. They'll be okay," Lina promised.

Sasha wasn't worried about his dads as much as he worried about making it home. He was afraid he'd never see his parents again, but he didn't really want to speak those fears into existence. Instead of speaking, he just rested his head on top of Lina's, letting the worries chase him into sleep.

Sasha woke up before Lina or her familiar did the next day. Well—night. He smiled softly at his sister-in-soul as he realized she'd tucked him in after he'd fallen asleep, and Fiadh was curled between both of them.

They had finally reached a point where they'd need to go to a village to barter for supplies today, so they needed to be at their best. Letting them sleep was the best thing he could do.

After making sure Lina was still tucked in and warm, he slipped back out to where he left his sunbrew relo. The water was a dark brown, the ground-up bark floating around in the mixture unappetizingly. Sasha sighed, then grabbed the bowl and went back into the cave. He found a fairly clean piece of cloth in his bag, covered their metal pot with it, and strained the liquid into the pot. The pot went on the ashes of the fire, and Sasha took the grounds to bury somewhere they would help plants grow.

When he returned, Lina was awake and digging through her pack to find some breakfast.

"We're venturing into a village today," Sasha told her. "We need to trade for food."

"I noticed," Lina replied dryly. "What are we trading with?"

"We've got some pieces of jewelry we can take apart," Sasha said hesitantly. "I'm a little nervous about getting robbed later with our story, though."

Lina appeared deep in thought, brow furrowed as she nibbled on the dried meat. She looked down at it, then at her familiar.

"Fiadh," she started hesitantly. "Would you be willing to hunt for us? Obviously, you'll get some of the meat too, but if we can prep some wild meat and other essentials from them, maybe we can trade those. It's obvious we can get that legitimately. Find us when we stop for lunch?"

Fiadh dipped her head, then disappeared.

"Good idea, Raya." Sasha grinned at her. "Once we're a little closer to the capital, it won't be as weird to have some jewelry to trade, but out here? Gold is a massive luxury."

"No money system?" Lina prodded.

"They have a money system," Sasha began slowly. "But there's not much outside of the capital and the closest villages. There aren't even any other cities aside from Stroyne."

"Just one city?" she asked with wide eyes. Sasha was still taken slightly aback by the fact that her eyes were blue with the glamour.

"Everything else is villages, maybe a town or two outside of the capital," Sasha confirmed.

"That's... problematic," Lina said as Sasha dug the pot of relo out of the ashes of the fire. He poured it into two sturdy clay mugs and handed the mess to Lina.

"Yeah," he agreed. "Enjoy," he added, making a face. "The sunbrew is less strong than firebrew, but it's still... rough."

Lina almost choked when she sipped the drink, but took a few quick gulps to force the rest down. Sasha just took it all down at once. He didn't hate the relo, but the taste and smell reminded him of Dad, and that was... more than he could handle right now.

Thankfully, within a few minutes, the female seemed to perk up a bit.

"It does its job well," she admitted as they were packing up their camp.

"Unfortunately, it's popular here." Sasha made a face. "Though honestly, high-quality relo is good. It's just hard to get outside of that wealthy central circle."

"Like pretty much everything," Lina said sourly.

"Like pretty much everything," Sasha echoed.

The two of them hurried up and left the cave. With Fiadh hunting, they'd find a spot outside of the closest village so they could process whatever meat the disguised fae-lioness brought them.

In the meantime, they walked down the narrow dirt paths winding around wide-based mountains, the trees mostly orange and red now with only a few lingering green leaves. Sasha wasn't sure how close they were to the autumn celebration, but it was likely that the holiday would pass while they were on the road.

He hoped they could find a village to celebrate in; Lina deserved to enjoy the joys that fae life had to offer. And anyone who tried to say she wasn't fae could fuck right off. With her current disguise, it was probably the best chance they had to actually *celebrate* without some bigoted drama to handle.

It would be better if he could spoil his little sister without worry, but he'd find *something* they could do.

Sasha absently swept some leaf litter off his shirt, shoulders drooping as his hands brushed the tumbled amethyst wrapped in leather under his shirt. Goddess, he missed his dads. Part of him was angry. He wanted to celebrate autumn with his dads, dammit! But he had to do this. And another part of him knew that this was going to be an important turning point in his life. His ability to function without his parents. Even though he was *technically* an adult by fae standards, he was cognizant of the fact that he was a fairly young adult. And due to the training required for his status as a Prince-in-Waiting, he still lived at home.

Oh, he could have found himself a house or apartment somewhere in Skovfore and gone to his dads daily for training, but what was the point? He loved his dads and was happy to live with them. No reason not to, frankly.

But it definitely made adventures like this one harder, as he desperately tried not to cry while walking down the path.

Lina, in the way she had of seeming like *she* could read *his* mind, pushed up next to him and grabbed his hand. He gave her a half smile, which she returned with sad eyes.

At least he wasn't all alone.

Soon, they found the spot they'd designated on their map. Amusingly enough, Fiadh was curled up in the center of it, with two large deer, a few quail, and even a boar.

"Oh, excellent job!" Lina gushed to the big cat, running to give her a few pats. Sasha evaluated all of them and realized that Fiadh had taken care to hurt the animals minimally. So even the hides could be used.

"Thank you," Sasha said to the cat with a tiny smile.

It took them most of the rest of the day to process the animals, leaving them with lots of smoked meat, hides, and feathers. Sasha even carved a few little figurines from the bones.

"We didn't get very far today," Lina said, wringing out her wet hair in front of the fire with a frustrated expression. There was a hint of light on the horizon; they'd have to go to bed soon.

"We won't get very far at all if we don't have a wider range of food," Sasha pointed out, though he sympathized with her frustration.

"I know," Lina sighed. "I just... I don't know. The lack of forward movement is stressful."

"It can be." Sasha made a face. "But we shouldn't have to do this again. We can sell some of it here and keep some for our own food, then we can sell more farther down if need be. Travel gets easier once we leave the mountains."

"That's true." Lina relaxed slightly. "Thanks, Grisha. I hope everything goes okay tomorrow with all the trading."

"It'll be fine," Sasha assured her, trying not to show his own worry. Lina was stressed enough as it was. They both went quiet, leaving Sasha to cast around for something to discuss. "Autumn Moon is soon. If we can figure out when it is, I'd love to take you to a festival on our way south."

"Autumn Moon?" Lina's curiosity clearly distracted her from her brooding.

"That's what they call the autumn harvest festival here," Sasha explained. "It's usually a few nights of merriment with performances, stalls of handmade foods and trinkets, bonfires... stuff like that. It's a major holiday here; even the small villages have something happening."

"That would be fun." Lina gave him a barely-there smile.

"Now's probably the safest we'll ever be at a festival like that," Sasha admitted.

"That's true." Lina made a face, then stared into the flames of their fire.

"Get some rest," Sasha told her, putting his hand on her shoulder.

"Only if you do," Lina shot back with a hint of her normal cheer.

"Of course." Sasha smiled, then reached over and ruffled the little female's hair. A barely audible giggle warmed his heart before they both settled in to rest for the night.

29

Lina

By the time Lina woke, Sasha was already up, packing up their campsite and the last of the meat they had processed. Unfortunately, it seemed that she'd missed the sunset—it was full dark now.

"Hey, sleepyhead," Sasha said. "We're going to eat in the village since it's not far from here."

"Alright." Lina shook her head and rubbed her eyes before she got up and began working through her share of the packing up. They packed fairly light; no tent, just blanket bundles that they called bedrolls. Some of the meat was packed away and hidden with their valuables, and the rest was wrapped up in one of the spare blankets. Lina was still a bit surprised by how much Fiadh managed to bring down for them.

In less than an hour, everything had been returned to their bags, and they were walking in a row down the dirt road toward the village.

Lina was more surprised than she felt she should have been when it appeared in their view. It was larger than she'd anticipated, and from their vantage point at the top of the bowl-shaped valley in which the village was built, she was able to see the bustling square in the middle of the mess of dirt streets and wooden buildings, all well lit with dancing torches.

"Looks like it's market day," Sasha observed with a quick grin. "We should be able to get a good price for these."

Lina shivered; it had barely been two months since they'd been attacked on their way to the center of Skovfore, but the memories and the slight worry in the back of her mind remained. Her mother's constant watchfulness came to mind, and Lina forced the anxiety down. She was *not* going down that road. Not now. Not ever.

Fiadh bumped her face gently into Lina's back, reminding her that she was safe here—no one knew who she was. And she wasn't alone. Lina reached back and scratched Fiadh's soft ears without looking.

Finally, they arrived at the edge of the market square.

"Let me lead," Sasha whispered to her, before grabbing her hand and tugging her over to a butcher.

The male's brow rose when the two clearly young fae stumbled up to his booth. All Lina could smell was the coppery scent of blood emanating from the stall, its source clearly the meats hanging behind the butcher himself.

"May I help you?" he snapped. Lina's brow rose before she could stop it. He must be the only butcher here with that attitude; otherwise, people would definitely go somewhere else.

"I have meat to sell you," Sasha told the male, seeming unfazed by the butcher's attitude.

"As you can see, I have plenty," the butcher sneered slightly, looking down his nose at them.

"And as I can see," Sasha shot back, "you don't have what I've got." The butcher rolled his eyes.

"Let me guess," he said dryly. "You've got some rabbits? Maybe some fish?"

"Deer, quail, and boar." Sasha crossed his arms.

"Yeah, right," the butcher scoffed. He was larger than most of the fae Lina had seen, and she shrank into Sasha's shadow. For once, she was glad of her human blood and how it made her a little shorter than the average fae female, something the enchanter who did their disguises couldn't change.

"My sister's familiar is a fae-panther," Sasha said proudly. "They hunt together."

That was a stretch, and the butcher knew it, too. He snorted out a laugh, but the sound petered out as a little growl brought his attention to the big cat hovering behind them both.

"Oh, alright," the butcher grouched. "Show me what you have."

Sasha brought out some of the uncooked meat, haggling back and forth with the uncooperative butcher. Soon, they left with a pouch of gold and silver coins.

"Tightfist." Sasha frowned. "We should have gotten more for that. Hopefully, the next few vendors will be more friendly."

Unfortunately, it seemed that they were not. Sasha bargained and haggled, getting what he swore was only half the worth of what they sold. Though they did get a good amount for the little bone figurines from an enchanter—that allowed them to get plenty of journey bread, fruits, and vegetables. As a bonus, the uncured but well-cut hides were able to get them a room and two meals at the local inn.

Much later, their bags were tucked into their room, being guarded by Fiadh. Lina sat silently next to Sasha in the inn's common area as they scarfed down their thick stew and soft brown bread. A younger fae dropped down in the booth across from them, mischief on his face. He had a short tousle of black curls on his head and almost alarmingly red eyes.

"So, you're the newcomers that made such a fuss this evening." The male leaned back, crossing his arms.

"Not purposefully." Sasha seemed very nonchalant, more than the gentle tap on Lina's foot suggested. Their signal to get ready. "Just needed supplies to continue our journey south."

"It's not often we see travelers," the male said. "Where are you heading?"

"Our uncle lives outside of Stroyne." Sasha shrugged. "Our parents are dead now, so we're heading south to stay with him."

"Do you speak?" The male, who had yet to tell them his name, turned on Lina.

"Sometimes," she shot back. The male grinned at them both.

"I'm Boriss," he told them.

"Grigory," Sasha said.

"Raisa," Lina added. Boriss snorted a laugh.

"Bullshit," he said. Sasha raised a brow.

"What was that?"

"My specialization is knowing truth." Boriss gave them another grin. "Now, I'm not terribly powerful; I'd be in Stroyne if I were, but I do my part to keep my people safe. Try again."

Lina appraised the male again, then saw the way the rest of the room was deliberately not looking. She reached down and poked Sasha's leg, and he glared at her but let her lead.

"We're traveling south," she stated clearly. "We only wanted to sell enough of our wares so that we could get the rest of the way to our destination. We have no intention of harming anyone here, as long as no one harms us first. We wish to eat our meal, sleep, eat breakfast, and then leave."

Tension that she hadn't noticed leaked out of Boriss.

"Alright." He nodded once. "And that's as much truth as you'll give me?"

"Is that not enough truth to know that we mean no harm to anyone here and plan to be leaving after the sun sets again?" Sasha shot back.

"It is," Boriss admitted. He pulled something out of his pocket and tossed it to Sasha. It was a leather pouch that jingled. Sasha peeked in, and his face relaxed slightly.

"Really?" he asked wryly.

"Gotta protect ourselves somehow," Boriss snorted. Soon, several more people appeared, dropping a few other packages of assorted things on the end of their table.

"Makes sense," Sasha said. He eyed Boriss before speaking again. "We're both halfers. Born on the other side of the water. Parents are gone, and the village turned on us."

Boriss held his hand up.

"No more," he begged, almost grinning. "Mixing truth and falsehood gives me a *headache*," the male complained. Boriss stood and slid out of the booth. "Whatever your reasonings, thank you for the meat. It'll help us as the weather cools. Safe travels, and be wary of soldiers."

With *that* foreboding warning, Boriss left them to finish their meal in relative peace.

30

Sasha

The rest of the journey passed more easily now that they had resources. Somehow, the little village they'd stopped in had sent word to additional villages on the way, which helped them avoid the issues they'd experienced previously. The taverns and inns they stayed in were clean and quiet, with at least decent food, and gave them good breaks from sleeping on the ground.

After another month on the road, both Sasha and Lina had acquired a taste for relo, which Sasha just *knew* was going to make Dad incredibly smug ~~if~~ when they got home. Both of them had really settled into using their false identities as well; sometimes, Sasha caught himself thinking of Lina as Raya first.

Today was going to be the biggest test of their new identities; they'd be meeting their new 'parent.'

Lina's hand slid into his as they joined the crowd of people entering the city at sundown. Sasha squeezed her hand and gave her a little smile as they wove in and out of the crowd. Fiadh was outside the city; they'd decided to meet back up with her afterwards. Flashy familiars were easy to remember, and they wanted to be invisible.

The emotions and stray thoughts from the people around them pounded against his mental shields before he took a moment to reinforce them. It had been weeks since he'd been around that many people, so his shielding had lightened. As a distraction from the clamor, he mentally recited the instructions that Da had gotten from his cousin before they left.

You're going to be meeting them in Ganlyoversk. Go to a tavern called The Gorgon's Eye in the artisan district, and ask for Bogdan. Tell him that you're looking for a sponsor, and your names. They'll connect you with whoever Wen sends.

Doing his best to brush aside how much he missed his dads, Sasha pulled Lina aside as they got inside through the gates, leading her over to a quiet spot out of the crowds.

"Everything okay?" Lina asked, tearing her gaze away from the gray stone buildings and wooden carts of merchandise that cluttered the square around the gate. He wished they had more time to meander around; Lina had seen so little of their world. Only the parts with no other people. Now that she was disguised, she had a better chance of having a somewhat positive experience. (And didn't that piss him off...)

"Just needed to look around a bit," Sasha reassured her. "I'm trying to make sure I know where we're going."

"Artisan district, right?" she verified.

"Yeah." Sasha nodded. "Just gotta find it." A small, mischievous smile crossed her face after a moment of thought.

"I got this." Lina smirked. She tugged on his hand, dragging him through the square until they were standing in front of a vendor that most people weren't paying attention to. They had a massive pot of boiling oil and a mess of little hand pies.

"Two, please," she told the male, bouncing on her toes with the excitement of a younger fae.

"What kind?" he grunted.

"Hmm." She looked at the selection and pointed to what Sasha was fairly certain were pork and cabbage ones. "Those!"

The male snagged a few of the flavor she requested and dropped them in the hot oil. As he supervised them, she spoke again, sounding somehow absentminded.

"Can you tell us where the artisan's quarter is?" she asked. "Dad sent us here alone this month since Ma and our baby brother aren't feeling well. He makes little talismans to sell there! But we've never been here without him." Lina managed to look embarrassed somehow.

"We'll find it, Raya," Sasha told her with a scolding tone. "Don't worry him. He's busy."

In truth, he'd picked up exactly what she was doing once she cornered a not-busy food vendor. He knew his role, so he just said his lines and let her work.

"But Dad told us to be careful!" she protested. "He used to tell us not to go a certain way because he doesn't want us in the assassins' quarter until we're older."

"Until *you're* older," Sasha corrected with a little smirk. "I'm old enough if I wanted to."

"It's in the Southside," the vendor told them, handing them cooked pirozhki wrapped in paper. "You'll want to go through the West End rather than the East," he added. "East is where the Assassin's Guild is. And don't go straight through town; the central area is for royals."

"Thank you!" Lina beamed, paying the vendor. If there was a little extra there, neither of them mentioned it. She handed Sasha a pirozhki, and they left.

The vendor's directions made it much easier than Sasha expected to maneuver the city; the side of the city they were on was very clearly residential. Thankfully, in keeping with their cover story, Lina kept her rubbernecking to a minimum. He could tell she desperately wanted to soak up the new environment, but consistency was key, just in case someone followed up.

In the spirit of that, they wandered in and out of the talisman shops in the artisan's quarter, selling a few of the trinkets that Sasha had made using his dad's techniques and a couple of his simpler ones they had packed. At the last one, Lina asked the store proprietor where The Gorgon's Eye was.

The female seemed to have a soft spot for Lina, giving them more than the others had all day and even giving them very specific directions to the tavern.

Thankfully, the tavern was clean and well-lit. Sasha led Lina up to the bar and waited for the bartender to show up. He eyed them a bit suspiciously when he realized how young they were.

"I'm looking for Bogdan," Sasha told him.

"Order something. He'll find you," the bartender grunted.

"Relo for both of us," Sasha said.

The bartender didn't speak again aside from grunting out the price of the drinks, sliding the thick, steaming mugs across the bar when he got the money. Handing one mug to Lina, Sasha jerked his head for her to follow. They found a booth in a corner, Sasha sighing in relief when they dropped down on the bench.

"Now we wait," he murmured.

Neither of them spoke as they sipped their drinks, waiting for someone to show up. Even with both of them taking their time, both mugs were almost empty when someone slid into the booth across from them.

"What are two little ones like you doing looking for Bogdan?" The voice was androgynous, and the person's cloak had a deep hood that covered their face.

"That's between us and Bogdan, isn't it?" Sasha's brow rose.

"Good thing I'm Bogdan," the other chuckled.

"I'm Grigory," Sasha said. "This is my sister, Raisa. We're look-ing for a sponsor."

"Ahhh, gotcha." A flash of white that made Sasha wonder if the other had grinned or something more sinister. "So, you're the two looking for Ykaterina. I'll take you to her once you're finished with those."

Sasha pushed his mug away from himself, and Lina tipped hers up to grab the last of the brew.

"I think we're ready," Lina said when she put her own mug down.

"Fair enough," Bogdan said, sliding out of the booth and pausing for barely a moment before he began walking toward the door. Sasha grabbed Lina's hand again, pulling her along so they didn't lose track of each other. Carefully, he cracked open the walls that kept the thoughts of others out of his head.

Be careful. I don't trust him, Sasha sent on a thin thread of thought to Lina. She nodded once, not looking at him. Neither of them spoke as Bogdan wove easily through the city, toward the center. Sasha felt himself getting more and more tense as the buildings' exteriors began to show more wealth. Soon, they found themselves by the servants' entrance of an elegant manor.

Bogdan knocked carefully in a pattern, then paused and did it again. The door opened, and a hand with well-manicured nails reached out, grabbed Sasha's free hand, and pulled them both inside. They didn't see any of the house, or the fae who grabbed them, as they were pulled through dark servant's passages, Lina's hand tightening on his the only outward sign of her fear.

A door was thrown open, and the room they emerged in was well-lit, though the curtains were drawn tightly. For the first time, Sasha saw the female whom he was fairly sure was Ykaterina.

The first thing he noticed was that she had a mass of violet hair, brighter and more eye-catching than his original color. Her skin was incredibly pale, and her dark eyes were almost hidden behind bangs. The female's eyes flashed bright purple as she stared, and the walls of the room flashed the same color.

"There," she said in a voice that was practically a purr. "Now you can speak freely, little ones."

"What did you do?" Lina's voice only wobbled a little bit, but it was enough for Sasha to squeeze her hand. He could barely speak; for all their care, they'd been backed into a corner. They only had third-hand approval as to whether this woman was safe. She hadn't even introduced herself. He and Lina had no way to know if the male they followed was Bogdan, and no way to know if this female was who she said she was.

"My specialization is shields." The female smirked. "Physical, mental, and emotional. *No one* can get in that I don't want to."

Sasha and Lina met each other's gaze. That wasn't anywhere near as relieving as she seemed to think it was.

"Cat got your tongue?" The female's brow rose. "Or rather, *fae-lioness* got your tongue?"

Sasha's heart raced as he stared at the woman in what he hoped was well-disguised horror. How did she know? Fiadh was outside the city. Who *was* this female? They hadn't heard Ykaterina's name before they met Bogdan. And neither of them knew if Bogdan was who he was supposed to be. The two of them had made it all the way to right outside of the Unseelie Kingdom's seat alone.

Part of Sasha wondered if their time travelling and hiding had made them a bit paranoid about trusting others. Especially after the assassination attempt back home. Relying on strangers to get into the city was terrifying.

"Love." A soft, laughing voice indicated that another female was in the room. "Stop antagonizing my nephew."

Sasha jerked his head so fast he would probably have a crick in his neck in the morning, but his eyes met a pair of vivid blue ones that weren't dissimilar to his and Lina's disguised ones.

"Are you Nadya?" Lina said, eyes wide, head tilted. Sasha absently wondered if she knew that she sounded like she was begging the other female to save them. Whether she did or not, he didn't blame her.

"In here, right now," the second female said with a soft smile. "With Katya's shield up, you can call me Auntie Wen."

31

Lina

Lina felt herself and Sasha both collapse to the ground like puppets with cut strings. She felt hot tears well up in her eyes, though she didn't let them fall.

"Katya!" Wen scolded. "You scared them to death!"

"Sorry, kiddos," the other said, sounding truly regretful, to her credit. "I'm Ykaterina. You'll be staying with me. I didn't realize I was frightening you so badly." Lina felt a bit of relief pulse through her as the female verified that she was, in fact, Ykaterina, and that they were in the right place. Safe.

Wen knelt down and put a hand on each of their shoulders.

"I know that right now you're going by Grigory and Rasia," the female said. "But will you tell me your names?"

"Aleksandr Mindwalker," Sasha choked out. "Sasha. Prince-in-Waiting of the Northern Forests."

"Adelina Halfhuman," Lina said, squeezing Sasha's hand. "Future Prince-in-Waiting of the Southern Highlands."

Wen's eyes widened.

"Half *human?* Southern Highlands?" she said in disbelief.

"Grandfather chose me," Lina said. The careful statement told the other female her relation to the current Southern Highlands Prince.

"We're going to have to keep you from Darek," Wen said. "I'm assuming you're disguised, since you two look basically identical and full-fae. But I don't know if he'd recognize your aura as like his."

"I've met him once before," Lina admitted. "Though I've seen more of *Ghoulbane.*" Even now, the male's name was practically a swear coming out of her mouth.

Wen's lips pursed.

"*That* one" was all she said before she turned to Sasha with a soft expression. "I've been wanting to meet you since I heard about you."

"Me?" Sasha stared.

"You're my cousin's son!" the older female protested. "I only found out about you because you became the Prince-in-Waiting!"

"Why haven't you talked to your family?" Lina asked, eyes narrowing. She remembered how... *wistful* Del had looked when talking about Wen.

"Deep cover," Wen sighed. "I was sent here to spy for the Seelie Court. I wasn't told I was going to be here for a couple of *centuries.* And I haven't even found anything."

"Who sent you?" Lina had a feeling she knew what Wen would say.

"Prince Donal."

With some unfortunate practice, Lina pushed away the ache in her chest at the reminder of her uncle.

"Then you need to be incredibly careful," Lina said softly. "We're... not sure exactly how deep it goes, but Prince Donal doesn't entirely have the people in mind, at least."

"He apparently undertook a massive censorship campaign," Sasha added. "Removed a lot of the history from before *He* came into power."

"That's troubling," Ykaterina said with a frown.

"He... he tried to keep me from telling Del when I was sent

here," Wen said slowly. "And technically, Del's the Seelie Spymaster. He should have been the one to make that decision."

"And he wouldn't have kept you here for this long," Sasha stated. "Not without being able to go home."

The two older females looked at each other, then looked back at the younger fae.

"We don't have much more time," Wen admitted. "Katya can't hold her shield for much longer, and when we're not under the shield, we have to slide our roles back on."

"We're ready," Lina said after exchanging a nod with Sasha.

"Then here's the final story," Wen instructed, suddenly sounding so much like her cousin that it hurt. "Katya found you two trying to sell her some of the little trinkets you were peddling today and decided to take you back to Stroyne with her. She thinks that 'Raisa' has the potential for a useful power, and 'Grigory' refused to let his sister go without him. He has a powerful emotion-sensing specialization, so Katya took you both.

"Since she's right on the line of 'too good for Unseelie,' no one will find it strange. You'll be able to use the time you're here to find what you're looking for. No." She held a hand up as Sasha opened his mouth. "Don't tell me. I don't need to know right now. If you need me to know, then tell me later."

"Final bit of information," Ykaterina added. "Nadya has adopted a male around the same age as you two. He's full-Seelie but was kicked out of his home for reasons outside of his control. If he decides to tell you why, that's his prerogative. Otherwise, just be kind to the poor kid."

Sasha and Lina both nodded. With that, Ykaterina's eyes—and the walls—flashed bright purple again, and the two women's bearings changed entirely.

"Let's get you two in rooms," Ykaterina said with a soft smile. "You'll meet Kostis at breakfast."

"Thank you," Lina managed.

Lina didn't have the energy to do much else besides wash her face and hands and change into the nightgown that Ykaterina had placed on her bed that night. Barely noticing the softness of the bed or pillows, she was asleep almost immediately.

The next evening, a knock at the door woke Lina from her deep, restorative sleep.

"Um... yes?" she called.

"I'm to help you get dressed," a kind, but no-nonsense voice called out. Lina shrank down slightly, all of her memories of her grandfather's house rearing their ugly heads.

"Come in," Lina said softly, twisting the blankets in her fingers as she sat up.

The first thing Lina noticed was the smile on the female's face, which immediately helped her relax. Once the tension dissipated slightly, she took in the female's golden hair and pale skin.

"Mistress Ykaterina said I'm to be your lady's maid," the female told Lina. "I'm Maria."

"Hi, Maria," Lina said with a little smile. "I'm Raisa."

"Nice to meet you, Miss," Maria said with a grin. "Now, let's get you ready for breakfast. It's a communal affair in Mistress Ykaterina and Nadya's households. Any color preferences for your clothes?"

"No, not really," Lina said, bemused. Maria was a much nicer lady's maid than Sofria was; she had half a mind to poach the female from Ykaterina after she was able to hire her own staff.

After Maria vanished through a nearby doorway, Lina was able to look around the little room properly. All the furniture was a heavy, dark wood, but the rest of the decor was in light blue and white to keep the whole thing from being too dark and overbearing. Her bed was on one wall; the one to her right had the door out and the table with the washing bowl and pitcher. The one to her left had a window, little bits of lamplight from the roads filtering in. Next to the window was a desk, a bookshelf on the other side. The final wall across from Lina had two doors, which she assumed were a closet and a bathing room.

At the thought, Lina got up and entered the room that her lady's maid hadn't entered, finding a small but nice bathing room.

When she returned to the main bedroom, Maria had pulled some clothes.

"We'll be heading back to the capital today," she told Lina. "The trip takes a few hours, but you'll be on a carriage or a boat the whole time."

The outfits that Maria had picked were all some form of dress that came to below the knee with thick leggings. Lina remembered what Clio had told her about the Unseelie court—namely, that females needed to be in dresses. She stifled a sigh and pointed out the deep navy dress with corseting and the dark brown leggings to go with it.

"Excellent choice. That will flatter your coloring," Maria praised, bustling around to put the other clothes away and then to help Lina dress. Her skin crawled slightly with the memories of the times that Sofria had helped her dress before Lina had put a stop to it, but Maria was gentle, for all she was moving quickly. The female had her sit at her desk to do her hair in an intricate braid down her back, then added a hint of cosmetics.

Lina was just as glad there wasn't a mirror for her to look in. It took her quite a while to get accustomed to what she looked like after her Coming of Age ritual, but now that she had the glamour, it was strange again. Few of her features stayed the same. Both she and Sasha had olive-toned skin now, like she'd inherited from her father. But the rest of her features were fairly Unseelie. According to Mikhail, it was because most hybrids in the Seelie Queendom that could pass as full-blooded did their best to. It was the same here. If you could pass as Unseelie, that's what you told people.

She understood the need for it all, but it was... odd. It was strange enough seeing Sasha look so different (and she knew he felt the same), but the person in the mirror was completely different. In some ways, the biggest losses were the features that made her look more human. They othered her here, but they were *part* of her. Lina thought she'd been human for the first half of her life. Losing it was like the loss of a limb.

"Thank you," Lina said to Maria, wishing she could be more effusive in her thanks for the kindnesses.

"Of course, Miss." Maria smiled. "Now, off to breakfast with you."

Following the instructions Maria left her with, Lina found herself in an elegant dining room on the main floor of the manor.

"Good morning, darling." Ykaterina smirked.

"Good morning," Lina replied.

"Your brother will be here soon," she told Lina. "As will Nadya. Come, sit."

Lina followed these instructions too, seating herself where the older female indicated. Before she could do anything, a servant appeared and began dishing food onto her plate. Again, memories of her time with her grandfather flashed before her eyes, and she just barely avoided flinching.

To her pleasant surprise, both the food and the mug of relo placed at her place were steaming hot. Part of her raged at how it took her looking full-fae to be treated like she was *normal,* but she buried that deep.

That would be something she could rage about when she returned to the Northern Forests.

Before she could take a bite of the delicious-looking food, Ykaterina spoke again.

"Raisa, dear, this is Kostis." The female gestured to the other figure Lina hadn't previously noticed. The male was likely around Sasha's age, if she had to guess, and very obviously full-Seelie. His skin tone was a deep olive-bronze that was slightly pasty, as if he hadn't seen the sun in a long time. A mane of golden curls capped his head, and his eyes... his eyes were *gorgeous.* They were the color of fresh honey and almost seemed to glow.

Lina tried to hide the blush that heated her cheeks, but by Kostis's smirk, she didn't do a great job.

"Good morning," she managed. "It's nice to meet you."

"It's nice to meet you as well," Kostis told her. Even his *voice* was nice!

She felt a warmth flaring in her palms, not unlike when she made faelights, which she twined together and hid. Lina buried her confusion at her strange reaction to the male; this was *no time* for her magic to start flaring! Even though her being a hybrid was pretty obvious, she knew there was no hiding her Seelie magic.

Thankfully, distraction soon arrived in the form of Sasha, who narrowed his eyes slightly at her when she turned pleading eyes on him, but easily swept Ykaterina up into conversation after also being introduced to Kostis. And Wen soon appeared as well, allowing Lina to have a silent, internal breakdown in peace.

What *was* this? Why did she keep wanting to *watch* the male? Why was she so drawn to him?

It wasn't simple attraction; she was no stranger to that. Even though no one had ever *reciprocated* her interest here (the half-human thing really turned people off), she'd had her share of crushes. It would have been weird if she hadn't; the fae were beautiful.

But Kostis... he was like the answer to every question she'd ever had. As a shy preteen, she'd had a huge infatuation with an actor who played a blond, bronze-god type surfer. Really, the only difference between Kostis and the surfer was that his tan was real and his eyes weren't blue. Was it weird that she preferred them not to be? That she preferred Kostis to the pretty actor?

What the *fuck* was happening to her?

The panic was also stuffed down to cry about later. Part of her desperately wished that Mikhail was nearby to ask if he knew what was happening. She reached to the neck of her dress and pulled out the amulet he'd made, tracing the shapes absently and letting the barest hint of the male's familiar magic soothe her.

"Missing your lover?" Kostis snarked, a brow up. A rebuttal fell out of her mouth before she could stop it.

"Nope, missing yours," she sassed, eyes widening in shock as she covered her mouth to hopefully stop more comments.

"Our mom enchanted that for her," Sasha said evenly from next to Kostis. He met her gaze, worried. She'd *never* spoken like that. Not even in jest. There was silence at the table for a moment.

"I apologize," Kostis said contritely, looking a bit confused himself. "I deserved that. It's none of my business either way."

"Apology accepted," Lina said before going back to her breakfast. Even though it was delicious, she had to choke it down. Thankfully, her strange outburst seemed to excuse her from the normal table conversations, so she could hide her confusion and her embarrassment in her relo and food. Hopefully soon, they'd leave so she could figure out what in all the hells that was.

32

—————

Sasha

Sasha didn't entirely understand what was going on between Lina and Kostis, but he could tell by her face that she didn't either. So he quietly committed to running interference between them until things evened back out.

He did his best to keep Kostis engaged in conversation, though he didn't mention the bewildered looks the male sent Lina. Nor did he miss the confused, sideways glances she sent in return. Sasha knew very well why she was grabbing at her pendant; she'd taken to fiddling with it when she was feeling out of her depth.

Honestly, Sasha was feeling just as out of his depth as their carriage stopped at the edge of the inland sea that housed Stroyne. He couldn't see the island through the fog as they all hurried into their rooms on the ferry, Fiadh thankfully joining them as they walked.

"The fog protects us," Ykaterina said firmly to both him and Lina. She gave them a slight warning glance. "Stroyne is hard to see until you get through to the other side. Stay below; the fog has… opinions. Particularly about halfers. Nadya will be staying below as well."

Sasha did his best to read between the lines. The fog likely had some sort of spells in it that would detect duplicity and probably didn't like Seelie fae in any capacity. He had no idea how Wen had gotten through it during her early trips, but his burning questions could be handled later. Preferably after Wen was no longer stuck in Stroyne.

"I'm going to check on Nadya, then order our lunch to be sent to us later," she continued. "Rest now. We'll be there in a few hours."

After the female left, both of them collapsed into chairs like puppets with cut strings. Thankfully, Lina was on a couch, because after their time apart, Fiadh was feeling cuddly. The giant jungle cat was curled up on the cushion next to Lina, head in the little female's lap.

"Wanna tell me what was happening this morning?" Sasha prodded after a few minutes.

"I..." Lina trailed off, shoulders slumping. "I don't know. He's just... interesting. And I don't know why."

"Interesting how?" Sasha felt his brow furrow.

"Like... pretty." Lina's face was flaming. Sasha fought a smirk. She was interested in the male? He filed this away to tease her with later. Right now, she needed a big brother. "Which doesn't make *sense*," she continued. "The fae are all just generally attractive."

"Have you not had a crush before?" Sasha asked, curiosity getting the better of him, even though he knew it wasn't really a good time.

"That's the thing," Lina murmured. "I *have.* No one has ever reciprocated, obviously."

He didn't really think that was fair. Sasha didn't really care if his partner was male or female, and he was of the opinion that Lina in her natural state was rather pretty, but he saw her as his sister rather than a partner. But he didn't agree that it should be 'obvious' that no one reciprocated, since it was entirely because she was half-human.

"People are stupid," Sasha decided. He gave Lina a significant look, hoping she knew he was talking about the lack of reciprocation. She gave him a fragile smile. "And this is different?" he added.

"It is," Lina confirmed. "And I don't know why."

They were both quiet for a while, deep in thought.

"I hate to say it," Sasha said slowly. "But this might have to be something we handle *after* the current crisis." Lina looked relieved.

"Thank the goddess," she murmured. "I can't handle more right now."

Sasha's heart went out to her; the pressure the little female was under was immense. D'Vita had laid a very difficult task at her feet, and now it was an active *thing* rather than an abstract idea. They'd be in Stroyne soon, and their false identities would be even more vital. There was no room for Sasha and Lina in Stroyne, just Grigory and Raisa. Hell, his aunt didn't even know what he looked like properly. Or Lina.

They were quiet the rest of the trip, and thankfully, Kostis and the adults left them to their ruminations. The meal Ykaterina had brought them was delicious, though Sasha caught Lina picking at her food, using some of the sleight of hand Da had taught her to feed bits of meat to Fiadh.

"Come up on the deck," Ykaterina invited them. "We'll be back soon, and you'll be able to actually see the city now that we're through the fog."

Lina and Sasha went with her, both curious about the city they'd only heard about. Nothing could have prepared them for the reality.

Sasha's breath caught in his throat as he caught sight of Stroyne. The city was nothing less than a mountain of gray stone. A sturdy, defensible castle rose out of the center, surrounded by a thick wall. Sasha caught sight of some elegant roofs between the castle wall and another, less thick wall that seemed to separate the royals from everyone else. The plain, sturdy buildings were all over the rest of the city at different heights. The moon cast a pale light over the city, washing it all in silver. He suspected that even without the graying moonlight, there wouldn't be much color visible.

The ferry they took began to dock, bringing Sasha's attention to the mass of carriages waiting there, and wagons hiding in the shadows to handle luggage. Even here, there was little color, the elegance of the carriages in their shape and size.

"Raisa, dear," Ykaterina got their attention, even though she was only speaking to Lina. "Please tell your familiar to come with us in the carriage. I know she'll likely be uncomfortable, but it's the safest for her until we can get her registered. Once she's registered here, she'll be able to wander freely, but I don't want her hurt between now and then."

"You can tell her if you'd like," Lina offered quietly.

"Oh no," Ykaterina brushed her off. "I wouldn't want to interfere with your familiar. It just isn't done."

The subtle warning wasn't lost on either of them. Things were different here. At home, they all treated Iron like a member of the family, and he mostly acted like what he was—an oversized house pet. But here, Fiadh was Lina's responsibility, and everything she did reflected on Lina.

"My apologies," Lina told the older female. "I'll take care of that now." And with that, she knelt down in front of Fiadh and began to whisper to the big cat. Fiadh butted Lina's forehead with her nose after the conversation, making the younger female smile before she stood back up.

The carriage ride was quiet, Wen and Kostis in their own carriage, leaving Lina and Sasha with their new guardian.

"Because you're new here, I'll have to introduce you at Court Dinner tonight," the female warned them. "I make an appearance there a few times a week. It's very formal. Both of your servants have been warned and will be dressing you appropriately." Sasha and Lina nodded seriously.

"Be careful what you say," Ykaterina continued, meeting each of their gazes. "I won't say be careful who you talk to, because you won't have much control over who speaks to you, and as younger fae, you'll be expected to be polite. You, particularly, Raisa, as you've not specialized. But it's important to be careful what you say to anyone who asks. Lace every lie with truth; there are some who can tell when you lie.

"Don't draw the attention of the King or his direct subordinates if you can avoid it. And you." She turned to Lina. "For the love of magic, *please* avoid Darek at all costs." Lina made a face.

"Gladly," she hissed before smoothing her expression back out.

"Rest this afternoon," Ykaterina advised. "The dinners run until after daybreak most of the time. Early evenings are for meetings, late evenings are for preparing for Court Dinner, and then the rest of the time, people are politicking at court dinners." She stopped, then eyed them both. "And avoid the Valkyrie."

With that, they arrived. The security checkpoint at the gate of the nobles' ring was thorough, but soon, they were allowed to continue their journey. All of them were quiet until they were inside the elegant manor house, not dissimilar to the one they'd just left.

"We all have rooms at the palace as well, but I've sent them a message that I now have two charges," Ykaterina informed them. "I told them that for now, we'd be staying at my manor house, and we'd all be in the palace once you'd been trained properly. You'll need to accustom yourselves to how things run here before I drop you in the palace as well."

"Thank you." Sasha gave the older female a small smile. "We appreciate your thoughtfulness." Lina nodded in agreement. Ykaterina's gaze flickered between them, then she waved a servant over.

"Grigory and Raisa." She pointed to each of them in turn. "They're here to stay. Show them to their rooms."

The servant bowed, then gestured for them to follow her up the stairs and into the depths of the house.

33

Lina

Lina was only slightly surprised at the elegance of the suite of rooms she'd been given. It was much like the room she'd stayed in in the other manor outside the city, but somehow even more elegant.

The color scheme was similar, dark woods and light blue fabrics, though there were also thick tapestries on the stone walls. Most of them were starry skies and elegant sunsets, though one looked like it might have a story behind it if she were brave enough to ask. The dark wood floors had warm rugs to protect her feet, ones that looked soft enough to bury her feet in.

She only had a few moments to look around with Fiadh before Maria reappeared.

"Hello." The servant smiled at her. "Would you like to choose your gown now or later?"

"Later, please," Lina said softly.

"Then I'd recommend getting some rest," Maria suggested. "Court Dinner is always long, and after all of your travelling, you'll want to be at your best."

"Thank you. I'll do that," Lina decided. She followed Maria into the bedroom and took her shoes off as the female turned down the blankets and lights until the only light was from the fireplace in the corner.

"Sleep well, Mistress Raisa," Maria said.

It felt like sleep had only just taken her when Maria gently shook her shoulder.

"It's time to get ready for the dinner," she explained. "I've brought you a tray of snacks and some relo to revive you."

"Thank you." Lina blinked, and her head spun slightly. This was more than she'd ever experienced. At the manor house in Skovfore, they did most things for themselves. And in her grandfather's manor? She was lucky if one of the servants would do *anything* for her. Much less all of this.

Maria relit the lamps, and Lina got out of bed and went over to the little table on the opposite wall, where a tray of food and relo sat. As she helped herself to the delicious little snacks, Maria bustled around getting things ready. And starting a bath, from the sound of it.

Lina was correct; Maria helped her into the bath and washed both her and her hair, letting the dark locks that she *still* wasn't used to dry as Lina soaked in the warmth and enjoyed the rest of her relo. Interestingly, Maria used her palms to dry Lina's hair the rest of the way.

"How did you do that?" she asked the other female.

"Oh!" Maria flushed. "I... my specialization is fire and heat, unfortunately."

"Unfortunately?" Lina tilted her head and furrowed her brow.

"I'm... not fully Unseelie," Maria whispered, head bowed. "My grandmother was Seelie."

Lina reached out and laid her arm—a pasty shade that was the result of someone with olive skin not seeing the sun—next to Maria's. The female looked at her in confusion.

"So was my father." She murmured the words—not technically a lie, as Darek *was* a Seelie fae—but they tasted sour in her mouth regardless.

Maria relaxed, smiling slightly.

"I wasn't sure," she admitted. "I had hoped... not that you had dealt with the same, but that you wouldn't be put off."

"I'm no such thing," Lina promised easily. "I think that's a clever way to use your magic in your work."

Now, Maria beamed.

"Thank you, Mistress," she said, sticking her hand into the tub and reheating the water before she returned to where she was now beginning to style Lina's hair. Lina just closed her eyes and let the female's gentle fingers lull her into a half-doze. When her hair was done, Maria helped her out of the bath and dried her off before bringing out three dresses, which seemed to be her pattern.

The first dress looked... interesting. Not her. It was a vibrant red, with a deep dip between her breasts that went almost to her navel. It clasped behind her neck, leaving her entire back open. The dress looked like it would cling to every dip and curve.

The second was a soft periwinkle—fitted through the bodice and flowy through the skirt. It had little cap sleeves, and while it was pretty, it also felt a bit young for her.

The third dress was the one she liked best. It was a dark rose, fitted in the bodice and loose at the skirt again. There was gold detailing on the bodice, the skirt, and the long sleeves that clung to the arms and then widened out at the elbows, leaving her forearms bare. The flowy sleeves and the skirt had a second layer of gauzy fabric in a lighter rose shade.

"I think that's a good choice." Maria smiled as she helped Lina dress. Afterwards, there was the messy business of cosmetics, though thankfully, the other female kept it light enough to not cake up her face. Then, to her horror, *jewelry* appeared, which Maria only managed to convince Lina to wear by telling her that her appearance reflected on Ykaterina.

She consented to simple pink earrings that didn't hang long and a simple gold necklace with a rose-shaped pendant. The amulets

Mikhail had made went into a deep pocket in the side of her dress, one that Maria closed up to prevent loss.

Maria seemed content, leading Lina to the entryway where Sasha was waiting, their host not having made her appearance yet.

"You look nice, Raya," he said with a soft smile.

"Thank you." She grinned slightly. "You clean up nicely, too."

And he did. He was wearing a formal tunic in a deep navy blue with dark brown pants. His usually unruly hair had been tamed a bit, no longer sticking up but tied back at the back of his neck in a tiny tail. The shirt under his tunic was a pristine white and caught at the wrists.

"Good to know," he snorted.

"Excellent, you're ready." Ykaterina swept into the room in a gown not dissimilar to Lina's red one, but this one had slits up both legs and was the deep purple-red of a fresh wine. "You look lovely." Ykaterina gave Lina one of what she was fairly certain were rare true smiles.

"Now," she said as she looked between them, "I—and even the court—won't expect perfection today. But you'll be getting more training. And whether you need it or not, *act* like you need it." Again, the warnings between the lines. She knew who they truly were, but others could not. Not if they were going to succeed. "Raisa, bring your familiar. Not only will it speed the registration process along, but it's also a show of power. You don't have a specialization yet, so they'll be looking for a show of it. Grigory, stay close to her. The only people I would trust her alone with that aren't in this room are Nadya and Kostis."

"What about Grisha?" Lina fretted. "Won't he be in danger too?"

"Females have to show a lot of power here before they're given respect," Ykaterina said bitterly. "Otherwise, you're just an object to them. Males don't have that problem. And his specialization will help too."

Lina frowned, but nodded. With that, the three of them (and Fiadh) were back in the carriage and heading inland toward the foreboding stone wall.

The security checkpoint was even worse here than to get into the nobles' ring. They all had to get out, and the carriage was thoroughly searched. Fiadh was given lots of dirty looks from the security fae, but no one came near her after Ykaterina told them she was a familiar.

Finally, they were given leave to return to the carriage, this time driving through what looked to be a forest, before the castle reappeared in view, looking just as concerning as the wall. Lina clasped her hands together, trying to hide the shaking.

This was it; this was what she'd been working for since the moment she'd woken up in that forest after her Coming of Age. A chance to sneak into this castle in the center of an island on an inland sea. A chance to find the Seelie Queen, wherever she was hiding.

34

Sasha

Sasha wished he could help Lina more as he saw her expression waver between worry and determination, and noticed her free hand holding onto her skirts for dear life. He wished he could tell her she was safe, that there was nothing to worry about, that everything would be okay. But that was a lie. They *were* both in danger and would be the entire time they were here. Nothing he could say or do would stop that. The only way she'd be safe is if she teleported home, and frankly, there was no way to know if that would actually keep her safe.

Not to mention the absolute cesspool of whatever was going on in the Southern Highlands and Aledale City. That was its own brand new set of problems that he was firmly ignoring until he returned home.

Besides, from here, there was little he could do about it. Even though he was worried for his dad and da, he trusted them and Prince Clio. And even Prince Liam, to a degree. For all the male was a bit odd, he had a very distinct sense of justice.

Only part of him was focused on the coldly elegant entryway they were in, or the soft look his aunt gave Ykaterina. The rest of him was focused on whatever the hell was going on between Lina and Kostis. The male couldn't seem to keep his eyes off of Lina, but flushed and looked away any time their eyes met. Lina was doing similarly, and he felt her stress in the way she held his arm. The longer he was in their presence, the stronger his suspicion became, but again, there was nothing they could do about it right now. He wished they didn't have to do all this, but he knew it was necessary. They would have never gotten in here otherwise.

But it didn't stop him from wishing he could just go dig the Seelie Queen out of whatever goddess-forsaken pit Lifebringer had tossed her in and take both her and Lina back home right now. Where they had a *chance* at being safe. Instead, they were walking through Lifebringer's castle, about to go eat dinner with his courtiers. They were in the fae-lion's den now. Where they'd stay for the goddess only knows how long.

Finally, *finally,* they began to make their way to whatever room would house the dinner. Lina's hand tightened on his bicep again, but he was incredibly proud of her composure. Fiadh was walking on her other side, eyes flickering around in a way that made Sasha feel safer than he had previously. The fae-lioness, disguised as she was, wouldn't allow them to be hurt. Not Lina, at least, and Sasha suspected that her protection extended to him after what happened in Skovfore before they left.

Despite Sasha being fairly comfortable with the palace at Aledale City, this was beyond anything he'd seen before. The room they entered was huge, designed like a ballroom. Half of it was covered in tables, most of which were spotted with nobles. The rest was a sort of dance floor, an open space. The ceiling went up at least three stories, with sturdy black chandeliers dotted across it for light. Elegant mosaics took up huge chunks of each wall, scenes of the night sky, volcanoes, and the creatures of the Unseelie Kingdom.

At one end of the room was a dais, which had a throne on one side and a long table on the other. Thankfully, it looked like the King was not in attendance. At least, not yet. The long table had quite a few rather snooty-looking nobles dotted across it, and unfortunately, it seemed that they were headed to that table, rather than one of the lesser tables.

In some ways, it was incredibly helpful to be able to peek into Lifebringer's inner circle. In others, it was incredibly dangerous. If they made one wrong move at the wrong time, they were done. Even without Lifebringer being there. These people were cutthroat, from what Dad remembered, and would not hesitate. Sasha couldn't forget that this was the court that had sent the people who would be his grandparents to the Wild Hunt because they were *too kind.*
Lina's fingers tightening subtly on his bicep again helped ground him away from the fear that he suddenly felt at the sight of that table, that throne. She looked up at him, a question in her eyes. He dipped his chin slightly. He could do this; he could handle it. She gave his arm a soft, barely-there squeeze again as they began to walk up the dais steps.

Ykaterina put a hand on each of their shoulders, guiding them to their seats. He was seated on Lina's left, Ykaterina on her other side. Across from Ykaterina was Wen, and across from Sasha was Kostis. So far, no one had claimed the seat on his other side, and Sasha did his best to keep his relief off his face. He took a quick glance around to see if there was anyone he had heard of or recognized at their table.

Artfully tousled green curls caught his eye.

Sasha did his best to take in the other's appearance quickly, doing his best to avoid notice. The male seemed to be flaunting his green hair and Seelie heritage with a bright smirk. But for Sasha, it wasn't the Seelie blood that made him hate the male on sight; it was the green eyes he'd gotten so used to seeing in his heart-sister's face.

Darek Sonslayer.

Lina's father.

Blood freezing in panic, Sasha shifted in his seat, adjusting himself so that he was blocking any possible view the male would have of Lina. Logically, he knew there was no way for Darek to recognize his offspring. Lina looked full-fae right now, and while she was intended to be a half Seelie and half Unseelie, the looks they both had skewed them towards Unseelie. Only the bronzy undertone of their skin marked them as part Seelie.

Sasha barely noticed the dinner arriving, nor the announcement that the King would not be dining with them that night (though he sensed the relief that flooded the room afterward, and the rowdiness that ensued). But when he noticed the food, he made a point to fumble a few of the utensils and a couple of what he knew to be correct court manners.

The part he and Lina were playing suggested that they'd have *some* manners, but not the knowledge of intricate court graces that they did have; Sasha, in particular. In some ways, it was a relief not to have the pressure on like that yet, but he also knew that they were being watched closely. Newcomers always were, in any court. Carefully tucking away his worries about Lina, he focused on the conversation that Ykaterina was having with her seatmate.

"Where on *earth* did you find these two?" a surprised male voice asked.

"Oh, they were in Ganlyoversk," Ykaterina replied, a clear smug tone to her voice. "The male is a talented empath. The female hasn't specialized; she only just did her Coming of Age recently."

He was glad she'd spoken; Sasha had almost forgotten that they'd swapped his power from thought sensing to emotion sensing. He could do both, but most people knew that the Prince-in-Waiting of the Northern Forests had a thought-sensing power and was half Unseelie. Even here. Focusing on the emotion sensing would keep them all a lot safer. Especially when their disguises leaned fairly heavily on his past and his appearance.

Including Lina, who was definitely in more danger with Darek here. Part of him wanted to peel the male's skin off for how he had treated her. From his murder of Lina's mother, and the continued bullshit she received from Egan and the servants. But that was her kill to claim, her vengeance, especially now that she was physically capable of doing so. Though even if she was, now was not the time.

Unfortunately, all too soon, the multi-course dinner was over. And then the hoards descended upon them both.

35

Lina

Lina had barely tasted her food, desperately missing the relo and little snacks she had eaten before this terrifying dinner. Even with Sasha making himself a wall between her and Darek, she had underestimated how afraid of him she was. How much her hands would shake when she caught a glimpse of green curls, so like the ones hiding under her glamour.

She did her best to listen to the conversations around her and subtly watch Ykaterina and Wen for cues on how to behave. Overall, her goal was to stay quiet and unobtrusive. Blending into the background would be harder on the dais, but between her anxiety and the knowledge that Darek was *right there,* it was necessary. She'd been calmer when she was presented to the Council of Princes all those months ago!

Unlike then, though, there was a giant disguised fae-lioness behind her chair, glaring daggers at anyone who looked at her with too much interest. Fiadh's presence gave her the courage to put up a front of normalcy and eat carefully but with curated mistakes. And the focus needed gave her a reason to avoid speaking much to those around her.

She and Sasha were watched the entire time, both by their table mates on the dais and by those at the "lower" tables. The "watching" sensation made her skin crawl, and the tension made her hands shake. Lina focused mostly on keeping the trembling under control; it was more visible to the masses.

Even with how torturous the meal itself felt, Lina knew that the worst was to come. She and Sasha were newcomers; there was every chance they'd be inundated when the courtiers socialized. And the warning not to let her be alone... that scared her more than she'd let on.

At Ykaterina's silent gesture, they stood, leaving everything where it was on the table, and she led them into the open area. The spot she led them to had a couple of chaise lounges and a drinks table between them. Kostis and Wen showed up in their corner soon after, handing wineglasses to Ykaterina, Sasha, and herself. Lina allowed Sasha and Kostis to bear the weight of the conversation until others began intruding on their bubble.

The first to appear was an imposing trio. The central figure was a haughty male with his all black ensemble unbuttoned to halfway down his chest. His hair was black as well; the only color about him was his blood-red eyes. A small part of her wondered if this male was responsible for the vampire legends in the human world, but the rest of her just tried not to meet his gaze or attract more of his attention. On his arms were a pair of females with black and brown hair, respectively. Instead of dresses or pants, they were covered only by scarce pieces of fabric and gossamer that revealed miles of translucent-pale skin and willowy frames.

"New blood!" The male smirked, revealing artificially sharpened canines. Lina avoided shivering with every ounce of courage she had left. "Perhaps lovely Katya will allow you to... *visit*." He was looking directly at the skin bared by her dress.

All Lina could think of was how nice it would be to stab his covetous eyes with a fork.

"Down, Bloodletter." Ykaterina sounded bored, but there was a hint of ice in her tone. "They are *mine*. And I think you've learned the hard way that me and mine do *not* share."

The male, appropriately called Bloodletter, actually pouted.

"I still think you two would be just as lovely with me as you are together," he complained. The females under his arms both hissed, glaring daggers at Lina, Wen, and Ykaterina.

"Your courtesans disagree," Wen noted, seeming to look down her nose at the females. Her gaze ran up and down the women, then drifted away as if they were as inconsequential as a common stone.

"I am the *Duchess of Steria*," screeched the black-haired female with eyes so pale they looked almost white.

"I am the *daughter* of the *Count of Adiel*," the brown-haired one with yellow eyes that looked frighteningly similar to Mikhail's announced at the same time.

"My mistake." Wen nodded slightly to them in apparent apology. "You must purchase your... *gowns* from them, then."

Lina stifled a snort of amusement, which made Sasha send her a warning look and Ykaterina a fond one. The two females gave her scathing glares, then proceeded to ignore her, which was perfectly fine as far as Lina was concerned.

"Raisa." Ykaterina gestured lazily to Lina. "And Grigory." She pointed at Sasha.

"What are their specializations?" Bloodletter's brow rose.

"Grigory is an empath," Ykaterina said. Thankfully, she'd warned them in the carriage that it was much more socially acceptable—even required—here to talk about specializations than it was in the Seelie fae lands. "Raisa hasn't specialized yet, but the signs point to a very strong specialization." She glanced pointedly at Fiadh.

"I don't understand why you won't *share*," Bloodletter complained, but then straightened up and ended the conversation, sweeping away to allow more Unseelie fae to greet them.

Names and faces blurred in Lina's mind, dark hair in shades of violet, navy, maroon, brown, and black mixed with eyes in shades of yellow, red, deep brown, deep blue, and even colorless silver to the point that Lina wasn't sure she'd recognize any of these people the next day. Or night. All she could do was hang tight to Sasha's arm and smile politely, making what small talk she could manage.

They were there for what felt like hours, and their only saving grace was the fact that Darek never approached. Well, that and the lack of Lifebringer's presence. Kostis and Wen vanished partway through the night, Wen with a gentle squeeze to each of their shoulders and Kostis with a sympathetic expression.

Finally, *finally,* Ykaterina excused them, then bundled them into the carriage.

"You did well," she told them seriously as they made their way back to the manor. "I'm proud of you. I won't say that gauntlet is the *most* difficult thing you'll experience here, but it will easily be high on the list. It will mostly get easier from here. Unless Lifebringer appears, which happens about once every few months or so."

"Why does he attend so rarely?" Sasha asked, surprising Lina with how... *perky* he was, given that the sun was on the edge of the horizon.

"The usual assumption is that he has better things to do." Ykaterina rolled her eyes. "We don't see him much, thankfully; those nights are... hard."

"Does he have an heir?" Sasha prodded further. "It's odd that he doesn't have a representative at these meals."

"Supposedly." Ykaterina shrugged. "But no one even knows his name. He's confined to Fyedor Peak up north most of the time for safety. About a third of the Valkyrie squadron is stationed there at all times, sometimes even more. Though it's rarely spoken of, most of us at Court think it's a ploy to keep us away from what he's actually doing up there. And to keep his hold on the throne."

"Good to know," Sasha replied thoughtfully. Lina was fairly certain his gaze was far away, but she wasn't sure, given that she had her eyes closed and her head on the soft material of his overtunic.

The remainder of the ride was quiet enough for Lina to drowse, waking to the gentle shake she received from Sasha and stumbling through the house. Thankfully, Maria was waiting in her rooms. She helped strip Lina of her dress and put her into a nightgown, removed her cosmetics, and took her elaborate hairstyle down to braid it into a simple tail down Lina's back.

Giving Maria a mumbled thank you was the last thing she remembered before falling into a deep sleep.

36

Sasha

The manservant that was assigned to Sasha, who was fairly certain the male's name was Geoff, woke him up not long after the stars
came out. Breakfast was waiting on the table in his sitting room, along with a large mug of relo. Also waiting at the table across from
his food was Kostis, with his own large mug of relo.

Sasha blinked at the other male, confused, but sat down anyway
and took a few large gulps of his relo for fortification. Kostis just sat
quietly as Sasha began to eat, waiting for something Sasha wasn't
sure of before he finally broke the silence.

"Do you need something?" Sasha prodded, brow up. Aside
from court dinners, he and Lina hadn't seen much of Kostis during
their first week with Ykaterina. Kostis's face flushed, though it
wasn't obvious on his deep olive skin.

"Sorry," he said quietly. "I wanted to talk, but I also wanted to
give you a chance to eat first."

"Alright," Sasha said guardedly. "I've had enough that I won't
mind if you talk, and I can focus on it."

"Well," Kostis said awkwardly, "I firstly wanted to apologize again for being a total asshole to your sister. Obviously, I'll be apologizing to her again, but I know how being an older brother can be."

"You have a younger sibling?" Sasha asked. A hint of heartbreak crossed Kostis's face, quickly controlled with a blank expression.

"I did once," he admitted after a deep breath. "Before I was exiled from the Seelie Court."

"You were exiled?" Sasha knew some of this, but had been trained in information gathering by an assassin. He needed more to evaluate the kind of male Kostis was; the other male could possibly be an ally.

"I..." Kostis's shoulders were somewhere in the vicinity of his ears. "I accidentally killed my best friend. But I was deemed dangerous."

"It seems odd that you were labeled dangerous for an accident," Sasha mused.

"It was my magic," Kostis murmured. "I never specialized, and it's just... overpowered. We were playing together, still faelings. Showing off little magics. And mine... it exploded outward. I was unscathed, but... Eryn was gone."

Sympathy warmed Sasha to Kostis.

"Where were you from?" Sasha asked.

"The Eastern Mountains," Kostis said. "I'm lucky, really; the whole village was calling for my death, even my own family. They brought me to the Prince, and he was boxed into a corner. He tried to convince them to settle for exile to a different part of the Seelie Queendom. He wanted to send me North."

Sasha didn't say anything, but he knew if Liam had sent Kostis North, he'd have another brother.

"But the village rose up," Kostis murmured. "Said I needed to die, by their hand or his. So he exiled me to the Unseelie Kingdom. The village believed that all Unseelie fae were monsters that hated Seelie fae, so they assumed I'd die here. But Prince Liam sent me here, to Nadya."

Sasha vaguely remembered his da mentioning this when they were preparing for their journey here, but didn't realize how much he and Dad had helped Kostis. The male didn't know, and might never know. But he privately decided to try to befriend the older male. Kostis needed more people in his corner.

"That's shit," Sasha told Kostis. "I'm sorry you dealt with that. I get it, though. My mom was an Unseelie assassin, and my pa was a Seelie blacksmith. They were lifemates and stayed together long enough to have me and Raya. Then, Mom went on missions again, until the one she never returned from. Pa didn't make it more than a decade after that.

"Our village decided that with the protection of our parents gone, we were prime targets." The bitterness in Sasha's voice was real, even after all this time. "After they attacked us, we packed our stuff and left. We grew up in the Northern Forests, in a village near Queensrest. So we snuck across the strait and came south."

"That's also shit." Kostis gave Sasha a small smile. "But to answer your original question, I was the oldest of three faelings. My sisters were twins, and we all protected them like they were made of gold."

In some ways, they were. Faelings were treasured, and twins were like a sign from the magic itself of their favor.

"Wow." Sasha blinked. "That's... rare."

"You're telling me." Sasha heard a hint of bitterness in Kostis's voice. "I loved them desperately and would have done anything for them. My parents kept us apart after a while because they were afraid of my magic. When the village rose up against me, they almost looked... relieved."

Sasha wondered how much trouble he'd get in for throwing Kostis's parents off a mountain when he got home. Knowing his parents, not much, and only if he got caught. A memory from the day he'd first met Lina crossed his mind—there were Gorgons in the Eastern Mountains. He wondered if they were still there.

"That's awful." Sasha frowned. He looked more closely at the other male, who seemed... resigned. Sad. He made a decision then and there. "Do you know how to use daggers?"

"No?" Kostis stared, looking a bit confused by the turn the conversation had taken.

"Good," Sasha told him, draining his relo and standing. "Come on, we're going to teach you how to survive."

It was evident to Sasha immediately that Kostis had been given a small amount of terrible weapons training. Thankfully, it wasn't enough to fully imprint bad habits on him, but it was enough to frustrate both of them; Sasha because he had *standards,* dammit, and Kostis because he wanted to be good at it immediately.

"Shit!" Kostis swore loudly as he lost his dagger to Sasha.

"You're almost there," Sasha told him. "Keep trying."

"I'm hopeless." Kostis shook his head.

"You're not," Sasha promised.

"You're definitely not," echoed a more feminine voice, announcing Lina's presence to Kostis. She'd been there through the last three rounds; Sasha had sensed her, but Kostis had been clueless.

Amusingly enough, Kostis flushed when he saw Lina.

"Remember, Sasha and I have both been training for a *long* time," Lina continued encouragingly. "Our mom was an assassin, so she trained us from a young age."

"Um... thanks," Kostis stumbled over his words, the well-spoken male from earlier nowhere to be found in Lina's presence. Sasha reined in a snort of amusement. A suspicion formed, but he decided to watch and wait.

"Here," Sasha rescued the other male. "Watch Raya." He jerked his head at his sister, who snagged one of the spare daggers he had hanging around his waist. "Couldn't get your own?" He raised a brow.

"Yours are right here," Lina teased, then dropped into a ready position.

Sasha moved towards her, making sure to slow the entire thing down so Kostis could see what they were both doing. Lina kept him on his toes for a minute, blocking his disarming attempts before flipping the script on him. Within a moment, she had two daggers. Her eyes widened slightly, and she beamed at him before turning to Kostis.

"Use your height," she advised. "Grisha is a bit short, so he doesn't have the reach you do. You don't have to block like you would with a sword; you mostly need to do more dodging."

"Good call," Sasha praised Lina. "We'll practice dodging first." Lina looked down at her dress and frowned slightly.

"I should probably go back inside. I'm not dressed for this," she sighed. "Have fun." Without further ado, she handed Sasha the daggers, waved at both of them, then turned and went back into the manor.

"She seems... really nice," Kostis said, still watching where Lina had disappeared back inside.

"Most of the time," Sasha chuckled. "Ready for another one?"

"Let's do it." Kostis turned back to him, a determined expression now on his face.

The two of them spent another few hours out in the space behind the manor before Wen called Kostis to go back to theirs to prepare for another goddess-forsaken Court Dinner. After that first night, things seemed to get even worse. The two females that Lina had irritated semi-accidentally often dropped by their corner to snipe at Ykaterina, Wen, and Lina. Sasha had a bad feeling about those two females. They already didn't like Ykaterina or Wen, but they at least knew this place, these people, as well as one can. They had respect and/or fear. Ykaterina had told them not to leave Lina alone for a reason, and Sasha was going to avoid doing so at all costs.

The dinner itself was... fine. A bit like the ones he'd attended in Aledale City a few times with Dad and Da. But between trying to stay between Lina and Darek and anticipating the social hours after the meal, Sasha admitted (if only to himself) that he was a bit...

stressed. He had no idea where they should start looking for the Seelie Queen, and with all of the hostility pointed their way, he didn't know when they'd be able to start looking, either.

Sasha knew that keeping their heads down was a good way to start, but he was... honestly exhausted. They'd only been here for a week, and he just felt overwhelmed. They'd traveled for a month and a half to get here, going the longest way possible, and things were only just beginning. Sasha missed his dads. He missed training, he missed classroom time, he missed their meals together... He just missed *them*. He was desperately in need of the safety that he'd always had with them, because safety wasn't guaranteed right now.

Hell, he missed hearing his *name*. Grigory, Grisha... those weren't his names. He missed hearing someone call him Sasha. Even Aleksandr. He'd been wearing Grigory's face for so long that he felt like he'd almost forgotten what it was like to be Aleksandr Mindwalker, Prince-in-Waiting of the Northern Forests.

Part of him was desperate to see Wen, just for even the barest hint of connection to his family. For the hints of Da in how his aunt smiled and made people laugh. He just... he wanted a *hug*, dammit. A proper one.

A knock at his door pulled him out of his own head a bit.

"You in there?" Lina's soft voice was a lifeline in that moment.

"Yeah," he said, the barest traces of his feelings in the sound of his voice. "Come in."

Lina opened the door and swept in. Her expression fell slightly. Instead of speaking, she simply sat down next to him and delicately put her head on his shoulder. He stayed still, knowing her maidservant did her hair for the night's dinner. Even though he would have rather dropped his head on top of hers.

"I miss them," he breathed. Quiet, and keeping his words as vague as possible so that a potential spy wouldn't understand.

"I miss them too," she whispered in reply.

A small, calloused hand slipped into his and squeezed. Sasha took a few deep breaths.

"I'd give a lot for a hug from them," he murmured wistfully.

"Me too," Lina's voice was small. "This is... it's been a lot."

"It has," Sasha replied softly.

Both of them were quiet.

"I bet Nadya would hug you," Lina suggested.

"And you," Sasha responded.

"I'll be alright," she smiled, a worn, tired thing.

"Hugs aren't a finite resource," Sasha reminded her.

"True." Lina squeezed his hand, then stood. "I'll be right back."

Sasha returned his focus to his breath, but it was hard to focus on anything more than what he missed. *Who* he missed. Every time he focused on his breath, his memory travelled to Dad. Or Da. Or Iron. Leander. Cook.

In some ways, he missed Lina too. Because she wasn't *Lina* here. She was Raisa. Raya.

Just like he wasn't Sasha.

A hand on his shoulder jerked him out of his head. Looking up, he saw Wen closely for the first time in a while. Her bright blue eyes were fraught with worry.

"Your sister suggested I come visit you," Wen told him gently. He gave her a trace of a smile. "Oh, kiddo," she murmured.

That did it. Despite her not having been in the Seelie Queendom in almost two hundred years, part of her still sounded like them, talked like them. All he could see, all he could hear, was his dad. He buried his face in his hands and let the tears flow, though he didn't allow a single sound past his lips.

Wen, to his surprise, tugged him into a tight hug. The familiarity of the gesture made the tears worse. She just rubbed his back, rocking back and forth without words. She leaned down and breathed a dangerous sentence into his ear, but one that calmed him more than anything.

"I miss them too, Sasha."

They were both silent for a while, Sasha allowing himself to soak in the affection from the aunt he'd only just met, in that connection to his parents—frayed as it was.

"Keep an eye on my sister, too," he asked Wen. Begged, really. Let his aunt see the truth in his eyes; the truest words he'd spoken were when he was calling Lina his sister.

"Of course." Wen smiled softly. She examined him for a moment. "My brother would have loved you both dearly," she told him.

"Your... brother?" Sasha mentally filed through his memories. He only vaguely knew about Wen's brother; neither Dad nor Da mentioned him much.

"His name was Faolin," she said, voice quiet. "He was killed. Hundreds of years ago. He *begged* our parents to take in our cousin. And then dragged us a little foundling a few years later."

He read between the lines: his parents. Sasha smiled up at Wen, hoping the request for more showed in his gaze.

Thankfully, it did, and she obliged.

"My cousin loved books," she told him wistfully. "He read our entire library by the time he was twenty. Even before he moved in. We used to buy him books for every holiday. He loved to learn.

"When we were all faelings together, we used to compete to see who could climb the highest." She snorted a laugh. "I was never much of a tree climber, but I couldn't let little faelings thirty years my junior beat me! It took more practice than I'd like to admit, but I *finally* beat them."

Sasha smothered a laugh; he was fairly sure he'd heard this story before. And knew how it ended.

"Unfortunately," Wen continued, "it was all for naught. As I tried to get down, I slipped off a branch and fell. I'm lucky it was just my leg I broke, frankly. Our little foundling was hilarious; he was the only one who didn't participate in the climbing contests. He looked at me where I landed and just deadpanned, 'That was stupid,' before he trooped back to the house.

"My brother and cousin were panicking—absolutely *losing* their shit. My cousin just kept spouting off random things he'd read about bad injuries, and *that* led to Faolin doing something weird with his magic that stuck me in place."

"Oh no." Sasha felt himself smiling now. "I bet that made healing... tricky."

"The healer ripped all of us a new one," Wen admitted freely. "Me, Faolin, and my cousin for climbing trees that high, Faolin for sticking me to the ground so closely he could barely do the healing, and me for not telling them to set the leg. Our foundling, on the other hand, got a brand new set of tools for making enchanted jewelry and some unique supplies."

"That's hilarious," Sasha said, a little wistful himself. Though thankfully, the bulk of the homesickness seemed to have calmed. The little amulet Dad had made to send them home still called his name, but nowhere near as strongly.

"Feeling a bit better?" Wen asked softly. Sasha nodded.

"Thank you," he told her.

"I get it." Her smile was bitter. "I miss them too. I should have been relieved centuries ago. I don't know who made that call, but I'd like to give them a piece of my mind."

Sasha had a strong suspicion he knew who had done it, and *why,* but this was not the place or the time to air such things.

When he got back, he would absolutely be sharing his suspicions with Da, though; his investigation into the male likely responsible needed more fuel. Something was massively wrong with whatever Donal was doing, and whether it was related to Lifebringer or if it was the older male being opportunistic, it was going to impact *how* everything came to fruition.

Hopefully, the rest of the Council would do something—they'd have to somehow get Cormac on board, though. And *that* wouldn't come easily. Idly, Sasha wondered how much his da had uncovered in the weeks since they'd been gone (ignoring the sharp pain in his chest as he remembered that it'd been that long).

Sasha sighed.

"Something tells me that's going to be addressed sooner than you might think" was all he said to his aunt, whose brow rose but let the comment pass unchallenged.

"We need to get ready to go," Wen said softly. "They'll be expecting us at the palace soon." She was quiet for a moment, a hesitance in her demeanor. Sasha just waited. "Once we move back into the castle, we'll have to be more subtle, but I can probably tell you a story or two about my family more regularly."

"My sister too?" Sasha asked, hardly believing the words.

"Of course," Wen promised warmly. "She's family." The words warmed him more than he could say, but he didn't show most of it. As far as most of these people knew, she was his actual sister, not his heart-sister.

"Time to go," Lina's voice broke in, a little smile on her face at the sight of them.

"Let's get going, then." Sasha shrugged. "Wouldn't want to be late."

"No." Wen's expression sobered more than he expected. "We *definitely* wouldn't want to be late."

37

Sasha

Weeks crept by, then months. Nights were spent at court, and days were spent sleeping. During his free time, Sasha trained Kostis the way Dad trained him. In some ways, it was a balm to the homesickness, and in others, it made it worse.

Lina helped when she could, but in the Unseelie Court, females were expected to wear dresses and only fight with magic. Aside from the all-female Valkyrie, anyway.

So Sasha and Kostis were left alone, and Sasha was able to learn more about his mysterious cousin.

The more he learned, the more furious he was about what the other male had been through. A simple magical accident had derailed Kostis' whole life and had absolutely destroyed his self-worth. Kostis never used magic, only draining it when he absolutely couldn't avoid it anymore.

All Sasha could do was encourage Kostis to the best of his ability.

After Sasha and Lina had been in Stroyne for four months came the announcement that Sasha had almost forgotten was coming. "Tonight, we're skipping Court Dinner," Ykaterina told them both. "Tomorrow, we're moving into the palace. You're ready."

Sasha saw the blood leave Lina's face. Hoping to help her relax, he kept his tone relaxed when he spoke.

"Why now?" Sasha asked.

"They're asking questions," Ykaterina said soberly. "And because the Winter Masque is coming up. We need to be settled before the Solstice."

Sasha winced. Another reminder of time passing; it was almost the Winter Solstice. Autumn had arrived and—with travel and their busy nights here—almost passed. Out of the corner of his eye, he saw Lina's hands tighten in the skirt of her dress. She was still, too still.

He focused most of his attention on Ykaterina, asking questions about their role in the solstice celebration to give Lina a chance to recover herself, but his sister-in-heart seemed stuck.

"Raisa?" Ykaterina's voice broke in. Her gaze caught Lina's. "Are you okay?"

"Of course." For the first time, Sasha *saw* Lina shut herself down. The fear that covered her face and filled her eyes vanished in a blink. Lina's eyes were empty, and her face carefully neutral. "Of course," Lina repeated. Her voice was steadier and clearer now.

Sasha tried to meet her gaze, but she kept her eyes on Ykaterina.

"Your servants will pack your things for you," Ykaterina told them, gaze lingering on Lina before she moved on. "We'll be leaving at sunset, settling in for a while, and then Dinner tomorrow.

"Be careful," she added. "The castle is cutthroat, and you need to take care of each other."

"We will," Sasha said, Lina only nodding.

After Ykaterina left, Sasha did his best to reach out.

"Want to go train a bit?"

Lina nodded again.

"Please," she said in that empty voice. "I won't be able to any more after this."

Sasha eyed Lina, but went into the courtyard with her. They did practice spar after practice spar, wearing each other out until they were both ready to drop.

By the time he was cleaned up and fed, Sasha had decided to try to talk to Lina. He searched the house, finally finding her in the library, surrounded by books.

"What's wrong?" he asked bluntly, dropping down into a chair next to her.

"Nothing," she lied.

"Bullshit," he responded pleasantly. "Try again."

Her avoidance of the problem would only hurt her in the long run. Sasha did his best to keep his worry off his face or out of his body language, but he wasn't sure he managed.

"I'm scared," she finally said softly. Sasha relaxed as he realized he'd gotten through to her.

"Me too," he admitted.

"I feel like I've been scared forever," she murmured, looking down at her hands where she was twisting her fingers together. Sasha frowned, reaching over and tapping her twisting fingers.

"Gentle on yourself," he reminded. Pain flared in her gaze for a beat, and Sasha suddenly remembered Dad saying the same thing to her when they worked on magic. Thankfully, she pulled her fingers apart and fisted her hands in her skirt.

"I've been scared since we landed on this continent," Sasha added, the words little more than a breath.

Lina reached for his hand, and they squeezed each other's fingers tightly.

"I want to go home," she breathed. Sasha nodded, chest tight and eyes burning slightly.

"We'll get there," he swore. "We'll do it, and we'll get there."

"There's no other choice." Lina shrugged slightly, shoulders drooping as if the weight of the world sat across them. "The world must be returned to balance. If it doesn't, there's no future to prepare for." A slightly hysterical laugh burst from her. "I haven't even specialized yet. I'm barely an adult."

"You're not alone," Sasha murmured. "You don't have to do this alone. I know you're scared." He squeezed her hand, determination flooding him. "But you're strong and capable. We can do this."

The dampness lining Lina's eyes overflowed at his words, a tear tracing a gentle path down her cheek. She looked up at him, a plea in her gaze. Sasha just nodded, gently releasing her hand and holding his arms open for her. Lina tucked herself into his shoulder and sobbed into his shirt, bringing to mind that awful night after Da's mate bond rage. All he could do was hold her, rubbing between her shoulder blades as she cried.

"It's going to be okay," he whispered. "I promise."

He'd do everything in his power to make it so.

Moving into the Unseelie King's castle was a surreal experience for Sasha. He'd been hearing about this place off and on since he was a faeling. Dad had been in his twenties or thirties when he'd been run off, still just a faeling. But old enough to *remember*. Dad hadn't been quite old enough to really be part of things, but Sasha was young enough to remember how much children see.

He vividly remembered a tale his dad had told him decades ago about what this court had done to someone who fed the feral cats in the courtyard rather than using them for target practice. The "weakness" had been punished with a public flogging, then the male who'd been accused was locked in a small room for a week with starving cats. What was left of him left the court and was never seen again.

It was intended to be a ghost story from his dad, a world he never needed to worry about. But today? Today, he was going to be *living* in it.

He used the "settling in" time to try to remind himself of what he was fighting for, why he was putting himself (and his heart-sister) through this. Of what would happen if they failed. And tried not to think about his grandparents, or about the male who had fed feral cats.

A knock on his door startled him out of his worries.

"Come in," he said. Ykaterina and Lina entered the room. Ykaterina closed the door firmly and gestured to Lina to sit next to him on the couch.

"I..." She seemed lost for words, worry overtaking her features. "The King will be at dinner tonight."

A tiny gasp escaped Lina, and Sasha absentmindedly grabbed her hand and squeezed.

"Keep your shields tight tonight," Ykaterina warned them, fear in her eyes. "Keep your faces clear. Show only the emotions you wish him to see. And whatever he says, whatever he does, do *not* react. If you do, you could damn us all."

Sasha nodded, seeing Lina do the same out of the corner of his eye.

"Don't draw attention," the older female told them. "Everything will be different tonight. People will either do anything they can to get his attention, or they'll do their best to remain unnoticed and unseen. You need to be the latter. Whatever you're here for, you can't do it if you're under his gaze."

"Got it," Sasha managed.

"Get dressed," Ykaterina told him, then gestured to Lina, who gave his hand one last squeeze, and then followed her out.

Sasha felt like he blinked, and suddenly, Lina was on his arm. Supposedly, he was escorting her, but he could feel her leading him around by the arm. Gratitude flooded him. He squeezed her hand between his bicep and side gently, receiving a tiny squeeze of her hand in return.

The room felt... different today. While there had been no formal announcement, the whole room knew the King was here. Would be attending dinner. There were far more fae than usual, the cavernous hall feeling almost crowded tonight. Ykaterina led them to a quiet corner, and there they stayed until a small bell rang.

"Kneel," she breathed, tugging them both down with her. Sasha helped Lina, who was struggling with her dress. As they'd been taught, both of them stared at the gray stone floor in front of them.

"King Lifebringer!" the herald's voice echoed in the silence. "Long may he reign!"

"Long may he reign," the people called back, no mumbles among them.

Sasha heard footsteps at the front of the room. The hair on the back of his neck stood up. This was him, the male who had been the faceless shadow enemy in the west for centuries. Millenia, even.

"Rise, my children!"

Sasha obeyed, reeling at how... *normal* the male's voice sounded. Subconsciously, he had expected some hint of the depravity the King was capable of. The barest hint of the monster within. But instead, all he heard was a deep, melodic male voice. Sasha allowed his gaze to brush over the King, carefully not staring at the other male.

The King was incredibly pale—that was the first thing Sasha noticed about him. His all-black ensemble should have washed him out, but somehow, it just emphasized the paleness of him. His skin was so clear as to be practically translucent, and his hair was bone white. Even his eyes were a colorless gray-white shade. The only bit of color about him was the blood-red ruby sitting on a circlet that Sasha would bet was white gold or platinum.

The next thing Sasha noticed was the Valkyrie. They stood at intervals against the walls, and several stood behind the King. They were practically clones, each identical to the next. Beautiful women with deep brown skin and gleaming white hair, dragon wings peeking over their shoulders. Their clothes were even identical: chain mail shirts combined with thick, wine-colored leather that looked like what Dad had given him and Lina. The only difference between them was their weapons. Some carried swords of varying sizes, axes for others, bows, maces, daggers, weapons he'd never even seen before.

He'd never felt safe here, but now he felt like someone had an arrow trained between his shoulder blades. As if one wrong move would kill them all.

It could, but Sasha was trying not to think about that.

Lina, like him, ate sparingly at dinner. Both of them kept their ears peeled for anything interesting, but no one said much of use. The sycophants were flattering the King, either directly or loudly to others. Everyone else was doing whatever they could to stay out of his way and out of his notice. It seemed a losing battle, as the quiet ones were the ones the King watched. Sasha felt the King's gaze on him more than once, but he simply ate his food. He desperately hoped that the King and the other nobles believed their silence to be fear of one so powerful, a commoner's fear of royalty. Not the fear of wolves in sheep's clothing approaching the shepherd.

The meal ended with little fanfare, but the social hour was going to be even worse. Sasha was worried that the King would notice them and say something. Even with his power, he wasn't sure how possible it would be to hide.

Ykaterina placed a gentle hand on his shoulder for a breath as she guided him and Lina toward their usual spot, where Wen and Ykaterina held court in their own way. Kostis glanced at both of them, worry hiding behind his blank expression, but Sasha couldn't reassure him. He could barely reassure himself. This time would be different. He didn't know why or how, but the emotions he was getting from the room promised it.

38

Lina

Lina was desperately worried about Sasha. Her brother-in-soul hadn't been himself ever since hearing about the King. And since the male appeared in the room? He had been half comatose.

Unfortunately, she didn't have time to do anything for him because most of the females in the room were nearby, seeming to feel the need to be even crueler than usual. Lina dodged barbs about herself, her magic, and her brother with now practiced ease, hiding the feelings behind a mask.

"Oh, hello." The male that she now knew as Adryian Bloodletter appeared with the same two females on his elbows. "Have you given any more thought to my proposal?"

"No more than the last time," Lina shot back, tone bored.

"Adryian," a smooth, terrifyingly familiar voice cut in. "Are you bothering this poor little female?"

"I would never!" Adryian smirked as Darek made his appearance for the first time.

"You would," Darek shot back, brow up. "And she knows how you work by now. Ykaterina has been bringing them for months." He turned to Lina, whose mouth was dry, and fear was icy in her veins. "Don't mind this asshole," he said smoothly. "We're still working on teaching him manners."

"Of course," Lina replied, tilting her head slightly. "I'm sure it's a long process."

Darek, to her surprise, burst out laughing. Lina's skin crawled.

"While I don't believe we've met, you seem somewhat familiar," Darek said. It took all of Lina's training not to show her panic at that statement. "I'm Darek."

"I'm Raisa." Her voice didn't tremble, and her curtsey was neat. Her hands were holding her skirts tightly enough that they couldn't show their shaking. "Lovely to meet you." The words were ash on her tongue, but everything was locked down deep.

"A little young for you, Darek." Ykaterina's voice was icy. Bile flooded Lina's mouth, but she kept it shut.

"Oh, I'm not interested," Darek snorted. "I'm a bit... impaired anyway, remember?" His words were bitter, and his smile was sharp.

"That's right." Ykaterina had never sounded this cruel before, and Lina felt both terrified and amused, seeing her father put in his place. "Got what was coming to you, *Sonslayer*."

Darek just laughed, an ugly sound.

"It's not like they were people," he snorted. "Just mortal roaches. Even the halfers are nothing but pests. Flies on a rotting carcass."

"But one of those 'flies' took your place, didn't they," a silky voice cut in.

The King.

Darek's expression darkened, but he dipped his chin to the King.

"Not for long," he swore. "Egan hasn't seen the little brat in months, but he's still looking."

"Well, his effectiveness is questionable anyway," the King dismissed. "He's been trying to get himself settled in a Council seat for how many years? And that business with Nikolai and Annika's son." The King shook his head, seeming to ignore the fury rising on Darek's face. "What was his name? Leshki? Alois? Ah, Mikhail!

That was it. One of the only people who has ever fully evaded the Valkyrie. And as a child!"

The Valkyrie behind the King hissed.

"Yes, Dear One," the King said to her. "You're still angry about the death of your sisters. I don't blame you. But he'll get what's coming to him."

Lina's blood ran cold, though she kept a facade of disinterest on her face.

"He should have known better," Darek muttered. "Egan embarrassed us all."

"Well." The King patted Darek on the shoulder. "I'm sure you're not so hypocritical as to be angry that he was thinking with the—well, let's say the *wrong head*. It's the reason you're here, after all."

"Of course not," Darek bit off. "If you'll excuse me." He bowed a bit and swept away with a dark look at the whole group of them.

The King sighed.

"He could be such an asset," the male mused. "But I suspect he's outliving his usefulness."

Sasha cut in with a derisiveness that Lina felt that she should have expected.

"I'm surprised he was useful in the first place," he sniffed.

To everyone's surprise, the King laughed.

"Even Seelies have their use, little halfer," he admonished with a grin that softened the blow.

"Oh, not because he's Seelie." Sasha shook his head. "Begging Your Majesty's pardon. It's because he just seems like a bit of an idiot."

This got another laugh for Sasha, who seemed to be playing a dangerous game. Lina snuck a look at her brother-in-soul, but even she couldn't read anything in his expression. If she didn't know him, she'd assume he was perfectly comfortable in his current conversation. But she did know. And she knew that this was probably one of Sasha's deepest fears he was facing. The creature from his nightmares.

"Well, I fear I must repeat myself." The King smirked. "Even idiots have their use."

"Of course." Sasha bowed.

"Thank you for the... *stimulating* conversation, youngling." The King dipped his chin a fraction. Just enough to get soft gasps from the fae around them. Then he continued on his way. Lina saw Ykaterina put a hand on Sasha's shoulder for a moment, the touch startling him out of where he was watching the King with a blank expression.

The blankness broke when his eyes met hers, worry and fear battling with a fierce protectiveness. She reached over and squeezed his hand for a moment. All she could spare to remind him that they'd survived, they were okay.

Conversations blurred into a constellation of words and sounds for the rest of the night, Lina relied on her training and a bit of auto-pilot to get her through until they could leave—unfortunately, that time was later than it once was now that they were living in the castle itself.

Finally, *finally*, Ykaterina excused them, bringing all three of them directly to her suite and locking the door.

"That was dangerous," she said bluntly to Sasha.

"I apologize." His shoulders slumped. "I shouldn't have said it. Especially not after what you said earlier. Keeping the eyes of the King off us is vital."

"I can't even agree with you," Ykaterina sighed, draping herself over a divan. "Because that little nod translates to having the King's favor. That's something that extends to at least the three of us, and even Kostis and Nadya to a degree. You just made our lives here ten times easier. Not whatever you're doing, unfortunately, but our day-to-day at least."

The older female rubbed her face, a crease between her brows as she thought.

"Go to bed, both of you," she told them finally. "You did well tonight, and not just because of all that." Ykaterina waved her hand in the general direction of the door. "But you'll need your rest for tomorrow."

Lina grabbed Sasha's hand as they left, tugging him into her suite before he could disappear.

"You okay?" she asked him, holding his hands in hers.

"I think so," he managed, pulling one hand away to run his fingers through his hair in an absentminded, yet familiar gesture. The other gave hers a gentle squeeze. "That was... a lot. I shouldn't have said what I said."

"I think it will end up working out for us," Lina said slowly. "I think we can make this help us once we understand better what it means." She was quiet for a moment before grinning up at Sasha. "And... thank you."

Sasha gave her a little smirk.

"You're welcome." He reached out and mussed her hair before he turned and left.

As she summoned Maria, Lina did something that she hadn't done much since they'd arrived; she pondered her task. Finding the final Seelie Queen.

The King frightened her more than she knew how to express, precisely because of how *normal* he seemed. He'd spent millennia butchering Seelie Queens and generally bathing the world in blood, and yet he laughed at jokes. He called his people children. He gave advice to younger fae.

And that normalcy? It was terrifying. Because if he could seem so normal, then what atrocities were others capable of? Who else was an enemy in an ally's skin?

It was frustrating, too—everyone knew someone who'd been sent to the King's famous dungeons, but no one had actually *seen* them. Everyone spoke about them, about the terrors therein, but no one knew anything for sure. This was likely purposeful, and she suspected that the Queen was in there. But the problem was in *getting* to her. They were here, so what next? How would they find her?

Maria let Lina stew in her thoughts as the servant took the stabbing pins from Lina's hair and helped her out of her court dress. Perceptive as good servants usually were, Maria simply said a soft goodnight as she left Lina curled into a small couch by the fire.

A soft face in Lina's palm startled her from her absent contemplation.

"Hello," she murmured to Fiadh. "I've missed you."

The fae-lioness didn't speak, but she did give the impression of someone exploring, poking her cat-curious nose into whatever suited her fancy. Little of it was important to Lina aside from the faces of the two fae who had attempted (and failed) to hurt her. Those two would need to be taught a lesson in etiquette, and soon.

Fiadh jumped nimbly up onto the couch, curling up next to Lina and laying a massive head in her lap. Lina just scratched the soft ears for a few moments, slowly drowsing on the couch wrapped around Fiadh. They'd figure it out; they had to. Maybe the fae-lioness could look more while everyone was busy. Maybe she and Sasha could go for some sort of walk to explore the castle, using their ignorance to their advantage.

Thoughts swirled in her head as she drifted slowly off to sleep.

The next day saw a *pile* of invitations delivered to their little part of the castle. When Lina met Sasha and Ykaterina for breakfast, the older female had three stacks of envelopes and fancy papers. There were also two piles of fancy bags and boxes on the couch. An additional stack of envelopes was sitting by Lina's spot.

"What's all this?" Lina asked, eyes wide.

"The effects of your brother's favor," Ykaterina told them, vaguely amused. "Those," she said and pointed at the ones by Lina's plate, "are marriage proposals. I'm going to write polite rejections on your behalf as your guardian, but if you're curious, they're there."

Lina grabbed the top one and slid the paper out, then made a face as she skimmed it.

"It's from Bloodletter," she explained, seeing the curiosity in Sasha's expression.

"Yikes," Sasha chuckled.

"I'm good," Lina said, sliding it back on top of the stack.

Ykaterina waved over one of the servants, who grabbed the stack and removed it.

"I'll work on those later," she told them. "I've also checked the gifts. Anything that wasn't dangerous to you is there. You can have it all. The downside is, again, thank you notes."

Lina nodded.

"And we've also received quite a few invitations for luncheons," Ykaterina continued. "Some for all of us, some for just the two of you, and some for just one or the other. I'll be teaching you two how to manage your own correspondence, how to check your gifts and mail for danger, and how to decide which invitations to decline and which to accept.

"For today, I intend to accept one of the invitations for all of us, one from another highly favored of the King. The etiquette for who should write the refusals is thus: if it's for all of us, then I write them as your guardian. If it's for both of you, Sasha will have to handle it. Everything else is handled by the individual."

Sasha made a face when he learned that he'd have to handle the paired ones, but he nodded in understanding.

"Nadya and Kostis also got an invite to this luncheon," Ykaterina said. "They've accepted as well."

Relief suffused Lina, though she didn't know why. She barely knew Wen and knew Kostis even less.

"Thank you for helping with this," Lina said to the other

female.

"You're welcome." Ykaterina smiled. "Let me know if you need help actually writing the letters."

"I will," Lina promised. Ykaterina waved more servants forward, and they began breakfast.

39

Sasha

Somehow, even with the favor of the King causing everyone to breathe down their necks, Sasha and Lina found time to look for the Seelie Queen. In some ways, the favor made it easier. They could ask questions that would have otherwise been suspicious, and they convinced interested parties to bring them to otherwise prohibited locations.

However, it was a slower process than he expected. Over the past several months, they'd been all over the Unseelie King's castle, asking questions, searching rooms and halls covered in dust, and being careful not to make nuisances of themselves.

And their time was limited—beyond just the Court Dinners, they now had proper events to attend to. He, Lina, and Kostis usually gathered in one of their three sitting rooms after breakfast to read over the invitations and decide which ones would be best to attend. Sasha was incredibly entertained during those sessions; the way Lina and Kostis would jump back and forth between sniping at each other and gentle flirting kept Sasha from going insane as their task continued with no end in sight.

At this point, Sasha was a bit frustrated. Even with all of this, they had no real clue where the Queen was. Both of them had a feeling she was in the King's Dungeons, but that wasn't something they could access given their status as newcomers, as halfers, or even with how young they were. Their questions, their work, their time... all of it felt a bit useless.

He could tell Lina didn't agree, though she was fairly quiet about it. Sasha just hoped that Lina was right in this situation.

It didn't help that his homesickness came and went in waves. Some days, it was hard to get out of bed with how much he wanted to go home. Other days, he was able to push it to the back of his mind.

Today was one of the bad days.

On days like today, he envied Lina how she could just... handle it. How she could roll with the punches. He buried his face in his pillow with a groan.

"Grisha?" Lina's soft voice seemed to grate in his ears.

"Fuck off," he growled.

He could tell that she froze halfway to him. Part of him felt guilty; he'd *never* spoken to her like that. But he just... couldn't handle it anymore. She spun around and left.

Guilt and anger battled for dominance as he groaned into the pillow. Suddenly, he felt Lina reappear.

"I've spoken to Ykaterina," she said in a businesslike tone. "She shielded this room and says we have around a quarter hour. So tell me what's wrong, Sasha."

The sound of his name for the first time in a few months made him flinch. Fury won out, and he sat up.

"What's wrong? What's *wrong?*" he snarled at her. "What's *wrong* is that we're on a futile fucking quest. There's no way to get to the Queen; all these months have been for *nothing*. I've been gone for almost a *year* and have accomplished nothing."

His fury soared as he saw that Lina's expression hadn't even changed. She just stood there.

"Do you even *care?*" Sasha demanded. "Do you even care about us? My family? My life?" He snorted. "Of course you don't. We're a means to an end to you."

"That's enough," she said in a cold voice. "I'm sorry I'm so used to not having anyone to give a shit about me that I am handling this place better than you. I'm sorry I'm putting my faith in the goddess's choices and staying optimistic so I don't go *insane* here."

Sasha laughed, an empty sound that sounded the way his heart felt.

"There's a difference between optimistic and stupid," he told her. "Why are you even bothering?"

"Why am *I* even bothering?" Lina crossed her arms. "Why are *you* even bothering? You have the same way out that I do. And you may actually have some kind of future, even if I fail. If you're so desperate to go home, then fucking *go*. I don't need your help if this is how you're going to give it.

"And for your information, I miss them desperately. I just am better able to compartmentalize it because, as I said, *I've lived this shit for years.*"

Before Sasha could reply, she spun on her heel and left, slamming the door behind her and leaving him with the remnants of his fury and guilt. He buried his face in his hands. He didn't know how long he had been sitting like that before he felt a hand on his back.

"This is a hard life." Wen's voice was soft. "This life is hard for me, with all my centuries. You're barely more than a faeling doing the same thing."

"I miss them so much." Sasha's voice cracked. "I don't... I don't even know how to *function,* it's so bad. I've never been gone this long. Never."

"I miss them too," Wen sighed. "I'm so grateful I got this time with you, but it never should have been like this."

Sasha just let the tears come. Wen gathered him to her shoulder and smoothed his hair as he cried.

"I've been an ass," he said into the safety of his aunt's shoulder.

"I got that impression." Wen's voice was gently teasing. "I didn't hear the discussion and wasn't given any details, but I'm not surprised."

Sasha now felt even worse. Part of him had assumed that she'd gone and essentially tattled on him to his aunt. Instead, she'd sent him someone to help comfort him. He didn't deserve her.

"I... she just *stood* there and took it." Sasha sat up and rubbed his eyes. "She didn't even seem like it phased her. And I was just so... I don't even know. I wanted her to feel like I did, and then she didn't even seem to care, and I just couldn't handle it anymore."

"Sasha." Wen saying his true name was always a jolt, but a good one. One that reminded him who he was. "Sweetheart. I don't pretend to know anything about your relationship. I don't know how you two met or how you ended up here together. And for now, that's good. I don't *need* to know. But what I do know is that of all the lies you've had to tell here, the one thing you've said that's never been a lie is that she's your sister."

"Lina... she's my sister in every way that matters," Sasha admitted, voice hoarse.

"Exactly." Wen wrapped an arm around his shoulders. "And it's okay for siblings to fight, just like it's okay for them to see the world differently. Faolin and I were such opposites."

Sasha hung his head.

"I need to apologize to her," he said. Wen squeezed his hand and stood.

"When she gets in here, you'll have about a quarter hour to talk," she told him. "We've been stretching Katya's limits here, and—more importantly—risking a lot with the King. I know this is important for both of you. But don't take any longer than you need."

Sasha nodded. The familiar-foreign sensation of a soft kiss on his forehead almost undid him as she left, but he just stared at the blanket on his bed.

It wasn't long before Lina reappeared. She didn't speak, and Sasha didn't look up at her yet. He didn't have the courage.

"I'm sorry, Lina," he whispered. "I was cruel. And an ass. You were right in everything you said, and I responded like a child."

He heard footsteps, and a slight weight sat down next to him. She pressed a hand to his chin, pushing it up gently.

"I'm not angry," she said softly. "I can see your perspective. And, honestly, I'm a bit jealous. I wish I were so accustomed to that kind of love that it breaks me to lose it. But I'm not.

"I miss them too," Lina added. "I want to go back so badly it's not even funny. I cry myself to sleep most nights. I want to go *home,* Sasha." The plaintive tone made Sasha's heart lurch in his chest. He'd never even considered how private a person she'd always been. How long it had taken her to open up any of her emotions to them, and how it was usually something pushing her deliberately to the brink that did it.

Sasha didn't say anything, just opened his arms. Lina, who he now saw had reddened eyes and dark circles that she must have been covering with cosmetics, threw herself into his chest. He rubbed her back.

"We really only have each other here," he said. "Auntie Wen and Ykaterina have some understanding, but they're in the dark for a reason. I'm sorry I hurt you."

Lina was quiet for another moment.

"You're right," she said. "And for the record, I forgive you. It did hurt. But I get it—at least, as well as I *can* understand."

"Thank you." He held her tighter. "Hopefully, it'll be over soon."

"Hopefully," Lina agreed.

They stayed like that for another moment or two, then both of them got up and readied to exit the room.

"Ready?" Lina asked grimly.

"As I'll ever be," Sasha replied with a sigh.

40

Lina

Wisely, they refrained from Court Dinner that night, Ykaterina telling them to do something relaxing. Lina didn't really know what to do for fun at this point, thanks to the fear and focus they'd been living with for so long. Sasha, to her amusement, ended up pulling out a set of little pieces of stone carved with unfamiliar shapes.

"What are those?" she asked, leaning back against the couch from where she sat in front of it. He dumped the stones out on the table between them, careful not to knock over their thick mugs of tea.

"Runes." Sasha grinned. "They're a divination tool common here. True future telling is an extraordinarily rare power, but runes or cards with a little magic can give you some insight into how the energy is flowing around you or the person you're focused on."

Lina eyed them, then picked one up to examine. The stone fit neatly in the palm of her hand, smooth and flat like a skipping stone. It looked like an amethyst polished to a mirror shine. The rune itself was carved, silver paint in the carvings to accent them.

"I wonder if they have any connection to similar divination methods back... where I was born," she mused, tilting it back and forth. "When I was around... ten? eleven? Not long before I found out about my heritage, I had a tarot phase. I'd love to look at divination cards sometime."

"Could be." Sasha shrugged. "I'm sure if we say something to Ykaterina, she'll take us shopping. You never ask her for anything."

"Actually..." Lina trailed off. "Let me go to my suite really quickly. I think someone may have given me a set recently." She got up and slipped next door, digging through the piles of gifts that she hadn't had a chance to do much with recently. Finally, a velvet drawstring bag met her fingertips. Opening it up, she saw cards.

Not taking anything out of the bag, she just re-stacked everything and went back into Sasha's suite.

"I found them," she announced, waving the little bag at the male.

"Are they like the ones you had when you were younger?" Sasha asked, looking interested.

"Not sure yet," Lina admitted, dropping back down in her spot. She blindly reached in and pulled out a card. Her blood ran cold; it was the Tower.

"What?" Sasha asked. She swallowed, then put the card in the center of the table.

"These are the same cards I used as a child," Lina told him.

"Not entirely surprising." He nodded. "Something we can look into later."

"Yeah," she murmured. Lina stared at The Tower for a moment, then swept it back into the deck. On a whim, she pulled her magic to her hands and began to shuffle.

"Doing a reading for us?" Sasha asked, brow up.

"Something like that," Lina replied, distracted, finally stopping and pulling the top three cards. She flipped them one at a time.

And there it was, the first card: The Tower.

The second, Judgement.

The final, The Hanged Man.

"What does it mean?" Sasha asked after a moment of looking at them.

"Something's coming," Lina murmured, running her fingers over the cards. "Change." She paused on The Tower. "Awakening." She brushed Judgement. "And sacrifice." The Hanged Man seemed to meet her gaze as her fingers rested on the final card.

Sasha's carefree expression faded into a look of concern.

"Try again?" he offered.

"No." Lina shook her head, placing the cards back into the bag and slipping them into the deep pocket of her dress. "It won't give us anything else, I can tell."

"Hmm." Sasha eyed the deck as she put it away. "That's concerning."

"If it's as true as it feels," Lina replied, "something big is going to happen very, very soon."

"Yeah," he replied slowly. "That seems... right. I don't know why, but it does."

Lina sighed.

"Unfortunately, all we can do is keep our eyes peeled," she said. "And do our best to be ready."

"As well as we can, not knowing what's happening," Sasha grumped, giving the cards a glare. He stared at the runestones, then dumped them back in the bag, shaking them. A violet glow lit his hand as he reached into the bag, grabbing a few stones and dropping them unceremoniously on the table. He frowned as he looked at them.

"Anything interesting?" Lina prodded.

"Nothing new." Sasha shrugged. "Essentially the same thing your cards said. Something's coming. Change. Nothing concrete about what."

"Maybe our time here is coming to an end, and our quest will be fulfilled soon," Lina suggested.

"I don't like the sacrifice line," Sasha admitted. "It worries me."

"We'll be alright," Lina soothed absently, thinking on the three cards she'd pulled.

"We have to be," Sasha replied grimly. "We have to."

The rest of the night was spent in quiet contemplation, but in each other's company. Fiadh showed up soon after, tucking her back end in Lina's lap; wrapping her tail around her person's wrist, and dropping her head in Sasha's lap. The delighted smile on his face when he got to scratch Fiadh's ears was a balm to Lina's soul. Sasha had been struggling more and more the longer they were in the Unseelie Court. Hopefully, something would change soon.

After a good day's sleep, both felt a lot more normal. Not relaxed, not with the readings they'd gotten the previous morning, but steady. Prepared. The early parts of the day moved at a leisurely pace, with Lina curling up in Ykaterina's sitting room and Sasha accepting an invitation to a luncheon to make up for his disappearing act the previous day.

Ykaterina and Wen were tucked into a couch together, chatting with Lina about mundane things like dresses and shopping, when it happened.

Kostis burst into the room, eyes wide and fearful. Lina half stood, ready to fling a hidden dagger at whoever was chasing the other male.

"Kostis?" Wen's gaze snapped to her adopted son. "What happened?"

"I... I saw something," he managed. "A little female. She looked... young. Maybe my age? Or Raisa's? She was covered in iron burns..."

All three of the females stared at Kostis. Gone were his usual teasing lilt and easy grin; an uncharacteristic worry had taken their place.

"Where did you see this?" Wen asked.

"I was walking, and they were escorting her somewhere," Kostis reported, biting his lip. "I was over in the Northern Courtyard."

"That one is usually empty," Wen mused. "At least, after the incident a few centuries ago."

"Did anyone see you?" Ykaterina demanded.

"I... I think the female did..." Kostis was hesitant. "But she didn't say anything. She just... smiled? A little?"

Lina shoved down the strange hint of jealousy and asked the burning question.

"What did she look like?"

"I think she had blonde hair," Kostis reported, confused. "Her eyes were blue."

Something shifted inside Lina, her magic almost *pulsing*.

"I think she needs help," Kostis whispered.

"Where were they taking her?" Lina's tone was businesslike as her mind raced.

"They said something about a cell at the top of the Red Tower?" Kostis said, a question in his voice. Lina didn't answer it; she just turned to the older females.

"Where's the Red Tower?"

"Nowhere you need to be going," snapped Ykaterina.

"Well, that's just too bad," Lina shot back. "Because apparently, I have to. Now, are you going to help me, or am I going to have to figure this out myself?"

"People who go in the Red Tower never come out," Wen said softly. "Not unless they are to be used as a message." Lina just looked at them both.

"The Red Tower is on the west side of the island," Ykaterina said after a pregnant pause. "And it's guarded by a whole contingent of Valkyrie as well as fae guards."

"Thank you," Lina told them.

"This is what you've been looking for?" Wen asked. Lina nodded, chewing her lip. "How did you know?" Lina eyed her.

"How attached are you to what you're doing now?" Wen's gaze

darted to Ykaterina and then back. "That's kinda what I figured." Lina smiled a little to soften the blow. "I promise you'll find out."

"Wait, wait, wait," Kostis broke in, panic on his face. He dropped a hand on Lina's shoulder to stop her from moving. "What the hell is going on here?"

"I'm going to get her out," Lina said, a dark promise underscoring the words.

"Who *are* you?" Kostis whispered. She could see in his expression that he was starting to realize that Lina wasn't who she said she was.

"Someone who can promise you a place if you decide to return" was all she said, offering a sad smile. Before more could be said, she looked to Wen and Ykaterina. To her surprise, Ykaterina looked… broken. Before she could stop herself, Lina leaned over and hugged the older female.

"Thank you," she whispered again. "Thank you for all you've done." Lina stood back up. "When he gets in," Lina said in a more normal tone, "can you send Grisha to me?"

Wen nodded, pride and worry battling in her gaze.

With nothing left to say, Lina went to plot.

41

Sasha

When he came back to their group of suites after lunch, Sasha didn't expect to find the two older females on a couch in Ykaterina's suite whispering together in a way that reminded him desperately and painfully of his parents. He also didn't expect Kostis to look at him with a breath of betrayal in his gaze, or for the females to send him to Lina.

"What the hell is going on?" he asked as soon as he entered her rooms and closed the door. He froze when he saw what she was doing; she was sharpening their blades.

"It's time," she said simply after finishing the dagger she was working on.

He felt his eyes widen and jaw drop.

"You found her?" Sasha breathed, almost unable to comprehend the fact that *their mission was almost over.* After how long they'd been there, it was... almost incomprehensible that they had actually found the Seelie Queen. That they were going to actually *move.* With some luck, they'd be home within days.

"Kostis did." Lina nodded. Sasha's heart went out to her. He could sense that the conversation she'd had with Kostis and the older females had made her sad, though he wasn't sure exactly why. He had a suspicion that it had to do with the slightly odd relationship she had with Kostis.

"When do we move?" Sasha asked.

"After Court Dinner," she told him. A rush of joy had a smile breaking over his face. He could see his dads as soon as tonight! "We stay late," Lina continued. "And then we go straight from there to the Red Tower."

Sasha felt the blood drain out of his face and the joy shift straight to panic. The Red Tower was a prison, and one that he'd heard horror stories about for decades. That's where they held Dad's parents before handing them to the Wild Hunt.

"We're going *there*?"

Lina explained what had happened earlier in short, succinct notes.

"Damn," Sasha murmured. "So what, we're just gonna storm it?" He knew the doubt and worry he was feeling were evident in his face, but he didn't have any idea how they'd manage something like this.

"Not quite." Lina met his gaze, a bit of humor now dancing in it. "We're going to sneak in."

"How do you expect us to do that?" Sasha asked, curious now, and dropped down to the floor next to her. He grabbed one of his familiar daggers, happy to have them in hand again, then snagged the other whetstone to hone its edge. Lina began to explain, and the longer she spoke, the more impressed he was. She'd learned more than he'd realized during their time here, things that would serve her well when she took on her role publicly. She would be a good leader if her people would give her the chance to be.

As they prepared, they talked in low voices, barely comprehensible phrases passing back and forth between them as they spoke in the sort of code you could only achieve when you knew and trusted someone implicitly. The half-spoken words and unfinished phrases allowed them to follow each other's train of thought to the end, as well as any battle-ready pair would.

"I hope... I hope we can finish this soon," Lina whispered after a bit of quiet. "I want them to come see us. I want Auntie to come home. I want Da and Dad to meet Ykaterina. Da would heckle Auntie, and they'd pick at each other, and Dad would help Ykaterina adjust to their chaos. And Kostis..." She trailed off, not finishing the statement.

Sasha's chest tightened. He wanted that too; he wanted his whole family together.

"We'll do it," Sasha swore, likely rashly, but he couldn't help trying to cheer her up. "We'll do it, and then we'll go *home*."

Her eyes were bright with worry and unshed tears, and Sasha had a feeling she was thinking of the same thing that he was.

The Tower.

Judgement.

The Hanged Man.

...

Change.

Awakening.

Sacrifice.

"We'll get through this," Sasha reiterated, reaching over and grabbing her hand, squeezing.

"We have to," Lina replied quietly. "The balance requires it."

With those sobering words, they turned back to their task. Finally, they'd sharpened and prepared everything they could. Sasha slipped away to prepare for Court Dinner and grab the one or two things he wanted to keep with him. His bag of rune stones went into a pocket after Sasha tugged on his frankly uncomfortable court wear. A single book found its way into the invisible pouch on Fiadh's back.

One sharpened dagger went into his boot, hiding under the leg of his pants. Another up each sleeve. Two hanging inside the pockets on each side of his decorative vest. The last down the back of his neck. A strip of leather for his long, unruly hair went in the runestone pocket. The pendant that would take him home in the other. Sasha just sighed as he double-checked that his vest was still hanging properly in a mirror.

A soft knock pulled him out of his musings.

"Come in," he called absently, tugging at the offending vest, worrying about the daggers.

Kostis slipped into the room, meeting Sasha's gaze through the mirror. He gave the other male a little half smile and turned.

"This is it, then?" Kostis said quietly, sadness in his face. Sasha's half smile dissolved faster than sugar in tea.

"We always had a purpose," Sasha murmured, not meeting Kostis' eyes. "Always."

"Was any of it real?" Kostis asked, half angry, half wistful. Sasha looked up, forced himself to meet the other male's gaze properly.

"The only thing that wasn't was my story," Sasha promised. "And even that has some truths in it. We... didn't want to lie to you. You're our friend, Kostis, no matter who I am or who Raisa is."

"Raisa... she told me..." Kostis seemed very young in that moment, looking to Sasha like he had more answers than he did. "She said that she was someone who could give me a place. if I wanted to go somewhere else."

"She is." Sasha nodded. "As am I."

"You're..." Kostis seemed to lose his voice here. His shoulders drooped. Sasha gestured him closer and put a hand on the younger male's shoulder.

"I'm going to give you two names," Sasha said seriously. "And I want you to guard those two names with your life. If you're willing to hold that burden."

"What will those names do?" Kostis eyed him.

"They will open doors for you," Sasha replied bluntly. "The mountains are forever closed to you, but there are more safe places

than you think. More safe people. You made your way here origina-
lly because of some of those people." Kostis nodded once.

"I'd like those names," Kostis murmured. "And I swear to protect them."

Sasha leaned in and whispered to Kostis. "Adelina Halfhuman
and Aleksandr Mindwalker," he said to the other male.

"Who..."

"People who care for you." Sasha smiled slightly as he cut the
male off. "More than you'd think. More than you know. They are
people who would give you a place if you wanted to go elsewhere.
People who have seriously considered finding a very deep crevasse to
put your parents in, because what happened to you was *wrong*.
People who could get away with it." Sasha's smile grew to show all
his teeth.

Kostis's golden eyes widened as he realized what he'd been given.
And then widened further as the names sank in.

"Take care of yourself... cousin," Sasha told the male, putting a
hand on Kostis's shoulder and squeezing.

"Raisa. Is she..." Kostis couldn't seem to finish the question
Sasha knew he wanted to ask.

"Not by blood," Sasha admitted. "Just here." He tapped his fingers to his chest. Kostis's chin dropped.

"Thank you for your trust," he whispered. "And... here. For
her." Kostis dropped a simple hair clip in Sasha's palm. The little
item *sang* with hidden power. "I have too much power," he
admitted. "So I have to divert it sometimes. After earlier... I took this
and diverted everything it would hold. It's just a power store."

"Thank you." Sasha closed his fingers around the simple access-
ory and squeezed the male's shoulder again before letting go. "No
matter what you hear," he added, "you are always welcome."

Kostis nodded, then turned and walked out, leaving Sasha alone
in the silent room. Sasha tucked away the emotions the encounter
had brought to the surface; he'd have time to deal with them later.

Right now, he had a dinner to attend.

42

Lina

Dinner went painfully slowly that night. Lina could barely taste the usually delicious food that she was consuming, not with the weight of the garment she'd decided to call her battle corset under the top of her dress. Not with the weight of daggers hidden all over her person.

Not with the plan she had laid out for herself and Sasha.

But if she'd learned anything these past months, it was how to keep her feelings to herself, no matter what she saw, heard, or felt. And Lina knew that her face and tone didn't breathe a word of her next steps through the agony of the dinner and beyond.

Time moved slowly and quickly at the same time, seeming to move in strange, jumping increments. She seemed to lose the end of dinner entirely, but when she checked the time after what felt like hours talking to catty courtiers, it was barely thirty minutes.

The massive room was mostly empty when she and Sasha finally took their leave. They followed their usual path through the palace, not deviating until the very last moment.

"Now," she breathed before they exited into the courtyard they'd be using to get to the Red Tower. As Wen had shown her weeks earlier, Lina tied up her dress to more easily move. Sasha tied his hair back with a piece of leather, then dropped his transport pendant around his neck. Lina did the same with her own pendant, running a gentle finger over her protective amulet before continuing to ready herself. Daggers went into their sheaths on either side of her lower back with the handles in easy reach. All she was missing was her sword, and *how* she missed her favorite weapon!

Sasha met her gaze, and she just nodded. He put his hands on her shoulders, and she held her hands over his.

"Move," he whispered to her harshly. And she did, pulling him behind her as he created a sort of shield of disinterest, a tactic he'd read about in Ykaterina's library and had practiced with Lina until he could do it consistently—if not easily. Anyone who saw them would assume they were there on purpose and be uninterested in their presence. It was incredibly subtle and powerful.

As promised, the courtyard to the Red Tower was full of Valkyrie and fae guards. Lina wound carefully between them, using all her lessons in stealth to keep silent. Noise made the shield harder to maintain.

Lina was glad that they didn't have to worry about getting *out* of this fortress tower; getting inside was hard enough. She pulled her magic to her, pulling at a loose stone on the other side of the courtyard until it fell to the ground. The sound grabbed the attention of all the guards just long enough for her to slip inside the tower with Sasha behind her.

She gasped when she got over the threshold, barely seeing the empty room before she felt a sharp *snap* that reverberated through her skull. Lina fell to her knees hard, the echoing pain feeling a bit like a dislocated joint being replaced—pain, and then sharp relief. A groan pulled her attention to Sasha, who was holding his head. She reached her hand out to put it on his head, and she gasped again, seeing freckles on her olive skin.

"Sasha," she whispered, a hint of panic in her tone.

"What the hell was—" He looked up, and Lina got a good look at his *real* face for the first time in over a year. The dark circles, his *much* paler skin, eyes darkened a hint to violet blue. "Lina," he whispered. "The spell broke. Mine must have broken, too. We need to hurry."

"What are we going to do?" she said, quiet but horrified.

"We keep going. I'll find the ladder," Sasha whispered. "Recover, spells breaking like that never feels good."

Lina nodded, and Sasha began to search the ceiling with a dim green faelight. Fiadh, who was supposed to be following them invisibly, must have been caught in the spell too. The newly revealed fae-lioness tucked herself around Lina as she recovered from the shock. It only took a few minutes for Sasha to find the trap door, and the ladder was attached to the ceiling next to it.

"Pull it down," Sasha told her, pointing to the ladder. "I'll catch it." Lina's brow rose, but she complied, tugging at the fasteners with her magic. Soon, the ladder tumbled down, landing with a soft th-ump on top of Sasha. Lina stifled a laugh as she helped him get out from underneath it, leaning it against the wall closest to the door.

"From what I learned," she breathed, "there aren't many guards on each floor. But we're going to have to fight our way through. Quietly."

"I'll go first," Sasha said with a nod. "I'll get you a sword; you're better with an ill-fitting sword than you are with daggers."

"Got it." Lina nodded. Sasha began to climb, a dagger held in a hand and another between his teeth. Lina came behind him, doing her best to stay out of his way as he pushed the trapdoor open and immediately threw the dagger in his hand, grabbing the one in his mouth at the end of the movement. He disappeared through the gap, leaving Lina to crawl up behind him.

By the time she hit the top, the two guards were dead, and Sasha was holding a short sword out to her hilt first.

"Perfect." She grinned as she gave the blade an experimental swing. "Hopefully I haven't lost any of my touch."

"Dad will kill you if you have," Sasha said soberly, amusement dancing in his eyes before he scanned the room. Lina followed suit, trying to figure out the best next steps.

There were three hallways like spokes out of this central hub, and a twisting spiral staircase heading through the middle of the room with a door at the top.

"Kostis said something about a cell at the top of this tower," Lina told Sasha grimly. "I think we'll need to get up to the top."

Sasha made a face.

"Do you think you can shield us again?" Lina suggested.

"Not in close quarters like this, not when it'll be obvious that *someone* is there." Sasha shook his head. "As much as I hate it, you're going to have to lead. You have a longer reach, and I can throw daggers from behind you."

"No problem." Lina brushed off his concern, hiding the terror that had been building since their visual spells were broken. Fiadh shoved her nose into Lina's free hand in a clear attempt at comfort.

"Lina," Sasha grabbed her shoulder in his free hand as he spoke, "we get out of this."

"We get out of this," she repeated, the words tasting like ash in her mouth as the Hanged Man flashed in her mind's eye.

"Believe in us," he demanded. "If you don't, we're fucked."

Lina nodded, shoving down the panic, fear, and worry and tucking them away before stalking up to the stairs.

"Ready?" she whispered when she was in front of the door.

"Kick it in," Sasha whispered back.

And she did. The wood buckled under her shoe, swinging open quickly. Lina had her sword out in front of her through the door before she could even think. A cry echoed as she felt the slight but telltale resistance that indicated that her blade had met flesh.

The next while was a blur of blood, swords, daggers, and magic. Lina, Sasha, and Fiadh fought their way up the tower, leaving a trail of corpses behind them. No one seemed to have sounded an alarm yet, so they were able to fight their way through. Lina could feel her sword arm getting heavier and heavier, and she'd noticed that someone had gotten through her guard and left a deep scrape across her shoulder. Her dress was in ribbons, the corset keeping her from deeper, more problematic wounds.

Finally, they reached the top, the fae breathing hard. Fiadh just sat down and began to lick blood from her coat.

"What now?" Sasha panted.

"We search each row," Lina said grimly. "As fast as we can. Eventually, our luck is going to run out."

"Split up?" Sasha asked. Lina shook her head.

"We can't; we have to know where each other is," she told him. "Do your mind magics work in here?"

"As long as it's just within the tower," he confirmed.

"Maybe check for more guards down each hallway," Lina suggested. "Then, we know if we have to be quiet, or if we can just hurry."

Sasha's brow furrowed, gaze far away. Confusion flickered over his features, becoming more and more prominent as he searched.

"There's no one up here," Sasha reported, brow furrowed. "Not a single person."

"No, that can't be right." Lina shoved down panic again. They couldn't have failed; there was little to no way they'd ever be able to get this close again. She strode towards one of the halls until she found a door. The door was metal, rust pockmarking it. She peered into the tiny window.

Bile hit the back of her throat. The fae inside was clearly dead, eyes wide and sightless. Eyes were one of the only parts of the poor creature's body that she could recognize; the rest of them was a mess of thick burn scars. Several blackened fingers and toes were missing as well.

"Fuck," she swore, bracing her hand on the door.

"Get away from there!" Sasha said, eyes wide.

"Huh?" she asked, head tilted.

"That's *iron*," he hissed. Lina blinked, then her eyes widened as she gently pulled her hand off the door.

It was fine.

"That's right." Sasha stared at her palm. "You can touch it. The iron is why I can't feel anyone. And I'm not going to be able to go down those halls; I don't have the right protection."

"The fae in there," she said and pointed, "is very, very dead."

"Shit," Sasha muttered, gaze locked on the tiny window. "Are you going to be able to manage?"

"I have to be," Lina replied grimly.

In some ways, this was worse than the fights. Those were, to a point, clean deaths. This was torture and pain that would live in her heart for the rest of her life, however long it would be. Lina found many prisoners in those halls, living and dead. Every single one of them was burned and beaten, all of them putting the smallest amount of themselves possible on the surrounding iron.

All she could do was keep looking for the Queen, swearing to herself that she'd burn this place to the ground one day. That she'd get vengeance. That the iron would be torn out and used on the creatures who had done this.

Her hands were shaking, and tears were streaming down her face by the time she hit the end of the hall. And there, in a tiny metal cell, was the Queen. Their gazes met, the Queen the only one with a hint of sanity left.

Lina read the female's lips as she spoke, though she couldn't hear through the iron door.

"The One Who Was Promised."

The words sent a shiver down Lina's spine, but she tugged out the lockpicks that had been hiding in Fiadh's bag and began to work the lock. It was almost absurdly easy, but when she opened the door, she saw why; there was no handle inside. The door threatened to swing closed behind her, but Lina propped her sword up to hold the door open.

"I'm here to get you out," Lina swore to the frail, burned figure.

"Alright." The Queen nodded.

"What's your name?" Lina asked, scooping her up.

"Here, I'm called Oksana," the female whispered. Lina abandoned her sword as she carried Oksana through the hall, shielding the Queen from the iron as well as she could.

When she reappeared in the main area, she froze.

In front of her was Sasha, daggers out and guarded. Fiadh was behind him, golden eyes glowing. And in front of Sasha was Darek.

"You," he hissed, catching sight of Lina.

"Me," Lina replied evenly, wishing she could have carried Oksana and her sword.

"You useless bastard." Darek took a step forward. "You're damn lucky that your slut of a mother managed to protect you for as long as she did."

"Shut the hell up about my mum," Lina fired back. "You're just a spoiled brat who blames the world for not letting him do what he wants with no repercussions."

Instead of replying, Darek rushed them. Sasha darted back in front of them, protecting both her and Oksana from Darek's wrath. She placed Oksana down behind her, being sure to sit her on the stone instead of the iron. Lina spun to help Sasha, just in time to see him down on a knee with a sword sticking out of his middle, Darek jeering.

"No!" Lina screamed, the Hanged Man flashing behind her eyes again for a moment. She sprinted over, pulling daggers out of her pockets, and immediately began throwing at Darek. "You *fucker*!" She stood between her brother and her father, a knife pointed in the older male's direction.

"Should have been faster, *daughter*," Darek spat.

Lina screamed again, arm and wrist snapping forward in a flawless throw that hit Darek in the middle of his chest. Fury stained his cheeks as he pulled the weapon out, blood spurting with each quick beat of his heart. Lina easily evaded him until he dropped to the floor, the puddle of blood growing. She ran back to Sasha, who smiled sadly at her.

"Take—" He coughed slightly and winced. "Damn, that hurts. "Take care of Da and Dad, okay?"

"You're not dying, you asshole." Lina worked furiously, barely noticing Oksana slowly dragging herself over to them. A dagger ripped a thick chunk of Lina's dress off, which she folded over and over on itself. She braced herself and Sasha both, pulling the dagger out and shoving the pad over the injury. Lina barely noticed her hands glowing green as she held the pad to Sasha's middle.

The rattling of weapons and armor startled her out of her daze. Lina looked around, desperate for anything to save them all. She took Oksana's hands and placed them over the pad.

"Press this on the wound as best as you can," she ordered. Oksana followed instructions as Lina grabbed his amulet. "Hold on to his clothing," Lina added. "You're going somewhere safe." She sent a heavy burst of magic through the pendant, activating it and leaving her reserves depleted. Fiadh was between her and the soldiers beginning to burst into the room.

Sasha's eyes opened and flashed with horror just as he and Oksana winked out of existence, leaving Lina and Fiadh in the Red Tower.

43

Sasha

"Lina!" Sasha screamed as the familiar comfort of his dads' living room materialized around him. The sound pulled something in his middle, and he groaned in pain. The deep ache distracted him enough that he almost didn't hear the thumping footsteps of his dads from wherever they'd been in the house.

"Don't strain yourself," a soft, female voice told him gently. The Queen. Her blue eyes met his. "You're still injured, though I think The One Who Was Promised healed you." Before he could think more, say more, he was wrapped in familiar arms. A flash of dark hair told him who was holding him.

"Dad," Sasha sobbed, burying his face in the other male's shirt and finally letting the tears flow properly. "Dad, I missed you."

"Oh, kiddo." A hand rubbed up and down his back soothingly, then paused. "Sasha, where's Lina?" Sasha could hear the worry in Dad's tone, and it broke something in his heart.

All he could do was cry harder, fisting Dad's shirt in his hands that shook.

"I don't..." he sniffled. "I don't know. I got hurt, and then I think she healed me and then sent me and Her Majesty back."

"Shit," another familiar voice muttered, though Sasha guessed that Da was helping the poor Queen, whose name he still hadn't caught.

Sasha slowly left the safety of his dad's shirt, revealing the male himself, dark circles worse than ever, and bloodshot eyes. He must have been training, because Dad's hair was tied back at the neck with a strip of leather, just like Sasha's. Dad rubbed his back again, and Iron nosed the back of Sasha's neck gently.

"Hey there." Da smiled softly, contradicting the sadness and worry in his gaze. A few stray tears glinted on Da's face. He had an arm around the Queen, who seemed to have melted into his side. She wasn't speaking much, just looking around with large, clear blue eyes. "Nice to see you again," Da added.

Sasha felt his lip quiver slightly. Lina should be here by now. She should be *home.* He'd promised her that she'd make it home, that they'd get here together. Part of him wondered if she'd known, that the expression of worry on her face had been because of what the cards had said.

That *damned* Hanged Man.

"What was that?" Dad asked sharply, bringing attention to the fact that Sasha had accidentally spoken aloud.

"She... We..." Sasha swallowed, trying to get his thoughts in order. "We found out that the fae introduced the cards to the human world. She'd seen them before, used them as a child. Did a pull. The Tower, Judgement, and the Hanged Man. Change—"

"Awakening," Dad finished, surprising Sasha with his knowledge. "Sacrifice." Dad's face was white, and he pulled Sasha closer.

"What..." Sasha stopped as Dad placed a finger over his mouth.

"I will tell you," he swore. "But not now. You need to get to the infirmary. Both of you. We already sent someone for Maryn. She'll be here soon."

Sasha nodded, and his dad helped him up, letting Sasha lean on him. Da was holding the Queen under her knees and behind her back. They were just about to troop down to the infirmary when they all heard a familiar female scream. When Sasha whipped his head to the sound, there was Lina, several arrows sticking out of her shoulders, thighs, and chest. There were large tears in her dress, revealing the hidden leather that had likely saved her life. Sasha felt ill when he caught sight of a thick gouge in the material. Fiadh was wrapped around her, teeth bared, and an arrow sticking out of her flank.

"Fuck," Dad said sharply, looking around for a way to hold them both. But Da was already on it. He began to whistle, a simple little song that lifted Lina up and held her still. She tried to thrash around, gaze blank, but Da kept her still while carrying the other female.

They made a strange parade through the house, Leander coming up to Sasha's other side and helping Dad hold him up. As they trooped down into the basement infirmary, hurried footsteps came behind them. Leander and Dad scooped up Sasha, practically running to get out of the healer's way.

"Move, *move*!" Maryn shouted, drawn to pain like a moth to flame. Da hurried to put both females on beds, though he kept up the humming that was keeping Lina still. As Leander and Dad helped Sasha onto his own bed, Maryn dumped a potion down Lina's throat. She was asleep within moments.

"Keep her still," Maryn commanded Da. She took a cursory look at the Queen, who quietly told Maryn her name was Oksana, and then Sasha. Her fingers gently brushed the fully healed skin of his middle. "She's a healer all right," Maryn murmured. "You just need to rest," she told him, then turned to Oksana.

"This will take a while to heal," Maryn told her. "And frankly, I'll be able to do more and better once Adelina is healed and can assist me. What I'll do is give you pain relief and an assisted sleep. Your body will begin the process of healing itself."

Oksana just nodded, taking both of the potions she was given. As with Lina, the female was asleep in moments.

"You're not going to let me put you to sleep right now, are you?" Maryn's voice was haggard already. Sasha shook his head. "Thought not." She turned to Dad and Da. "One of you will need to help me pull the arrows out one at a time so I can heal her. The other will be staying to keep an eye on Aleksandr to make sure he doesn't strain his injuries."

"I'll do it," Da volunteered. Dad sat on the edge of Sasha's bed, arm around him, and eyes on Lina. Sasha took a moment to appreciate hearing his name again; he never wanted to hear Grigory or Grisha ever again. And he wouldn't, if he had anything to say about it.

Carefully, Maryn snapped the arrowhead sides off of each arrow with a sharp knife, leaving just the fletching ends sticking out of Lina. One by one, Da pulled out the arrows indicated, allowing Maryn to half-heal each wound. Dad's arm left Sasha's shoulder, and his hand slipped into the younger male's, both of them squeezing tighter every time an arrow was pulled out or every time Lina made a noise of pain.

Finally, Sasha buried his face in Dad's shoulder. His dad leaned in, resting his head on top of Sasha's.

"I'm so glad you're home," Dad rumbled softly. "All of you. And I'm so proud of you."

This started the waterworks again, slow tears trickling down Sasha's cheeks and hitching his breath. He never realized how much of a privilege it was to cry, to feel. His whole life, he'd not worried much about it, never showing anyone much of anything except at home. But after having to hide even the tiniest feelings, with no safe place, it was a relief.

"Auntie misses you and Da," Sasha murmured into Dad's shirt when he trusted his voice again. "And she hasn't forgotten about the tree incident."

A short bark of a laugh escaped his dad, a soft hand squeeze accompanying the gentle kiss to his forehead.

"Branwen *would* bring that back up," Dad said with a sigh.

"I needed the laugh," Sasha admitted to his dad's shirt.

"I imagine you did, kiddo," Dad murmured. "I imagine you did."

"We need to get her home," Sasha told him. "Soon. Her and her…" Sasha paused. "Partner? I think? They're not subtle about it, but not vocal, either. I never asked, because it felt rude."

Dad smoothed his hand over Sasha's hair.

"We'll get there. We'll talk to Oksana once she takes her place; there's a good chance she'll recall Branwen."

"Also," Sasha added, "someone needs to do something about Kostis's parents. They're the worst sort."

"Liam has been making their lives difficult ever since he was forced to exile the child," Dad assured him.

They were quiet until Maryn's voice rose higher than a murmur.

"She'll be alright after some rest," the healer finally announced. "I've partially healed all of the arrow holes, and her body will take care of what I don't. I really just needed to patch them so she didn't lose more blood." Sasha left the safety of his dad's arm and looked at Maryn, who was exhausted.

"Leander," Dad rumbled. "If you would take Maryn upstairs and give her food, drink, and a guest room? I doubt she'll want to be far from her patients."

"I don't wish to leave this room." Maryn crossed her arms.

"One of us will be awake at all times," Dad promised. "And we will get you *immediately* if anything changes. You can't help them if your own magic isn't restored."

"Fine." Maryn shook her head. "Stubborn, the lot of you."

"You love us," Da teased. He smoothed Lina's hair back, then came over to Sasha. Maryn was leaving with Leander when Sasha tumbled into Da's lap and began crying all over again into another shirt.

"Oh, Sasha-sweet," Da murmured, chin on Sasha's head. "We've missed you."

Sasha vaguely felt the bed dip as Dad stood up, likely to go sit with Lina so she wasn't alone.

"I missed you too," he managed, holding tightly.

"You're home, son," Da whispered into Sasha's hair. "You're home."

And Sasha drifted off to sleep in his Da's arms.

44

Mikhail

Neither he nor Del got any sleep that night.

Mikhail sat between his children, watching their chests rise and fall. Thankfully, they'd been able to convince Sasha to take his sleeping potion and allow his body to recover from the ordeal he had been through.

Even beyond the injuries, which were many, the faelings' time in the Unseelie Court had left its mark. Sasha had deep circles under his eyes, and his already pale skin was even paler thanks to the effects of the glamour. His hair was limp, greasy, and *long,* falling below his shoulders. Lina was no better off. Blonde and green curls were lank, falling almost to her waist. Her olive-tinted skin was also pasty, making her look even more ill than she was.

And then the female. Oksana.

The Seelie Queen.

The young female had long, pin-straight hair, a pale blonde that would be striking against her bronze skin once she'd seen the sun, but currently just made her look washed out. And the scars... Goddess, the *scars.*

Mikhail knew exactly what made scars like that: iron. The little female had been tortured, left in contact with iron for far too long. When Maryn woke up, she'd likely have to help counteract the iron sickness if she could. Though, frankly, Lina probably would be better off for that, given that iron didn't hurt demi-fae like her.

He smiled slightly. A healer. It was... poetic, in a sense. That Lina would be one of the rare healers. It would help elevate her status among the fae as well, though Mikhail hated that it even mattered. He'd have preferred for her to be accepted just as she was. But this was their current world, and they just had to live in it.

Iron was curled around Fiadh, who'd been divested of her little backpack and was snoring softly in the corner. The fae-lioness somehow also looked tired, likely from helping shoulder the faelings' emotional load.

Or from helping shoulder the power burden of instant travel; this was why no one did it without formal portals. Exhaustion and major potential for mistakes. And why Mikhail had encoded the destination and spell all in there with the faelings just needing to provide the power to initiate it.

Maryn appeared soon after, looking significantly more refreshed.

"Good morning," she murmured. They gave her quiet replies and let her work, checking on each of the three faelings.

Unsurprisingly, Sasha woke up when she checked on him. He gasped, shooting straight up and staring around in a panic before his eyes locked with Del's, and he relaxed back down to his pillow.

"I want you sleeping in your own bed tonight," Maryn ordered. "You're no longer injured, but I want you to take it easy for at least a week. Rest, recover. Eat and sleep. And bathe."

Sasha gave her a little half smile at the last comment. As she moved on to Oksana, Leander and a few additional servants came in with breakfast trays. Sasha's was set up as a table over his legs, Mikhail put his on the little nightstand between Sasha and Lina's beds, and Del's was on the one between Lina and Oksana's beds.

A tiny groan came from the Queen, who was now sitting up and letting Maryn look her over better.

"You have Iron Sickness," the healer told the female. "I don't know where you came from or how you came to have it, but that's something we need to address. As well as the iron burns.

"What I'll likely do is give you some fortification potions and nutrition replacements," she continued. "Your body will be able to heal and overcome the sickness more easily if it's strong. I can't touch the Iron Sickness because it involves leeching the iron from the body, but I can help with the burns. When Adelina wakes up, she'll likely be able to help you with the Iron Sickness since she's demi-fae."

"Thank you," Oksana told the healer quietly.

"As with Aleksandr," Maryn said, "rest, recover, eat, sleep, and bathe. I'm going to heal some of the worst of the iron burns, and then you'll be able to sleep in a real bed, rather than an infirmary cot."

"There are better ones?" Oksana asked, clearly curious.

Mikhail's heart broke for her. He didn't know where she had been kept, but it was vile what had been done to her.

She and Maryn discussed the potion regimen she'd be taking, and after Oksana took her first potions, Maryn began the healing. Soon, Oksana looked a bit brighter and had her own tray of breakfast.

Maryn went over to Lina, who was still sleeping, breathing even.

"Most of her injuries are healed completely after sleeping," she whispered to Mikhail. "But she's also been through a lot. Her body may be keeping her asleep to help her process everything she's seen and experienced."

"There was a prison," Sasha said softly. Mikhail, Maryn, and Del all stared at him. "It was called the Red Tower."

Mikhail's blood ran cold. He knew that name.

"According to her, there were iron box cells," Sasha continued. "I couldn't get close enough to the halls to see what was in there, but she could."

"They were torture devices," Oksana said bitterly. "You couldn't exist in the room without touching iron. Most of my burns are on my feet for a reason—I tried to stand as long as I could before I collapsed."

Mikhail wrapped an arm around Sasha.

"The Red Tower is a cursed place," he agreed. "I hate that you had to go in there. And that you were imprisoned there," he nodded at Oksana. She tilted her head sideways at him.

"You are Unseelie," she said.

"He is my lifemate," Del told her. Oksana unexpectedly smiled.

"Perhaps you can help me understand your people better," she said. "I will eventually have an Unseelie lifemate as well."

"Not the current King," Mikhail said.

"Of course not." Oksana's eyes glittered with rage. "He has destroyed the balance that is our task to maintain. That is the purpose of the Tethered Thrones: to maintain the balance and Mother D'Vita's connection with our people.

"She saved her strength for a decade so she could speak with The One Who Was Promised," Oksana continued. "She was our last chance at restoring the balance. The balance will teeter back in our favor once I am enthroned, and then I will deal with the Usurper."

"We," Del corrected. "*We* will deal with the Usurper. And help you get on your throne. You're not alone. Most of your Council will be ready to bow at a moment's notice."

"Most?" Oksana's brow rose.

"I've been digging for the corruption," Del assured her. "Myself and the other two that I know for sure will be loyal to you. We're well-positioned to root out the corruption as soon as you give the word."

"Why do you call Lina that?" Sasha asked after having been quietly listening.

"That's what she is," Oksana replied simply. When they all stared at her, she continued. "Mother D'Vita told me about her, the female who was our last hope to save our world. I am the last of the

Lost Queens." Oksana laced her fingers together. "Mother D'Vita never told me how many of us there were, how many of us he destroyed. She just told me I was the last, no matter how it ended. When the magic is out of balance, so is she."

There was a quiet; Mikhail could tell they were all processing before Del spoke.

"If you're interested," he said, "we have some journals of previous Queens and old documents that might be helpful for you. You're welcome to read them."

"I..." Oksana looked at her feet. "I was not given the privilege of learning to read."

"Then we will teach you," Mikhail told her firmly. "If that's what you want."

A little smile from the young Queen.

"I would love that," she said.

"It would be a good activity for the coming days," Maryn approved. "You need to be resting, but being too idle is worse for the mind, which affects your body's ability to heal and rest."

Oksana and Del began to discuss the particulars, while Mikhail's mind wandered over everything that he'd heard so far. The mention of the Red Tower had shaken him; it had been centuries since he'd even thought about the hell prison. He cast a worried glance over Lina; what had she seen? What had she learned? What horrors were forever printed on her subconscious?

Mikhail sighed, reaching over and smoothing her hair. Sasha reached over and grabbed his free hand, holding tighter than he had since he was a little faeling first come to their home.

"You managing?" he asked his son, rubbing a thumb over Sasha's hand. A tiny, sad smile was his reward.

"Mostly," Sasha admitted. "I'll feel better once Ra—*Lina* wakes up." Sasha shook his head a little, as if to dislodge the false name from his mind.

"We all will," Mikhail said, squeezing Sasha's hand gently. "And we'll be there for *both* of you, every step of the way."

Ultimately, it was only a few more hours of quiet and soaking up the fact that they were *here* before Lina woke up.

The little female sat straight up with a gasp, eyes darting around until they landed first on Sasha, then Oksana. Only then did she meet his and Del's gazes for a moment before bursting into tears.

Mikhail immediately tucked her under his arm, which had the desired effect of convincing her to cry on him instead of into her palms. He just murmured soothing nonsense and rubbed the back of her head. The other three did their best to be as normal as possible, but Sasha and Del kept sneaking worried glances at him and Lina.

All told, it took him a good half hour or so to calm her down and extract her from Mikhail's hold, by the end of which Maryn was waiting to examine her.

"Hello, youngling." Maryn smiled softly at the faeling, not commenting on the bloodshot eyes and reddened nose. "I'm glad you're awake, and the others are too."

"Me... me too." Lina gave Maryn a tiny attempt at a smile.

"Now, would you like the good news or the better news?" Maryn asked the little female.

"Good, then better?"

"Good choice," Maryn praised. "Good news is that you're mostly healed. Once you rest up a bit, you'll be absolutely fine. Better news is that you've got a specialization."

"I do?" Lina's eyes were wide. Mikhail just patted her head.

"You're a healer, sweetheart," Maryn said with a smile. "You healed Aleksandr completely. I saw the rip in his shirt, and I sensed the magic, but he was completely physically healed when he got here."

"I... I did?" Lina looked softly hopeful.

"You did," Maryn affirmed. Lina looked around at them, and

practically *glowed* when she saw the pride on Del's face, and yes—his own as well.

"Well done, youngling," Del praised. "Fae healers are rare these days. We're lucky to have Maryn here; there are only a handful in each territory."

"Oh." Lina's mouth dropped open slightly. "That's... wow."

"That about covers it." Mikhail nodded. "It's impressive."

Lina's face was pink at this point, so they redirected to the next steps of healing.

"Now that you're all awake, I'd like you moved to proper rooms," Maryn declared. "You're as healed as you'll be in an infirmary. Oksana," Maryn said and turned to her, "I'll check on you daily to see how your body is healing. Please avoid doing too much activity for the foreseeable future. Aleksandr, Adelina." The other two had her attention now. "You also need to avoid too much activity, but for you, Aleksandr, I'd wait at least three days. Adelina, a week since you weren't fully healed when you got here." Both faelings nodded.

"What that means," Del chimed in, "is that Misha and I will be giving you something to reach out with, so that if you want to go somewhere or need something, either one of us or Leander can come help. Or at least make sure you don't get hurt further."

Mikhail snorted at the face Sasha made; he'd never liked being stuck in one place much. But he hated dependency even more.

"Just because you have to rest doesn't mean you have to stay in your room, kiddo," Mikhail told his son. "We'll help you get to where you want to go. And if you want privacy, we'll give you what we can, though forgive us for checking on you regularly. We've been..." Mikhail trailed off.

"Worried sick," Del finished the sentence firmly.

Sasha's cheeks flushed with chagrin.

"I don't know if I'll want too much time alone," Sasha admitted. "Not right now, not when you're finally *right here*."

Mikhail's heart clenched at the words. It was both gratifying and heartbreaking to hear how much their son missed them. He hated how long the separation had been; it was just as hard on them as it had been on Sasha. And not to mention Lina, who might not even say how much she needed the company. Mikhail had a gut feeling that she was going to have to open back up again a bit, that the time apart had made her tuck back into herself quite a bit.

But they would heal; all of them would. At least, if he had anything to say about it, they would.

45

Lina

It was... strange. Being back in her own bed. Odd.

The bed itself felt almost wrong; it wasn't far off from the beds she'd been sleeping in for the previous months. Her bed was no softer or harder (excepting the sleeping arrangements on the road), the pillows no different. But even with her eyes still closed from her deep, potion-assisted sleep the previous night, she knew where she was.

Perhaps it was the sense of safety. The smell of the fresh sheets that felt like home. The deep dip in the bed where Fiadh curled against her legs and torso. The soft sounds of the house and lack of a maidservant were probably part of it as well. The knowledge that she could wear pants if she so desired also probably played a part, if she was being truthful with herself.

Lina gently opened her eyes and felt her lips curl into a smile. The soft rays of the sun filtered in through the curtains, a sight she'd missed desperately for so long. The light, honey colored wood of her furniture reflected the light, making the room feel larger.

Fiadh didn't open her eyes, but Lina felt the fae-lioness begin to purr.

"Hello," she murmured, sitting up enough to rub over the top of Fiadh's head. Fiadh opened an eye just a slit, then closed it. Lina giggled quietly before getting out of bed. She knew that she probably ought to ring the little bell on her nightstand, but she smelled breakfast, and a cup of tea sounded delightful. Waiting, on the other hand, did not.

Lina never got to the dining room; instead, she followed her nose to find the rest of the household curled in chairs in the living room, platters of food making a buffet on a table against the wall.

"Good morning!" Del's cheerful voice greeted her from where he sat on the couch across from where Oksana perched on a chair, looking almost baffled by her plate of food.

"Help yourself," Mikhail grunted, nodding to the spread. He was using a sleeping Iron as a sort of chair on the floor in front of Del's couch spot.

As Lina got closer, she saw Sasha curled in a chair next to Oksana with his own food, though he seemed to be ignoring it in favor of a cup of steaming tea that smelled of fruit and flowers.

There was a plate for her by the food, which she piled high with her favorites: cheese biscuits, sausage balls, cut fruit... Every familiar sight, smell, and sound helped her settle back into her life. Into the familiarity she'd missed so much.

Soon, she was settled into the opposite end of Del's couch with her food and a cup of tea. She didn't really bother with participating in the conversation, instead just listening to Del and Sasha explain what the different foods were on Oksana's plate. The older fae would take a while to acclimate, but Lina knew that if anyone could help the Queen, it was Del and Mikhail. Lina reached down with her foot and scratched Iron's wide spine just in front of the tail joint, causing an increase in the volume of the deep purrs coming from the mngwa and a slow blink from Mikhail.

"I'm going to go get some relo." Lina's face heated; the drink had grown on her. "Do you want some?"

This blink was less slow and more baffled, but a little smile soon replaced it.

"Please." Mikhail sounded like he was still half asleep. "I just take sugar."

"No problem." Lina returned the smile, then got up to grab plates and go see Cook.

Only a few minutes later, she reappeared with two mugs, one of which she passed off to Mikhail.

"Thanks, kiddo," he murmured, eyes lidding as he sniffed the brew. "Got yourself attached to the stuff?" Mikhail asked her after taking a sip.

"You drink it long enough." Lina shrugged. "Though Sasha seems to be an exception," she added, noting the younger male seemed to be half asleep with yet another cup of tea cradled between his palms.

"He's consumed plenty of relo over the decades," Mikhail snorted. "Pro tip: if you decide to stop drinking it, taper off. It can give nasty headaches if you just stop drinking it."

"Good to know." Lina winced, then took a sip of the warm and —somehow, despite everything—comforting brew. "It's weird that this stuff still feels... comfortable. Cozy."

Mikhail sat up, eyes flashing fully open to meet her gaze.

"What you and Sasha—and Oksana—lived through, went through, will always be a part of you." His voice was deadly serious. "And even in times like that, times of stress and pain and fear, there will be good moments. Joy. It does not negate the pain and suffering, and it does not change the strangeness that you'll feel with the changes.

"All that to say.." Mikhail smiled slightly at this. "Enjoy your relo, Lina. It's okay for you to enjoy it, and not strange at all."

"Thanks." Lina smiled softly in return, closing her eyes to inhale the rich smell of the high-quality relo. Mikhail was drinking the *good* stuff. Even with her limited experience, she could tell that. The drink was warm in her chest and stomach, and the company warmed her soul.

"If you all are willing," Mikhail said after a moment of thought, eyes flickering over the room, "I'd like to share something that you three younglings should know."

Lina noticed Sasha and Oksana refocusing on Mikhail in an almost confused manner, with Del's expression encouraging.

"Sasha." Mikhail nodded at his son. "You've known better than anyone that I've been keeping something fairly large and important to myself for quite a long time." Sasha nodded. "Del knows," Mikhail continued, "but only because he's my lifemate. I couldn't have kept it from him if I tried. I... I've not been truthful about my specialization."

"You're... not an enchanter?" Sasha asked, confused. "But then..." He just held up his wrist with the protective bracelet that Mikhail had made decades ago.

"I am, but not..." Mikhail made a face. "I'm a foreseer. One of its manifestations is in creating enchanted objects and jewelry to help change a future or keep it on its path."

One of the only people who has ever fully evaded the Valkyrie. And as a child!

The King's words echoed in her head.

"That's how you did it," she murmured. Mikhail stared at her until she continued. "That's how you escaped the Valkyrie. Iron helped, obviously, but that wouldn't have done it alone. If it had, then..." Lina winced, realizing what this meant. "If it had, then the King wouldn't know your name."

Mikhail's already pale skin went white.

"Explain," Del demanded, also pale.

"We... we met him," Sasha said. "He... well, he actually got us out of a sticky situation with Darek trying to talk to Lina."

"He's terrifying." Lina shivered. "He seems so... normal. But the things he's done, what I saw..." She wrapped her arms around herself, heedless of the mug that splashed drops of relo on her nightdress. "But he was talking about... about *Egan*." The name was spat out, as it always was. "About how he was outliving his usefulness. Darek, too. Then, he mentioned something about 'the business with Nikolai and Annika's son' and mentioned you by name and how you were the only person who'd successfully evaded the Valkyrie."

"Fuck," Del hissed, reaching down and putting a hand on Mikhail's shoulder.

"I don't think he has guessed you're a foreseer," Sasha told Mikhail quickly, as reassuring as possible. "I... I get the feeling that right now, he considers you a curiosity. Something interesting, but unless he connects us, there are other things that he's going to see as more important. Even then, I don't think it'll be a danger."

"He's not wrong," Mikhail sighed. "And frankly, it was naive to consider that my escape didn't at least pique his attention." He reached up and grasped Del's hand, causing the other male to thaw slightly.

"My *father* and his *friend* probably didn't help." Lina released her arms, frowning at the spots of relo on her clothes. "They brought you back under his nose in some capacity."

"So did being mated to one of the Council of Princes," Mikhail pointed out. He shook his head. "All that to say, I have foresight, and it manifests differently depending on what's happening. Sometimes I just get a feeling, like the day you two got hurt at the market. Sometimes my foresight speaks through me. It used to be a lot simpler. I'd have foresight-dreams some nights; I only remember those dreams. Occasionally, I'd get the urge to make an enchanted object and send or give it to a specific individual."

"Mother D'Vita speaks to you as well," Oksana noted. "She kept me company throughout my imprisonment. Taught me to speak, taught me my purpose, and helped keep me... myself. It is easier for her to speak to me because I am of her more directly—but her connection to you is impressive as well."

"My foresight is related to the goddess?" Mikhail asked, sounding curious now.

"Are not all of our magics related to her?" Oksana asked. "She *is* the magic. But you are closer to her than anyone I've ever met before, other than The One Who Is Promised."

"A fair point," Del said, looking very deep in thought. "And if the goddess has been putting together plans that would lead to Oksana's rescue for this long, it stands to reason that you were gifted with those powers."

Mikhail had his face buried in his mug. And before he could answer, pure *power* washed over the room. All of them looked around, confused—except, Lina noted, Oksana, who looked relieved. A figure faded into view in the center of the room, who commanded all of their attention.

Even years later, Lina wouldn't be able to describe D'Vita clearly. She knew the other was tall and saw hints of curly hair. The way the light reflected off the goddess left half her body in shadow. Hints of bronze skin that faded to pale in shadow, hair that shifted from a light brown to black. A pure white sleeveless dress somehow accentuated all of her shifting colors. A single silvery blue eye and a single golden one swept over them.

As one, the room bowed in their seats to her.

"No, no," the goddess's rich voice almost echoed through the room. "You do not bow, my loves." She smiled. "You have overcome a hurdle that has been insurmountable for millennia. You have brought my daughter home.

"Unfortunately," the goddess continued, "your task isn't over. Finding Oksana gives us more time, but it doesn't restore the balance completely. She needs to be crowned, and soon. And then..." D'Vita hesitated, then sighed. "I'm afraid that you'll need to find a way to deal with the current King. The balance *cannot* be restored properly until we have a mated pair on the Tethered Thrones."

The room was completely silent. Lina stole a glance at the

others, all of whom looked some combination of determined and frustrated. Except Oksana, who simply looked… resigned.

"But I have a little bit of news that will help you," D'Vita added. "The King on the Unseelie Throne is *not* the rightful King. The 'Prince' he keeps hidden away is actually the Unseelie King. Once the Unseelie Throne is empty, we can find my daughter's other half."

They all looked at each other in shock; not the true Unseelie King? That changed *everything*.

"I have a gift for you, my daughter." D'Vita turned to Oksana. "Two gifts. The first is your truename." The goddess gently tapped the top of Oksana's head, and the little female teared up and dropped her chin. "The second," D'Vita said as she reached down and tilted up Oksana's chin, tears streaming from blue eyes and into white blond hair, "is a new usename. My daughter, I name you Aurora Sunbringer."

"Thank you," Oksa—*Aurora* whispered to the goddess.

"Rest well," D'Vita said to all of them. "And be ready for war."

And with those parting words, the goddess disappeared. Leaving them staring at each other. Unsurprisingly, it was Del that broke the silence.

"Looks like we've got a lot to do," he said. "So let's get to it."

Epilogue - Vikentiy

"What did you say?" Vikentiy asked his newest zonbi.

"It was my daughter," the body of Darek Sonslayer replied woodenly. Fury made it hard for Vikentiy to keep the bastard on the plane of the living since he wasn't anchored. "Adelina Halfhuman. The other was the Prince-in-Waiting of the Northern Forests."

"How did they get in?" Vikentiy demanded.

"Unclear," Darek admitted.

"I ought to destroy you again," Vikentiy grated, jaw tight. "But it's enough punishment to have had your throat slit by your bastard daughter."

Vikentiy contemplated Darek's appearance. The sliced-open throat had been haphazardly sewn closed to keep Darek's spirit in its body for now. The formerly dead male was now under his control. Even Darek's snarl was completely under Vikentiy's control. Allowed because he was feeling generous.

Reaching his hand into his pocket, he found one of the pieces of obsidian that he used for permanent reanimations. Vikentiy held his hand over Darek's head, then pulled the male's spirit into the crystal. He relaxed for a moment, taking a breath as Darek's body collapsed again.

Sabira, one of the Valkyrie allowed into this room, hissed.

"Oh, fuck off," Vikentiy muttered to her. They never truly enjoyed listening to him, but after torturing every Unseelie King until he turned over control of the throne and the Valkyrie, they were used to it.

By this point, it didn't take much harm to the new King for them to roll over and listen to him. Only Vikentiy's favorites were permitted to guard the true King; the rest were stuck with him.

Vikentiy shook his head, kneeling down by Darek's body and shoving the crystal down its throat. A quick preservation spell on the body, and he was ready. Vikentiy stood.

"Bring this filth to his rooms," Vikentiy sneered down at the body. "The preservation spell won't wear off until the obsidian attunes to his body, so you don't have to hurry."

Another Valkyrie snarled, but did as he bade. The creatures never vented their frustrations around others—at least, not if they wanted to keep their heads. The one that had snarled in front of the girl—Raisa —had been put down that very night.

After his reappearance at court, the two newcomers had faded into the background. He'd tortured them, of course, and their keeper, but they had nothing for him on how Adelina and Aleksandr had penetrated the walls. Frustratingly, it seemed as though their pleasant company had been all bravado. Ykaterina was tiring of them, too, it seemed; their bodies would make good food for the birds.

No one left this island if they were not deemed trustworthy by his standards.

Vikentiy took a deep breath, savoring the metallic scent of blood that gave this tower its name.

"This will become a boon for us," Vkentiy said. "I have been looking for a palatable reason to invade the Eastern Continent for centuries. I believed that the Unseelie Court wouldn't hold with an invasion with no purpose they could see. Those foolish faelings just gave me the key to the East."

Only a bare few hours later, he was standing on the dais in front *of his entire court. No one was absent, not even Darek, with his neck hidden in a scarf. Instead of his usual attire, he wore black armor.*

The courtiers gossiped, as he expected, but no one dared ask.

"My children!" he called to the assembled fae. Vkentiy ensured none of his contempt for these preening peacocks showed on his face. They immediately silenced and dropped to their knees. "Stand."

Vkentiy waited, then spoke.

"Somehow, members of the Seelie nobility managed to sneak onto our island sanctuary." Vkentiy shook his head. "While here, they snuck into one of our most secure facilities and broke out a dangerous prisoner." Truth and lies, wound together into something the sheep would believe.

"What they have done is unforgivable," Vkentiy declared, tone dark. "It's time we show those elitist Eastern fae what happens when they wake the beast." He turned to Ykaterina. "Ykaterina, lovely child. Come."

He saw her face pale, but she stepped forward and knelt before him.

"Ykaterina, you have been a loyal member of my court for centuries." Vkentiy leaned over and had her stand. "But weakness cannot stand. We are to go to war, child. And your foundlings are a weak link. They aren't worthy of their places here."

"Yes, your Majesty," she replied, violet eyes still not meeting his. Vkentiy didn't let his glee show on his face; someone like her would have looked down her long nose at him when he was a lowly street urchin.

"Raisa, Grigory, come."

Both faelings came and knelt.

"I'm sorry that it must be this way." Vkentiy let false sympathy suffuse his tone before he nodded to the Valkyrie on either side of him. "Hold them," he commanded.

Ykaterina's eyes widened, but she still said nothing else.

"Sabira." Vkentiy held out his hand. The Valkyrie handed him a

dagger. He held it out to Ykaterina, hilt first. "Kill them," he told her. Vkentiy absently noted a little tremble in her hand, but she took the blade and ripped it across the faelings' throats. First, the male, then the female.

Their silent tears hadn't even dried on their cheeks when the Valkyrie holding the two younglings dropped them, letting their blood spill down the steps. He dismissed Ykaterina with a nod.

"This is only the beginning of the blood we will spill," Vkentiy swore. He smirked as the cheers of his people began to grow. He didn't speak aloud, but he did reach out to Darek's mind and gave him a single command:

Darek, contact your friend Egan. It's time for him to show us if he's worth the time we invested in him.

Loved Seeking the Dawn?
Excited about the next
installment?

The second book in The Tethered
Thrones duet will be available Fall
2026

Follow me on Instagram
@e.lisabeth.writes
to keep up with latest news and updates on
book 2!

Acknowledgements

I cannot believe my first book is finally out in the world! Thank you to all of the lovely people who helped me make it its best.

Thank you to Meghan; you're my best friend in the whole world. You were the first to step into Lina's world, and you have always given me fantastic feedback. Even when it was hard to hear! (I still can't believe I had to cut so much of my beloved Del and Mikhail.) My book is so much better because of you, and so am I.

And an extra thank you for the work you did putting Lina on the front cover. You saved my butt last minute and I'm so grateful.

Thank you to my beta readers — you convinced me that my book was worth publishing and that it would find its audience if I was patient enough. Your feedback was incredibly helpful to improving the story, and your compliments reminded me that yes, some strangers already liked my book!

Thank you to Brigid Kemmerer and the Missed Deadlines Discord! As a baby, unpublished author, all of you in the Discord encouraged me and reminded me that NYT bestsellers and unpublished alike, we're all writers together. I would never have finished this book without the writing sprints I did with you guys.

Thank you to Ashleigh Worley, the most awesome editor in the world, who has made my writing better both in this book and in my future books. Your little notes and reactions gave me the push I needed to keep working on this book when I was worried it would flop. The editing process was – dare I say – fun when I worked with you!

Thank you to everyone who gave me advice about independent publishing and what I needed to do; I can be sure you saved me so much tripping over my own feet.

I would be remiss if I didn't mention the hundreds, possibly thousands, of authors whose writing influenced mine in some capacity or another. Whether it was David Eddings and Robert Asprin's irreverent approach to fantasy, Mercedes Lackey's strong female leads before it was cool, or Sarah J Maas' igniting my love for writing fae, faeries, and the like, everything I've read has left an imprint on my heart, mind, and writing style.

And yes, this does include the vast library that is Archive of Our Own. Thank you to the team there for maintaining a space for people to play and write in worlds that aren't their own. My skills as a writer are a million times better than they could have otherwise been thanks to the fifteen or so years I've been writing and publishing fanfiction.

Thank you to my parents and siblings, who read my book, listened to me rant about publishing, and cared for my toddler when I was writing. You guys always enthused and celebrated with me, even when it probably sounded like I was speaking in tongues. Special thanks to my dad, who created a monster when he handed me Pawn of Prophecy by David Eddings.

And last but CERTAINLY not least, thank you to my husband. Not only did you introduce me to the hyperfixation that inspired this world, you've been with me every step of the way as my writing grew. And listening to me talk about writing styles and fan theories with a patience that you like to think you don't have. Without your support and encouragement, this book wouldn't exist. I love you and our precious daughter with all my heart.

Elisabeth Valienne

Elisabeth Valienne is a fantasy and romantasy author who blends mythology, danger, and a spark of humor. Her debut novel, Seeking the Dawn, launches readers into a world of fae, magic, and family. She lives in Virginia with her family, too many books, and a very energetic toddler. Find her on her website at elisabethvalienne.com